ME AND YOU

Claudia Carroll was born in Dublin, where she still lives and where she has worked extensively both as a theatre and television actress.

By the same Author

A *Very* Accidental Love Story
Will You Still Love Me Tomorrow?
Personally, I Blame My Fairy Godmother
If This is Paradise, I Want My Money Back
Do You Want to Know a Secret
I Never Fancied Him Anyway
Remind Me Again Why I Need a Man
The Last of the Great Romantics
He Loves Me Not . . . He Loves Me

CLAUDIA CARROLL

Me and You

AVON

This novel is entirely a work of fiction.
The names, characters and incidents portrayed in it are the work of the author's imagination. Any resemblance to actual persons, living or dead, events or localities is entirely coincidental.

AVON

A division of HarperCollins*Publishers*
77–85 Fulham Palace Road,
London W6 8JB

www.harpercollins.co.uk

A Paperback Original 2013

A catalogue record for this book is available from the British Library

ISBN-13: 978-1-84756-274-6

Set in Minion by Palimpsest Book Production Limited,
Falkirk, Stirlingshire

Printed and bound in Great Britain by
Clays Ltd, St Ives plc

Acknowledgements

Huge and heartfelt thanks to one of the most hard-working people I know and yet one of the calmest and kindest. Marianne Gunn O'Connor, what would any of us do without you?!

Massive thanks to Pat Lynch, who's always such a pal.

Thanks also to the wonderful Vicki Satlow in Milan, who does so much in getting my books translated and published overseas. You're a star, Vicki.

I really don't know how to even begin thanking my fabulous editor Claire Bord. Thank you so much for all of your wonderful thoughts and suggestions with this book and for always being so encouraging and enthusiastic. You're a pure joy to work with, Claire, you really are.

To all of the wonderful team at Avon, HarperCollins, or the Avon Gals as I call them. You're all just so amazingly supportive and it's a pleasure to be part of such a hard-working team. Very special thanks for being so lovely and welcoming whenever I'm in London . . . now if I can only scheme a way to get you all over to Dublin more often! Special thanks to the fabulous Caroline Ridding, Claire Power, Sammia Rafique, Helen Bolton, Becke Parker, Cleo Little, Caroline Hogg and Keshini Naidoo. And of course, thanks to Sam Hancock who's always on the other end of a phone whenever technical things get banjaxed.

Huge thanks to the fantastic HarperCollins overseas sales team, especially Catherine Friis and Damon Greeney.

A massive shout-out to the legend that is Moira Reilly who I only wish would let me move in with her, so she could organise my life every day. And Tony Purdue, you work so hard and I'm so grateful to you.

Huge thanks, as always, to Mum, Dad, who are so unfailingly supportive . . . and also great crack to go out with. And to my lovely family and amazing gang of old pals.

A special thank you to my old pal Fiona Lalor, who listened so patiently to all my demented ramblings about plotlines and characters and love triangles (in this book, I hasten to add, not in real life). See you in the Roundy very soon, Fi!

Warm thanks to readers everywhere, who thanks to Facebook and Twitter are kind enough to get in touch and tell me whenever they're reading something I've written. It really makes my day to hear from you all and please stay in touch. It's the perk of any author's job.

Old friendships are very much the theme of this book, and this book is dedicated to my oldest friend of all. We've come through Primary and Secondary school together, we've survived college, we shared a house for the best part of a decade and never once in all that time, have we had a single cross word.

This one's for you Karry, with love.

To my old pal, Karen Nolan.*
With love and thanks, always.

**though when I say old, she's actually really young.*
**(Ok, so maybe she told me to write that last bit.)*

Hands trembling, heart palpitating, she recognised the handwriting instantly.

I'm fine. I'm sorry.
Please take care of him for me.
And maybe one day I'll get to explain.

PART ONE

THE LADY VANISHES

Chapter One

Christmas Eve, The Sanctuary Spa, 9.30 a.m.

My birthday. My actual *birthday* and I've just been stood up.

No hang on, keep reading, it gets worse. By my best friend. In the same week I was turfed out of a flat I really loved, (and v. annoyingly, after the landlord had finally got round to getting Sky Atlantic in). In the same month I lost a job I loved even more. In the same year I got dumped by the man I loved most of all. Bastard not even having the good grace to leave me for someone younger or thinner.

Will spare you the details. Whole other story for a whole other day.

9.44 a.m.

Maybe Kitty's just a tiny bit delayed? Then suddenly I think, maybe it's me? Maybe I got the day wrong?

Remind myself; it's my birthday. Got the day right. No question.

Have to accept it; definitely in stood-up territory here.

9.52 a.m.

V., v. weird. Can't quite get my head around the fact she'd *do* this to me. Today of all days. Getting a bit wobbly lipped and almost on the verge of tears now.

9.53 a.m.

Wouldn't mind, but this whole spa day was Kitty's idea, not mine. She booked it, made appointments, even made brekkie and lunch reservations at the Spa Café, the whole works. Not a chance in hell of my being able to afford it right now, for starters. But Kitty insisted, said it was my birthday treat. Said it was something she really wanted to do, to make it up to me for having had the single shittiest, *annus horribilis* anyone ever had to suffer. Kitty's like that, though, ridiculously generous. Would gladly give away her last bean. Can't even walk down a street without running into the nearest Starbucks to buy a sandwich and a hot drink every time she sees a homeless person. But now . . . is it really possible that she just hasn't turned up? Has even forgotten?

Anyone else I know, not a chance. Absolutely none whatsoever. But reluctantly, I have to admit with Kitty? Meh. Very distinct possibility.

9.55 a.m.

This is ridiculous! I'm a complete and utter bitch for not even giving my best friend in the whole world the benefit of the doubt! Because she *will* get here, I just know it.

9.56 a.m.

She doesn't, though. Kitty was supposed to meet me for a big birthday brekkie at eight this morning; she's really, seriously late now. So late, I'm actually starting to palpitate, but then I remind myself Kitty's done this before. Is, in fact, famous for it. Sometimes it's not her fault, she's just held up at the restaurant where she works and can't get away. Genuine excuse. But I have to admit there's been other times, and plenty of them, when she just went out on the piss night before, then slept it in. More often than not, in all her clothes and full make-up from the previous night, knowing her.

I've nagged her about this carry-on loads of times, but she just laughs at me, tells me to stop acting like such a designated-driver type and to get out there and start enjoying myself a bit more. Can almost hear her catchphrase ringing in my ears: 'Sure, we'll be a long time dead!'

So that's why I'm not overly worried about her. Just a bit disappointed that she'd do this to me today of all days, that's all.

Wobbly bottom lip starts to get a whole lot wobblier now, even thinking about it.

It's akin to smashing up unwritten commandment of friendship, then dancing barefoot on it.

9.58 a.m.

Blanket ban on phones in here, there's a big snotty sign above reception saying so, so I step out the Sanctuary door into the street outside, to try calling her. Practically immune by now to the weird looks I'm getting, in the ridiculously over-sized dressing gown and white fluffy slippers.

Icy cold air's calming me down a bit and I'm starting to breathe a bit easier. Like a bleeding sauna back there.

10.00 a.m. on the dot

Ring Kitty's mobile for about the twentieth time; still no answer. Ditto her landline. Ring Byrne & Sacetti's Restaurant, where she works, and ask if she's there. Yet again.

Same voice as before answers. Remembers me. Even with a crappy mobile phone reception and with 'Santa Claus is Coming to Town' blaring away in the background, I can still hear how hassled this one sounds. Tells me, v. curtly, Kitty definitely, definitely, *definitely* isn't there. She's already checked the roster for the second time.

I've a strong urge to gnash my teeth and say, 'But she just has to be! Can't you check the roster just one more time? Then remind myself, it's Christmas Eve. Poor girl's probably working under conditions last seen in field hospitals, circa World War One. And after all, who in their right minds wants to be working today, when they could be out on the piss with all their mates instead?

10.02 a.m.

Try calling Simon, Kitty's boyfriend. Maybe he's seen her, or at least knows a bit more than I do? Impatiently, I bring up his number on my phone and dial.

No shagging answer. Voicemail. Why isn't anyone answering their bloody phone today? Does nobody realise this could be a serious emergency?

10.03 a.m.

Seeing as I'm on the phone anyway, decide to do ring-around of all our mutual buddies, on the off chance anyone's seen or heard from Kitty. Call the whole gang – Sarah, Jeff and Mags – but no one picks up. Now I love my friends dearly, but at this point, I'd gladly do time for the whole shower of them. Why won't anyone answer their phone?!

Bloody last-minute Christmas Eve shoppers, whole lot of them.

10.20 a.m.

Eventually, I have to admit defeat. Arrived well over two and a half hours ago and now I've to face up to the cold, hard fact that Kitty's just a no-show. Shuffling uncomfortably in disposable slippers, I head back to the reception area to explain all.

Manager gives a long, exasperated sigh, then coolly points out that there's still the matter of a last-minute cancellation fee to be coughed up.

Knees almost buckle under me. Was deeply afraid of this. Mainly because I've no money. Not a red cent, nothing, *nada.* The price of the bus fare home, that's about it. In a wobbly voice I ask how much for exactly. For the full amount, I'm crisply told. All cancellations are charged at the full price unless they're made at least twenty-four hours prior to your treatments. They're *very* clear about that at the booking stage, apparently.

OK, as of last week, when I was propelled back onto a dole queue, I've no credit card. It's in the bin at home, slashed through with scissors, so I wouldn't be guilted into buying last-minute Christmas pressies or led astray by the January sales. And if I give her a cheque, it'll only bounce . . . So what in the name of God am I supposed to do now?

Somehow, though, kindly manager must sense the blind, sweaty panic I'm now in. Tells me a little bit more politely that it's OK, they automatically charge the credit card of whoever made the booking. Says she still has all Kitty's card details in their system.

Oh Kitty, am so, so sorry to do this to you . . . All that bloody money you worked so hard for . . .

Then the receptionist leans in towards me and says in a low voice that seeing as this is already paid for, there's absolutely no reason why *I* can't stay to enjoy the facilities. Shame to waste it all, just because your friend is no-show, is her gist.

I just look at her, dumfounded. Out of the question, I tell her, a bit haughtily.

Mother of God, how could I ever hope to relax or enjoy myself? Something is wrong, very wrong, and this one thinks I could possibly spend a pampering day having hot stones rubbed into the small of my back, while freeloading off Kitty's credit card?

Not a bleeding snowball's chance.

10.30 a.m.

Mercifully I'm now out of the highly uncomfortable, disposable, G-string/dental floss knickers combo, fully dressed in my depths-of-winter coat and back out on the busy, icy-cold street again. Bloody mayhem here, like something you'd see in Stalinist Russia circa 1939. Whole place is completely thronged as Christmas shoppers with pinched, hassled expressions, laden down with overstuffed shopping bags all shove past, impatiently banging against me.

Carol singers on street corner are joyfully belting out 'Ding Dong Merrily on High', but I'm so stressed out of my mind, I nearly want to wallop them, just for having the barefaced cheek to show Xmas cheer.

10.45 a.m.

Starts to snow lightly, that lovely stage where you think, ah look, lovely, beautiful snow, how romantic and gorgeous and Christmassy. Though in approximately an hour, when cars start piling up against each other and all the buses stop running, I'll doubtless be snarling, 'OK, we've all had enough of this mayhem! When will the bloody snow ever give up?'

Yet again, I call Kitty's mobile and landline. Yet again, *nada.* Yet again I try ringing all the gang and – holy miracle of Christmas – Mags actually answers. (Mags is the proud mother of three kids, all under the age of six, so it's almost the seventh wonder of the world whenever she can even *find* her phone, never mind pick up.)

'Mags? Hi, it's me, in a bit of a panic here . . .'

'Angie! What are you doing calling? I thought you and Kitty would be lying stretched out on massage tables, getting hot aromatherapy oil rubbed into your unmentionables by now! God, I get so mad jealous every time I think of you pair of complete dossers . . . And here's me, trying to defrost a turkey with one hand, while glazing a ham with the other, before eagle-eyed mother-in-law-from-hell lands in on top of me. Just so the aul bitch can do her annual Christmas Eve inspection of my kitchen . . .'

Jeez, am inclined to forget how hard it can be to get a word in edgeways with Mags. Like she spends so much time round kids, that whenever she gets a chance to talk to adults, she physically won't let them off phone.

'I deliberately didn't call you to say happy birthday till much later on!' she says, still not letting me talk. 'I was sure your phone would be on silent for the whole day . . . God, you single people have the life! Never get married, do you hear me? And NEVER have kids, ever!'

'Mags, will you just hear me out?' I'm almost shouting in frustration now, purple behind the eyeballs probably, from the need to talk. 'Kitty never showed up.'

A short, stunned silence.

'She *what*?'

'And I've rung just about everywhere I can think of and there's no sign of her. So I was just wondering—'

'That is so terrible!'

'I know—'

'On your *birthday*?'

'Well, yeah—'

'You're joking me!'

'I wish!'

'Can't believe she'd just leave you high and dry like that!'

'I know, but— '

'But nothing!' she says firmly. 'Now you just listen to me, love. I know it's unforgivable carry-on, but I really wouldn't invest too much time worrying about Kitty, there's bound to be some perfectly simple explanation for this. Like . . . maybe she just slept it out, or something? You know what she's like.'

'But I must have rung the girl's landline about a dozen times so far this morning. And her phone is like a bloody foghorn! How could anyone alive possibly sleep through that?'

Remember distinctly Kitty having to get the most blaring bedside phone ever known to man installed; she'd just got the job at Byrne & Sacetti and once got so bollocked out of it once for sleeping through an early shift, that she'd no choice.

'I know,' Mags persists, 'but then, this is *Kitty* we're talking about. Look, I know we're kind of clutching at straws here, but she's nowhere else to be found, so why don't you just call round to her house and keep hammering on her front door, in case she's there? Or . . . I dunno . . . maybe pelt her bedroom window with stones till she eventually hauls her lazy arse out of bed? Why not, Ang? I mean, where else could she possibly be?'

11.05 a.m.

I've a good twenty-minute wait at a freezing bus stop, before a number ten that miraculously isn't stuffed pulls over and I squeeze my way in. Traffic's dire; Christmas Eve – I'm inclined to keep blanking it out. And nearly an hour later, I'm puffing and wheezing my way down Berkeley Street off the South Circular Road, where Kitty's been renting a gorgeous, cosy, two-up-two-down for about two years now, only about a ten-minute walk from restaurant on Camden Street, where she works. One of those recently renovated Corpo redbricks in a neat row of terraced houses, all just like it. Bit like Coronation Street, minus the Rovers and The Kabin and neighbours having bust-ups in public.

Mags is right, and thank God at least one of us is thinking clearly. I mean, where else could Kitty possibly be if not at home and still crashed out in bed? In fact, the more I think about it, the more I see how easy it would have been for her to go out on the batter, with a gang from the restaurant after work last night, for a few Christmas drinks, which somehow turned into about fifteen Christmas drinks, knowing her. Highly probable. With Kitty more than likely the ringleader, but then she's a divil for dragging everyone off to the pub, 'just for the one!' And where Kitty leads, the party invariably follows. Then five hours later, of course, everyone's still there.

So the chances are v. high she could well be lying under the duvet now, sleeping it off and totally dead to the world. Aren't they? Admittedly, I'm still a tiny bit snippy with her for whole birthday standing-up thing, but still . . . It's the season of goodwill; I'm prepared to forgive this one, tiny blip.

And, yeeessssss! That's when I see it! Her car, her pride and joy, an ancient, battered little banger of a run-around Mazda that she insists on calling Doris, neatly parked right outside her house. It's the miracle of Christmas! She *is* home and all is well! Wait till you see, I'll knock her up out of bed now and everything will be fine, the birthday will be salvaged and we'll still have a lovely Christmas Eve together. Just wait till you see. How could I ever have doubted her? Jubilantly, I hammer on her door.

But there's no answer. Knock again, wait. Ring the doorbell, wait some more. Knock again, ring again, nothing.

On cue, worry sweat restarts.

'Kitty?' I yell through the letterbox. 'It's me. You awake? Come on, love, get your lazy arse out of bed and let me in, will you? It's bloody freezing out here!'

Silence.

OK then, hope you're decent girlfriend, 'cos I'm coming in . . .

Kitty's due to go away with Simon on Stephen's Day and – thank you, God! – she gave me a spare key to her house when I saw her last, so I could nip in and feed the stray cat who drops in from time to time, while she's away. I fish her keys out from the bowels of my handbag and just as I'm letting myself in, out of nowhere fresh worry suddenly strikes.

Supposing she was broken into last night? And suppose she was in some way hurt and is now lying unconscious in a heap on the floor inside?

Another wave of panic, as yet more worry sweat starts pumping out of me with a vengeance. Must smell like bin day at a meat factory by now.

Fling the hall door open, calling out her name. But the alarm is on, beep-beeping away at me. So, no break-in then. Which is good news. I mean, 'course it's good news; obviously no burglars have been here, for one thing. But if the alarm is on, it means Kitty's not here, simple as. She only ever switches it on when she goes out; know this for a fact.

I punch in the code she gave me to silence shagging thing, then look around, taking v. deep breaths and trying my level best to stay nice and calm. The whole house is worryingly quiet. Don't think I've ever been in this house when it's so scarily silent before.

'Kitty? Are you here? It's me!' I call out, but I know it's a useless waste of time. Wherever she is, it's not here.

Place is so, so silent, a bit like the *Marie Celeste.* I head down the tiny hallway and into her cosy little galley kitchen-cum-living room, straight ahead. And as you'd expect from

Kitty, and probably on account of the mentally long shifts she works, the place is complete, Cath Kidston chaos. Even when she claims to have tidied up a bit, the house still looks identical. Not a hit-by-a-bomb mess, more like general disorganisation, but in way that's somehow full of charm, if that makes any sense. Books she's been studying for her evening classes are abandoned on the ironing board and a mountain of dirty washing is dumped beside the machine, that kind of thing.

V., v. weird and a bit spooky. Like Kitty's presence is somehow everywhere even though she's not. There's a pile of dirty dishes still on the kitchen table, but with Kitty you can never tell if it's breakfast dishes or late-night supper. Often both are the same thing in this house, pizza being a case in point. (Leftover pizza is a big staple of any waitress's diet, I'm reliably informed. Can't blame them either, the hours they work to support themselves, let's face it, they need the carbs.)

Starting to feel bit shifty now for snooping. Remind myself that if you were to go into my flat whenever I'm not expecting anyone, I'm not sure quite how tip-like place would be, but knickers lying strewn around the floor and knackered greying bras shoved down the backs of radiators, would be a v. definite given.

Sorry. Meant to say my ex-flat.

Keep forgetting.

Over in the corner, a Christmas tree is up; a proper real one, none of your fake, tinselly crap for our Kitty. A beautiful, perfectly symmetrical tree that smells like pine toilet freshener, but in a nice way. She told me she and Simon chose it together last weekend; apparently he insisted. Presents are littered round underneath it, some still in the bags and waiting to be wrapped. I'm well impressed; still haven't even got round to buying half my presents yet, but then being smashed broke and unemployed tends to be something of a major impediment to Christmas shopping.

Next thing, there's a sharp banging noise from behind me and I let out an involuntary yelp. Jump round to see who or what the hell it is, but it's OK, it's not an axe-wielding psycho, only Magic, the adorable tabby cat Kitty found on street outside starving and sick, so she took her in and nursed her back to full health. But then, Kitty's v. like that: a natural magnet for waifs and strays.

Magic lets herself in through a cat flap at the back door and immediately heads over to me, curling herself round my ankles.

I pick her up and pet her gently.

'Hey, Magic! Where is she? Where's your mommy? Have you seen her? Any ideas?'

The cat just licks her lips at me and jumps down, strutting over to the cupboard under the sink where I know Kitty keeps tins of Whiskas, then glares imperiously at me as much as to say, 'Haven't the first clue, love. Now would you stop talking to a mute animal like a complete moron and just feed me?'

So I do, and while Magic's wolfing down a bowlful of cat food, I take a good nose around the house. Just in case there's something, anything that might give me some idea of where Kitty could be. I head into her tiny study, the only other room downstairs and have a good gander at the noticeboard on the wall, littered with Post-it notes. Maybe some really important appointment she had this morning that she forgot all about till the very last minute, then had to rush off to?

Nothing out of the ordinary, though. Just row upon row of yellow stickers all covered in her scrawly handwriting with hastily scribbled reminders like, 'Collect dry-cleaning.' 'Root out passport and check expiration date.' 'Pay phone bill or will get cut off.' 'Cancel papers.' 'Put out bins!!' No indication she'd anything urgent on at all today, not a single thing.

So then I check upstairs, but it's exactly the same thing: absolutely nothing strikes me as odd. Hard to tell if the bed has been slept in or not. It's unmade, but then Kitty's not really the bed-making type. There's a big pile of her clothes carelessly flung across a chair by the wardrobe; a bright red plastic mac, pink flowery leggings and a load of T-shirts. December, I know, sub-zero outside, I know, but this is honestly the kind of thing Kitty would go out in without giving it a second thought. She's by a mile the nuttiest dresser I've ever seen. Like she just falls out of the bed first thing every morning and does a wardrobe lucky dip, grabbing whatever comes to hand without, God forbid, doing anything as conventional as colour co-ordinating. And still, by the way, managing to look stunningly fab in an artless, couldn't-particularly-be-bothered kind of way, not like a candidate for care in the community, as someone like me surely would.

'Kitty, where the hell are you?' I say aloud, then slump down onto the bed, so I can have a good think. Nowhere that she's supposed to be, and yet her car is here. So if Kitty did stay here last night, then got up as normal this morning . . . why didn't she just drive to the Sanctuary to meet me? She always drives everywhere around Dublin, except to work, because she reckons it would physically choke her to have to pay for the shagging parking.

Curiouser and curiouser.

Unless something happened to her on her way home from work late last night? But what? Image after image floods my worried mind: a hit and run accident? Mugging?

Right, that's it, then. Sod this, am done with all this bloody agonising and trying to second-guess what has or hasn't gone on. I'll just have to call the police, right now, I've got no choice. And yes, they'll probably have a right laugh at me or threaten to arrest me for wasting police time, but I can't help it. Just have to know if something, anything's been reported.

I call directory enquiries and get connected to the right number. A copper at the local station answers. So I tell him whole works: that my friend's just disappeared off the face of the earth, isn't answering her phone and isn't in work either. And that I'm in her house now, and still no sign.

Just hope he doesn't ask about her next of kin. There isn't time.

'And how long has your friend been gone for?' he says flatly, in a disinterested monotone.

'Well, we were to meet this morning at eight, but she never showed, so of course I panicked . . .'

OK, now I swear can almost hear him trying to suppress a dismissive snort.

'Eight this morning was barely four hours ago. She'll turn up, trust me. Besides, I'm not authorised to open up a missing persons report until a subject has been gone for a minimum of seventy-two hours. And, of course, assuming they've actually gone missing and aren't just out doing a bit of Christmas shopping.'

'But supposing there's been some kind of accident?'

Why isn't he taking this seriously? I thought he'd at very least put out APBs or whatever it is you call them, like they do on *CSI* the minute someone vanishes. But no, the subtext is v. clear: get off the phone now, you bloody lunatic time-waster.

'If there had been,' the copper tells me, talking down to me like I'm a bit soft in head, 'I can assure you that we'd know all about it. But I can tell you we've had no incidents or disturbances reported in the South Circular Road area so far today.' And with that, doing a mean hand-washing impression of Pontius Pilate, he adds, 'Well, if that'll be all then?'

Useless! Bloody useless! I want to snarl down the phone, 'Is this what I pay taxes for?' then remember: I've no job. I'm no longer an upstanding taxpayer at all. So I just keep my mouth shut and hang up instead.

One last, final look at the photos dotted all over the bedside table. Lovely one of Kitty and Simon when they went on a big, splash-out hollier to France last year. Kind of thing you only ever do when in the first stages of love. Whereas buying Christmas trees together clearly indicates they've reached the tenth stages. Said as much to her and can still remember her laughing, saying yeah, in two years time, they'd probably be screeching at each other, 'But I went out and got the shagging tree last year! Now it's your turn!'

Both of them in the photo look like something out of a Tommy Hilfiger ad. Clear-skinned, lightly tanned, athletic, long-limbed, skinny, totally gorgeous. Kitty, as always in photos, turning her head slightly sideways, the wild, abandoned tangle of Rebekah Brooks curls falling over her face to hide a kink in her nose she hates so much. Really has issues with it; she claims that if she ever won the Lotto, first thing she'd do would be to straighten it out once and for all. Says it gives her the look of a young Barbra Streisand; the *Yentl* years.

Major source of debate between us; mainly because if I had plastic surgery funds, the first thing I'd do would be to get my lardy arse sorted, once and for all. (As an aside, this is entirely possible; I've read about far worse cases than mine on back pages of *Marie Claire.*) Though I have to say, the only one who even notices Kitty's bumpy nose at this stage is her; if you ask me, it gives her even more character. Couldn't imagine her without it. Even blokes say it makes her look sexier and more appealing. (Curse my straight nose, *curse* it!)

Anyway, she and Simon are like Mr and Mrs Perfect Couple in the picture; they somehow even look a bit alike. Glowing, pictures of health and vitality, like Darwin's natural selection in progress. Made for each other, everyone says so.

Behind that, I spot a photo of Kitty and me. Bless her, she even went to the bother of framing my skinny photo. Ashamed to say, taken so long ago, I'm wearing jeans I haven't fitted into in a minimum of three years, in spite of all my best efforts plus a serious amount of yo-yo dieting. Also I've a v. unfortunate over-heavy fringe that I got talked into by a hairdresser when I was feeling a bit vulnerable and which turned out to be a BIG mistake that's taken ever since then to grow out. (Not really my fault; I was going for a Zooey Deschanel look, but ended up more like Kathy Burke (appearing as Waynetta Slob on *Harry Enfield*, that is).

Check the boxroom beside Kitty's bedroom, just in case.

Nothing out of ordinary, just piles of cardboard boxes and bags of clothes, which I'm guessing must belong to Simon, who's due to move in with Kitty after the holidays. Guy spends ninety per cent of his time here anyway, so both of them figured it was easier and cheaper just to go whole hog and live together.

So now what? Then, a sudden light bulb moment. The restaurant where she works is only about a ten-minute walk from here. I could maybe call in and try to furrow out some of Kitty's waiter pals? Maybe they know something I don't? Better yet, maybe Kitty's been there all this time and whoever answered phone to me earlier is either a complete dope, or else operating on a severe hangover and got it arseways about Kitty being off duty?

Check Magic is OK, and has enough food, milk, water, etc. Even try to cuddle her before leaving but the cat knows I'm not her mammy, leaps out of my arms like she's been electrocuted, and struts haughtily out the cat flap again, away on her travels. Kitty's a terrific cat person; me, not so much.

Snow's getting far heavier outside now; it's bloody freezing and slippy, with old ladies skidding and sliding all around me. Seriously starting to regret wearing totally inappropriate shoes – they're as good as destroyed after approx five minutes out in this.

My feet are now soaked and even my heavy-duty winter coat is getting a right battering.

Least of my worries.

12.05 p.m.

Eventually I batter my way through the elements to Byrne & Sacetti's Italian Bar and Restaurant to give it its proper title, right slap in the middle of busy, packed Camden Street.

It's a massive, sprawling place, set over four storeys, a bit like a family-run mini-empire. The entire ground floor is a food hall-cum-coffee-shop; first floor is the main restaurant, second floor is for private functions, weddings, fiftieth birthday piss-ups, etc., while the basement level is a wine bar, much favoured by single women, on account of its deserved reputation for being a high-end place to bump into eligible guys.

Many, many romances, according to Kitty, have started over chat-up lines such as, 'Excuse me, by any chance do you know where the charcuterie counter is? I hear there's thirty per cent off Parma ham and slabs of parmesan this week! And by the way, if you could possibly recommend a decent white wine to go with them, I'd be so grateful. Hope you don't mind my asking! Oh and . . . by any chance is that seat taken?'

Byrne & Sacetti is one of those Italian eateries that never seem to close, ever. They start with brekkie at dawn, lunch from twelve, afternoon teas, coffees, cakes, etc. in the food hall throughout the rest of the day, the evening restaurant proper opens at six, while wine is available downstairs in cellar bar till closing time. Gold mine, in other words. Even in the depths of recession, this place is still pulling 'em in.

Kitty's been working here for close to two years now, but still, in all the many, many times I've met her here after her shift before she'd drag me off for a night out, I've never seen it quite this jammed. Like the bleeding last days of Rome in here. Christmas revellers, already half-cut from too much daytime boozing, are staggering and clattering downstairs from the restaurant, while in the food hall section, last-minute shoppers panicking about tomorrow's dinner are nearly arm-wrestling each other over the last of the Panettones.

Gonna get ugly before too long, I can just feel it in the air.

12.22 p.m.

Still wandering round Byrne & Sacetti, one level at a time. I'm snooping round the basement wine bar now, weaving round stuffed-to-the-gills tables of Xmas boozers, trying not to trip over their abandoned shopping bags. There's a big gang of the ladies-who-lunch brigade in, all dressed in fashionable nude colours with nude, Kate Middleton heels to match and all looking like human Elastoplasts, if you ask me. All of them unanimously shoot irritated looks at me, as I almost stumble over expensive-looking handbags, abandoned carelessly at well-heeled feet.

Apologise, but don't really mean it. I'm only here on the off-chance I get lucky and chance on some waiter pal of Kitty's who might know something; *anything*. I would have met a good selection of her buddies from work, including a lot of the Sacetti family, from a few nights on the razz that Kitty's dragged me along to over the past few years. With karaoke nights featuring v. large; the Irish-Italians are very fond of their karaoke, it seems.

No joy, though. Can only see Xmas revellers starting the celebrations early, laying into their celebratory glasses of Prosecco and antipasti platters.

Mine is the only stressed-looking face; everyone else is having a rare old time, like the whole world has clocked off for the holidays.

Even Kitty.

12.45 p.m.

Finally . . . success!

I'm just nosing around the packed function room on the very top floor now, weaving in and out of groups of invitees clutching champagne flutes and trying not to look like I'm out to gatecrash a private Christmas party, when suddenly I hear my own name being yelled out loud and clear.

'Angie? Angie Blennerhasset? That you?'

Delighted, I turn round to see Joyce Byrne, part-owner here and a good pal of Kitty's. Married to Stephano Sacetti, other half of the Business Empire. Hardest working couple I think I've ever met in my entire life. Lovely, perpetually smiley, happy Joyce, still radiating Xmasy good cheer in spite of the fact she's probably been slaving away and on her feet since sometime before I went to bed last night.

I give her a big hug and fill her in.

'You mean Kitty just never turned up at the Sanctuary this morning?' says Joyce, horrified, and, I swear, the shock in her voice is almost reassuring. See? Proves I'm not mad, for one thing. I'm on the right track. Something awful *must* have happened.

'You're kidding me! She was so looking forward to it! She was full of chat about the whole thing; you should have seen the girl! She was all excited . . .'

'You mean . . . Kitty's definitely not here now, then? Hasn't been moved to work in the kitchen or anything?'

'No, definitely not. If she were, I'd know. Been here since the crack of dawn. Besides, I was only just thinking how quiet the staff room was without her.'

'And the last time you saw her was . . .?'

Starting to feel v. Hercule Poirot-ish now.

'God, let me think. It was definitely last night, seriously late, I think it must have been well after one in the morning. She was just finishing up after a party in the restaurant and I was doing the till. She gave me a lovely bottle of wine for Christmas, said she'd see me soon, then bounced out of here, all excited about seeing you. And, of course, going off on holidays with gorgeous fella of hers.'

Hard to put into words the feeling of total deflation. I was so hopeful Kitty might have been here all along and just through some complete fluke, I hadn't spotted her yet.

'So where do you think she might be?' Joyce asks me, worriedly.

'Well, let's work it out. You last saw her at around one o'clock this morning. And she's definitely not at home now, but her car *is* there . . .'

'Yeah . . .'

'So wherever she is, chances are she hasn't gone too far . . .'

Oh God. Sudden shock goes through me like I've just been electrocuted. Suppose Kitty was on her way home from work, and then got abducted by some sick, pervy sociopath who now has her locked up in a cellar somewhere?

Joyce really must be a mind-reader. She immediately grips my arm, quickly grabs a glass of still water from a passing waiter and makes me gulp down a few mouthfuls.

'Angie, the worst thing you can do is let your imagination run away with you. Trust me, there's some perfectly innocent explanation for all this. Have you spoken to her boyfriend?'

'No, he's not answering his mobile either. I can't get a hold of him at all . . .'

'Oh, that's right, of course. Kitty told me he's gone home to his folks down the country for Christmas and that she wouldn't be seeing him till Stephen's Day.'

'Unless . . .'

'Unless what?'

And there it is, the simple bloody answer to all this! Been staring me in the face all this time. Why didn't I think of it before now?

'Maybe there was some emergency with . . . well, with her foster mother? Something so urgent that Kitty just had to drop everything and run?'

The sudden relief at saying it aloud is almost overwhelming. Of *course* that's what must have happened. Explains away everything, doesn't it? I was an utter gobshite not to have guessed earlier!

It's a v., v. long and complex story, but the brief potted summary is that Kitty has no family to speak of, never even knew her dad, and her birth mother passed away when she was just a baby. She grew up in one foster home after another but says none of them ever really worked out and she just drifted around from Billy to Jack, rootless. Then when she was about fifteen, she was placed with an older, widowed lady called Mrs Kennedy and the pair of them just idolised and adored each other right from the word go. To this day, Kitty considers Mrs K., as she affectionately calls her, to be the only real family she ever had, even though she was only homed with her for over a year.

But when Kitty was only about sixteen, the poor woman started to become seriously ill with Alzheimer's, followed by a series of strokes. Awful for her and just as bad for Kitty too, though she never let on. Instead, she just did what Kitty always does: tried to keep the show on the road single-handedly for as long as she could.

Anyway, it got to stage when authorities decided Mrs K. couldn't care for herself any more, never mind a sixteen-year-old, so on what Kitty calls the most Dickensian day of her life, they broke them up and packed Mrs K. off to the best-equipped care home going, for someone with her condition. Meanwhile, Kitty was sent off to yet another foster family, and from that point on, she just completely clams up whenever I gently probe her for more about her back-story.

Mrs K. is being well looked after, though, and to this day, Kitty still visits her at the care home every chance she gets. Only trouble is, it's just outside Limerick, a bloody two-and-a-half-hour journey from here. Kitty's amazing though; drives down to see her every day off that she can. I've even gone with her a few times, but find it all just sad beyond belief. There are days when Mrs K. doesn't even recognise Kitty; confuses her with one of staff nurses in care home and for some reason keeps calling her Jean.

Also, I'm just not a born natural round ill people, like Kitty is. Kitty will laugh and joke and even bounce round other wards to visit all Mrs K.'s pals; you can always tell what room she's in by the loud sound of guffaws that follow her about everywhere. Like a one-woman Broadway show. Whereas I never know what to say or do, just sit tongue-tied in corner, then end up coming out with weak, useless crap along the lines of, 'Well, she's certainly looking a whole lot better, isn't she?'

Even worse, the days when Mrs K. doesn't know us are lately becoming the good days; sometimes she won't talk to us at all, just sits rocking away to self and singing theme tunes from TV shows, bird-happy, away in own little world.

Keeps confusing me with one of the tea ladies called Maureen, and every now and then will screech at me, 'How many times do I have to tell you, Maureen? I hate bloody egg and onion sandwiches!'

Heartbreaking. My own family may not exactly be the Waltons, but Kitty's story at least makes me appreciate what I have that bit more.

So maybe I'm finally on the money here. Because if something did happen to Mrs K., I just know in my waters Kitty wouldn't think twice about hotfooting it all way to Limerick, would she? And she couldn't phone me to explain on account of . . . well, maybe there being no mobile signal down there?

Has to have been what happened. And the only reason it didn't occur to me before now is that for past few years, although Mrs K.'s mental state is deteriorating fast, she's been so physically strong that not even Kitty was worried about her for the longest time.

'Joyce, I think I should call the care home. Now.'

'Of course,' she says firmly. 'You can use the phone from my office; you'll have a bit more privacy. It's just off the kitchens. Come on, I'll show you.'

Obediently I follow her and the pair of us weave our way through the Christmas boozers, worry now vom-making in my throat. Don't know what Kitty will do if anything's happened to Mrs K. Especially not now, at Christmas. She's the only person in the whole world that Kitty considers family; it would just be too bloody unfair by far.

Joyce efficiently brings up number of Foxborough House care home on her computer and even dials for me. Hands trembling nervously now as the number starts to ring.

'Foxborough House, how may I help you?' comes a polite, breezy, unstressed voice.

'Hi, there, I was wondering if I could enquire after Mrs Kathleen Kennedy? She's in room three eleven on the ground floor.'

'May I ask if you're a family member?'

Gulp to myself, stomach clenched, somehow sensing bad news. The worst.

'Family friend.'

'Well, I'm happy to tell you that Mrs Kennedy is absolutely fine, just ate a hearty dinner, in fact.'

'Sorry, you mean . . . She's OK then? There's no emergency with her?'

'No, none at all.'

'And, well . . . I was just wondering if Kitty Hope had been to see her at all today? She's my best friend and—'

Receptionist's voice instantly brightens tenfold at the very mention of Kitty's name.

'Oh, yes, I know Kitty well! Such a fantastic, lively girl, isn't she? We all love it so much when she comes to visit, she really cheers up everyone's day round here. But you know, the last time I saw her was about a week ago. I remember distinctly, because she mentioned that she'd be away for Christmas, but that she'd be in to see her mum as soon as she got back. At New Year, I think she told us.'

Joyce looks hopefully at me and I shake my head. So, no emergency, then.

Kitty's still gone AWOL.

1.05 p.m.

Right then. I've been in Byrne & Sacetti for ages now, can't loiter round any longer. Also, it's not fair to delay poor old

Joyce any more, not when it's like Armageddon in here. So I hug her goodbye and she smiles her warm, confident smile and tells me not to worry a bit. That Kitty will turn up safe and well and we'll all look back on this and have a good laugh.

Attempt to give watery grin back at her, but I'm an appallingly unconvincing actress.

1.08 p.m.

Then, just as I'm facing back out into the snowy street outside, my mobile suddenly rings.

Check to see who it is, hoping against hope . . . Not it's not Kitty, but it's the next best thing! Her boyfriend, Simon! He *HAS* to have news, just has to . . .

I dip into the doorway of a fairly quiet pub, away from the noisy street and the blaring sound of Christmas Eve traffic before answering.

'Simon! Can you hear me?'

'Hey, Angie, how are you?! I'm sorry about the delay in getting back to you, but I'm back at home, plus I'd to take a whole clatter of nieces and nephews to see Santa today and to buy all their Xmas presents. Bloody mayhem in Smyth's toy store, there were near riots over the last of the Lalaloopsy Silly Hair Dolls. Tell you something, I've never needed a stiff drink so badly in my life!'

Such a relief to hear his soft Galway accent. Strong. Reassuring. Bit like a pilot making an announcement on an Aer Lingus flight. For first time today, I feel safe. Calm. Somehow, it's all going to be OK. I'm far too stressed out to cop why he's on about Lalaloopsy Dolls, then remind myself: Simon comes from a massive family with approximately fifteen nieces and nephews, or whatever it was at last count.

'Simon,' I interrupt, a bit rudely, 'is Kitty with you?'

'With me? What are you talking about?'

Stomach instantly shrivels to the size of a sultana.

'You mean . . . you don't know where she is then?'

'No, isn't she with you? I thought you pair were having your lovely, relaxing, girlie treat day today? That I've been explicitly banned from, and told not to even call till hours later, when you're both roaring drunk on champagne?'

Fill him in. On everything, on how I've been everywhere and phoned just about everyone, looking for her. I even tell him bit about cops, who all but laughed at me and politely told me to bugger off the phone.

Long, long silence. Not a good sign. Starting to get weak-kneed and a bit nauseous now.

'Last time I saw her,' he says slowly, 'was yesterday morning, just as I was leaving the house to get on the road to Galway . . .'

'*Yesterday* morning?'

No, no, no, no, no. This not good news. Not good at all.

'Yeah. I came down here as early as I could, to try and beat the holiday traffic. Then I called her at about lunchtime to say I'd arrived safely and that both my parents were asking after her and are dying to see her as soon as we get back from holidays.'

No surprise here. For some reason, people don't just idolise Kitty: they want to carry her shoulder high through villages. Simon always says from very first time he took her to the West to meet his folks, they instantly preferred her to him. She's just one of those people that absolutely everyone adores, even people she's only met for five minutes, like barmen, taxi drivers, etc. You even see hard-nosed, intransigent dole officers eating out of her hand, after just a few minutes in her company. V. hard not to. Kitty's the mad, bad, dangerous-to-know type, totally magnetic and just the best fun you can possibly imagine. Kinda gal you meet for a few drinks, then end up the following morning in Holyhead. (Actual true story. Happened to us the night of her thirtieth birthday.)

'She was on her way into work,' Simon goes on, 'and couldn't really talk, so I told her I'd call her back later on. But when I did, she didn't answer her phone. I wasn't particularly worried, though; there wouldn't be anything unusual in that if she was working late. So I just left a message and said we'd catch up this evening, after her spa day with you.'

'So where do you think she's got to?' I ask, voice now sounding weak as a kitten's. The image of a sick perv locking her up in cellar suddenly now very real in my mind's eye.

'Well, she can't just have vanished into thin air,' says Simon confidently. 'Leave it with me, will you? Let me make a few phone calls. Maybe she just crashed out in another pal's house last night after a few Christmas drinks? I mean, you know what she's like!'

'OK then,' I tell him, trying my v., v. best to sound reassured. 'Well, you know I'm back living with my parents now, so you'll know where to find me if there's any news.'

'Don't worry, I'll call you the minute I hear from her.'

Am just about to hang up when he says, 'Oh, and by the way, Angie?'

'Yeah?'
'Happy birthday!'
My birthday.
It had totally gone out of my head.

Chapter Two

Christmas Day, 9.30 a.m.

Hardly slept a wink. Keep waking in the middle of the night to check my phone, in case there might be some message from Kitty. But nothing, still absolutely *nada.* Tried doing an early morning ring-round of all our mutual buddies yet *again*, but of course, the morning that's in it no one's even thinking about answering their phone. Course they're not; what was I thinking? My married pal is doing Santa Claus stuff with the kids, my single pals are all still in bed.

On the plus side, I've had three texts from Simon so far. One to tell me there's no news as of yet, but that I'm still to relax and try to enjoy a family Christmas. (Yeah, right. Only someone who hasn't actually *met* my family could ever possibly come out with a statement like that.) Second text is to say he's still with a big gangload of his relations now, and can't talk, but will call soon as he can. Third says if there's still no sight or sign of Kitty by tonight, he's coming straight back to Dublin, as soon as he can reasonably get away.

All three messages stress that I'm to keep nice and calm, that she'll turn up safe and well. This he promises.

'Course, that doesn't do anything to stop the sickening worry, but still, v. reassuring to know someone else is taking the whole thing as seriously as I am. Plus, I keep reminding myself Simon works as a trend forecaster. Which is a bit like weather forecasting, according to Kitty, except it's all about economic projections, ERSI figures, etc. He's part of the team that waved red flags, wagged fingers and warned us we'd all end up broke, and stay broke, barefoot and living off tins of Heinz beans, till sometime after our great-great-grandchildren all end up emigrating in coffin ships.

(Apparently there's v. big money in predicting bad news, but then, unlike horoscopes that say you'll have an utterly magical day, people are far more likely to believe you if you tell them that nothing but horrors and destitution await. Myself included.)

So Simon's basic job is telling the future.

So if he says Kitty will turn up and all will be well, then somehow, I trust him.

I've no choice.

11.35 a.m.

Right then, time to meet the Kardashians. Namely, the annual Xmas Day ordeal *chez la famille* Blennerhasset. My usual survival plan involves turning up as late as possible without incurring the wrath of Mother Blennerhasset, busying myself in the kitchen under the guise of 'helping', then skedaddling the minute the last Quality Street has been gulped down, to get back home in time for a nice juicy Xmas blockbuster movie. (So I'm free to watch it in the comfort and peace of my own flat.)

Except not this year. My usual escape hatch has now been totally sealed off. The official story to the rest of my extended family is that I'm 'temporarily crashing out with my parents, as I'm in between leases on two apartments.' Which I thought made me sound like a reasonably together person, not a twenty-eight-year-old no-hoper, newly unemployed, broke and forced into a humiliating crawl home with my tail between legs, etc. The inner circle, however, (Mum, Dad, older brother and sister,) all know the shameful truth, and in the case of my beloved sister, Madeline, rarely miss the golden chance to score a point.

Decide to time her, to see how long she lasts without managing to get a dig in. Just for the crack.

Midday

Mother Blennerhasset's annual Xmas midday drinkies for aunties, uncles, cousins, friends of parents, freeloading neighbours, etc. Drawing room's completely thronged. Everyone v. successfully and politely avoiding questions about my jobless state. But you can always rely on Madeline.

Ah, Madeline. Older than me by just two years, but already following in the family footsteps by working for a top law firm and making more money than I've ever seen in my whole life; with a mortgage, a pension and a flash-git style Mercedes *fully paid off.* Weighs approximately same as her coat and keys put together. (And just as an aside, as you'll see, the whole family have P. G. Wodehouse names. Which has to be borderline child abuse. Who in their right mind lumbers kids with names like Madeline, Toby and Angela when you're unfortunate enough to have a surname like Blennerhasset?)

'So, Angie,' she coos, wafting up to me with a glass of Prosecco in one hand and mobile clamped to the other. (Claims she's a very busy and important person who's still working. On Xmas Day. I know, I know.)

Then in full earshot of Mrs Higgins, Mother Blennerhasset's most competitive friend, with a v. successful daughter exactly my age already running her own business, fires her opener.

'Any prospects of gainful employment coming your way in the New Year?'

And, ladies and gents, we have a new record. Not ten minutes into the drinks do and already her inner bitch is out of the traps. And yes, Madeline really does talk like this. Like some Victorian matron in a bonnet-y, corset-y, Dickensian drama.

'Gimme a second, I just want to put out some more of these,' I smile weakly, indicating a near-empty tray of vegetarian vol-au-vents that I'm trying to squeeze my way back to the kitchen, to replenish.

She follows me though; clearly seeing this as green light to have a go at me. Angie-baiting being what she excels at, like an evil cat toying with a defenceless mouse. Bloody expert at it. Started when we were kids, when she'd go out of her way to make me the butt of her gags just for the laugh, but now that we're older, it's somehow got nastier. Then my brother Toby wafts in after two of us, wanting nothing more than grub and to make an escape from the arse-numbing tedium of the party, knowing him. Both come after me into the kitchen and slam the door shut.

'Come on then, answer the question, Angie, don't obfuscate the issue,' Madeline persists, instinctively knowing she's hit on my weak spot. And now that she has, she'll keep on and on at it till she's drawn blood. 'Are there or aren't there any jobs coming your way, sometime this century?'

'I just have to get these into the oven . . .' I mutter vaguely.

'Stop changing the subject,' she says, perching up on the kitchen table now and elegantly picking at a single grape from corner of cheese platter. Probably all she'll eat for the entire day. 'Because sooner or later you've got to get yourself back out there into the jobs market. Got to up your game a bit. So you've had a few knocks – who hasn't? Pointless hiding out at home, lazing around the house all day, just passively waiting on work to come to you.'

Look appealingly over to Toby, who's sitting in an armchair by my mother's Aga, flicking through yesterday's *Times* and stuffing his face with a large batch of cheese frittatas. Toby's generally far more humane than Madeline. Will tease me to tears, then surprise me at the oddest times by actually sticking up for me.

'Toby, tell her to back the feck off,' I say pleadingly to him.

'Aah, don't be so touchy,' he says, mouth stuffed, far more interested in the TV listings than in what's going on over his head. 'Mads just wants you to get a bit of work for yourself, that's all.' Then he thoughtfully adds, 'But you know, in all fairness, sis, she does have a point. The longer a gap any potential employer sees on your CV, the less attractive you become in their eyes.'

'Gee, thanks so much, Toby. "Et tu, Brute", and all that,' I hiss over at him, with what I hope is withering scorn.

'All I'm trying to impress on you,' Madeline drones on in that affected nasal whine that grates on my nerves so much, 'is that you've just got to get up off your backside, get out there and make it happen. Can't keep scrounging off the Aged Ps for ever, now can you?'

I've been trying v., v. hard not to rise to the bait, but at that, the saliva in my mouth suddenly turns to battery acid. Is this honestly what this one thinks I've been at? Arsing round watching daytime soaps, when in fact I've practically been hammering doors down trying to get some work? *Any* kind of work?

Oh, to hell with her anyway. I snap up from the oven, where I was shoving in yet another fresh batch of mini beef Wellingtons.

'Excuse me,' I tell her v. firmly, hands on hips, like a character out of a spaghetti western. 'I've already had a job interview this week, I'll have you know, thanks very much.'

'Oh, really? What for?' she scoffs. Can practically sense her getting riled up to test out what she thinks is her rapier wit on me.

'For . . . a position. A really good one, as it happens. Something secure, just till I get back on my feet again.'

'Where?'

'Never you mind where.'

I turn and bury my face deep in the fridge-freezer to avoid eye contact, pretending to rummage round back of it. Needless to say there's absolutely no offer of help from Madeline, but then because she's a lawyer, she clearly considers herself a cut above menial labour. Whereas, in her eyes, I may as well be the hired help with an apron on, saying 'Just hand me a broom and call me Daisy from *Downton Abbey*.'

'Stop avoiding my question, Angie, and just spit it out!'

'No, now go away and leave me alone. The mini pizzas

won't defrost themselves, now will they? Toby? Call her off, will you?'

'Jesus, I came in here for a bit of peace,' Toby mutters disinterestedly, this time between gobfuls of mini gherkins. 'So for feck's sake, just tell Mads what your big interview was for and then the pair of you can shut up. Besides, bar you applied for a job as an exotic dancer, what's the big deal anyway?'

Deep sigh. Because he's right: I know only too well that Madeline won't let up with the third-degree questioning till I come clean. She's worse than the KGB like that. I fully realise from years of dealing with her that it's easier just to let her have all the jibes she wants at my expense, and get it over with. Quicker in long run.

'Right then, have it your way. The job I applied for is in a catering company, if you must know.'

'A *catering* company?'

Then a short, two-second time delay while Madeline puts two and two together. 'Oh my God, don't tell me you mean like, buttering batch loaves in one of the sandwich bars your friend Sarah runs!'

If I'd said the interview was for a job scrubbing public toilets and that the main perk was that after two years I'd be issued with my own brush and a bottle of Domestos, Madeline couldn't possibly sound like she's enjoying this any more. She guffaws at me, like an Ugly Sister from *Cinderella* as I look pleadingly over to Toby for back-up, but no such luck. He's far more interested in the sports pages now, not to mention the plateful of mince pies he's devouring.

Thank Christ, am saved from further torture by Mum briskly swishing in, all swingy scarf, big, bosomy tweed suit and sensible shoes, looking even more like Ann Widdecombe than Ann Widdecombe herself. In she breezes, not a scrap of make-up on her, despite having a houseful of visitors to entertain. But then, Mum's proudest boast is that she hasn't put on foundation for minimum of forty years. No time.

As usual, her eyes are like hawks, taking in everything in one quick up-and-down glance.

'So here you three are!' she eye-rolls at us. 'Now come on, girls, stop all your bickering. I need some help. Chief Justice Henderson has just arrived; Toby, would you be a pet and entertain him? And, Madeline, I know Douglas McGettigan has to be the single most boring man in the Northern Hemisphere, but he's sitting all alone; anyone that's actually met him before won't go within six feet of him. Can you look after him for me, please? Chat to him about his golf handicap, he enjoys that.'

As the other pair scarper, I get thrown a familiar, vaguely exasperated look.

'Angela, you let your sister goad you, and you really shouldn't, you know. You just got to stop rising to the bait every single time. How often do I have to tell you?'

I mumble something vague into dishwasher along the lines of Madeline being a back-knifing cow and Toby being worse than useless, but Mum swishes off, too much in distracted hostess mode to pay much attention.

The minute she's out door, I pour myself a very large glass of Prosecco and knock it back in a single gulp.

Then check that there's plenty more bottles in fridge. If I'm to survive today, I'll be needing lots, lots more where that came from.

Dining room chez Blennerhasset, 3.45 p.m.

Dinner served. Determined somehow to survive and live to tell the tale. Mum and I jointly cooked, but then we're the only ones round here who eat normally and still gain weight. The other three are like bleeding rakes.

3.55 p.m.

Conversation turns to a personal injury case Dad presided over in the District Court few months back, where Toby was a junior counsel for plaintiff. Toby won, record settlement. Got in the papers and everything, one or two scuzzy tabloids even lapping up the whole father/son thing. Dad was utterly mortified by all the fuss, but I'm prepared to bet good money Toby still has all press cuttings framed and mounted in his downstairs loo. Strongly suspect he thinks it'll boost his chances of landing a quick shag.

But if you weren't involved in said case, and if you don't happen to get the legal terminology, it's all deeply, deeply boring, so while Toby's telling yet another 'hilarious' lawyerly anecdote, I surreptitiously whip out my mobile from my jeans pocket and check it. Just on the off chance Simon has news. Or better still, in case Kitty herself has miraculously resurfaced. Who knows? Maybe having crashed out on someone's sofa for past twenty-four hours? And now with nothing more than a minging hangover and a hilarious tale to tell?

Course I've tried to check if Kitty is by any chance visiting her foster mum, but can't. Already made two sneaky phone calls to Foxborough, Mrs K.'s nursing home, when I was holed up in the kitchen loading the dishwasher. No answer, though. 'Course not, it's Christmas Day. Who in their right mind would be working on reception Christmas Day?

Mum's straight on to me. Asks me why I keep glancing down at my phone every few seconds. Then tells me to put the phone away, that it's rude.

3.56 p.m.

Golden chance for Madeline to get yet another jibe in.

'You know, Angie, you can just say if all this legal chat is a little bit above your head. We can always change the subject and talk about, ooh, let's see now . . . what's happening in the lives of the Kardashian sisters? Would that be a little more up your street? Or maybe the latest news from the catering industry?'

'I was actually checking to see if there was any word from Kitty,' I fire back, throwing her what I only hope is a scalding look.

The whole table give long sighs and eye rolls. Yet *again.* All in lawyerly agreement I'm totally overreacting to whatever's going on. The gist of what they think is that Kitty's spending the day doing whatever suits her and clearly has better things to do than making phone calls. Yes, even to the best friend she stood up on her birthday.

Relations between *la famille* Blennerhasset and Kitty are as follows: both Mum and Madeline are the only people I've ever met totally and utterly resistant to her laid-back, chaotic charm. Instead, the pair of them have her down as a notoriously unreliable, uneducated, lunatic flake-head from the wrong side of the tracks, whose worst crime in their eyes is that she's a bad influence on me and has been ever since the day we first met. They hold her wholly responsible for my not obediently trailing after every other Blennerhasset since the Civil War and subsequently spending my days mouldering away in the law library. (Where I'd doubtless have ended up either an alcoholic by now, or else on hard drugs. Fact.) Mainly because it was Kitty who first encouraged me to stop always doing what was expected of me, but instead to follow my own dreams, and to live my best life.

Which is why, not long after graduating, I took myself off to post-grad film school, to study as a freelance director. Which is kind of why, after years of great gigs coming in, I'm now suddenly unemployed. (Film production is what you might call a soufflé business, and this is not a good economy to be in the soufflé business, trust me.)

Dad and Toby tend to be slightly more under Kitty's spell, though every now and then Dad will remind me he still hasn't forgotten about the time she filched a bottle of his Château Margaux for a piss-up we were both going to. Happened when I invited her to stay here one Christmas all of four years ago and he still hasn't let it go. And I know right well Toby has a crush on Kitty, I can tell by way he blushes like a wino whenever she's here and he keeps asking her if she'd like to swing by his flat sometime, to check out his fifty-two-inch Blu-ray plasma screen.

'She's clearly gone to visit that foster mother of hers down in Limerick,' Mum is telling me, 'so just relax and don't let that girl ruin your Christmas, like she ruined your birthday.'

'She didn't ruin my birthday,' I say loyally, to an exasperated eye-roll back at me.

'I'm sorry, love, but it's no secret that Kitty Hope is not exactly my favourite of your friends.'

'Mum's quite right, you know,' Madeline pontificates, 'so just stop harping on about what did or didn't happen to Kitty and wait till she gets back to you. Knowing her, she probably forgot all about you and spent the day at some more interesting Christmas Eve do. Be perfectly typical of that nutcase you insist on hanging around with. Oh God, will you ever forget the time that she—'

But Dad interrupts. 'Scan not your friend with microscopic glass; you know his faults, so let his foibles pass.'

Dad's a great man for quotes, but I rarely have the first clue where they come from. Nice, though, to think he's temporarily forgiven Kitty over the nicked Château Margaux incident.

'Thanks, Dad,' I smile gratefully back at him.

'You know, I'm certain there's absolutely nothing for you to worry about, pet,' he says, leaning forward and gently patting my hand. 'One of a thousand things could have happened to Kitty yesterday, you know. She'll be in touch, you just wait and see. Never assume something is wrong until you have concrete evidence in front of you.'

Subject dismissed as far as everyone concerned.

Long pause, the table filled with sounds of *nomnomnom* noises, then Mum suddenly pipes up, sounding worried now.

'Are you absolutely certain that you and she didn't have some kind of falling out?'

I nearly splutter on a Brussels sprout.

'Mum! There was absolutely nothing like that, I promise! Come on, you know how close Kitty and I are. We've never had a single cross word in all the years I've known her!'

Almost the truth. Only ever had one tiny blip with Kitty, in seven otherwise row-free years. In my defence, it wasn't entirely my fault either. It was Kitty's idea to shoplift two lip glosses from the Top Shop cosmetic counter just for the laugh, when she thought the place was so packed, no one would notice.

Bloody CCTV cameras.

It was v. scary, we were taken into a security office and threatened not only with the police being told, but even more intimidatingly, with being barred from every Top Shop branch on the planet for life. I was all of twenty-one years old at the time and while Kitty brazened it out with all the swaggering confidence of someone who's had to fight all her own battles from a young age, I collapsed under questioning and just sat there, bawling hysterically. End result? We were let go with a caution, but to this day I still can't cross threshold of any Top Shop without breaking into a cold, clammy sweat.

Mum's implication is v. clear though. That somehow, even without realising it, I did something to piss Kitty off, and now she hasn't disappeared at all. She's just not speaking to me.

7.35 p.m.

Dinner over, thank Christ. And now we're all sprawled round the fire with Mum point-blank refusing to switch on the telly, even though I'd kill to see lovely, life-affirming *It's A Wonderful Life* and banish the horrendous shittiness of last twenty-four hours temporarily out of my head. The others are all back to chatting about mutual colleagues that they know and I don't, to the background track of Dad snoring like a passing Zeppelin.

So, so bored. And still so worried about Kitty.

I'm just thinking about her when my mobile rings . . . Simon! Suddenly wide awake and on high alert, I race out to the hall to take it, away from the riveting background debate on the gripping subject of *Flynn vs. Sullivan* and whether or not sentencing was overly lenient.

'Simon? Can you hear me?'

My heart's nearly walloping off my ribcage by now, cartoon-like.

Please have news, please, please have good news, please can Kitty somehow have surfaced and be with you and please tell me that all is well . . .

'Hi, Angie, look I'm so sorry to bother you on Christmas night, when you're with your family . . .'

The line's v. bad, he's already cracking up on me, but even so, I can clearly hear the deflation in his voice. Not a good sign.

'Simon, are you still there?'

Have to shout this a few times before he comes back into coverage again.

Come on, come on, come on!!!!

'Yeah, look, Angie,' he almost has to yell now to be heard, 'I'm still with my parents down in Galway and the signal is rubbish at their house . . . Have you heard anything yet?'

Oh shit. If he's calling me to see if *I've* any news, then we're really in trouble.

'No, not a word, I was hoping you might have by now! What about Mrs K. in the nursing home? Did you have any luck getting through there? I tried earlier but no joy.'

'Me neither. So look, here's the plan . . .'

Good. A plan. I'm a big fan of plans. Everything works better with a plan. Weddings, murders, everything.

'I'll keep ringing every friend Kitty has that I can think

of tonight,' he says, sounding more and more crackly by the second, like he's calling from inside the large Hadron Collider at Cern.

'Great, I'll do likewise . . .'

'. . . And if there's still no sign of her by first thing in the morning, I'm going to drive straight to the nursing home in Limerick, to find out exactly what's going on for myself.'

'And . . . well, what if Kitty's not there either?'

My voice is sounding tiny now, like a small child's, and the worry sweats have restarted with a vengeance.

'Then I'll just come straight back to Dublin and I guess we'll take it from there. The main thing to remember, Angie, is not to panic. I'm sure she'll turn up safe and sound and that there's some perfectly reasonable explanation for this.'

As ever, when told not to panic, my shoulders seize and my breath starts to come in short, jagged bursts.

'But, Simon, what then? What'll we do if we still can't find her?'

Too late, though. His phone's gone totally out of coverage. Line's now totally dead.

And he never even answered the question.

Chapter Three

Stephen's Day, 7.01 a.m.

Another sleepless night alternately spent tossing, turning or else staring at the ceiling, hoping against hope that my phone would just ring and it'd be Kitty. Then I switch the light on, check the mobile on my bedside table, thinking maybe, maybe, maybe the Miracle of Christmas has actually happened . . . Keep telling myself that you just never know with her . . . But nothing. So I lie back down again, try to sleep, can't, then repeat the whole palaver all over again at regular thirty-minute intervals.

At first light, I check the phone for about the thousandth time, but it's a total waste of time, the screen's completely blank. Automatically I hit the re-dial button and call Kitty's number, almost through force of habit at this stage. I know it's like eating a whole tube of Pringles and that it's ultimately v. bad for me and will end up driving me mental, but I just can't stop myself. And, of course, her phone clicks straight to voicemail.

'Hi there, it's Kitty! Sorry I can't take your call, but leave a message and I'll ring you back. Providing of course that you're a) good-looking, and b) that I don't owe you any money!'

Completely weird hearing her disconnected voice like this. It's almost a shock how bright and bouncy and full of energy she sounds, while we're here, agonised out of our minds about her. I check the number of times I've called her since the whole Christmas Eve/aborted birthday fiasco. Fifty-two. And not one single message returned. Even find myself turning to prayer, something I only ever indulge in when I'm really sick with worry.

Listen God, I know you don't exactly hear from me all that often, and I appreciate you've probably got miles more important things to get on with, such as sorting out famine in Africa, etc., etc. But if you could just see your way to keeping Kitty safe wherever she is and maybe if you could get her to turn up anytime now, we'd all be so, so grateful. Come on, God, you can do it! It is, after all, officially the Season of Goodwill, isn't it? Any chance this could be my miracle of Christmas?

P.S., hope Baby Jesus had a really lovely birthday yesterday.

The only straw of hope we've got is this: at end of day, it is Kitty we're dealing with here. I have to constantly repeat it over and over, like a mantra. Therefore, the rules that bind ordinary mortals like you and me just don't apply.

True, she's my best friend, but still . . . I remind myself of the sheer number of times in the past when she's flaked off like this before. Honest to God, you'd marvel at how entirely possible it is to love another human being dearly, and yet want to strangle them with your bare hands at same time. No question about it: Kitty's the type who could have taken off anywhere, or who absolutely *anything* could have happened to. Easily.

Might possibly even have ended up drunkenly crawling

on a flight to Rio, with a gang of people she accidentally got swept up with, and now can't get in touch with us . . .

Highly unlikely, but you'd never know . . . I keep saying it over and over, like it's playing on a loop in my mind.

With Kitty, you just never know.

7.02 a.m.

Snap out of it immediately. Course she's not on a flight to Rio. As if! I'm suddenly aware my excuses for her now becoming increasingly more far-fetched. Jeez, I'll be imagining alien abductions next. I tell myself Simon is right: there has to be some perfectly simple explanation. *Perfectly* simple. We'll look back and laugh when she turns up. After I physically reef the curly mop off her head first, for putting us through all this crap.

And if it does actually turn out that she flitted off to South America to do conga lines in the sun, then I'll personally wring her neck with the knicker string off her own bikini.

Not an idle threat, by the way.

9.14 a.m.

A text from Simon. I nearly drop the phone, my hands are shaking so much as I try to read it.

> HAVE JUST LEFT NURSING HOME. STILL NO NEWS. KITTY HASN'T BEEN HERE SINCE LAST WEEK. I SAW MRS K., WHO'S UNAWARE OF WHAT'S GOING ON, BUT IN GOOD SPIRITS. ON WAY BACK TO

DUBLIN NOW, NO SIGNAL HERE, WILL CALL YOU SOON AS I GET THERE.

9.30 a.m.

My brain's completely scrambled. I'm finding it so hard to function normally, to colour in between the lines. Between panic attacks, I keep thinking, oh, OK, now I get it, I'm in hell. And once I accept that, surprise myself by getting through whole minutes at a time.

9.35 a.m.

OK, two choices here. Either I can continue staring worriedly out the window like a stray character from Chekhov, or I can actually make myself useful and get back to doing a ring-around of just about every mutual friend Kitty and I have. Which, given that it's Stephen's Day and normal people are all out visiting relatives or else hitting the January sales, is a lot easier said than done.

Call my buddy Jeff, but it's only his voicemail. Probably up climbing a mountain today or something equally shamingly healthy. (Jeff's one of those outdoorsy, Patagonia-clad fitness nutters.) Then Sarah, who at least answers, but then she's been queuing up to get into the Harvey Nichols sale probably since sometime before midnight last night. Sarah's the type who'd v. happily drive through a warzone if she thought there was even an outside chance of a discount store, where she'd save a fiver off leggings.

She tells me she hasn't seen Kitty in well over a week, but promises to call back as soon as she bags a Marc Jacobs trench coat she's had her eye on for months and been saving up for, as a Christmas self-gift.

'Reduced by SEVENTY-FIVE PER CENT, can you *believe* it?'

'Yeah, but the fact is that Kitty's still missing and I'm starting to get seriously worried now . . .'

'Oh, come on, I wouldn't worry about Kitty. Sure, you know what that one's like! She'll turn up safe and well with some mental far-fetched tale to tell, you wait and see!'

Her v. last words to me before hanging up.

And Mags' phone goes straight to message minder, but then I know she's got a houseful of visiting in-laws and will only get back to me at what she calls 'wine o'clock'. In other words, when her kids are in bed and she can actually hold an adult conversation, without banana being rubbed into the good furniture.

So in a nutshell, no one seems to have seen or heard from Kitty. Course they haven't. By now, they all know the distress flares are up. So if they had, wouldn't they have just called me?

12.05 p.m.

Simon phones again. Says he's nearly on the outskirts of Dublin now and asks if we can meet, to decide where we go from here. Am delighted; two heads are most definitely better than one. We arrange to hook up at Kitty's house in an hour. Don't know why, but it just seems like the most logical place. Also to be v. honest, am bloody thrilled to be getting out of here. My family are all starting to treat me like I'm bit soft in the head for investing so much time and worry on Kitty. Mum and Madeline clearly of the 'no doubt about it, that one hopped on a plane to Rio on a whim and true to form, didn't bother telling anyone. Would be typical of her' school of thought.

Which is not only mean but v. unfair. Don't care what they say, flitting off to Rio definitely isn't something she'd do.

And the more I keep saying it, the more I actually manage to convince myself.

1.20 p.m.

Bit late, bloody skeleton holiday bus service, not helped by icy roads, meaning the driver can only do approximately two miles an hour. Then, skidding and sliding from the bus stop down to Kitty's little terraced street, I nearly sob pure, salt tears when I turn the corner and see Simon's black Audi parked neatly outside, right beside Kitty's banger. Like the two of them are home; like old times; like absolutely nothing's wrong. Like I'm swinging by for nothing more than a lovely glass of wine and big, comforting plate of pasta, while dissecting some of the more rubbishy pitches on *The Apprentice.*

But at least Simon's here, I have to remind myself with an inward sigh of relief. It's a big step forward. And who knows, maybe he'll have good news or else he'll have figured out some way to find her?

Everything's going to be OK now he's here, I think. Am certain.

1.22 p.m.

Simon lets me in, looking like he only just got here ahead of me, still in a heavy winter coat and deep in chat on the phone. By the sounds of it, am guessing to someone v., v. High Up at Byrne & Sacetti, possibly even Stephano Sacetti, the man himself. Co-owner, with a bit of a Silvio Berlusconi complex, according to Kitty.

Simon smiles quickly at me, leads me into the tiny living room and motions for me to grab a seat, miming me a gesture that he's trying to wrap up the call. He keeps making lots of 'ah huh' noises and saying, 'OK, OK, yes, I see,' a lot.

Rip off my heavy winter coat and plonk down, fidgeting with my gloves and pretending not to earwig.

God, am inclined to forget just how authoritative and impressive Simon can be, even on the phone. If handsome, lovely Simon can't find Kitty, then no one can! Would be v. surprised if he's not getting a big pile of information out of Sacetti right now, including really personal stuff, like bank account numbers, star sign, current relationship status, etc. He's just one of those guys people naturally trust and open up to. Bit like a senior consultant. Or a hairdresser.

Doing me the power of good, though, just to see him. Can't begin to describe the huge relief at just being around another human being who's actually being proactive and prepared to take this seriously and not just write me off as a near-mental case for worrying myself into early grave.

Look at him distractedly in all his gorgeousness while he talks on. Simon's v. tall, by the way, even taller than Kitty, but with the same lean, leggy build as her, which short-arses like me are so envious of. Classically dark and good-looking, in a Pierce Brosnan circa-when-he-was-doing-the-Bond-movies type way, right down to the deep sea-green eyes, always v. focused and intense. But I must stress in an attractive way, not a Christopher Walken-weirdo way.

I drift off a bit while he keeps talking down the phone. Funny just how different he and Kitty are personality-wise, and yet how well suited at the same time. Like a textbook case of the opposites attract theory in practice. Whereas she's wild and abandoned and reckless, and by a mile the funniest girl on the planet, Simon's a more conservative, stable, strong, silent type. Oddly enough, the combination works though and works beautifully. She's able to knock a bit of craic out of him and lighten him up, whereas he's had a v. steadying, calming influence on her. Everyone says so. He's tamed her down a bit too; right up till she met him, the very second she sensed a guy was getting overly serious on her, she'd bolt screaming for the hills. Was famous for it.

But she's been with Simon for over eighteen months now, her longest relationship ever, and I should know, I was there on fateful night it first happened. It was like something out of a movie; he just took one look at her and that was that. I might as well have turned into background flock wallpaper. Just like everyone who meets Kitty instantly falls under this inexplicably strange, charismatic spell she's able to weave. It's extraordinary; even gay men seem to get crushes on her. I've invested many, many hours trying to study exactly what it is that she has, so I can somehow impersonate it, in much the same manner as politicians running for President are said to study JFK and ask, 'What was it that made him so special, and how do I in some small way, channel it?'

But no chance. Kitty's a unique one-off.

Eighteen months on, and the pair of them are more loved-up than ever; the Christmas tree in the corner that they went out and bought together is a big reminder. Not to mention the fact that Simon's officially about to move in here. And they're completely fab, one of those couples you point to and think, you see, YOU *SEE?* True love isn't just excuse for weak rom-com vehicles tailored around Jennifer Aniston! It actually exists and is out there. And Kitty and Simon are living, walking proof! So there!

He mimes a 'sorry about this' gesture at me and throws his eyes to heaven, like he's been trying to get off this call for ages now and just can't. Have to say, though, whoever he's on to, he's certainly doing a terrific job.

'No,' he's saying calmly down phone, 'as I've already explained, the last time I saw Kitty was early on the morning of the twenty-third, when she was leaving the house for work . . . Yes, yes, of course, we already tried that, that was the first thing we did, but no joy . . . Besides, you're right, I think you've got to be missing for a minimum of three days before they'll finally take you seriously . . . Though if it comes down to it by this evening, then rest assured, the police will certainly be my next port of call . . .'

The police? Hang on a minute. Did he just say the *police*? Suddenly I'm panicky. I thought Simon of all people could fix this, could find Kitty and make it all go away! So if he's now talking about going to the worse-than-useless cops, then my whole confidence base just spectacularly imploded. I throw him a sharp, horrified look, but he just makes a 'calm down, it's fine, relax' hand gesture back at me.

'No, she's most definitely not with her foster mum in

Limerick either, I'm afraid,' he's saying now. 'I've just driven up from there, in fact. She hasn't been down to see her in over a week . . .'

Another eye-roll at me, though if he's beginning to lose patience at the daftness of the questions he's being asked, you'd never know by him. Simon's always unfailingly polite.

'Yes, yes, of course, we've been trying to get in touch with all our mutual friends for two full days now, but you know how hard it is getting anyone to answer their phone on Christmas Day. Or even today, for that matter. No, no, I'm quite sure you're right and that there's absolutely nothing for us to worry about, but as I say, if I could possibly get my hands on a list of anyone she was working alongside at the restaurant on the night of the twenty-third, that would be really useful to us at this point . . . Brilliant. Huge thanks for this . . . And yes, of course I'll be sure to call you the minute we do find her . . . Right, well, see you shortly, then. And once again, I really do appreciate everything you're doing to help.'

A big thumbs up sign to me, then finally he wraps it up.

'Well? Any news?' I ask, on edge of seat, bowels knotted and palms sweating, too antsy even to say hi properly.

'I'm so sorry about that, Angie,' he says, not answering my question and instead coming over to give me a big, warm hug. I hug him back and for a moment, we hold each other v. tight. And it's comforting. He smells lovely too, but then Simon always smells delicious. Citrussy.

Then he slumps down in the armchair beside me and rubs his eyes like he's ready to flake out with exhaustion. Unsurprising really, given that the poor guy must have left Galway at some ridiculous sparrow fart of an hour this morning, to drive all the way to the nursing home in Limerick, not to mention coming straight on to Dublin.

'Simon, you mentioned the *police*?'

'It's not going to come to that, trust me. She'll have materialised by then,' he says. 'But if we've no more news today, then I think maybe it's our best option.'

Then he clocks the stressed-out-of-mind look on me and softens. Even sits forward and takes both my hands in his. Feels warm and reassuring.

'Oh, now, come on, Ange, you've got to keep calm. Chances are she's safe and well, and, for whatever reason, just can't get a message through to us. Maybe she's been staying with someone she works with who lives down the country, where there's no phone signal, for instance.'

'You honestly think she could just crash out with friends and not even go to see Mrs K.? On Christmas Day? You really think she'd be capable of doing that? Because I, for one, just aren't buying it!'

'I know, I know,' he sighs, letting go of my hands and staring straight ahead of him now, the gorgeous green eyes focused, v. on-the-case. 'Believe me I know that none of this adds up. But all you and I can do for the moment at least, is take this one step at a time. Worse thing is jumping to conclusions. And the second worse thing we can do is panic.'

I nod, a bit numbly.

'By the way, I guessed you talking to Sacetti just now? Any news?'

'Yeah, that was Sacetti all right. Ever met him through Kitty?'

I shake my head. Though I've often heard her talking about him. Apparently, although happily married with five grown-up kids who all work for him, he has a terrible eye for the laydeez, and Kitty claims he's an outrageous flirt, particularly with the younger waitresses. Even tried it on with her once, but was swiftly met with a sharp knee to the groin and a stern lecture about how he should try being a bit nicer to his gorgeous and v. hard-working wife.

'Well, like just about everyone else, he hasn't seen her in a few days . . .'

'Oh for God's sake! When will someone turn up with news that can actually help us?'

'No, hang on, there's more,' Simon gently cuts across me. 'I asked him for a full list of all the staff who were working alongside Kitty on her last night there.

'OK. Well . . . good thinking.'

'And Sacetti immediately agreed, said he was glad to be of help. They're actually open today and he's in work, so we can call in, if you've time. Then maybe the two of us could come back here and do a ring-around of all her co-workers to see if anyone knows anything.'

I nod eagerly.

'Because,' he continues, sounding supremely confident, 'someone just *has* to. She could easily have gone to another work colleague's house after she clocked off her last shift, maybe for a few Christmas drinks and somehow ended up staying there. Maybe she figured Mrs K. was fine, so she just decided to hang out wherever she was for Christmas. She and I aren't due to go away on holidays till tomorrow, so for now at least, let's just assume the best. We might even hear from her later on today; you of all people know how scatty Kitty can sometimes be. She's well capable of just bouncing through the front door this evening like absolutely nothing's wrong and start flinging stuff into a suitcase for the trip. You know what she's like. So until then, the best thing you and I can do is stay focused and keep our heads. Just remember, there's dozens of perfectly reasonable explanations for this.'

Simon sounds calm, self-assured, completely confident. And, amazingly, given the state I'm in, some of it manages to rub off on me. Even though I know deep down in my bowels this is a big load of horse manure. My best pal in the world would NOT stand me up on my own birthday. It's unthinkable. Just not possible.

'So, are you free to come to the restaurant with me right now, by any chance?' he asks, hauling himself up and rooting around for his car keys. 'Sooner we get that list from Sacetti, the sooner we can start ringing around. Be a helluva lot quicker if we work together.'

''Course I'm coming with you,' I tell him firmly. 'You think I'm going anywhere till all this is sorted?'

He looks gratefully down at me and smiles.

'You're a good friend, Angie. Kitty always says you're the best and it's only the truth.'

'She'd do exactly the same for me. I know she would.'

'So apart from all this,' he says, helping me on with my heavy, winter coat like the perfect gentleman he is, 'how are you doing? Holding up?'

'Been better,' I shrug up at him. 'People keep telling me to relax, that she'll turn up, but I can't listen to them. I just know in my bones that there's something seriously wrong. And I don't care what anyone else says, nothing about this feels right, not even for Kitty.'

Then I can't help myself.

'Simon, if I ask you a straight question, will you give me a straight answer?'

''Course I will. You know that.'

'And I want the truth from you now, and none of your spin.'

'Truth and nothing but,' he says, the eyes boring into me.

'You seem so calm and reassured and that's brilliant, but, well . . . just how worried are you at this point in time? Because you must be, just a bit. I mean, deep down.'

Desperately need him to say, 'Worried? Me? Not a bit of it! In fact, I'm so supremely confident she'll walk through the door this evening, that I'm fully intending to start packing ski gear and snow boots for our holliers tomorrow, the very minute I get back from the restaurant.'

But instead, he goes quiet. Worryingly quiet.

Which is wrong, all wrong! I'm the one having a wobbly here; he's meant to be rock of sense that talks me in off the ledge!

'At this point in time?' he eventually says, 'I'd give it a four out of ten. If I ever make it all the way up to ten, then I'll really start panicking.'

Have to bite my tongue clambering into his car. It was a trick question! He was supposed to say zero out of ten!

Cosmic shift in that moment. And I've now officially gone from absorbing his calm aura, into hand-me-a-Xanax territory.

2.25 p.m.

Stephano Sacetti turns out to be short, round and welcoming. Kisses us both on both cheeks, Mediterranean style, and waves us into his private office on the top floor. He's actually a v. charming man, twinkly-eyed and sallow skinned, with an expensive-looking silk suit and the faint whiff of cigar smoke off him.

Says all the right things, all the stuff I needed to hear: that we're not to worry, that Kitty is a v. responsible person. (Eyes went slightly goggly at that. Kitty's many wonderful things but responsible is most definitely not one of them. But then given that this is her boss-man, I figure she must have put on one hell of an act in front of the guy.)

Anyway, soon as we arrived, he immediately printed us off a long, long list of all the staff, waiters, bar staff, delivery men, kitchen staff, right down to Polish guys that scrub down the loos, who were all around during that same last shift as Kitty. Way more than I'd ever have thought, but then you must need a small army of staff to run an ever-growing empire like this. Plus, as he tells us, it was the night before Christmas Eve, the place was packed out; it was a case of all hands on deck.

Jeez, scanning through it, the list runs to almost two full pages, literally dozens of names and their contact numbers. He's even thrown in the contact details of diners who'd booked in that night and who'd left their phone numbers when making reservations. Everything we need and absolutely no stone unturned, in other words.

On the way out, we do a quick scan on each level of the restaurant, just in case there's someone working that either of us might recognise. Place is surprisingly busy; there's a whole clatter of young girls in Ugg boots with gel nails and too much false tan, all chattering excitedly over coffee and buns in the Food Hall Café about their Christmas sales bargains. Meanwhile the entire restaurant level is bustling with families having a post-Christmas lunch/hangover cure, or else diners who just couldn't have been arsed cooking another big meal two days running. Simon just strides through every level confidently, me racing after him to keep up.

Only see one person we can ask though, a young part-timer who works down in the Food Hall. Francesca Sacetti is a cousin of Stephano, but then approx. fifty per cent of the staff in here all seem to be cousins of Stephano. (If you ask me, the Sacetti family are a bit like the Corleones, only legit.) We head over to where she's busy restacking tins of olives on the shelves and ask if she's seen Kitty at all.

No, she blinks innocently back at us. Says she's been in Palermo for past two weeks. First day back at work today.

Should have guessed by her shagging suntan. Then she asks, wide-eyed, 'Why, what's the matter? Is something up with her? Is Kitty OK?'

Not off to a v. good start.

4.05 p.m.

Back at Kitty's, stuck on our phones, the pair of us. Bit like a telesales conference in here. Lists covered in biro marks surround us, scattered all over the floor. My ears physically sore and raw red from being on the phone for the past few hours. At this stage, we've a system of sorts going. We've both crossed out the names of people we actually got to speak to but who were no help to us, then made dirty big red marks beside the names of anyone who didn't actually answer their phone, but who we've left messages for, practically begging them to call us back urgently.

Net result to date? Sweet feck all.

8.20 p.m.

Still here, with my voice nearly hoarse by now from talking on phone.

On the plus side, between the pair of us we've at least managed to make some kind of headway and now have a good long list of people we've left messages for and who are to get back to us; people who might just be able to shed a bit of light on the whole thing. On the minus side, though, in spite of everyone we did actually manage to speak to, we've got absolutely nowhere. In cop-show-speak, no leads to talk of. No one's seen or heard a whisper from Kitty in days, and no one's spoken to her on the phone either. No texts even to say Happy Christmas, nothing.

As if she's just vanished into thin air.

9.05 p.m.

Eventually, Simon slumps forward, holding his head in his hands and looking about as shattered as I feel. He has to be feeling the uselessness and futility of this, I just know. Know it without being told.

'Listen, I've an idea,' I tell him tentatively, not wanting to panic the guy, but at the same time, anxious to do more than keep on cold calling a bunch of total strangers late on Stephen's night, when everyone we talk to would far rather be stuffing their faces with Cadbury's Selection Boxes, while watching *Mamma Mia!*

He looks over to me, red-eyed with tiredness by now.

'Don't freak out on me,' I say, 'but I really think it's time to start checking around hospitals. Just in case . . . Well, you know. She might have been at some party and maybe something happened to her on the way home? And say she was taken to a hospital somewhere and no one has a clue who she is?'

He looks worriedly into space for a second, then nods his head.

'I'm only praying you're wrong,' he says, jaw clamped tightly, 'but it's certainly worth a shot.'

Sick with nerves now, I get back onto the phone, go online, look up the number for Vincent's Hospital and dial.

9.20 p.m.

Bloody waste of time! Hospitals turn out to be a total dead end. Didn't take me long to ring every single one with an A&E unit in the greater Dublin area as there's not that many. And once I navigated my way past 'Are-you-next-of kin?' type questions and explained the situation, I pretty much got the same response from all of them.

V. sorry for my trouble, but it's impossible to give that information over the phone. Have I tried contacting the police, is all I'm asked, over and over.

Right then. Nothing for it but to call into each and every hospital we can think of, first light tomorrow, as they say in search-and-rescue TV shows. Better than sitting round here ringing a total bunch of strangers who know absolutely nothing, feeling useless and with all confidence fast draining from me.

Anything's better than that.

9.35 p.m.

Agree we need to call it a night. As Simon v. wisely points out, calling people we don't know at this hour just isn't a good plan. He offers to drive me home and promises to call during the night if she turns up.

Which I just know by him, he's still secretly holding out for. All night long, whenever he hears a car door slamming or fast footsteps pounding down street outside, he'll jump up a bit, then look confidently towards the front door like a lost puppy, silently praying she'll slide her key into lock and bounce in like nothing happened. Honest to God, the hope in his eyes would nearly kill you.

Am wall-falling with tiredness by now. Gratefully accept his offer.

9.45 p.m.

On the way to my parents' house, we pass by the local cop shop on Harcourt Terrace.

I catch sight of a copper striding out of there, which means at least they're still open. It's a sign. Right then, in a flash, the decision is made.

'Simon, pull over the car,' I tell him firmly, when we're stopped at traffic lights.

'What did you say?' he asks, looking at me like I've finally lost it.

'I know this is the last thing either of us wants to do right now,' I say, whipping off my seat belt and getting ready to jump out, now that we've stopped. 'But I just think there's no harm in calling in and telling the cops everything that's happened to date, that's all. Let's just bring them up to speed and keep them informed. I mean, they've got access to all sorts of resources that we don't, so . . .'

I trail off a bit here and it would melt a heart of stone to see just how crushed the poor guy's starting to look. Can practically hear him thinking: bringing in the coppers now means Kitty's really, really gone and isn't coming back.

He parks the car and I reach over to pat his arm sympathetically.

'Look, I know how sick with worry you are,' I tell him a bit more gently. 'And I know how much you were looking forward to your skiing trip tomorrow and that you're secretly hoping against hope that she might yet do some kind of eleventh-hour resurfacing act in the middle of the night. Don't get me wrong, I'm praying for that too. But we're here, is all I'm saying. And we have spent all afternoon and evening pretty much doing their bloody job for them. So let's just see if they can help us out! Just humourise me, Simon. Come on, what's wrong with that?'

Long pause, and I swear I can physically see the eternal optimist in him wrestle with his inner realist.

Astonishingly, the realist wins out.

'You're right,' he sighs, for first time all day sounding defeated. 'We're here. For what it's worth, let's do it.'

10.35 p.m.

Police are *useless*! Total and utter waste of time! I storm out of there fuming, and even calm, level-headed Simon's pissed off at just how lackadaisical they were. Now I know it's Christmas, etc., I know the sixteen-year-old copper on duty would far rather be home in front of a computer screen chatting up girls on Facebook, rather than listening to a borderline hysteric and the shell-shocked boyfriend of a missing woman, demanding that something be done immediately to track her down.

First question: did Kitty have a history of drug or alcohol abuse? I gave him an adamant no. Almost snapped the face off him. I mean, sure Kitty likes a drink the way we all do, but drugs? Never once, in all the long years I've known her! And that is a long, long, time, probably since well before you were toilet trained, I stressed to the acne-faced copper.

Second question: did she have a history of depression, or was she in any way prone to suicidal tendencies? Almost guffawed in his face, and Simon was at pains to point out that she's a respectable student, waitressing her way through night school; the jolliest, most positive, outgoing type you could ever meet, who'd probably never once in the whole course of her life entertained a solitary dark thought. 'Course, I was nearly thumping on the table by then and kept demanding to talk to someone – *anyone* – more senior, who might see the severity of the situation and take it that bit more seriously.

Simon had to haul me back by the elbow at this point, and even had the manners to apologise to the young kid on my behalf, politely explaining that we'd both had a v. stressful day of it. At which point I went back to standing sulkily on the sidelines, arms folded, occasionally lobbing in, 'But she never went to visit her foster mother on Christmas Day! *And* she stood me up on my birthday! So why aren't you writing that down in your logbook, sonny? Unheard of for her!'

Totally wasting my breath. Child-copper told us that standard procedure is that a missing persons report can only be filed when someone's been gone for a minimum of three days. I nearly had to be held back at that and had to resist the urge to holler, 'So going AWOL over Christmas is no cause for immediate concern, then?'

Simon calmly pointed out that, as far as we know, the last person who actually saw Kitty was Joyce Byrne at Byrne & Sacetti, who said goodbye to her at about one in the morning on the twenty-fourth, just as she was finishing up her shift. About seventy hours ago, roughly. For God's sake, we're almost there, almost at magical three-day mark!

But the copper was v. insistent. If she still hasn't surfaced by tomorrow, he told us, then we could come back and they'd take it from there. Around six in the evening is the best time, he added, as the sergeant would be back on duty then. Like we were making appointments at the hairdresser's.

But then – And this is bit that almost made me gag – he v. coolly, almost dismissively, informed us that the vast majority of people who disappear for a while usually resurface again safe and well. Well over ninety per cent of them, in fact. Clearly it must be a well-known statistic they apparently teach you in your first year at Garda Training College, because he kept stressing it over and over again, like a broken record. Then told us to just go home and even managed to add insult to injury by calling after us, 'And try not to worry.'

Had the strongest urge to smack him over the head with the butt end of my umbrella, but Simon clocked it in time and hauled me out of there, before I got the chance to inflict lasting damage.

11.10 p.m.

Front driveway of my parents' house. Sleeting down v. heavily now, lashing. The two of us barely spoke the whole way here; too punch drunk by it all. Just as I'm about to clamber out of the car, Simon grabs my hand and pulls me back.

'Thanks, Angie,' is all he says sincerely, the green eyes focused right on me in that v. intense way he has. 'You're keeping me sane in all this. I just want you to know that.'

'Ring me,' I tell him, 'anytime at all in the night if she turns up.'

'You know I will.'

Am too exhausted to say what I really think.

But what happens if and when she doesn't?

Chapter Four

27 December, 8.20 a.m.

I'm in a deep, dead, exhausted sleep when I'm woken by the phone, beside me, ringing. And in a nanosecond, I go from early-morning grogginess to wide awake and on high alert.

Please be Simon with news . . . Please can the pathetic, frail little hope he was clinging to – that Kitty would just stroll through the front door during the wee small hours – have actually, miraculously come to pass . . .

It's not Simon, but the next best thing! My buddy Jeff, ringing me back to say he got all my hysterical voice messages yesterday and of course now v. anxious to find out what in hell is going on with Kitty. What's the story? Has she turned up? Quickly, I fill him in and bring him up to speed.

'OK then,' he says in his decisive, man-of-action way. 'Just tell me how I can help and I'll be there.'

Jeff's amazing. Jeff's a true pal. This is exactly what's needed right now. Fresh blood. Reinforcements.

8.25 a.m.

Call Simon. The phone's picked up after approximately half a ring, if even that.

'Hello?' he answers.

Shit. I just know by the overly hopeful note in his voice he was praying this might be Kitty. But Simon's always the perfect gentleman and at least has the good grace not to sound a bit deflated, when it turns out it's only me. My heart goes out to the guy. Am actually afraid at one point he sounds dangerously close to tears.

Please, for the love of God, don't cry, I find myself silently praying. Don't think I could handle it if I had to be strong one in all this, while Simon fell apart. Thank Christ he doesn't, but the underlying tremble in his voice is nearly worse.

He says he and Kitty were meant to be leaving for their big skiing hollier in just under three hours' time. His Xmas gift to her. He tells me that just a few short days ago, before the whole world somehow fell apart, he thought he'd be arm in arm with her right at this very moment, skipping through Duty Free with bottle of champagne tucked under his oxter and with nothing but a fab, romantic week in Austria arsing around the slopes to look forward to. Says never in his wildest dreams did he think he'd spend this morning ringing up a gangload of total strangers, in the slim hope someone, somewhere might have had even a fleeting conversation with her on that final shift and that maybe, *maybe* they might be able to shed a bit of light on this.

It's a flair of mine to say the wrong thing at times like this, and true to form, Angie strikes again.

'Simon . . . this is just a thought,' I say tentatively, 'but I don't suppose there's any point in turning up at the airport, just in case?' Then in a classic Freudian slip, I manage to mumble out the single most annoying comment, the same one I was gritting my teeth down the phone over, every time I heard it yesterday.

'I mean, you know what Kitty's like,' I blurt out, barely pausing to think. 'So just say she did end up buried deep in some stranger's house over Christmas, someone who we've not made contact with yet, then . . . well, maybe she'll just turn up at Departures later on this morning, with a credit card in her back pocket and nothing else?'

I regret the words the very second they're out of my mouth. Am a stupid, bloody, moronic, tactless *idiot.* I shouldn't do this to the guy, when he's going through so much! It's downright cruel. False hope can be a v., v. dangerous thing.

Still, though. On the other hand, it wouldn't be unprecedented carry-on for our Kitty. Can't help thinking back to that one particular, now-famous occasion—

But Simon interrupts my train of thought, sighing exhaustedly.

'You know, I'd sort of been hoping for that too,' he says. 'In fact, I was thinking almost exactly along the same lines as you. But at about four o'clock this morning, I couldn't sleep, so I got up and started rummaging through her desk, in case there was some clue there as to what's going on. An address of where she might be staying, a phone number, a name, maybe. Something we've overlooked that just might explain all this.'

'And?'

'Well, put it this way: she's most definitely not going to casually turn up at the airport this morning and that's for certain.'

'You're absolutely sure?'

Not meaning to contradict him so baldly, but she actually *has* done it before. With me, as it happened. Years ago. I thought she'd stood me up for a last-minute trip to London, and next thing she bounded into airport, no bags, no luggage, nothing, and full of the most outlandish story involving a hit-and-run driver, a sick cocker spaniel with a mashed front paw, a wailing child and a last-minute dash to the nearest vets. One of those completely mental, nutty excuses, so utterly off-the-wall that you just knew it could only be the truth. Vintage Kitty, in other words.

'Yeah, I'm pretty certain,' Simon is saying, 'because when I was rummaging through her desk at stupid o'clock this morning, I came across a couple of things.'

'Like what?'

'Like a list of restaurants in the resort that we were meant to go to. A German phrase book I'd bought her for the trip, as a joke. And right beside all of that, I found her passport.'

9.25 a.m.

Jeff picks me up and v. kindly says he'll drive me to Kitty's house, then help to give Simon and me a dig-out for the rest of the entire day. Says he'll do whatever he can to help, bless him. Claims he's prepared do anything to find our gal, even if it's only running around distributing milky mugs of sugary tea, patting shoulders and saying, 'There, there, dear,' at regular intervals. A true friend, in other words.

Anyway, he collects me in his little runaround Skoda, typical Jeff, dressed like he's on his way to a gym. Bit too tight Lycra gym leggings with trainers and a v. clingy sweatshirt, with suspicious overtones of a recent spray tan, just a shade too mahogany for it to be natural. In December. When it's freezing.

To his great annoyance, Jeff's often mistaken for gay, reinforced by the fact he works as a freelance make-up artist, hence the addiction to spray tans. But he's not; he's straight as they come and actively seeking a GF. And he really is a total sweetheart, inordinately generous, the kind of bloke who'd gladly do anything for you. If he was in a movie, he'd most likely be cast as the reliable-best-buddy-of-leading-man. You know, the sort of roles Paul Rudd makes a v. healthy living out of. Such a lovely guy, Kitty often says, that it's almost a racing certainty he'll ultimately end up with a complete bitch. Always the way; the sweeter and more genuine they are, the more horrendous the girlfriend. Sad fact.

'I just can't believe Kitty would pull a disappearing trick like this!' he tells me after a quick peck on the cheek, as I clamber into the car beside him. 'It just doesn't seem possible, not even for her!'

I nod mutely back at him in agreement.

'So that's not only Christmas that she's missed,' he goes on, 'on top of your birthday, but now the chance to head off on a holiday with Simon, too? Jeez . . . Dunno about you, honey, but I'm now working on the definite possibility that something serious must have happened to her on her way home from work. I'm thinking . . . maybe some axe-wielding psycho now has her locked up in a cellar somewhere in the bowels of the South Circular Road?'

He has the tact to shut up instantly when he catches me doing an involuntary shudder and offers me a bottle of ayurvedic water. (Still water, by the way. Jeff's theory is that carbonated bubbles are an indirect cause of male cellulite. Don't get me wrong, I love the guy dearly, but he can be tiny bit image-conscious like that.)

'Congratulations,' I tell him, gratefully snapping open water bottle and taking a big slug. 'You've now arrived at stage one. Disbelief combined with a willing acceptance that whatever happened to her must be gruesome beyond belief. I'd a full day of that yesterday, thanks very much, while you were hauling your skinny arse up the side of a mountain.'

'So, dare I ask what stage you're now at, hon?'

'Since early this morning? I'm officially at stage two.'

'Which is?'

'Bizarrely, it's ridiculous belief that everything's going to be OK, in the face of almost overwhelming odds. Which is why I'm about to suggest you and I take a quick detour on the way to Kitty's.'

10.01 a.m.

Vincent's Hospital, the biggest one over my end of town. Jeff pulls into the car park and we stomp our way through the icy grounds towards the A&E department.

'Simon thinks this is a total waste of time,' I explain briskly on the way, 'but I'm saying, let's just rule out all possibilities, that's all.'

'Quite right.' Jeff pats my arm a bit patronisingly, like I'm some hysterical old dear who needs agreeing with at all times, else she's likely to get a fit of the vapours. Truth is, though, I'm not particularly bothered whether Jeff understands or not. Just need to be doing something. Need to keep being proactive.

Keep telling myself over and over again: if it was the other way round, Kitty would probably have SWAT teams out patrolling the streets, searching for me by now.

10.17 a.m.

A&E unit is v. quiet. Miracle. Was half expecting it to be like a field hospital at the Battle of the Somme given that it's the Christmas holidays. Head to the main desk and speak to a v. helpful receptionist. A lovely young one who must be able to sense waves of urgency practically pinging off the pair of us, as she goes out of her way to be helpful.

'We're looking for a patient who may possibly have been admitted early on the morning of Christmas Eve, thirty-one years old, five feet ten . . . em . . . really skinny . . . Oh yeah, hazel eyes and waist-length long, black, curly hair. Name of Kitty Hope. Might they have anyone who even comes close to fitting that description?' is our not v. well-thought-out opener.

But no joy. Receptionist is nothing if not persevering, though, and as soon as she's checked on her system that no one of that name's been admitted, she then volunteers to ask around for us, just in case. Even disappears off into the A&E to double check; really goes the extra mile for us. Then comes back through double doors where we're sitting tensely on plastic seats in the waiting area and shakes her head sadly at us.

She doesn't even need to open her mouth. The look on her disappointed face tells us all we need to know.

10.32 a.m.

Back in the car when Simon calls wondering where I am. Sounding agitated and panicky. V. worrying. And now I'm starting to feel a bit shitty about leaving poor guy alone this morning, to deal with all this by himself. Just doesn't sit right with me, somehow.

Suddenly I'm concerned that he and I seem to have switched personalities: whereas he was the pillar of confidence and strength yesterday and I was the screw-up, today we're in near-perfect role reversal. He seems to be falling apart, so it's up to me to be Miss Bossypants Assertiveness. I tell him that we're on our way back, then saintly Jeff v. kindly offers to drop me off at Kitty's and continue doing the trawl of hospitals on his own.

I thank him warmly. So fab to be able to delegate. Then I've a brainwave. I suggest to Jeff that we should start rooting out photos of Kitty from her house, so we have something to show to the world, and in particular, to the hospitals. Not to mention the coppers, who are bound to want decent headshots of her later on, if it comes to that. I'm now working along the lines that Kitty could be lying in a ward somewhere, suffering from deep concussion and not knowing who she is or how she got there.

Then, of course, my imagination totally runs away with me and I get an immediate vision of her bandaged from head to foot with just tiny slit holes for her eyes, so no one can even see who she is, never mind what she looks like. Bit far-fetched, maybe, but as I said to Jeff, quoting Basil Rathbone in the old Sherlock Holmes movies, once you've eliminated the impossible, then whatever you're left with, however improbable, must be the truth.

Makes sense. Doesn't it?

When the pair of us arrive at Kitty's, Simon answers the door. Soon as I catch the state he's in, the sudden urge I get to cradle him tight and tell him everything will be OK, even though it clearly isn't, is almost overpowering. He actually looks like a lost little boy. The dark circles under his eyes have now gone even darker; poor guy looks like he never even got to bed last night, never mind slept and, unusually for him, he's still streeling around in yesterday's clothes. He gives me a hug and I instantly feel the roughness of his face against mine. Unheard of for a man like this, I think distractedly. Simon's normally all smooth and lotion-y with a lovely, lemony smell of expensive aftershave off him. Well turned out, as Mother Blennerhasset would be wont to remark. Heartbreaking to see.

Even Jeff gets bit of a shock at just how badly Simon's taking it.

Soon as we head inside, Jeff skites off to Kitty's study to whip a few decent photos off the wall and Simon automatically goes to stick on the kettle, offering us both coffee.

'I feel daft even asking you this,' I say gently to him, 'but how are you feeling right now?'

He gives a weak, watery smile back at me. 'You know what I've spent the last hour doing?' he says hoarsely. 'I've been on the phone to the hotel in Austria where Kitty and I were due to be checking in around now.'

'Cancelling the booking?'

'Cancelling everything. The reservation, the candlelit dinner for two I'd booked for tonight, the . . .' He breaks off here a bit. 'Well . . . let's just say, I had a surprise arranged for her, a very special surprise, but now I guess that's all gone by the wayside too.'

'Oh, Simon, I don't know what to say,' I tell him gently. 'I hope at least that the hotel were OK about it?'

'Oh, yeah, very sympathetic. The reservations manager spoke fluent English and she was incredibly understanding. She wanted to know . . .' but he trails off again, like the end of that sentence is too painful to even articulate. I instinctively move a step closer to him, but he focuses on putting Nescafé into mugs and composes himself in time.

'She said she was sorry if my girlfriend and I had broken up. And I just couldn't find it in me to get the right words out, so instead I hung up the phone.'

Then Jeff sticks his head around the door, with a stack of photos for us all to check. V. hard to find one of Kitty without a drink in her hand, or where you can actually see her nose full-on (she was expert at turning her head in photos, as she'd say, to minimise general Barbra Streisand-ness of it), but eventually we settle on about a half a dozen that'll have do.

Right then. Jeff sets off on his mission and Simon and I get back to manning the phones, picking up exactly where we left off yesterday.

12.45 p.m.

Getting on bit better today. Spoke to one junior chef who distinctly remembered seeing Kitty on that last shift and having a long chat with her. Apparently about how much she was looking forward to her skiing trip.

V. strange look from Simon at hearing that. Would nearly break a heart of stone.

2.20 p.m.

Our buddy Sarah arrives, fresh from doing an early shift at her family's sandwich bar where she practically runs the place single-handedly; doing everything from PR to sales and marketing to working on the tills, if she has to. Bless her, she strides in laden down with basket of fresh sambos, croissants, muffins, etc.

Carb hit, just what we need. Sarah's completely amazing, like a ray of light round here, positive energy beaming all round her. Great 'can-do' attitude, v. Dunkirk spirit. If you were casting Sarah in a biopic of her life, you'd go for an efficient Women's Institute/ICA type, as played by a young Penelope Keith.

Kitty and I know her all way back to her post-grad college days, when Sarah used to trawl round the place in Doc Martens and denim overalls, famous for never shaving under her arms. Then, the minute she graduated and went to work in her family's catering company, overnight she suddenly morphed into a female Alan Sugar, crossed with a Karren Brady-businesswoman-type, dressed in stilettos and scarily smart black pantsuits, and living off a combination of fags and nerves. It's in the blood and genes will always out, as Kitty used to shrug.

Really delighted to see her now, though. Like a burst of vitally needed energy.

3.45 p.m.

It was exhausting, it nearly bloody killed us, but somehow between us, Simon, Sarah and I, we've now managed to work our weary way through to the v. last name and get to speak to everyone we could on that everlastingly long contact list. Don't know how we did it, but between Sarah's Prussian efficiency and my insane, misguided optimism in the face of overwhelming odds, somehow we get there.

Absolutely *nowhere,* that is. No one has seen or heard from Kitty since her last shift in work, no one knew of any late-night parties she might have pitched up at, not a bleeding sausage. Just dead ends everywhere we turn.

Poor Simon's really worrying me now. Like a shadow of the same guy I knew from only a few days ago. He's jumpy, tense, even a bit irritable, so unlike his usual über-gentlemanly self. Has already asked me about five times to come with him to police station later on this evening.

'I really need you there with me, Angie,' is all he says, with a pleading look, like a lost little puppy.

He's actually starting to treat me like I'm his lifeline. Even Sarah noticed.

5.10 p.m.

Fast approaching the 6.00 p.m. deadline to get back to the cop shop, and Simon and I are about as organised as we'll ever be to finally file a report. We've covered absolutely everything; we even rang up Foxborough House care home again, in vain hopes Kitty may somehow have surfaced there. But nothing.

Weird just how quickly you become inured to disappointment.

Between the whole lot of us though, I think we're fully prepped for all eventualities. Sarah, being Sarah (bit ghoulishly I thought), even went and unearthed a whole missing persons website and saw that the first thing police apparently look for are mobile phone details, as well as bank account and credit card statements. So after a fair bit of rummaging through Kitty's desk, the pair of us stumbled on a few old bank statements as well as a mobile phone bill (Kitty's *never* a great one for clearing out her desk, it seems). Felt a bit like tempting fate even taking all this stuff with me, but as Sarah kept reminding me, far better to arrive fully prepared.

All in all, getting organised for this was relatively easy.

So now for the hard part.

Harcourt Street Police Station, 6.00 p.m. on the nail

Utterly *mental* in the cop shop tonight. Like a riot just broke out before we arrived and Simon and I had the bad luck to walk right into the aftermath. Place is packed with underage-looking yobbos with buzz cuts and v. scary-looking 'body art', all out of their heads on meths or God knows what. I'm not kidding, every single one of them looks fully ready to start fisticuffs with his own shadow. Bloody terrifying.

I shuffle over to stand v. close to Simon, who instinctively grips my hand. Grip it back, tight. Grateful.

We wait meekly at the back of a tiny reception area, either till the yob-heads all get arrested or else someone notices us, but by a stroke of pure luck, the very same adolescent copper who was on duty last night chances to walk right by us with a tray of coffee. He sees us and immediately stops.

'You two must be back about your missing friend then, yeah?' he asks.

Pair of us nod.

'I take it she still hasn't turned up, then?'

It's all I can do to fire him an impatient look and stop myself from snapping, 'Eh, no, sonny, she's actually at home with the feet up watching tonight's Christmas movie, which I believe is *Avatar*. Sure, we just thought we'd swing by to drink in the homely atmosphere.'

But Simon, as always, is that bit more tactful than I am.

'Still nothing to report, I'm afraid,' he says politely. 'Can you tell me who's the most senior person on duty here tonight?'

'That'd be Detective Sergeant Jack Crown. If you just follow me, I'll get him for you now. He said if there was still no news about your friend this evening, then he'd like to interview you both together.'

Sudden surge of elation. The sergeant wants to interview us! You see? Finally, finally, finally this is being taken seriously! Jubilantly we follow the pimply adolescent Garda, as he leads us out of the packed waiting area and down a long, snaking corridor to a tiny interview room right at the very end.

A gloomy, depressing, dismal-looking kip of a place. Overly bright fluorescent light that'd nearly give you a migraine, walls painted hospital green, with the paint peeling off them, and only one tiny window with bars on it, about seven feet above us. Bit like a prison cell. Underage Garda leaves us there and says that the sergeant will be along shortly.

The door slams shut and Simon shoots me a concerned look.

'Don't be nervous, Ange,' he tells me gently. 'Remember

we've got all the facts in front of us and all we have to do now is tell the truth and nothing but.'

'To be honest,' I answer, 'right now I'm mostly just relieved that maybe now they'll get up off their arses and finally start to do something to help. Think about it: we've spent all of yesterday and most of today essentially doing the police's work for them! It's a complete disgrace, that's what it is! Don't know about you, but I've no intentions of leaving here without them promising to do what they're being paid to do and get the bloody finger out.'

Because I want this sergeant, whoever he is, to be an elder statesman, Inspector Morse type, who'll have this solved in a mere matter of hours. Or else a wise, elderly Miss Marple sort, as played by Margaret Rutherford, who'll offer us pots of tea and scones, ask questions that initially seem totally irrelevant, like, 'What was Kitty's mother's maiden name?' Or, 'Had she ever visited Bologna in springtime?' And yet still manage to trace Kitty by morning.

Failing that, I want Kenneth Branagh as Wallander to stride confidently in here, or better yet, David Suchet as Poirot, who'll waddle around, charm the arses off us, ask insightful questions, then whisk off and have Kitty back to us with nothing more than a funny tale to dine out on. I want someone who'll walk in here and immediately inspire confidence. I want to just look at him and know that if this guy can't track down Kitty, no one can.

What's more, I want whoever this guy is to give us his solemn word that highly trained SWAT teams are, as we speak, being deployed to come in and help. I want helicopters patrolling the area where Kitty was last seen, I want everyone she ever met in her entire life from the age of three upwards to be hauled in for a full police interview;

I want her story to be on one of those 'live police enactments' that you see on TV shows like *Crimewatch* (except with somebody thinner playing me, obviously).

I want whole entire units of coppers with trained Alsatians pounding on every hall door between here and West Belfast, asking questions and demanding answers. I want to paper-blitz whole country with a full poster and flyer campaign, so no one can possibly avoid seeing Kitty's unforgettable face staring out at them from billboards, bus stops and lampposts.

I want total media blanket coverage. And only when all that is done, will I . . .

6.35 p.m.

Mental ramblings are suddenly interrupted by arrival of Detective Sergeant Jack Crown, who instantly surprises me by not being a senior, Inspector Morse or even a Scando detective type, but a youngish guy. Not that much older than Simon, late thirties at most, and not a bit wise or experienced-looking at all.

Definitely not a Wallander or even a Poirot either; the guy's sandy-haired, freckly, chunky and with sharp blue eyes and an intent, tight-jawed look about him. Thick-set build too, with hands the approximate size of shovels. Puts me in mind of Simon Pegg, for some reason. Initial reaction? Bit disappointed, actually. Was just hoping for someone with more gravitas and authority about them, that's all. Whereas this fella looks like the type of guy who'd be far more at home in a theme bar with a big feed of chips and a few pints in front of him. Not what I was expecting and certainly not what you might call confidence-inspiring.

Glance over to Simon, who shoots a 'would you just give the guy a chance?' look back at me.

Funny; we've spent so much time together of late, it's getting so we're starting to communicate without speech.

Det. Sgt Crown shakes hands vigorously with both of us as we introduce ourselves, but he isn't exactly what you might call friendly or even particularly concerned for our welfare. Never says, 'Call me Jack', and no offers of tea from plastic cups either. Just dumps down a notepad with a thick wad of files on the desk in front of him and rolls up his sleeves, ready to write down anything we say that might, in some small way, help.

'OK, firstly I'm really sorry you both had to come back,' he starts off, efficiently whipping a Biro out of his uniform pocket. 'But I'm taking it that at this point in time Kitty Hope has been gone for over three days now? If you've an accurate date and time as to when she was last seen, that would be really useful, as a starting point.'

No chat, no 'So where you do think she went?' or 'Tell me how you've both been coping?' No preamble with this guy whatsoever. Just efficiently cuts to the chase, like we've come in about a missing passport and are now holding up a v. long queue.

Simon starts to fill him in, aided by me shoving notes I made earlier in front of him, with exact names of who last saw Kitty, where and critically at what time. I keep on red-pencilling around stuff, so he won't forget and impatiently tapping my biro off sheaves of paper in front of him to draw his attention to anything he's leaving out. Driving the poor guy completely mental, in other words.

Crown works his way through a whole list of fairly standard-sounding questions and we answer almost in unison, nearly tripping over each other to get our spake in first. It's a long, long list, and we tell him everything: Kitty's age, gender, height, build, hair colour, eye colour, the date she was last seen, where she was last seen, plus full details about her next of kin and, more specifically, all about poor Mrs K. and her condition.

Then I can't help myself butting in.

'So you see, by far the weirdest thing of all here,' I interrupt, overeager to get the story out, 'is that we know she was most *definitely* planning to visit her foster mum in the nursing home on Christmas Day. So that categorically *proves* that something awful must have happened in the meantime . . . because only something really disastrous would ever have prevented her from . . .'

'. . . Going to see Mrs Kennedy on Christmas Day,' Simon butts in, finishing the sentence for me. 'Which, of course, was when we both started to realise just how serious the situation was, because up till then, we'd thought . . . that is to say, we'd *hoped*, that maybe she'd just been out having a few Christmas drinks somewhere . . .'

'. . . And maybe crashed out at friend's house or something? So then, between the two of us, we phoned around just about everybody we knew, not to mention everyone she worked with, even random strangers who were booked into the restaurant where she was working that night . . .'

'. . . And we got absolutely nowhere. Total dead end.'

'OK, OK, guys,' Crown interrupts, waving at us to quieten down. 'Let's just hear one voice at a time and take the whole story from the very beginning. Why don't we start with you, Angie?'

Strongly suspect it's because he knows I won't shut up

or stop interrupting otherwise, but v. happy to have the floor properly opened to me.

'Now, I want you to take your time and tell me in your own words exactly when you last saw Kitty and when you first became alarmed at her disappearance. Remember, don't leave anything out. Even the most insignificant detail could prove to be vitally important to our investigation at this point. OK?'

'OK.'

I feel a bit like a star witness who's just been ushered up to stand in front of packed courtroom. But Crown's not making any eye contact with me at all. Which is not exactly what you might call encouraging.

'So,' he starts off, face buried deep into his blessed notes, 'let's take it right from the very beginning. Firstly, tell me how long exactly have you known Kitty for?'

And so I start talking. About how she and I first met, all of seven years ago now. Remember it like it was yesterday. I was fresh out of college and because I hadn't the first clue what I wanted to do with my life, I managed to get a part-time job working at telesales in a call centre. I can vividly see myself there on my very first day, nervously cold-calling and trying not to fluff my lines. 'Excuse me, may I interest you in taking a market research call that could possibly end up saving you hundreds on your household bills?' That kind of shite.

I was only at the job for about an hour when this bright, bouncy beautiful creature with long legs as skinny as two Cadbury's chocolate fingers, springs into the cubicle right beside me and yells an apology over to the male supervisor for being late. Roared at him, 'Won't say what delayed me this morning, Sean, but by the way, you can sleep easy!

The gonorrhoea test was negative!' 'Course the whole room cracked up, supervisor included.

Right from the start, I was completely mesmerised by her; this glorious ball of energy with enough personality for two people, wearing a bright blue fleecy sweatshirt over what looked suspiciously like pyjama bottoms. I remember having to stifle giggles when I overheard her dealing with a particularly rude person she'd just cold-called. Instead of apologising and getting off the phone a.s.a.p. like we were trained to do, she just laughed and said, 'Nah, don't worry, I don't blame you for telling me to feck off, love. After all, I work in a call centre, selling house insurance. So technically, that makes me the devil.'

And when she introduced herself and dragged me off to the pub after work, that was it. She and I just bonded and it was like my whole world suddenly went from monochrome to Technicolor. I knew we'd be mates and what's more, we'd stay that way.

'So you see, that's how I'm so certain that something really horrendous must have happened to her!' I find myself getting more and more upset now, borderline hysteric. Part relief that we're finally being taken seriously, part vom-making worry at what in hell's actually unfolding.

'Because I've known Kitty for that length of time, practically all of my twenties, she's like my sister! We've shared flats together and everything . . . And, OK, so she may be a tiny bit unreliable and scatty at times, but I know that vanishing over Christmas, when we'd all be out of our minds worrying about her, just isn't something she would ever do!'

'OK, OK, take it easy,' Crown suggests in a don't-argue-with-me tone. 'And remember that jumping to conclusions isn't helpful at this point.'

Which at this point slightly gets my back up, I have to admit. It's unsympathetic.

'I fully understand what you've been through,' he goes on, 'and how worrying this is for both of you, but trust me when I tell you, it's far more useful at this point to try and leave all emotion out of it. So how about we just stick to the actual hard facts?'

I take a deep, soothing breath, then nod curtly back at him. Jeez, what is this guy, anyway? Some kind of emoticon? I feel like snarling across at him, 'How would you feel if your best friend vanished into thin air over Christmas then, sonny? Or would you just "keep all emotion out of it" too?'

'OK then.' Crown looks up from his notes just in time to catch me glaring furiously across at him. 'So when was the last time you actually did speak to Kitty?'

Like this is some kind of test, I'm fully ready for him.

'It was just after lunchtime on the 23rd. About half-two.' Don't mean to snap, but that's how it comes out. Sorry, but this guy is seriously starting to get my back up now.

'That's very specific. You're quite sure about the time?'

'Absolutely. Because I was—'

I break off a bit here. Because I was actually in the dole office signing on, when she called me. Distinctly remember as I had to give up my place in the queue and head outside to take the call. But then I decide it's none of Crown's bloody business anyway and keep on talking.

'Em . . . I was in town when she called,' I continue, 'so we didn't chat for very long. She was on her way into Byrne & Sacetti to start her last shift before the holidays, and she was calling to confirm a spa day we were due to have together the following day. It was my birthday, you see. So we arranged to meet at the Sanctuary Spa at eight in the morning for an early breakfast. Then she told me she couldn't wait to see me and . . .'

I'm forced to break off a bit here. The threatened wave of upset has now given way to the kind of tears you have to choke back, and I'm absolutely determined not to get sobby, not in front of Crown.

Softie Simon notices, though. He tactfully rummages round in his coat pocket, then produces a clean tissue, which I gratefully take from him.

'Come on, Angie, you're doing great,' he tells me gently, leaning into me and squeezing my shoulder. 'But just try to take it nice and easy. There's absolutely no rush. You all right now?'

I nod weakly back at him.

'So if we can just get back to your statement,' Crown interjects and I half-glower back at him. Then notice he's not wearing a wedding ring. Now why doesn't that surprise me?

'Can you remember if Kitty sounded in any way distressed or stressed out about anything?'

'Not in the least,' I tell him defiantly. 'But then, she rarely ever did.'

'OK,' he says, head buried back in his notes and scribbling away. 'Now if you feel up to it, just keep on talking.'

And so I do, and before I know it, it's Simon's turn. He's completely brilliant, though, far more businesslike and far less of a hysterical seesaw than I was. V. detailed and factual. I can practically see the sheer relief on Crown's stony, emotionless face that at least one of us is making his life a bit easier, and not clouding the issue with tears and gulpy sobs, or with having to reach for Kleenex every two minutes.

Even though we're essentially both telling same story

except from two different viewpoints, this still takes us *ages.* Actually starts to feel bit like we've been stuck in this stale, stifling room for hours. But then, as soon as Simon's done with his statement and Crown's finally stopped writing on the file in front of him, our questions right back at him start all at once, in a barrage.

'So what happens now?' Simon wants to know. 'What exactly is the next step here?'

'Yeah! I mean we've got buddies out trawling the streets, knocking on doors locally and asking if anyone's seen or heard anything, and we could really use a bit of help. Proper, professional help,' I throw in, fervently hoping offer of SWAT teams and helicopters is only round the corner.

'Because we're now working on the theory that she left the restaurant at around one in the morning,' Simon takes up from me, 'on Christmas Eve, when her shift ended. We're assuming that she went to walk home, as she always did, and that something could have happened to her then. Maybe a mugging? An abduction of some kind? Maybe she's being held involuntarily against her will? So you see, the faster you guys act, the better.'

'And the more help we can get from the police, the quicker we'll find her! She could be in some kind of awful danger right now, while we're all just sitting around here doing nothing!'

Crown makes another one of those 'take it easy' hand gestures that frankly are starting to annoy me.

'I fully appreciate that you're both deeply concerned,' he says coolly. 'But please remember that we've dealt with literally thousands of cases like this before and have a whole set of procedures in place that we're obliged to follow first.'

'Like what?' Simon wants to know, sounding, for the first

time since we got here, a bit impatient. Tetchy, not like himself at all.

'OK, the first thing we're going to take a look at are her mobile phone records. Was she the sort of person who'd have her phone on her person or close by her at all times?'

A moment while Simon and I glance across at each other.

'Well . . . yeah,' we both say together. 'In case one of her tutors at night school needed to contact her,' Simon adds, 'or if the restaurant ever called to change her shifts.'

'But we've been ringing her mobile number for days now!' I chip in. 'And believe me, there's nothing! I must have left about five hundred messages by now and still not a whisper out of her!'

'When you call the number, does it go straight through to voicemail?'

'Em . . . yeah, it does.'

I'm narkily thinking: but what's that got to do with anything?

'Right then,' Crown says, scribbling away on the pad in front of him. 'In that case, we can safely assume her phone is probably out of battery. So the first step we take is to get onto her carrier and get them to put a triangulation trace on it a.s.a.p. Pinpoint the exact location of her phone, is the theory, and there's a chance we'll have a good starting point as to where to start the search for Kitty. With luck, she won't be too far behind. Been very successful in cases like this before. We may not be able to nail down her specific location, but we certainly should narrow it down to within a one-mile radius.'

Simon and I nod back at him, a bit more enthusiastically now. Maybe not offer of SWAT teams I'd been hoping for, but still. It's positive. It's something.

'Secondly,' he continues, 'I'll need to take her home computer to run a few checks on it, as well as all her bank records and credit card details, if you can access them. The first thing anyone who goes missing will always need is access to hard cash.'

That, though, we're prepared for, and I have them whipped out of the big mound of Kitty-related documents from my handbag barely before he's finished talking. In fact, the only reason I haven't called the bank myself before this, is that they're all still closed for holidays.

'And thirdly,' Crown goes on, 'I need to ask you both one or two personal things about her, if that's OK?'

We nod and sit forward, both on the edge of our seats.

'You've already stated that Kitty Hope doesn't have any history of drug or alcohol abuse . . .'

'Most sober, reliable, upstanding girl you could ever hope to meet,' I interrupt, to a raised eyebrow from Simon at the sheer outrageousness of the exaggeration.

'So in cases such as these there's about a ninety per cent chance that she is, in fact, safe and well. And just for whatever reasons, felt she needed a bit of time out. Was she under severe pressure at work or maybe at the night school she attended?'

We both shake our heads.

'Well, I mean, she worked long hours and when she wasn't working, she was always studying,' I throw in, 'so the odd time she'd complain about being bone knackered, but apart from that . . .' I trail off a bit here. Mainly because the exact phrase Kitty always uses is, 'These fecking books have my brains turned into baked Alaska.'

'Was she under any financial strain?'

Again, we tell him no more so than any of the rest of us. No mortgage, low rent, no major credit card debts, no big whacks of cash outstanding to any shady loan sharks, nothing. She earned good money at the restaurant and always said Byrne & Sacetti's customers were consistently the best tippers in town. Sure, she'd overspend a bit; but then Kitty's outrageously generous and would often find herself broke and counting days till payday or until some whoppingly generous tip would tide her over. But doesn't that just make her an ordinary, normal person?

'Any gambling addictions that either of you know of?'

Almost want to guffaw at that one. I once went dog racing with Kitty (under the misguided impression that it might be good place to meet blokes). I can still remember her roars of laughter, claiming that the mutt of a thing she bet on would probably still be panting towards the finishing post at midnight that night. Said anything she put money on was instantly cursed and doomed to the greyhound equivalent of early paralysis. So that one, single night was the beginning and end of her gambling career.

'Was there a chance she may have been in the early stages of an unwanted pregnancy?'

An angry flush from Simon at that, followed by a firm no.

Did she appear to be suffering from depression lately?

No, we tell him, stressing what a happy, open person Kitty is naturally.

More questions come thick and fast, as Crown ticks off a long, long list in front of him.

Had she been acting in any way strangely up until the night she disappeared? Was she bringing home large sums of money? Had she recently appeared alienated in any way from her close group of friends? Were a lot of her clothes and personal belongings missing from her house? Any valuable jewellery suddenly gone missing? Or electrical items? Did she have an eBay account? And what about her foster mother, had she been to visit her in the days leading up to Christmas Eve?

We tell him no, a v. firm no to everything.

And finally he finishes writing, closes the file in front of him and sits back, eyeballing each of us in turn. One of those cold, unflinching glares. Serial killer-ish, I find myself thinking a bit nastily.

'So neither of you is aware of any personal reasons at all why she'd need to take off?'

'NO!' we chorus back at him, yet again. Don't know about Simon, but I'm kind of getting seriously sick of this guy by now. Worse than useless, if you ask me. And if he uses the phrase 'established set of procedures to follow here' once more, I'm seriously tempted to reach across the desk and thump him one. We're not exactly talking about a bloody wallet one of us left in the back of a taxi here!

I want far, far fewer questions and far, far more coppers to burst in, heavily armed and telling us they're now taking over the whole investigation. And that they confidently expect to have Kitty back home, with not a hair on her head harmed and looking for a shower, a glass of wine and a big feed of chips, in that order.

'Well, then, in that case,' Crown shrugs dismissively, 'the news is not necessarily bad. Rest assured, we'll do everything we can, but you should know that the chances of her turning up safe and sound are relatively high. In well over ninety per cent of cases like this, the subject is nearly always secure and will inevitably return when they're good and ready.

'However, given the worry and upset that Kitty's causing

to all around her, then unfortunately there's one hard, cold fact that remains. So I'm afraid I'll need you both to ask yourselves one unpleasant but unavoidable question.'

We both look at him expectantly.

'Why would she do this in the first place? She must have had a very good reason for wanting to leave. So what do you think it might have been?'

I ask Simon exactly the same question again in car on our way home.

He doesn't answer me, though, just goes v. quiet and stares out window into the night, completely wrapped up in thought.

By the age of fifteen, she'd already been with a grand total of eight foster homes, which had to have been some class of a record, she figured. They should be giving her a survival medal, like they did in Stalinist Russia, just for lasting this long in their poxy system. And here she was now, on the doorstep of number nine.

Initial reaction? Worst one yet. An old lady-type house in the back arse of nowhere, over-heavy with crappy-looking ornaments, family photos and, dear Jaysus help her, knitted tea cosies. And all those do-gooder social workers from Health must have seriously been scraping the barrel when they vetted the aul one, who was to be her new foster parent. This one was fifty if she was a day, with helmet-y hair like a wig, who answered the door to her in an actual suit. Feck's sake, a suit? Who wore a suit going round their own house, unless you were a complete weirdo?

*The care liaison officer had tactfully left, 'just so you two can get to know each other a little better', and with a stern 'you'd better be on your best behaviour' glare over in her direction, he was gone. Thank f**k. She'd accidentally seen a copy of her own file once and it had been impressed on her that she was lucky to have been homed at all, with her track record. But to hell with that shower of gobshites anyway, she thought furiously. They could feck off, the lot of them.*

*'Out of control,' her file had said. 'Complaints of a serious nature . . . shoplifting . . . swearing . . . smoking . . . underage drinking . . . wild . . .' Made her feel proud, though. She didn't want to fit in; she was sick to the teeth of all their rules and regulations, and being told how lucky she was to be homed at all, like she was supposed to be grateful. All she wanted was to hit eighteen, get out into the world and tell the whole shagging lot of them to go and f**k themselves.*

And yet here she was, arms folded defensively, sat sullenly at yet another kitchen table with this Old Dear opposite her. Mrs Kennedy; a widow, this time. Husband probably died of boredom, she thought viciously to herself, taking in the pin-neat house with cushions on the cushions and net fecking curtains. It felt like she'd been through the drill a thousand times. This was the bit where both parties were supposed to be on their best behaviour, tiptoeing round each other, while the house rules were impressed in on her. Don't this, don't that, please can you remember to x and y and z.

Mind you, the worst were the foster parents who cheerily told you, 'This is your home now, so please just try to relax and enjoy!' Then within hours, she'd find herself hauled over the coals for smoking in her room, or cursing in front of other kids, or any other rule-infraction shite they could think of to throw at her. In other words, we're saying that this is your home now, except it's not really and never will be, and we can turf you out on a whim. So don't you forget it, missy.

Fine, she wouldn't. In fact, she made a bet with herself, as Mrs Ancient here fussed around her and poured tea and handed her slices of gooey-looking cake. She'd see if she could equal her personal best of getting turfed out of a new home in under a week. Shouldn't be hard either. By the look of her, if she refused to go to Mass on Sundays, then this one would probably take a heart attack, start calling her the spawn of the devil and she'd be outta here in no time. Problem solved.

'Now please feel free to call me Kathleen,' Aul One was saying to her, pouring out tea into dainty china cups that barely held two dribbles and that were covered in a pattern that looked like dead scorpions. Later on, she'd come to

recognise this as the good, special occasion china, that only ever got wheeled out at Christmas and Easter, but for now she didn't give a shite. Would gladly have smashed it, if she could.

'Whatever,' she shrugged back, putting her feet up on the chair opposite her. Aul One seemed to notice, but said nothing.

'And remember,' Aul One went on, 'I really do want you to treat this as your own home.'

'Fantastic. In that case, can I have an ashtray and a lighter please?'

Again no reaction.

'Smoke all you like,' Aul One shrugged back at her, 'but I think you'd better do it outside.'

'House rule?' she sneered.

'Not really,' said Aul One. 'I just don't think it would be fair on the kittens. They're barely two weeks old and still nursing. I only wanted to keep the air nice and fresh for them, that's all.'

'Kittens?' In spite of herself, she was curious. 'Where?'

'In the kitchen, just behind you. Would you like to have a look? They're the most adorable little bundles you've ever seen.'

In spite of herself, she was intrigued. She followed Aul One into the tiny, galley kitchen and there they were, in a warm basket by the door. Eight little balls of the cutest, fluffiest things you ever saw. She picked one up and instinctively cuddled it. It made a tiny, weak little mewling sound, no mistaking it.

'She's meowing,' Aul One smiled down at her. 'I think she must like you.'

'Are you going to keep them all?'

'I wish I could, love, but I can't. They're too young to leave

their mother, but as soon as they are, I'm afraid they'll all have to be rehomed.'

'That's horrible! They should be with their mother!'

'I know,' Mrs Kennedy said sagely, taking her in from head to foot. 'And I agree. Farming them out is necessary, but awful.' Then after a half-beat, she added, 'unless . . . unless you'd like to keep one? As your own special little pet? You could name it and everything, if you liked.'

She looked up at her with shining eyes. Her very own pet; such a simple thing and yet she'd never had one before . . . or anything of her own, come to think of it.

'You'd have to take care of him or her, though. Kittens are a lot of work. You'd have to take on all that responsibility.'

She just nodded back and surprised herself by actually smiling.

And the two of them stayed there for the whole afternoon, lost in the kittens, playing with them, cuddling them, laughing at their antics. One of them, a little tabby tom cat, kept trying to climb up the curtains and they roared laughing at that. Another one climbed inside a paper bag and played with it for hours, while they looked on fondly, both of them loving it.

A long time afterwards Mrs K., as she'd taking to calling her, said that when she first saw this scrap of a teenage girl landed on her doorstep, all bovver boots and attitude, she was instantly reminded of the kittens. That's just what you were like, she'd told her. I thought you were like a young kitten who needed to be nurtured by a mom before being farmed out again. Or maybe not; maybe you'd found your forever home this time? She'd seen past the teenage sullenness that mistook rudeness for rebellion, and thought, I want to give this lost soul a chance. A proper home. And a proper mum.

Within days, she was settled, and within a week, she found herself actually rushing home from school, just so she could hang out with Mrs K. and the kittens.

Just the two of them.

Chapter Five

New Year's Eve

. . . and Kitty's still missing. But all of a sudden, everything's shunted up about sixteen gears and now we're actually being taken seriously. Bittersweet consolation that it all took this bleeding long to get here, but still. It's something.

Absolutely everyone's on high alert now. From staff at the restaurant where she works to other students and teachers at her night school in Rathmines, who've all been notified as well, even though it's officially closed for another week and everyone's scattered to the four winds. Locals around Kitty's area are all being urged to be extra vigilant too. And I have to grudgingly admit that the team of police Jack Crown's brought in to head up this inquiry have all been v. impressive to date. Though as Simon's quick to point out, they've done every single thing bar actually finding the girl.

According to Crown, all missing persons cases are categorised into two groups: acceptable and unacceptable. In a nutshell, 'acceptable' is if a person is suffering from depression, drug abuse or similar, whereas 'unacceptable' would be someone more like Kitty. The type with a normal job, home, friends, life, the whole works. The unlikely-to-take-off type, the sort of girl not usually classified as a 'flight risk'.

Which goes some way towards accounting for the reason they're finally pulling out all the stops to find her now. But I have to report that all progress is at best slow and at worst, soul-destroyingly frustrating. Like a perpetual game of one step forward and two steps back.

First bit of bad news: traces on her mobile phone turned out to be a total dead end. Oh, they tracked it down all right, through a v. sophisticated technique called 'pinging', which can place you within metres of any phone, even if it's powered off. (Am now getting au fait with copper-speak.) We discovered she made her last call – to my number, as it happened – at lunchtime on the day she disappeared, from within a one-mile radius of Camden Street, where the restaurant is. But beyond that, nothing. No outgoing calls have been made from her phone since then, or texts, emails . . . *nada.*

Coppers then narrowed the search down to within Byrne & Sacetti, then got security to force open her locker in the tiny staff room. For a whole, excruciating half-hour, Simon and I held out great hopes they might find something there, some clue as to what's happened. I'd gratefully have leaped on any tiny little thing at all: a computer printout of hotel reservation somewhere? Train or bus timetable? No straw, no matter how weak and puny, was beyond my clutching at it, like a holy relic.

But when security eventually did prise open her locker, there was absolutely zilch, bar a few out-of-date *Hello!* magazines, a slightly battered pair of trainers she always wore in work to help her stride around the place that bit faster, plus a half-eaten pack of chocolate digestives, (her on-the-run carb-hit of choice). And at the back of all that, shoved into the pocket of a bright red fleece jumper she often wore, was her mobile. Just sitting there.

Which rang instant alarm bells. Kitty was finishing work for the holidays that night. So why would she leave her phone behind? Made absolutely no sense! Suspiciously knowing looks were exchanged between coppers and I knew right well what they were thinking, even without them opening their gobs. They were wrongly assuming that Kitty's one of the 'voluntary missing', that she had this all planned, that she knew right well she could be traced through her phone and so had left it in the most obvious place she could.

'Total crap!' I felt like screeching at them. 'You've got it all wrong!' But Simon, level-headed as ever, cooled me down a bit. Yes, he agreed, it's total shite, what's at back of their minds. But for now, let's co-operate as best we can and just concentrate on getting her back safely.

Simon unfailingly always says the right thing, even if it's not particularly what I want to hear. Had a big, sullen lump in my throat for whole rest of day, though, directly attributable to Jack bleeding Crown. That any copper, no matter how well-intentioned, could even possibly think someone with as much to live for as Kitty would ever just take off without telling anyone? It's just unthinkable.

Yet more dire news: the bank turned out to be similarly useless. Apparently her last transaction was day before she vanished, when she stopped off at Tesco at about nine in the evening and used her Laser card to shop. 'A Goodfellas pizza, a sliced pan, a value-pack size of Andrex toilet rolls and three tins of cat food,' the copper who discovered this proudly announced, having spent the guts of an entire morning uncovering this earth-shattering discovery.

I'll grudgingly give the coppers this much though: they've really excelled themselves at door-to-door searches and have managed to get far, far more neighbours in houses close by Kitty's to open up to them, than we humble civilians could ever have hoped to. In fact, I'm constantly amazed at just how powerful the flash of an official-looking badge and a uniform can be.

Everyone's giving statements to them now, though to my disappointment, and Simon's impatience, the search has yet to turn up some bright spark who'll tell us, 'Yes! I recognise that girl from her photo and remember distinctly! I saw her going into number forty-two with that well-known perv who lives there! So let's batter door down and let the mighty sword of justice have its way!'

At least, not yet.

Have been working v. closely with the coppers for a while now and they've even carried out massive street-by-street searches in the local area, which hopefully may just throw up something. It was case of all hands on deck; dog units and subaqua diving teams were even called in; exactly what was needed.

The plan was to comb the whole area in and around Camden Street, where Kitty was last seen, in the hope of finding something, anything, that might give us some clue as to where she might have gone. I was v. hopeful something would turn up or someone's memory would have been jogged. It took hours and hours, cost God alone knows what, but the whole operation turned out to be yet another massive disappointment. Yielded absolutely nada, but I have to say in one way I was hugely relieved. The thoughts of police diving units being drafted in bloody terrified me. Because what if they did actually find something at the bottom of a river? Nearly got weak-kneed just thinking about it.

But Simon's always quick to ladle yet more mugs of tea down my throat to calm me down. 'She's absolutely fine, remember,' he keeps saying, gently talking me down, like I'm a five-year-old. 'Now repeat after me what the police are constantly telling us.'

'Ninety per cent chance of her coming back to us alive and well,' we singsong together.

Aside from all those setbacks, though, in one way it's actually v. reassuring to have full police back-up alongside us. To date, they've done things I never even considered: putting out appeals in the papers and on radio, for starters, though given that it's Christmas, they reckon not too many people will be paying attention to hardcore news. But Crown assures us we can do another media blitz after the holliers, when we're far more likely to grab the public's attention. They've even placed alerts on all 'points of exit' around country. Like at major roadblocks, where they're randomly stopping cars and whipping out breathalysers checking for drivers over the limit after a few Xmas drinks too many, that kind of thing.

Not only that, but Interpol have now been alerted, we're told, as well as international police forces. Also, staff have been placed on high alert at all airport passport control and ferry embarkation points, which I supposed they figured might actually have lead somewhere, till I had to point out to Crown that her passport was in fact sitting stuffed in her desk drawer at home.

No matter, I was told brusquely. It's 'standard procedure', apparently. And one thing I'm fast learning with this fella is, don't, whatever you do, even think about coming between him and his 'standard procedures'. Starting to wonder if the guy falls asleep at night with book tucked on his lap called *Garda Procedure: A Guide to Driving the General Public Mental by Relentlessly Banging on about It.* For a bit of light bedtime reading, that is.

If Kitty did actually have all this planned for a long time, is his ridiculous thinking, then she could easily have been travelling under an alias or even a false passport. Happens v. frequently, apparently. Could have all been worked out well in advance.

'Just think,' he told me over the phone, in that brisk, businesslike way that's frankly starting to drive me round the twist. 'Had she used her own passport with all her given details on it, then at every arrival point wherever she travelled, we'd not only have a record of her arrival, but most likely CCTV footage to accompany it too.'

'You're seriously telling me that Kitty went out and somehow acquired a false passport? And said nothing to no one?' *Are you deranged?* I want to tack on, rudely, but somehow don't.

'Angie, please, you have to trust me,' Crown insists. 'It's a lot more common than you might think.'

Utterly mental, as I pointed out during yet another blowing-off-steam chat with Simon. For one thing, there's no one worse in the world at keeping secrets than Kitty. Had she seriously been planning some big upheaval to Rio secretly without telling any of her nearest and dearest, you can be bloody sure she'd have left a trail of holiday brochures and bottles of mosquito repellent scattered all over the place. Kitty's a wonderful girl, but discretion never was her strongest suit.

Meanwhile, coppers are continuing to interview everyone who last worked with her at Byrne & Sacetti on her last night, just in case that might throw up a lead. And this time, for a change, it was Simon who got a violent urge to gnash his teeth when he heard and ended up quietly seething to me, 'But you and I have already covered all of that! What's the matter, don't these people give us any credit at all? Why are they wasting precious *time*?'

Police are going a step further than we ever did, though. They're now appealing directly to customers who were at Byrne & Sacetti that night, casual diners who either dropped into the coffee bar on the ground floor or else the cellar wine bar below, to come forward to talk to them. And believe me, given that it was two days before Christmas there must have been hundreds of them. Apparently they've been trawling through CCTV footage of inside every vast, sprawling level of the restaurant as well as exterior footage of the street outside. They even managed to find one single, final shot on wobbly stop/start camera that nearly broke my heart.

It was Kitty, striding in that long-legged, athletic, purposeful way that she had, all the way down Camden Street and away from the building at exactly 1.20 a.m., on the morning of Christmas Eve. Time and date were clearly burned onto top right-hand corner of screen; rock-solid proof in black and white that she did actually leave work that night, as normal. And then just vanished into thin bloody air.

Even though the shot of her was taken from, I'm guessing, about two storeys above her and all you really could see was a v. minuscule moving dot, there was still no mistaking our girl. Wearing the fluorescent pink Puffa jacket she loved so much, with jeans and cream furry snowboots, which her cat used to snuggle into whenever she'd abandon them on the floor. And then nothing.

The whole clip was only about fifty seconds long, but we must have watched it for a full hour, over and back again. Studied it like it was the Zapruder film of the Kennedy assassination. I'm not joking, I sobbed like a baby for the rest of day after seeing it. Could barely haul myself out of bed the next morning. Mother Blennerhasset is now getting seriously worried about me, and has started clucking on about getting local GP to prescribe me something 'just for your nerves, Angela love. No shame in it these days, you know. Sure half the judiciary are on Prozac.'

Can only assume she reckons this might cheer me up.

Simon's is now about the only voice on the phone that can get me out of the house and ready to face each day ahead. The last person I ever want to hear at night and the first in the morning, ringing me with updates, even if there aren't any, which there hardly ever are. His voice, or else Crown's, that is; though to date, only news the latter ever rings me with is unanimously bad.

Getting v. sick of constantly being told by the coppers not to worry. I'm finding it increasingly hard not to snap at them and come out with something like, 'Yes! Absolutely! Congratulations on cracking the case, Sherlock! I'll gladly abandon all worry now! Because the chances are Kitty is safe and well and checked into some remote hotel perched on a rock in deepest Kerry, where she can't be found! And you know what? You're quite right . . . Makes utter sense that she wouldn't give a shit about all the mayhem and anguish she's causing at home! Case closed, and now let's all go home and watch *Strictly Come Dancing* finals, and ring in a v. happy New Year for one and all!'

I'm convinced I must have worn my back teeth down to stubs by now.

During the blackest hours, I consciously have to stay focused on all the positives in this, as Simon keeps reminding me. Not that there's many, but if I didn't, I'd lose my reason altogether. One major plus: our gang of mates and a big group of Kitty's colleagues from work really have been unbelievable. It would gladden your heart to see how committed and dedicated everyone's being, especially seeing as it's still the holidays and everyone's giving up their family time, not to mention precious days off work to help out in the search.

Ever-organised Sarah and her assistant even put in a few extra hours at her family's sandwich bars' head office and, between them, printed off thousands of flyers with Kitty's picture emblazoned on them, along with all the bullet points of relevant info.

MISSING
SINCE 1 a.m. APPROX. 24 DECEMBER
KITTY HOPE
AGED 31 YEARS
HEIGHT: 5 FEET, 10 INCHES
HAIR: BLACK
EYES: HAZEL
BUILD: SLIM
LAST SEEN LEAVING BYRNE & SACETTI'S
RESTAURANT, CAMDEN ST.
ANYONE WITH RELEVANT INFORMATION
SHOULD CONTACT GARDAI,
AT THE CONFIDENTIAL NUMBER
LISTED BELOW.

This, emblazoned with the best photo of Kitty we could find, is now plastered on just about every lamppost in the area round where she lives and works. And when I say we've blitzed the place, it's honestly no exaggeration. Between myself, Simon and the rest of the gang, we've practically paper-bombed not only the whole neighbourhood, but most of the city centre too. It's nigh on impossible even to go into a newsagent's or pub by now, without seeing Kitty's unforgettable face and dancing hazel eyes almost flirting back at you; scarily white skin, no blue veins, no imperfections . . . flawless.

I can vividly remember the night that photo was taken too: it was about a year ago, the night of Kitty's birthday. She'd lugged the whole lot of us into Pravda bar in town for a karaoke night, then insisted on everyone drinking Black Russians, a.k.a., a hangover in a glass. Can't be certain, but I think the photo of her was taken after about her third or fourth, but before her seventh, which was around the same time the singing started. Led, of course, by Kitty, who hopped up on a table and started murdering 'Rumour Has It' by Adele.

Brilliant, brilliant night, but then it's impossible to go anywhere with Kitty and not to have a brilliant night. Car keys were lost, credit cards were nicked, heads were held down loos for hours the next day and everyone still reckoned it was the Best Night Ever. But then that's our Kitty for you. Even sitting on the top of a bus with her is like the best fun imaginable.

It really is an utterly beguiling picture of her, too. She looks like a movie star, even if we did have to Photoshop a full pint of Budweiser out of her hand. I even overheard the Garda liaison officer who's working on the case wolf-whistling when he saw it, and saying, 'Now there's a face I certainly wouldn't forget seeing in a rush.'

Hard not to smile at that. Kitty's not even here, and yet she can still provoke the exact same reaction from fellas that she's been doing ever since the day she first bounced into my life.

Neighbours are truly astonishing as well. I nearly get teary when I see sheer extent of people's goodness. Kitty's house is now a bit like Grand Central Station with all the comings and goings, but then, Simon and I have pretty much set it up as our HQ till we find her. And, no kidding, every few minutes, there's a gentle knock at the door and it's without fail some lovely neighbour with trays of sambos, giant tureens full of soup or big tray of home-made mince pies for the police.

One of them, Mrs Butterly, a hair-netted, grandmotherly type in her mid-sixties has been particularly magic, and it's almost starting to feel like she's moved in here at this stage. We've given her a set of keys, and every time Simon and I crawl exhaustedly back to the house after a day of postering and flyer-ing the town, she'll be standing at the sink washing up, or mopping floors; I even caught her doing the ironing once.

I know she means well, but it's v. strange the way she's tidied the whole house beyond recognition. With Kitty around, it always looks like charming but cluttered chaos; now it's sparkling and shiny, and you can actually see and find things, instead of having to root through mounds of stuffed binliners to find tins of cat food buried underneath.

Didn't like to say it to Simon, but it's actually starting to feel like her memory's slowly being airbrushed away from us. I don't mean to be ungrateful, though, particularly as Mrs Butterly only means well. Bless her, she even managed to bribe the whole clatter of grandkids she has away from their Christmas telly and their Wii games and Nintendos to help out with stickering Kitty's poster onto lampposts, bus stops, etc.

'I've no words to thank you,' I tell her, going to give her a big hug late one evening. Simon and I had just fallen in the door exhausted, and two minutes later she let herself in, weighed down with a cold turkey platter for the pair of us, and a flask of home-made vegetable soup.

'Least I can do, pet,' she says warmly. 'The thing is, I really love Kitty, you know. Best neighbour I ever had. Used to do my shopping for me whenever it got too icy for me to go out, and was always happy to babysit my grandsons, if ever I was stuck. She could referee a fight between the lot of them like no one I've ever seen, before or since.'

I nod, able to see scene play out so exactly. Just the sort Kitty was. I mean, *is.*

Sorry. Hard and getting harder not to start referring to her in the past tense.

To say Simon's v. up and down is major understatement. It's like he and I alternate our moods: on my bad days – and God knows, there've been a few – he's an unfailing rock of sense and confidence. Works the other way round too. At times when he's in the throes of depression and sick with worry, then I'm the one who has to have resolve enough for both of us.

Mind you, Simon's your typical West of Ireland, strong silent type. I know it would probably kill him to open up, so instead, on his bad days, he just goes totally silent on me. Brooding, intense, staring-morosely-at-the-wall-ahead-of-him type silence. Not altogether easy for other people to be around and only ever opening up to me, no one else.

He's virtually stopped eating, and in the space of the last few days has taken what the French call a *coup de vieux*. If possible, the guy physically looks about ten years older now.

Mrs Butterly's v. concerned.

'I left that fella in a whole tray of ham and cheese sandwiches last night,' she mutters darkly to me, when he's well out of earshot, 'and I found them all still there this morning, untouched. And it isn't right, you know. Last grown man who refused one of my ham sangers was my poor husband. On his deathbed.'

11.25 p.m.

Can't remember ringing in a New Year that I was looking forward to less. The gang's all here in Kitty's newly spotless house: Sarah, Jeff, Mags and her husband, Philip, minus the kids. It's absolutely not any kind of celebration, how could it be? Suspect we just all want to be under same roof to get through this awful milestone together.

V. strange, slightly muted atmosphere. No one's saying it aloud, but I know we're all thinking the exact same thing. Where is Kitty now? And though it's absolutely not something I could ever articulate, but the next, tacked-on worry is invariably, is she OK? And unharmed?

It's a stomach-churning thought and I have to use the full force of my will to banish it. So I keep reminding myself of what the coppers are constantly reiterating. That she's highly likely to be one of the 'voluntarily' missing. That, unbelievable at it may seem, this was all preplanned. Keep quoting Crown's one size fits all phrase: in well over ninety per cent of these cases, the subject will eventually come back, safe and well.

And have to admit, as odds go, they're fairly decent ones.

11.40 p.m.

Local kids on the street outside are having impromptu and, I strongly suspect, highly illegal bonfire and firework display. I've left Kitty's front door wide open and we all keep drifting in and out to watch. To watch, that is, or else to temporarily get away from Philip, Mags' awful husband, who's tolerated, (has to be, she's been our pal for years) though actively disliked by the whole lot of us.

Uncanny, every time Mags drags Philip out somewhere with her, within a guaranteed two minutes of his opening his gob, someone will have taken mortal offence at some of his more ludicrous pontifications. And sure enough, a bare ten minutes after they arrive, Sarah slips into the tiny galley kitchen beside me to have a good bitch about him.

'I mean, I know it's New Year's Eve and everything, but *why did Mags have to bring him*?' she quietly seethes into her glass of wine.

'Why did Mags have to bring him?' is like a catchphrase that forever follows Philip round, pretty much ever since the day they first met.

'You already know the answer to this, hon,' I hiss back at her. 'Because it's rare for pair of them to get a babysitter and have an actual proper night out together.'

Sarah doesn't answer me, though, just grunts into a bag of Doritos she's just found.

'Plus,' I loyally tack on, 'Mags is our mate and we love

her, therefore he must be endured, even if he is an arsehole. All there is to it.'

'Suppose,' she mutters sulkily under breath, mouth stuffed full of Doritos. 'I mean, we all put up with your arsehole of an ex-boyfriend, just 'cos we loved you, didn't we?'

I smile warmly back at her. Always v. reassuring when your mates are happy to slag off those who richly deserve it. The smile, however, freezes on my face when I get back to the living room, laden down with wine and what's left of the Doritos, in the nick of time to hear Philip come out with one of his legendary clangers.

'You know, I'm quite certain there's absolutely no need to overreact here,' he's ticking off Simon, who has the bad luck to be sitting right beside him. 'All I'm suggesting is that if Kitty has indeed taken off of her own volition . . .'

That phrase alone nearly makes me want to gag. And sure enough, there's worse to come.

'. . . then surely the police must have more pressing concerns, which their considerable resources could be put to far better use on? After all, they keep constantly reassuring you that she'll come back when she's good and ready to, so why not just sit back and let her?'

I glance over to Simon, who's reddening, but staying cool. Though he looks like he's doing an inner battle to physically restrain himself from punching the git square in the face, for having the barefaced cheek to come out with such a big load of insensitive shite.

'Oh, just give it a rest, Philip,' Mags snaps across the room at him, 'and drink your sherry. The police are doing everything they can, and I for one am bloody grateful for them.'

'I was speaking merely as a taxpayer,' Philip tells her

glibly. 'All this effort, not to mention expense, being poured into a possible black hole seems utterly wasteful, in my considered opinion.'

'In that case, thank God you're not the only taxpayer in this room,' Simon says curtly, jaw tightening, twitching slightly. Quietly furious, though you'd never know it if you didn't know Simon: he's rock-still.

'I wasn't finished,' Philip answers him, blissfully unaware of the offence he's causing (and yes, for someone who purports to be intelligent, he really is that thick). 'I'm merely trying to draw everyone's attention to the elephant in the room. If Kitty did indeed take off of her own accord . . . aren't any of you asking yourselves why? Answer that, and in my opinion, you'll get to the bottom of all this in no time.'

'You know, I think I might just go out and look at the fireworks,' Simon interrupts, rudely, for him. 'Anyone else coming with me? Angie?'

But he's already half-way out the door before I even get a chance to answer.

11.55 p.m.

At the impromptu New Year's Eve bonfire/firework display at the bottom of the street. The local kids are all having a ball for themselves, running around the place, hyper and out of their minds on cakes and soft drinks. Does me good to see it.

'Hey, missus!' one of them yells at me, a kid of about twelve, circling round the bonfire on a new-looking bike. 'Did you find your friend yet?'

'Not yet,' I call back at him as cheerily as I can, 'but don't you worry, we will!'

'Gimme money and me and me pals will go out on our bikes and help you!'

Kindness of strangers. Gets me every time. Even if the cheeky fecker did demand payment.

Half the street is out here tonight waiting on the chime of midnight, and I have to scout through the crowd for Simon, but eventually find him, right up close to the bonfire and staring intently into it, arms folded, utterly absorbed and miles away. I inch up close to him, so I'm standing at his shoulder now. Well, my chin is just about level with his shoulder, that is; Simon always towers above me.

'Pay absolutely no attention to Philip,' I tell him stoutly.

Silence.

'He's a total git,' I go on. 'Always was. And he's inevitably wrong, too. In fact, if he'd said he wanted to get involved in the search and that he was confident he *would* find Kitty, then I'd really be worried.'

More brooding silence. Then after a long, long pause Simon turns to me.

'What annoys me most about that moron,' he says, 'is that he actually had a point. Crown asked us the very same thing too, the first night we spoke to him, remember?'

I look back up at him.

'And believe me, I've been racking my brains about it ever since. Look, Angie, if she did have a good reason to disappear on us, then . . .' he breaks off here though, and goes back to glaring darkly into the fire instead. But the heat from it's almost too much now and I can feel my face burning bright red, even though it's well below zero tonight.

'Now you just listen to me,' I tell him as firmly as I can. 'There is absolutely no chance on earth that Kitty just ran for the hills voluntarily. She just couldn't have. I'd have known. You'd have known. No one was closer to her than you or I.'

'Angie, you're a good person and a loyal friend, and God knows I wouldn't be getting through all this without you,' he tells me, voice sounding thick now, emotional. Not like his usual stiff-upper-lip, stoic self at all. 'But you're completely missing it. You're missing the whole thing.'

'Missing what?'

'Just suppose there was some piece of the jigsaw that you weren't aware of,' he says, totally focused back on the bonfire now. 'Something that might just make some sense of all this. What then?'

'You're starting to worry me now!' I tell him, tugging at his arm. 'Would you mind telling me what the hell you're talking about?'

Can't hear what he answers back, though.

He's totally drowned out by the chime of midnight, by the crackle of fireworks and by the sound of celebrations breaking out all round us.

2.05 a.m.

Take ages, ages, an almost unbearable length of time, but finally others are all gone and it's just me and Simon back at the house, alone.

I find him sitting by himself in the living room, finishing off dregs of a glass of whiskey. He smiles at me and pats the seat beside him for me to sit down.

I don't faff around, just come straight to point.

'You in the mood to talk?' I ask him tentatively.

'To you? Always.'

'Look, I know tonight was a bit of an ordeal for you . . .'

An exasperated eye-roll here. 'Tell me about it.'

'But I have to ask. Whatever you were trying to tell me out at the bonfire earlier . . .'

'Let me get you a drink,' he interrupts me, but gently. 'I think you might just need one for this.'

Oh Christ. Whatever's coming must be bad, v., v. bad. I gird my loins and keep on pressing him.

'I'm OK, thanks, just anxious to know what's on your mind, that's all. We're all so worried about you. And if by any chance you've come across any new information that might help, then . . . well, you have to tell me. No matter what.'

'Angie,' he sighs deeply, looking over at me, red-eyed from deep exhaustion. 'Did you ever wonder why I was as cut up as I was over having to cancel the whole skiing trip with Kitty?'

'Of course I didn't! You were out of your mind with worry, like the rest of us.'

'No.' He sighs deeply. 'No, it was more than that. Far more. You see . . .' He pauses to rub bloodshot eyes and my heart just goes out to him. 'And for the moment at least, this is absolutely to go no further . . .'

'You can trust me. You know that.'

I'm on the edge of my seat now, wanting to screech, 'Just gimme the last sentence first!'

After another unbearable bout of staring moodily into the dying dregs of the fire, he turns back to me.

'While we were away on holidays, I'd planned on asking Kitty to marry me.'

My jaw drops.

'Even had it all worked out,' he goes on, 'right down to

the finest detail, worse eejit me. We were flying to Austria, as you know . . .'

'To Kitzbühel,' I interrupt automatically.

'Yeah,' he nods. 'But what Kitty didn't know was that at the end of the holiday, I'd planned to tell her I'd a very special surprise for her and that she was just to trust me. Then I was going to drive her to Innsbruck, where I'd booked us two tickets on the Orient-Express to pick us up there and take us onto Paris. Overnight sleeper, the whole works . . . I've been saving up for it for months now. Knew she'd never in a million years go in for a big white wedding, so I thought I'd splash out on the proposal and make it something we'd both remember for the rest of our lives.'

I gasp a bit here. Kitty's lifelong dream had always been to travel on the Orient-Express. 'I'll do it with my Lotto winnings,' she used to giggle. 'After I get this big hooter on my face sorted out first, that is.'

'We were to have dinner on the train,' he goes on, 'then a champagne breakfast the following morning. And when we finally arrived in Paris, I'd booked for us to stay the night at the Crillon Hotel . . .'

The Crillon. Have heard of it all right. Poshest hotel in the whole city, apparently. Must have seen a hundred movies using it as a background and in each and every single one, it looks like a bleeding palace.

'. . . Then later that night, I'd booked to take her to dinner in Maxim's . . .'

Jeez, I have to hand it to him. No expense spared. How could she possibly refuse the guy, when he'd gone to so much bother?

'There's more,' he smiles wryly at me. 'There's a live band at the restaurant and I'd even called ahead to tell them what I was secretly planning and to ask them to play her favourite song . . .'

'"Bat Out of Hell" by Meat Loaf?' I say, a bit stunned. (Kitty's taste in music is best described as eclectic.)

'No,' he grins, '"Wonderful Tonight", by Eric Clapton. OK, so maybe her second favourite song. And that's when I was going to ask her. If everything had gone according to plan, she and I would be an engaged couple by now.'

Instincts clashing. Involuntarily, I find my hand clutching my throat, like a dowager duchess in a nineteen fifties black-and-white thriller. I want to say, 'Oh my Gowd!' in a loud, annoying voice, I want to hug him and congratulate him and crack open champagne and beg to be bridesmaid and say all the things I'd say if . . . well, if circumstances were different. If this was an occasion to celebrate.

But instead, I land back to reality with aching thud.

'She'd have been over the moon, Simon,' is all I can tell him, simply. 'I know she would.'

The green eyes turn sharply away from the fire to focus firmly on me.

'You do? Because I'm not so sure about that.'

'Oh, come on! She was mad about you, you know that! You were her longest relationship in . . . in, like, for ever!'

But something in the way he's staring at me cuts the words off in my throat.

'You don't understand. There's more. A lot more.'

A long sigh, then he's gone back to staring into the dying fire embers.

'I was due to move in here after the holidays,' he eventually says.

'I know.'

'And as you've seen for yourself, I'd carted over a lot of

my stuff here beforehand, a few days before she disappeared. Just dumped it all, in bags and cardboard boxes into the spare room upstairs. I figured I'd get round to unpacking it all after the holiday.'

'So?'

'So, late last night, I couldn't sleep. I was restless and found myself wandering around the house at about three in the morning, just looking for something, anything, that might shed a bit of light on all this.'

OK, the suspense is nearly killing me now. And I'm deeply regretting that I didn't snap up his offer of a stiff drink earlier.

'And I found myself searching through the spare room, just in case. At first I couldn't find a thing, just all the bags and suitcases I'd left there myself, days before I last saw her. Then I remembered the ring I'd been planning to surprise her with. I've had so much else on my mind recently, I hadn't given it as much as a thought.'

'The engagement ring was here all this time?'

He nods.

'I knew it was safe here. And it was buried deep in the carry-on bag I'd have been travelling with, so I was certain I wouldn't go away without it. It was my grandmother's, you see, and I thought . . . well, after Kitty vanished, I figured the least I could do was keep it somewhere a bit safer, rather than still wrapped in its box at the bottom of a small suitcase. But when I went to root it out . . .' He breaks off here and I barrel over him.

'Don't stop! Keep on talking!'

My bum is clenched tight with worry now.

'. . . I discovered that the wrapping around the ring box had already been opened, then carefully resealed again.'

'*What?* You're sure?'

'Certain. The ring box had even been put back into its wrapping wrong side up.'

'You mean . . . you think Kitty found it?'

'That's exactly what I think, yes. Just think about it: it would have been the easiest thing in the world to happen. Some night when she was here on her own, she might have started to unpack some of my things and accidentally stumbled on it. Or she could have been rummaging round the spare room for stuff of her own and somehow come across it that way.'

Like a scene from a movie, I can actually see it play out in my mind's eye. Kitty has a v. inquisitive nature and I'm certain that if she were to find a ring box buried deep under a pile of Simon's clothes, no power on earth would stop her from opening it up to have a right, good gander at it. Be the very same myself. Couldn't sleep under same roof as something as huge as that without knowing exactly what it was.

'But she'd have been thrilled, Simon! I know she would!'

He looks at me for a long time, my face urgently trying to read his.

'You do? You absolutely certain of that? Wish I could be.'

'So what are you thinking?'

He hesitates. 'Angie, you and Kitty often laugh and say that before I met her, she was famous for just taking off the minute she sensed a guy was getting any way serious on her. If she was getting cold feet at all, she'd just up sticks and run.'

'Yeah, but that all changed when we met you! She's been with you for well over eighteen months now, for God's sake, her longest relationship ever, and I should know!'

'Well, maybe she didn't change as much as I'd like to think. The police are constantly at us trying to unearth some reason as to why she'd take off like she has, and maybe this is it.'

'So you think . . .'

'That she accidentally stumbled across the ring, instantly knew I was planning to propose on holiday and just couldn't hack it. So she reverted back to type and bolted.'

Chapter Six

New Year's Day, 4.15 a.m.

I've stayed the night in Kitty's. Couldn't bring myself to leave Simon, the state he was in. He v. gallantly offered me Kitty's bed while he said he'd sleep in the spare room, but I swear I could hear him up and about for most of the night, moving round and pacing restlessly. Don't blame him; I couldn't nod off myself either. Instead I'm just lying here in Kitty's bed, surrounded by Kitty's books and photos, bone-knackered and staring at Kitty's ceiling, thinking, where in hell are you right now? And have you the first clue what you're putting us all through?

If you saw me, you'd swear I was some kind of deranged, certifiable nut-job trying to reach out and contact her telepathically.

(Though not the worst idea, now it comes to me. Suggest to police that we hire a professional psychic? No, maybe not . . .)

5.45 a.m

Eventually manage to drift into fretful sleep, but then have the most vivid dream that it was Kitty and Simon's wedding day, I was chief bridesmaid in an arse-covering dress about as far removed from Pippa Middleton's as you can get, and just as we were all about to leave for the church, she vanished. And muggins here not only had to break the bad news to Simon, but then had to address a packed church and tell them the bride was probably halfway to South America by now. But that I was absolutely certain they could get refunds on all the lovely stuff they'd bought as wedding presents from IKEA, B&Q, etc.

Bit like in *Runaway Bride,* except this was most definitely not a romantic comedy.

6.05 a.m.

No convincing Simon about Kitty *not* having done a runner; he just won't hear it. I tried my level best last night; tried and failed. The guy's totally torn apart. He even produced the engagement ring to show me, like it was evidence in a murder trial. And I could quite clearly see for myself that the elegant silver wrapping around it had been opened and then carefully resealed. You could tell by way the Sellotape didn't quite stick right, where she must have replaced it.

The pair of us pored over it for ages last night, examining it like we worked in a forensics lab.

And the ring's absolutely stunning, by the way. A beautiful antique ruby, with two little diamonds, one mounted on either side. How any woman could have refused it, especially after the most romantic proposal known to man that he had all pre-planned, is totally beyond me.

Told Simon she'd have loved it. Sorry, correction, that she *will* love it.

6.06 a.m.

Simon's properly up and about now. I can hear him going downstairs and pottering around, putting the kettle on, etc.

Can't help thinking, not eight short days ago, this was the most confident, self-assured man I knew. The type of guy so brimming with positive energy and confidence, that if NASA were ever to announce they were looking for an inexperienced volunteer to fly the space shuttle, he'd be the first waving his hand in the air, saying, 'Yeah, no problem, I'm your guy! Sure, how hard can it be?'

But last night he was like a vague shadow of that person; not eating, not sleeping, just trailing round looking like living dead and radiating worry.

Can't describe how sorry I feel for him, how much I just want to hug him and mind him and tell him not to worry, that it'll all be OK.

But then, I too have been the rejected sap in my time. All too easy to sympathise.

6.07 a.m.

My thoughts wander. I've never even come close either to getting proposed to (pause to snort incredulously here) or, God forbid, ever proposing to a man myself. Probably a v. good thing too; would doubtless be in the divorce courts by now, no question. But I can't even begin to comprehend the utter pain and humiliation of laying not just my whole heart, but my whole future life on the line for another human being, then having it flung right back in my face. And without even having the decency to have a face-to-face chat, along the lines of, 'You're an amazing person, but marriage just isn't what I'm looking for right now . . .' etc.

But just running away like a coward instead?

Kitty wouldn't do it, simple as. Couldn't have. It DID NOT happen.

It's unthinkable.

6.22 a.m.

Minging thing to say, but if Simon's actually on the money about Kitty finding the engagement ring and bolting, then I honestly won't be held responsible for what I'll do to her when she decides to come back. In fact, the ice-cold fury I'm feeling towards her right now is giving me a whole new lease of life. If Simon's right, then it was an utterly unforgivable thing to do to the guy, not to mention to the rest of us eejits. Like subliminally telling him, 'Now do you see? This is the measure of how much I don't ever want to be with you!'

Notice I'm speaking about her in present tense now. V. good sign. Because if she has just taken off with herself, that proves one thing at least.

It means she's safe and well. And, after all, isn't that the answer to my prayers?

7.02 a.m.

Can hear Simon's turned the TV on downstairs now. Kids' movie, and by the sound of Michael Caine saying, 'Bah, humbug!' in a Cockney accent, I'm guessing *The Muppet Christmas Carol.*

Shag this, I can't sleep anyway, might as well get up. I

throw Kitty's man-sized dressing gown over me and head down to living room, where he's making coffee, white-faced and red-eyed. He offers me a mug and puts on some toast.

'How are you doing?' I ask, a bit pointlessly. Sure you only have to look at the guy to see the answer.

'It's a brand-new year,' he says. 'And already I hate it.'

7.15 a.m.

Simon thinks it's best if he and I go to see Kitty's foster mum in the nursing home later on this morning. Says we really have to, there's no choice. For one thing, he and Kitty should have been coming home from their holiday today and, of course, the two of them would have gone straight down to see her, so they'll be expected.

And not only that, but with any luck, after a re-enactment of Kitty's last known movements is broadcast on the *Crimewatch* TV show this week, this story will hit the news in a v. big way again; a second wave of publicity, as Crown puts it. Sure, coppers put out appeals to the public over Christmas, but all with zero per cent success. Mainly because it was the holidays and so people just weren't reading the papers or watching the news as regularly as normal. According to coppers, tomorrow's officially the best day to really 'go public' with the story; Christmas is properly over and people will generally start reading papers and listening to news again. I'm v. hopeful something will turn up or someone's memory will be jogged sufficiently when they see this plastered all over the media. Because Kitty can't have just vanished into thin air.

It's just not possible. Not unless your name is Lord Lucan.

So we can't take the risk of either Mrs K. or anyone in

the nursing home chancing on seeing Kitty's photo in the paper, then worrying themselves sick. It's only fair to fill in everyone there beforehand, as best we can.

I'm absolutely dreading it, but deep down I know that Simon's right. It's a case of welcome to the wonderful world of got no choice.

7.46 a.m.

Sarah and I have been working closely with coppers for the last few days on the PR angle of this too, aiming for full, blanket coverage. Apart from news, newspaper reports and radio bulletins, we're hoping to get people posting about this online and on social networks, the works.

Have to say, Sarah's been a complete wonder throughout all this, like a mini tornado of efficiency. She's doing all this to help out, in spite of the fact she's up to her tonsils with work; the only time her family's sandwich bars closed were Christmas Day, the day after and that was it. Seems there's still massive demand for cheese toasties and soya lattes, with all the January sales in full swing. And if my phone rings anytime before eight in the morning, it's almost guaranteed to be Sarah with some PR update.

Small wonder the girl isn't running the country. Could do it with one hand tied behind her back, easy. She even asked me how I was doing for cash these days. (Broke, broke, broke.) Then unofficially told me that even though I didn't get hired the last time I interviewed to work at one of the sandwich bars, she'd unofficially keep her ear to the ground in case any part-time work came up.

Bit nervous that my sister Madeline will wander in off

the street and find me with a hairnet on buttering sliced pans, but I'm deeply grateful otherwise.

Need dosh so, so badly. The costs of the search by now are seriously starting to mount. (Posters, flyers, bribing local kids to go out and plaster them on every bus stop, train station and any kind of shop for miles round, etc.) So far, Simon has forked out for just about everything himself. Absolutely insisted.

No doubt about it, the hunt for Kitty is now fast becoming a full-time job. Except sadly, one that doesn't pay.

9.21 a.m.

One miraculous thing about Simon: in spite of the hell on earth the poor guy's been living through, he's really surprising me now by being a lot more positive, for the moment at least.

Soon as we're out on the road to see Mrs K., he says it over and over, like a mantra: 'She's out there, Angie, I know it. She just *has* to be. She's safe and well and just got a bit freaked out, that's all. We need to find her and, what's more, we're going to.'

Almost like he's trying to convince himself.

Had a quick shower before we left, but I'm still in last night's jeans and had no choice but to borrow a jumper from the back of Kitty's wardrobe. Oversized on her, but a snug fit on me. I can still smell her perfume on it too; an expensive one Simon bought her as a gift when he came back from one of his business trips.

V. weird sensation, being able to smell her. Once we hit the motorway, I keep nodding off, then get a sudden whiff of Kitty and drowsily wake up, thinking in my half-asleep state that she's actually here in the car with us. And then remembering.

11.30 a.m.

Finally, finally we arrive, with my bum like a box of spanners after the long drive. We asked a lovely receptionist if we could have a quick word with Mrs Kennedy's consultant, one doctor Emily Hargreaves. Because even though the very thought of in any way upsetting Mrs K. is utterly gag-making, we both feel it's only right to fill in her doctor first to see what she advises. And we're certain she's on duty today. Simon had the foresight to ring ahead and let them know we were coming and would need to see her.

We're shown into a tiny office and asked to wait. I catch Simon's eye. It's the only time so far today he's been silent. He's over by window, staring vacantly out at the wintry garden, absorbed in watching an elderly couple, arms linked and wearing about fifty layers of clothes each, having an outdoor stroll. Even with the two of them padded out like Michelin Man against the cold, and even though they're barely able to hobble, never mind walk, they still look so companionable and so in love, arms linked and chatting happily away to each other.

I can almost tell what Simon's thinking, without him having to open his mouth.

He thought that in fifty years, that would be him and Kitty.

12.15 p.m.

Dr Hargreaves strides in, a big, bosomy, middle-aged woman, radiating kindliness and almost motherly concern. If you were making a biopic of her life, you'd definitely cast Brenda Fricker, or if she wasn't available, Miriam Margolyes. Insists on organising tea and sticky buns for us, as if we've just had a journey of epic Michael Palin-esque proportions, instead of a mere two hours on a motorway with many, many bypasses.

We've been speaking to her on the phone regularly since Christmas, but now that we're sitting face-to-face, we fill her in properly as best we can. Simon's incredibly careful to stress that we've good reason to believe Kitty is all right, but that she just got a bit freaked out 'by a personal situation', and is taking time out. He keeps hammering home the statistic about over ninety per cent of missing people coming back when they're good and ready to.

Dr Hargreaves is nothing if not a terrific listener.

'I can't tell you both how very sorry I am,' she eventually says, when Simon finishes. 'And how much I appreciate your coming down here, at a time like this. Horrendously worrying for everyone concerned. I'm very fond of Kitty, you know; we all are here. She's one of our most popular visitors. Never fails to brighten up the place every time she bounces in to see us.'

'So you see, we thought we'd better ask your advice as to how best to break it to Mrs K. – to her foster mum, that is.'

Dr Hargreaves nods gravely. 'I'm very grateful for what you're both doing,' she says, 'but please understand that it's highly unlikely Mrs Kennedy will be able to take in exactly what you're saying. You have to remember the huge toll the series of strokes she's suffered over the past few years have all taken on her, and on top of that, her Alzheimer's condition is sadly now at stage six.'

'Which means . . .?' I ask tentatively.

'She's now experiencing what we call severe cognitive decline. It varies from patient to patient, but in her particular case, it means that her memory has continued to worsen dramatically. There are some good days, when she'll still be able to remember her own name, but more often than not, she's simply not able to recall any of her own personal history. In other words, while there's a small chance she'll remember a face, it's highly unlikely she'll be able to remember the name of a loved one.'

'Even someone she loves as much as Kitty?' I ask worriedly.

'Perhaps it's best just to tell her that Kitty's missing at present,' is all Dr Hargreaves says, pointedly not answering my question, 'and that you're doing everything you can to help get her safely back home—'

'But you're saying there's a good chance she may not even know who we are?' Simon interrupts her.

'I'm saying there's a very good chance she won't even remember who Kitty is.'

12.40 p.m.

Just heartbreaking. Mrs K. looks exactly the same – looks unexpectedly well even – with a flush of colour in the pale, parchment-like skin. But hasn't first clue who we are or why we're here. We tell her exactly what Dr Hargreaves advised us to, then Simon looks worriedly at her while I shuffle embarrassingly around in background.

'Who are you?' she keeps on asking me. 'And where's Jean? What have you done with my Jean?'

I've absolutely no idea who Jean is, so I just keep telling her I'm Kitty's friend and that we've met before, but that gets no reaction at all.

Then she sits up in bed and starts looking beady-eyed at Simon.

'I know you, though.' She points at him. Says it again. Keeps repeating it over and over. A hopeful sign maybe?

Then she says triumphantly, 'I have it! You're off the telly! You're Simon Cowell!'

1.45 p.m.

Before we leave, we find Dr Hargreaves to tell her how we got on.

'She kept mentioning someone called Jean, by the way,' I tell her. 'Is that one of the nurses who works here?'

'Jean?' Dr Hargreaves says, shaking her head. 'No, I'm afraid we've no one by that name here. I shouldn't worry about it, though. Most likely just a name she picked up from watching TV.'

One good thing, as Simon says to me in car on our way home. At least Mrs K.'s spared all this worry.

It's bittersweet consolation, but I have to admit, marginally better than nothing.

'Now you do know why you're here, don't you? Jean?'

The disembodied voice came from directly behind her, a

flat, detached monotone; instantly put her in mind of this well-known battleaxe who worked at their local post office. A famously short-tempered one, who Jean and Mrs K. used to spend hours inventing glamorous exotic back stories, just for the laugh.

'She's actually a secret agent,' Jean would giggle, but then Mrs K. would override her and say, 'No, no! I've a better one! She's on the run from the law, but then she thought she'd hide out here, in a small country village where no one would know her . . .'

'. . . and from where she can operate her Al Qaeda sleeper cell in peace . . .'

Then the pair of them would collapse in fits of laughter. It was a weird thing about Mrs K., she often thought: even though there were decades between them, there was still absolutely no generation gap whatsoever. They were probably the unlikeliest pairing you could ever come up with, and yet somehow it worked.

'. . . So I just want you to stretch out nice and comfortably on the couch for me, now Jean, there's a good girl,' the monotone from behind her was still droning on. 'And remember, you're not in any kind of trouble at all. We're just here for a little chat. You've been through so much and we just want to help you.'

A bloody child psychiatrist's couch, that's where she'd ended up; God, Mrs K. would have fallen around at that. Jean's first instinct on coming in here had been to start acting like an out-and-out basket case, twitching and rolling her eyes and pretend foaming at the mouth like an extra from One Flew Over the Cuckoo's Nest. *Just to see if she could get some kind of a rise out of this one with her clipboard behind her, asking all these ridiculous questions. Anything, to relieve the tension, to take her mind off . . . well, what had happened. And what was very much still ongoing.*

'So, if you're ready then, Jean, maybe you'd like to tell me what's on your mind? In your own time.'

Jean lay back against the sofa and spent ages just gazing up at the Victorian ceiling overhead, heavy with coving and cobwebs, while the clock ticked on. Good fecking question. So how was she feeling? How could she even begin to put into words what was going through her mind? How could she possibly hope to make this one understand the sheer pain she'd been going through and was dealing with on a daily basis, when she was still trying to process so much herself?

'. . . Because you know, you'd been doing so well,' disembodied voice from behind her was saying now, after an interminable silence. 'We were all inordinately proud of you. Ever since you were housed with Mrs Kennedy, for the first time in years, you really seemed to settle down and you were absolutely blooming. Everyone could see that for themselves. Doing terrifically in school too; your grades have all been exceptional. And it can't have been easy for you, Jean, dealing with everything that came next. It must have felt so unfair, especially as it seemed your whole life had just turned a corner. So would you like to tell me about it?'

Would she? No, she decided. Too painful, to raw even to talk about yet, even though this one clearly meant well. Because how could she ever even hope to put into words what it had been like for her?

'How about we start six months ago? Tell me about when you first started noticing a change coming over Mrs Kennedy.'

Jean shuddered on the sofa, but said nothing. Couldn't. Besides, it wasn't just one single change in Mrs K., it was a pile of different things that all seemed to come together, in a bunch. The way she just seemed to tune out on her, how she'd just retreat off into her own little world, singing snatches from TV shows or ads with catchy jingles she'd heard on the radio. And what had Jean done to help? Absolutely nothing. Just papered over the cracks and tried to act like everything was hunky-dory. Nursed Mrs K., cared for her, organised all her own school stuff, kept the house going, did all the grocery shopping and laundry; she wasn't above even forging the odd signature on report cards, so to all outward appearances, Mrs K. was absolutely as normal.

They lived in a tiny town, though, and people had started to notice, to ask questions. Once, Mrs K. had got out of the house while she'd been at school and had been found strolling through Tesco in her nightie and hairnet, telling everyone she knew that she was on her way to London to meet Prince Charles. Another time, she was found on the bus to Cork, where she'd announced to anyone that would listen she was on the verge of running for the Presidency, but was a bit worried about all the intrusion into her private life. Word went out about plenty of other stuff too, and one day, Jean even had to threaten a girl in her class with a right walloping for openly referring to Mrs K. as 'funny talker' .

But like it or not, Jean could only keep the show on the road for so long. Like it or not, she was only sixteen. And pretty soon after, events took over.

'Of course, if you'd rather not talk about that,' the disembodied voice from behind her was saying now, 'then how about we talk about when Mrs Kennedy was first admitted into hospital? How did that make you feel?'

Jesus, how do you think? She wanted to snarl back, but then bit her tongue. 'Always remember, you'll catch more flies with honey than with vinegar, Jean love,' Mrs K. had repeatedly drummed into her, trying to do the best to curb the latent temper she had on her, which had got her into trouble so often in the past. Back in the days when she still acted like a proper, normal mum.

Was it really only three months ago, she wondered, since her whole life had turned upside down? Memories came back in sickening fragments: rushing home from school that day, seeing an ambulance at the gate and a concerned neighbour who told her what had happened. A stroke, she'd been told. They didn't know how serious it was yet, but were hospitalising Mrs K. anyway.

Early onset Alzheimer's, Jean was told at the hospital, after what felt like weeks of tests. All, of course, complicated by the stroke she'd just suffered, which left poor Mrs K. effectively paralysed down one side of her body. And sure enough, that had been that. She knew it was only a matter of time before the authorities tapped on her shoulder in the hospital and told her she'd have to be re-homed. Yet again. She'd yelled at them, screamed the air blue and told them she wouldn't leave Mrs K. Not when she was in this condition and needed her. We're all each other has, she'd kept trying to tell them, but no one listened. No one ever did.

And now here she was. On the flat of her back talking shite to yet another well-intentioned do-gooder who thought she knew what was best for her.

But only she herself knew the answer to that. And it was so bloody obvious, it was staring her in the face. She was sixteen years old now, almost seventeen. Wherever they placed her next, she'd run. Just run. Because what was her alternative? Try to fit in with another family who didn't really want an overgrown girl her age lumbering around the place? Feeling like an unwanted guest that had long outstayed her welcome?

There'd never be another home like Mrs K.'s, never. So why not just get the feck out now? Just check out like she was in a hotel. She'd always look after Mrs K. as best she could; she'd try to stay as close by the hospital as possible.

But the next chance she got, that was it. Mind made up.

She'd just walk out the door and never look back. And to hell with the lot of them.

Chapter Seven

2 January

As of today, our story officially hits the media in a big way. And not only that, but the re-enactment of Kitty's last-known movements went out on the *Crimewatch* TV show last night. I was a tiny bit worried about what effect it would have on Simon, seeing a model all gussied up as the woman he loves, bit like in that Hitchcock movie, *Vertigo*. But apart from a slight flush when he had to watch a replay of a total stranger posing as Kitty striding down Camden Street, he seemed fairly OK with it.

'You just wait and see,' I told him encouragingly as the pair of us sat side by side, glued to the telly. 'This will turn everything around for us. I just know it.'

The police PR department, in fairness, have been terrific, but they're no match for our Sarah, tornado of efficiency that she is. She called round to Kitty's not long after *Crimewatch* went out and, as ever, was like a badly needed burst of positive energy filling the whole house.

'You are both going to love me so much!' she said, handing out leftover croissants, which she'd filched from work and which I gratefully dived into. 'So far, just on the back of the re-enactment going out tonight, I've managed to land the *Times*, the *Independent*, the *Chronicle*, the *Echo*, the *Examiner* and pretty much all of the tabloids in the bag, can you believe it? This is virtually guaranteed to be the single biggest news story that goes out tomorrow! The *Echo* even said they'd use her photo on the front page, isn't that amazing? I've been faxing and emailing out press releases all evening, and the response I got was just incredible!'

Then, just as Simon stepped out of the room, all apologies, to take a call from one of his brothers, my mobile beep-beeped as a text came through. From Jack Crown.

> HI ANGIE, JUST CHECKING YOU AND SIMON WATCHED CRIMEWATCH TONIGHT. RING ME IF YOU CAN TALK. STORY SHOULD ALSO MAKE TV NEWS BULLETINS FROM TOMORROW, SOON AS IT DOES, WE'LL REASSESS PROGRESS FROM THERE. REGARDS.

'Who's texting you this late?' Sarah asked, suddenly all ears, but then Sarah misses absolutely nothing.

'Gobshite Crown,' I muttered darkly. 'Wants to see us tomorrow.'

'And what's wrong with that?'

'Sarah, the guy probably wants nothing more than a chance to rabbit on about police procedures yet again, and then to lecture me about how it's far better to let the professionals handle this and to just let them get on with it. Bloody neck of him.'

'Jeez, you've really made up your mind not to like him, haven't you?'

'No! I just . . .'

'Come on, you practically have slits in your eyes every time you look at the guy!'

'Well, he is annoying . . .'

'No he's not.'

'. . . And he has all the charisma of . . . of . . .' I randomly scout round for a suitable metaphor, but the best I can come up with under pressure is, '. . . of a Garda at a checkpoint.'

'He *is* a Garda. What do you expect?'

Had to shut up, she had me there.

'Come on, Angie, he's doing absolutely everything, and besides, he's not all that bad. If you ask me, I think he's actually doing as much as anyone possibly could, under incredibly trying circumstances. And he's always perfectly polite. All I'm saying is just give Jack Crown a chance, will you?'

Couldn't particularly be bothered, though, but then I'm more comfortable with prejudice. Once I've decided not to like someone, I've always found that it's generally far easier just to stick to that.

Sarah couldn't stay long and after she'd left, Simon and I stayed up late into the night, talking, talking, talking. Taking the whole thing apart, then somehow trying to piece it all back together again.

'Thank you,' he said to me at one point. 'If all this doesn't work for us, I honestly don't know what will.'

''Course it'll work. It has to. You just wait and see.'

I yawned and stretched and stood up to try and unstiffen my legs.

'You going home now?' Simon asked. 'Want me to drive you? Or you could stay if you wanted?'

'You wouldn't mind?'
'I want you to.'
'Be lovely, thanks.'

3 January, Kitty's house, 9.45 a.m.

Sarah wasn't joking. We are plastered *all over* the papers today, the whole unexpurgated story. Now that the Xmas silly season is over, this really seems to have caught the imagination of editors; an attractive young student working in a well-known Italian restaurant, without any prior history of depression, who, quite literally, vanished into thin air just before Christmas.

Headlines are varying, from sober ones like the *Times*: 'GARDAI CONTINUE TO SEEK PUBLIC ASSISTANCE IN SEARCH FOR MISSING WOMAN', to the slightly more sensational *Star*, which put us on page three (and no, the irony wouldn't be lost on Kitty, that she's finally a page three gal). The massive, banner headline was: 'MYSTERY SURROUNDING WOMAN'S DISAPPEARANCE. POLICE APPEAL TO PUBLIC. HAVE YOU SEEN HER?'

Wherever you are, I find myself silently willing her, for God's sake just turn on a TV or open a paper. And see for yourself just how much worry you're causing us.

12.59 p.m.

Me and Simon are glued to the TV for the lunchtime news, just in case. The pair of us are sitting right up on top of it, like it's Cup Final day at Wembley.

Come on, come on, come on . . .

1.01 p.m.

Headline is about pending property taxes and how half the country is refusing to pay up.

'Yes, we get it, now kindly move on!' I yell at the telly. A raised eyebrow from Simon shuts me up.

1.03 p.m.

Bum clenched with tension.

Aung San Suu Kyi is to leave Burma on a trip to Washington. Good for her, fantastic for world peace, etc., but absolutely shag all use to us.

1.05 p.m.

An inquiry has begun after a paramilitary left a gun and ammunition in a Belfast house . . . Jesus! Kitty's miles more important than any bleeding mislaid gun! Come on . . .

1.08 p.m.

Yes! Success! We're the fourth item! Just behind a trade delegation over visiting from China, but ahead of a transatlantic flight having to divert to Shannon on account of some halfwit leaving their mobile phone to recharge in the cabin loos.

'In other home news,' a v. Botoxed-looking newsreader says straight to camera, 'Gardai are appealing to the public for information about a missing woman, last seen leaving a well-known restaurant in the Camden Street area of Dublin in the early hours of December the twenty-fourth . . .'

Simon and I instinctively grab hands, lace fingers and cling tight, eyes glued to the screen.

Then up comes the same photo of Kitty that's in all the papers.

'Kitty Hope, aged thirty-one years, is described as being five feet ten in height, of slim build, with dark hair and hazel eyes.'

We grip onto each other even more. My fingers are now in danger of having the circulation cut off, Simon's hands are that strong.

'Kitty Hope was working at Byrne & Sacetti, a popular restaurant on Camden Street, and was last witnessed . . .'

My phone rings.

'For Christ's sake, who'd be ringing me in the middle of this!' I yell waspishly, but when I look at the number, I see that it's Jack Crown. Anyone else, I'd have ignored it and rung them back, but this might be important. Crown, after all, is hardly the type to ring up saying, 'Hi there, just checking in with you! Having a good day? Happy with all the publicity? Tired after the huge emotional roller coaster you must be going through?'

'Angie?' he says urgently, the minute I answer. 'By any chance are you free now?'

'Yeah, we were just watching the news actually . . .'

'Is Simon with you?'

'Yes, he's right here. He's beside me.'

'Then I think you'd both better get in here. The sooner you can, the better too. Believe me, I wouldn't disturb you, only it's important.'

2.22 p.m.

Jack Crown is already waiting for us as we arrive, nods a quick hi at each of us, then ushers us directly into a private room. And for the first time since this nightmare started, the guy actually looks hassled; a bit scruffy and unkempt-looking in shirtsleeves, like someone who's now going into the eighteenth hour of a gruelling working day. 'Look, I'm so sorry to haul you back,' he says, 'but I'm afraid I've brought you both in here to warn you.'

'Warn us of what exactly?' Simon asks, leaning forward on the tiny desk in front of us and eyeballing him.

'To date, we've had over fifteen very definite reports of Kitty Hope being sighted in various parts of the country,' Crown answers tersely, shoving a fistful of his thick, sandy hair out of his eyes and looking more exhausted than I think I've ever seen him.

I do one of those involuntary gasps and look back over to Simon, who's now completely frozen.

'Fifteen sightings! But surely this is fantastic news?' I blurt out. 'I mean, we only need for one of them to be genuine, and then we'll find her!'

'Yes and no, Angie,' Crown says. 'Yes, with great good luck, one of them may turn out to be accurate. But we have to bear in mind that it's physically impossible for her to be in all of these places at once. I just don't want either of you to get your hopes up at this stage, that's all.'

'Where exactly are these reports coming from?' Simon asks him urgently.

'From as far afield as Kerry, all the way to Belfast. And one, via our website, of a sighting in Amsterdam.

Which will, of course, take us that bit longer to investigate fully.'

'Amsterdam?' I ask, suddenly puzzled. Why would Kitty have gone to Amsterdam?

'Local police will follow up on all of these reports, on a case-by-case basis,' he explains patiently. 'But as I say, you have to remember that there's a high chance that the vast majority of these – and perhaps even all of them – will turn out to be little more than hoaxes.'

4 January, Kitty's house, 6.50 p.m.

Have been in a blind temper ever since this afternoon. Mainly because, so far, Jack Crown's turned out to be absolutely right. We've had absolutely nothing but sham reports that turned out to be worthless, or else out-and-out hoaxes. A retired farmer in Dingle reported seeing Kitty cycling through the town and onto the local hotel. I really got my hopes up at that; thought maybe Kitty travelled all the way down there and maybe checked into a hotel to get her head together. Plus she always loved Dingle, she loved nothing more than being close to the sea . . . Somehow the whole thing had the ring of truth to it.

But when coppers followed it up, it turned out that the woman who'd been sighted was actually, a) in her early forties, b) a redhead, and c) a guest in the hotel for her husband's surprise fiftieth birthday do. Turned out farmer who reported it was on a waiting list to get his cataracts done and had dodgy eyesight at the best of times. It ended up with him apologising profusely to the cops and sending everyone home with a few of his wife's home-made mince pies.

I was utterly incandescent. How could anyone mistake a redhead in her forties for Kitty? They wouldn't even look remotely alike! But as Simon patiently pointed out, at least we were finally reaching people. At least the public were on general lookout. And that it was just a matter of time before something solid turned up.

Simon's being a total rock of positivity these days.

Wouldn't have a blind hope of getting through all this without him.

5 January

More dead ends, including one sighting of Kitty in a petrol station on the 27th, just off the M7. Pair of us got v. hopeful at that; the M7 is the motorway you take to get to Foxborough care home. But the guy who'd reportedly seen her had the foresight to video her on his iPhone. I saw the footage for myself: a girl of about twenty-three or so, v. similar hair and build to Kitty's, but when you looked at the face, you knew it was just a bad lookalike.

Disappointment was crushing.

And so far, every other report has turned out to be little more than a wild-goose chase. All from well-intentioned people, clearly thinking they were doing their civic duty when they spotted someone even remotely resembling Kitty and quite rightly reporting it. But all roads lead to nothing more than one frustrating anticlimax after another.

Amsterdam's a real puzzler, though. For starters, I never bought into Crown's far-fetched theory that she'd been planning this for a long time and even went as far as to source herself a fake passport. I just knew that

Kitty, with the best will in the world, wouldn't be capable of keeping something as huge as that to herself. Simon made a v. good point too: we're pretty certain that she discovered the engagement ring only a day or two before vanishing. So if she did plan on making a run for it, that hardly gave her enough time to trawl the internet looking for dodgy websites that flogged fake passports, now did it?

No, the more we talk about it, the more we decide Amsterdam's just another hoax. But coppers are leaving no stone unturned, and apparently even Interpol are working with Dutch police checking out the lead from Schiphol airport. It'll take time, we're told, we're to be patient. Amsterdam's a primary gateway for flights 'out foreign', to quote Mrs Butterly. KLM use it as their major hub to connect worldwide, as well as United, Delta, Lufthansa; all the big boys.

So in the unlikely event of Kitty genuinely passing through there, where was her ultimate destination? And why even go there in the first place, when she'd so much more to live for here?

I steel myself to face yet another dead end. Mainly because I know deep down that's all this'll ever amount to anyway.

6 January

Simon's back to work today. So, so weird being without him during the day. Over the past week or so, we'd fallen into a sort of habit; he'd pick me up at my parents', drive me here, then the pair of us would spend the whole day doing what needed to be done. Answering calls, talking to police, setting up a website about the search, replying to emails and tweets, filling in Sarah, Mags, Jeff and all the neighbours who keep phoning all day, every day, all wanting updates.

Which so far, there never are.

7 January

And now Simon's at work from early till late and I'm doing all this on my own. I think he's grown to be every bit as dependent on me too, because he's taken to calling me at lunchtimes for long chats on what's been going on, what's come in, what, if anything, has been happening. Even if it's just a few random strangers posting sweet, concerned messages on our website promising that they'll keep their eye out and wishing us well. He'll always want to know and so I tell him.

Strange without him being here all day, though. Really feels like being without my right hand. But so far every day this week, while we're chatting away at lunchtime, without fail he'll come out with something like, 'Look, I'll be back at about seven-ish. How about I pick us up some take-out on my way home? And we could have a bite to eat together and just talk.'

I've said yes every time. And to take our minds off everything, we've even taken to watching movies after dinner. By then, pair of us are usually all talked out about what's been happening in the search for that day, so the distraction is a v. good thing. The only rule we have concerning film choice is nothing romantic: too upsetting for Simon. Action movies, we've decided, are perfect. Or thrillers, as long as they don't involve any kind of abduction scenario.

No doubt about it, evenings are getting to be by far the easiest part of my whole day. And after all, if I go home, what's waiting there for me? Home = sitting around dreading that Madeline might call, or else looking at the four walls worrying. Wishing that for once Mother Blennerhasset would permit the telly to be turned on, just for a bit of distraction.

And so I stay.

8 January

Amazing to think that not that long ago, we were a 'hot' story, but somehow it's all cooled off now. Sarah saw it coming, though. 'Today's newspapers are wrapping tomorrow's chips,' as she wryly put it, 'which is why we now have to concentrate on our digital campaign.'

A few more leads have shown up, but I can't bear getting all built up about them, only to be let down again. So on Simon's advice, I'm just letting the coppers get on with it and only allowing myself to get excited when Crown tells me they're chasing something definite.

Which of course so far, hasn't happened.

My days are falling into a sort of pattern now. Wake up at home, scuttle out of Mum's way as early as I can and come straight over to Kitty's. Simon's usually gone to work by the time I get here, so I let myself in, play with the cat for a bit if she's wandered in on the scrounge for grub, then head straight to the computer.

I've discovered an Irish website, *missingpersons.ie.* Would nearly break your heart. Some people on it seem to be gone years. There's a big, public notice board, where concerned family and friends all post messages that would make you bawl. All just pleading, begging for whoever they're appealing to, just to get in touch and let them know they're OK. How long, I can't help wondering, before I turn into one of those people?

One thing's v. clear from trawling through this site, though. No matter what reason anyone may have had to check out of their life and just bugger off without telling anyone where they were or why they left, it's just not fair on those left behind.

One woman, whose twenty-nine-year-old son has been missing since 2010, wrote that it was exactly like a bereavement. Only worse, because this way, you never get closure. You're almost afraid to go into full mourning because at any time, front door might ring and it could be them. So you never even allow yourself to start speaking about the person in the past tense, always the present.

And human hope is a v. dangerous drug. I should know.

9 January

Crown calls me. Says they're now widening the search. Widening it how, exactly? I ask him. Because aren't we already doing everything humanly possible that can be done? But no, apparently not. Now coppers want to do a full background search on Kitty.

He asks me about Kitty's life before we met so I tell him what I know, which isn't really all that much. But Crown keeps me on the phone for ages, insisting on coming back to the years after Mrs K. was taken into full-time care and before Kitty first came to Dublin. Not that there's all that much I can tell him. It wasn't something Kitty ever really went into. I knew she'd had a tough time of it, though; one drunken night she'd even told me she'd ended up living out of a suitcase in a hostel at one point. Kitty being

Kitty, though, just laughed and made a joke out of it. 'Terrible shame that I never went the whole hog and started sleeping on the streets, like Heather Mills. You never know, it might have been me who went on to marry and divorce Paul McCartney, and ended up twenty-five million quid richer.'

I can still remember her saying that, can still hear her big, hearty belly laugh.

But somehow Kitty managed to turn her life around after that; she got her act together, got work, found her feet again, got her life back on track. An incredible achievement by anyone's standards. Because if anyone started out on the bottom rung of life's ladder, it was Kitty. And now here she is, studying at night school, like she'd always promised herself she would, with a decent job that paid her reasonably well, a lovely home, boyfriend who adores her and friends who'd walk through flames for her.

'So there you have it,' I tell Crown. 'And I probably know as much as she was prepared to tell anyone about her past.'

I don't tack on what I'm really thinking, which is that it's her present I'm far more interested in.

'It's worth looking into,' Crown says thoughtfully. 'It could just somehow be in some way connected to her disappearance. But one thing is for certain, we'll never know till we dig a bit deeper.'

I drift off a bit at that, for the first time wondering if he could possibly be right. Is it possible those shadowy years that Kitty point-blank refused to get drawn down on have something to do with this?

'Angie?' Crown says down the phone, a bit more gently. 'You still there?'

'Oh, yeah, sorry. Just thinking. Well, worrying, actually.'

'Look, I know how hard this is on you, and on Simon too . . .'

Silence from me.

'And I also know that you think police procedures are getting us nowhere . . .'

Can't help myself flushing a bit at that.

'And so far, you'd be right. But please understand that I've seen a lot of these cases. And if we're ever going to find Kitty, believe me, this really is the only way. Thoroughness is what'll get us there in the end.'

'I know,' I manage to say, in a small and slightly mortified voice.

'All I'm saying is that I'm on your side, Angie,' he adds, but not sounding like he's in a nark with me.

'Yes. And thank you.'

'And I'm moving heaven and earth to get her back. But what I really need more than anything now is for you to trust me.'

I hang up the phone and make a silent vow. Better drop the attitude round Jack Crown from now on. I mean, quite apart from everything else, it's never a good idea to get on the wrong side of a copper, now is it?

10 January

Really, seriously starting to get bored now.

It's fine in the evenings when Simon's here, but the days are just so bloody long when you're unemployed. I find myself looking at the time on my phone every few minutes and nearly rejoicing when I find I've got through a whole hour. Then I tell myself, right, now I only have to last another sixty more minutes and that's yet another hour gone. That's how I'm getting through this on a day-by-day basis . . . and sometimes, it even works.

I thought habit and routine would save me, but it hasn't; instead it's just reinforcing the miserable state I'm in. Everyone else I know is back at work, bar me. Also, I haven't a single bean. Savings are running dangerously low and my dole's about to run out any day now.

And eventually I crack. In desperation, I call Sarah to remind her *re* the job at her sandwich bar that she promised she'd look out for. Any kind of job; I'm not above scrubbing toilets at this stage. Anything doing, I ask her, barely succeeding in keeping the pleading tone out of my voice. Because I'm actually going off my head here. Need something to distract me. Badly.

'Angie, this is total telepathy!' she says briskly. 'I was just about to call you! As it happens, I've a junior in our Baggot Street branch going back to college, so I've a vacancy. You free to start next week?'

Oh, bless Sarah anyway! Total lifesaver. Because, after all, buttering bread and slicing raw onions is infinitely better than worrying myself into early grave.

11 January

Finally, finally, finally, some actual hard news from Crown.

He calls me at about seven in the evening, just as Simon and I are about to order in from the Chinese down the road. Says he's just heard back from Dutch police at Schiphol airport.

'I just wanted you to know how sorry I am that it took so long,' he explains patiently, 'but you see Interpol had to interview staff at all airport departure points, just in case they'd seen or heard anything. I hope you understand, Angie.'

'Of course,' I say automatically.

'So finally we have news.'

I slump down onto the sofa beside me.

'And?' My voice comes out in a hoarse croak.

'It seems the lead came from an Irish aid worker who was transiting through Schiphol on her way out to Nairobi just last week,' he goes on. 'She'd read all about Kitty Hope's disappearance on her flight from Dublin to Amsterdam. She'd even seen her photo. Then when she arrived at Schiphol, she subsequently swore blind she saw a woman who exactly matched Kitty's description striding through the departures concourse at the airport. Interpol have questioned her and she's made a full statement. But I think by far the best thing is if you and Simon could get in here right away. I've something to show you.'

Harcourt Street cop shop, 7.44 p.m.

Police interview room, yet again. By now, I'm starting to spend so much time here that I might just bring a few scented candles with me for next time; may as well dot them round the place to make it that bit more homely. Crown is on the phone as we arrive, with a stuffed file in front of him that he keeps referring down to as he's talking. The minute he sees us, he brightens, then ushers us inside, awkwardly shoving a thick fistful of fair hair out of his eyes and mouthing at us that he'll be off the call and with us in just a moment.

'Now you're to be nice,' Simon mutters to me as we take our usual seats.

'Aren't I always?'

'No, not to me, to Crown. Look, Angie, I know you feel he's not doing enough for us, but trust me, he actually is. Frankly, I don't see how he could be doing any more.'

'I know, I know,' I tell him a bit sulkily, like a recalcitrant schoolgirl being hauled over the coals.

'The guy's all right, Angie. Just give him a chance.'

And I will. I promise. At least, I'll certainly try to.

Crown comes straight back into us, all sandy and chunky and a bit sweaty. He rolls up his sleeves, apologises profusely for having to take that call, then cuts straight to the chase. To their credit, seems Dutch police have been working closely with Interpol over the past two weeks trying to sift through hours of CCTV footage from Schiphol airport, and now finally, they've closed in on a shot of exactly who it was the aid worker saw last week.

'You see, it still has to be checked out,' Crown explains. 'Even if it does turn out to be just another dead end.'

Simon glances hopefully across and locks eyes with me, but I've been let down once too often to allow hope to get the better of me this early on.

'But the bad news is, though . . .' Crown goes on looking at me worriedly and suddenly I find myself thinking, Ha! You see? Always there's the bad news! And there's always going to be a 'but'!

'. . . that we've only been able to narrow it down to this one clear shot of Kitty, if it even is her. It's not that easy to tell. Here, have a look for yourselves. Tell me what you think.'

He whips out a large-ish black-and-white photo, grainy and slightly blurred, like it was taken from shaky video surveillance footage. Simon and I leap on it, nearly snatching it out of his hands. Look at it, squint at it, hold it up to the light, study it this way and that.

Turns out to be . . . well, not all that much, really. All you can see is the hazy outline of a tall woman, Kitty's height and build all right, with hair scraped under a woolly winter hat, patiently queuing up in a duty-free shop, one of those ones that are more like supermarkets, where you can buy anything from magazines to litre bottles of Jack Daniel's to Touche Éclat concealer. The CCTV camera must have been a good bit away from her too, as this girl's figure is tiny in the photo, v. distant.

Simon and I pass it backwards and forwards between us, scrutinising it from every conceivable angle. But it's nigh on impossible to tell whether it's Kitty or not, the picture quality is just too poor. Plus, the clothes this girl is wearing look wrong, all wrong for Kitty. For starters, they actually *match*. In all the years I've known her, don't think I've ever seen Kitty wearing what any reasonable person might consider co-ordinated clothing.

Most frustrating of all, though, is that you can't get a clear look at this girl's face, whoever she is. Would at least be able to make out her profile, only a v. overweight guy is leaning right in front of her to grab what looks like an oversized Toblerone bar from a stand right beside her. Totally blocking a clear shot of her; deeply frustrating.

8.15 p.m.

Back in the car with Simon.

'Dunno about you, but I definitely don't think it's her,' he says, jaw set firmly as he slams the door shut with an expensive clunk.

'No,' I snort back in agreement.

Sure how could it be? Kitty? Skiting off to Amsterdam?

Which she's never expressed so much as the remotest interest in seeing?

Without telling anyone, and travelling under a false passport? As if!

She'd had some horrendous jobs in her time, but this had been by far the worst yet. Smiley's Burger Bar, to give it its full title, was loosely modelled on Hooters in the States: loud and noisy, the kind of place where raucous teenagers went to celebrate being legally able to buy beer, or else finally getting the hell out of school. Menus were basic and geared towards keeping customers thirsty and therefore drinking yet more; pizza, chicken wings, guacamole dips all featured heavily, and fries came by the bucket load with just about everything. If you were dying of a hangover, you'd nearly be afraid to ask for a strong coffee, in case a vat of greasy chips was plonked down in front of you, to really make you heave.

All the staff unfortunate enough to work at Smiley's were united by several things. Being broke, needing the work, but mostly by a deep hatred of the job, which no one in their sane mind could possibly enjoy. For starters, there was the gakky uniform they were obliged to wear, electric blue shorts with a low-cut blue and white T-shirt that said 'Have a SMILEY day, now!'. The guys as well as the women, which meant that the whole lot of them pretty much went around looking like a bunch of tarts and rent boys for hire.

Then there was the 'Smiley culture', as the boss called it, which involved many, many regular humiliations that you just couldn't make up. All table staff were required to dance a conga line around the table of anyone who came in to celebrate their birthday, for instance, carrying balloons, streamers and hooters that all read 'Have a Smiley Birthday!'. Even the words to 'Happy Birthday' were changed, so the lyrics went, 'Smiley birthday to you . . . Smiley birthday to you-hoooooo . . .'

In other words, they were all obliged to make gobshites out of themselves on a nightly basis. And of course this invariably meant that you'd get regular piss-takers coming in and *pretending it was their birthday, purely to humiliate the staff. Jean had caught several students trying this on and even confronted one of them, collared him up against the bar and said, 'Oh so you're twenty-one today, are you? Ahh, so you must be a little bit like the Queen, then, and you celebrate two birthdays a year. Because a few weeks ago you came in here claiming it was your eighteenth. Now feck off and stop wasting our time, you dick!'*

Course she was reported and got a right ticking off from the boss for pulling that one off. She even had the threat of being fired dangled over her, but the rest of the staff applauded her in the staff locker room and even clubbed in to buy her drinks at the end of the night. Stunts like that somehow kept everyone sane, and Jean's antics in there had fast become the stuff of legend among the rest of the staff.

Her name had even become a byword in there for 'don't lose your cool'. 'Don't go pulling a Jean, now!' had fast become shorthand for 'Don't, at all costs, lose your head. Remember we all need this gig, so just grin, put up with it and think of the tips at the end of your shift.'

So in a nutshell, Smiley's was the sort of place where anyone over the age of twenty-five, or anyone still sober after nine in the evening, would stick out like a sore thumb. Sort of place where beer-drinking contests were the norm and the appetisers menu read, 'Onion rings; great to eat, but don't try proposing after them!'

Which was why he'd stood out so much when he first started going there. All the other waitresses had clocked him long before Jean had; this handsome, older guy, sallow-skinned and brown-eyed, slightly greying around the temples and, oddly for a Smiley's regular, always dressed in an expensive-looking suit. Hugely conspicuous against the rest of their clientele, who seemed to have an average age of about nineteen.

Another waitress, Suze, had a huge crush on him and would swap stations with whoever was serving where he sat, just so she could get to chat him up. 'My sexy, silver fox,' she'd call him dreamily. Joe was his name, she'd discovered, but beyond that all she knew was that he ran an engineering company that were working on a construction site nearby. That was it.

But not too long afterwards, he started asking Suze all about Jean. Who was she? Who do you mean? Suze had asked him right back, a bit pissed off that he seemed to fancy someone else over her. The tall, gorgeous-looking brunette, he'd told her. How long had she worked here and was she by any chance seeing anyone? And every time Joe dropped in, if Jean wasn't working that night, then he'd just up and leave. Got so everyone noticed and the rest of the staff started slagging her about her 'older admirer' .

Jean noticed too, couldn't fail to. Every time he was in, she'd feel his eyes practically burning into her, taking her in from head to toe, in the revolting Smiley's uniform; the tight electric-blue short shorts and the low-cut top that accentuated her boobs. She knew his eyes followed her everywhere she went; got so she could feel it.

'Surprise, surprise, Silver Fox wants you to serve him,' Suze told her sulkily one evening. 'Insisted on you and only you.'

Jean shrugged, strode over to him and without even looking at him, just said, 'Your usual, I take it? Organic beefburger with a side of spicy wedges?'

'It's Jean, isn't it?'

She just ignored the question, though, and tried her best to act all disinterested.

'Or would you like to see a menu?' she said coolly.

'If you'd like me to.'

'Well, personally, I wouldn't bother my arse.'

'Why's that?'

''Cos everything in here tastes the exact same. Lardy and gloopy with an occasional layer of congealed grease on top. And sometimes you'll even get our house speciality, which is a film of skin, depending on whether the grub's been microwaved or not.'

His eyes just twinkled at that as he pretended to study the menu.

'Tell me this, what does organic mean anyway?'

'Means it tastes the exact same, but costs a fiver more.'

He threw his head back and laughed.

'Why don't you call me Joe?'

'Fine, Joe, now if you're finished arsing around, can I just get you your usual?'

'No, as a matter of fact,' he said, putting the menu down and looking up at her with the greyest eyes she'd ever seen, 'what I really want to know is what time you get off work.'

'What's it to you?' she asked, glaring back at him defiantly. Not even sure why she was being this pert with him, only that the huge pull of attraction she suddenly felt was knocking her off kilter, confusing her.

'Because . . . I don't know. Except that you're interesting. And funny. And beautiful. And I'd very much like to get to know you better. Outside of here, that is.'

She looked at him keenly. Really took him in from head to foot. He was huge, this guy, well over six two and built like a rugby player with it. His shirt was slightly opened at the neck so she could make out the beginnings of a hairy chest and for a split second, she wondered what it would feel like to lie naked up against that chest, to feel those giant shovel-y hands touching her all over. She felt him looking intently up at her too, taking in the curve of her body, the length of her legs in the Smiley shorts . . . and she felt him wanting her, just sensed it. He was sexy, there was no doubt about it, and something about the way he looked at her was starting to intrigue her . . . but then reason got the better of her. This guy was early thirties, if he was a day, and she was only eighteen, for feck's sake! And yes, sure, he was attractive in an older-man-type way and, yeah, he obviously had a few quid, but . . .

'Sorry,' she shrugged and turned on her heel, ostensibly to get his order, but really just to get away from him. Because there was something about this animal chemistry slowly building up between them that was actually starting to frighten her.

'We just sell food in here, not staff,' she added haughtily, before she was gone.

He kept it up, though, for weeks on end. Every night she was working, sure enough, Joe would be there, never pestering her, but always asking for her, then telling her that when she changed her mind, he'd be waiting for her. Always polite, always respectful and always charm itself. Making all the guys she'd ever knocked around with up until then look like boys, she sometimes thought. Whereas this was a man.

'Persistent bastard, isn't he?' Suze used to snipe at her, a bit cattily. 'So why don't you just sleep with him and have done with it?'

Then one night, he caught her off guard. Jean had just started her shift and been given a message that the boss wanted to see her right away. She'd a good idea why, too, and knew what was coming: the mother of all barneys that had been brewing for a while now.

Joe was in, and in a blind temper she strode over to serve him first.

'Hey, what's up with you tonight?' he asked, sensing the simmering rage that was bubbling just under the surface with her.

'Do me a favour and just don't ask,' she groaned.

'But I am asking.'

Then she looked at him long and hard, as though weighing up whether he could be trusted or not. And decided, yes. So in spite of herself, she told him everything. Just in need of a sympathetic ear, that was all. The boss had been harassing her for a while now, she said, and more or less told her that she was expected to pose in a bikini for the Smiley annual calendar. The gobshite git was forever on at her, she said, coming out with patronising, sexist shite that she'd make a lovely Miss December in a red and white furry, Santa-themed Christmas bikini. Or maybe she could even be Miss March, in a Paddy's Day theme with shamrocks covering up strategic bits of her. She'd almost wanted to gag at that. As if! And the calendar was being shot next week, so this could be the only reason he wanted to see her tonight, she knew it.

'And I just don't know what to do,' she found herself confiding in Joe, really opening up to him. 'On the one hand, I want to kick the smarmy git's teeth in for him and on the other . . . well, crappy and all as this job is, I still need it.'

'No you don't,' he told her firmly, steely eyes locking into hers.

'Ha! Listen to you, Rockefeller! 'Course I need this shagging job, I've rent to pay and—'

'Jean, just hear me out. You don't have to do anything you don't want. So why not go up there right now, tell this tosser where to shove his job and I'll be waiting for you outside in

my car, so you can get out of here pronto? Trust me, you don't need any of this.'

'Eh . . . thanks very much for the offer, but where exactly would you be driving me to then? The nearest dole office?'

'Well, for a start, I've got a good pal who owns a hotel in town. He'd get you work there, I know it. So why put up with this crap when you don't have to? Not,' he added, the corners of his mouth twitching mischievously, 'that I wouldn't pay good money to see you pose in a Miss Smiley bikini, or anything.'

God, but she was tempted. Just by the lovely, lovely thought of getting out of this shithole and getting a decent job in a swish, upmarket hotel . . .

'You absolutely certain about this?' she asked him, sheer desperation getting the better of her.

'Not only am I sure, I'll meet you outside in the car park in exactly five minutes.'

And it had been as simple as that

'Ah, Jean, there you are,' the boss said to her as soon as she barged into his office. Or 'the captain of the Smiley crew', as this guy liked to style himself. Like they were some kind of religious cult and he was Joseph Smith. One Robert Procter. Nothing wrong with the name per se, *it was just that he couldn't say his Rs, so went around calling himself 'Wobert Pwoctor'. A fifty-something portly, sweaty, wine lover and general all-around sleazeball, who seemed to do nothing, only sit on his sweaty, oversized arse up in his lovely, cool, air-conditioned office, watching CCTV footage of whatever was going on downstairs like some kind of bargain basement James Bond baddie. All while dreaming up new and improved ways to make a holy mortifying show of his staff on a daily basis.*

'Glad you're here, Jean love,' Wobert said, focusing solely on her boobs and nothing else, 'because I have you down as Miss Apwil in the Smiley's calendar, and not only that, but this Saturday night I'll need you to compete in the Miss Smiley beauty pageant. I'm comperwing it myself this year, you know. You can be Miss Fish Wharf. There's even a sash in the locker woom that you can borwow.'

She just glared furiously at him, temper she'd been trying so hard to restrain now bubbling up to the surface like a volcano.

'. . . And I have to tell you,' he went on, seemingly oblivious to the furious bulging behind her eyes, 'without undue favour-wtism, that with legs like those, I weally do think the pageant would be a bweeze for you.'

And that was all it took. Break point.

'Wobert,' Jean said sarcastically. 'Oh, I'm so sorry, I meant to say Robert. Suppose I tell you to go and fuck yourself? And your poxy Miss Fish Wharf sash?'

He looked at her, astonished.

'If that's how you feel, then suppose I tell you you're fired?'

'And suppose I hand you your poxy uniform right back? Here and now?'

Two seconds later, she'd whipped off her hated Smiley T-shirt and flung it across the desk right at him. It even knocked over a half-drunk glass of 'wed wine' on his desk, spilling it everywhere.

Score. She whooped defiantly, turned on her heel and slammed the door so hard the glass in it actually shook.

Two minutes later, she was winding her way through the bar in only her bra and electric blue shorts, head held high. 'Course, by the time she made it to the main exit, the roar of wolf whistles and catcalls from students drinking at the bar, who couldn't believe their luck when they saw this beautiful, semi-naked woman stride by, was near-deafening.

And sure enough, Joe had been as good as his word. Two minutes later she was in the passenger seat of his luxuriously plush car, engine revving, sitting beside him in nothing more than her bra and shorts.

'Jesus, do you know what the sight of you dressed like that is doing to me?' he twinkled across at her. 'Here,' he added, whipping off his jacket and lightly tossing it over to her, 'cover yourself up, will you? Otherwise, there's a danger I might crash the car.'

'Just drive, Joe. Get me the hell out of here.'

'Where to?'

'Anywhere.'

'Fine by me,' he grinned. 'In that case, I'm taking you home.'

Chapter Eight

12 January, Kitty's house

Don't start work in the sandwich bar till next week, and at this stage, I nearly have the days counted. Swear to God, I never thought that looking forward to starting a menial job scrubbing floors and slicing onions would keep me going, but somehow it is. I so badly need to be active again, to be doing something, *anything*, other than sitting in front of Kitty's computer screen stressing and fretting. Still no news, but, as Simon says, no more hoaxers or wild-goose chases either, which has to count for something. Means we're finally starting to filter out the messers and time-wasters, if nothing else.

It's just coming up to lunchtime and, seeing as how food is my drug of choice these days, I automatically head to the fridge on the scrounge. Larder's pretty bare, though, so I'm just about to head out to grab a sambo when the doorbell rings.

Jack Crown. On his own and, unusually for him, not in uniform, just wearing jeans and a wintry navy jacket.

'Am I disturbing you?' he asks tentatively, but then I've been so snipey and horrible to him in the past, the poor guy is probably half terrified I'll cut the snot off him.

'No, not at all. Come in,' I say, ushering him into the kitchen and making a silent vow to force myself to be polite, like everyone keeps telling me I should be. He stands there awkwardly; one of those guys who dwarfs a room just by being in it, then shoves away a clump of hair that's fallen over his forehead and gives me what I can only describe as the weirdest look. Like he's got something to say to me, but just doesn't know where to begin.

Long, long pause while the two of us just look at each other.

'Em, well . . . Simon's at work,' I eventually say, puzzled beyond belief as to why he's here and what exactly is going on. Normally if Crown has news, he just phones. So what's all this about?

Then, just for the sake of filling dead air, I stupidly tack on, 'He won't be back till tonight.'

'That's OK,' Crown nods. 'It's actually you I came to see.'

Oh Christ. I find myself suddenly a bit panicky now; am I in some kind of trouble here? Do they now suspect me of burying Kitty under the patio out the back or something? And will people see me on the nine o'clock news being carted off in handcuffs to the Bridewell and mutter, 'You see? It's almost always a close friend who'll turn out to be guilty as sin.'

'It's just,' Crown begins uneasily as I stand opposite him, rooted to the spot and wondering what in hell he's trying to say. 'Well, I could be wrong, and forgive me if I'm speaking out of turn here, but I think that all of this is taking a huge toll on you. On an emotional level, that is.'

'I'm sorry?'

'Angie, it's unthinkable what you're going through, and of course what Simon is going through too, and I know it can be a nightmare to handle. But the thing is, the whole investigation has now taken yet another turn and we've reason to believe there might be news . . . And soon.'

'What do you mean?' I ask, panic suddenly making me weak-kneed. 'What are you talking about?'

'Hey, are you OK?' he says, looking seriously concerned now. 'Look at you, you're as white as a sheet. Do you want to sit down?'

'No, I'm fine, really just . . . please . . . give me the last sentence first. If you know something or if any new information has come in since yesterday . . .'

'At least let me get you some water,' he says, going straight to a pile of clean glasses on the draining board and in a flash filling one from the tap for me. 'Here, drink this. You'll feel better.'

I gratefully take a gulp and nod my thanks.

'Please,' I find myself almost begging as he just looks worriedly back at me, 'if you know something, don't keep it from me.'

But he just shakes his head. 'I wish I did, I really do. But at this point, I'm afraid there's nothing, at least nothing concrete. And I'm sorry to be so vague, but as soon as I do, I'll let you know immediately. In the meantime, though . . . well, I suppose what I'm ham-fistedly trying to say is that . . .'

'Yes?'

'You have to prepare yourself, Angie. And I'm so sorry to have to say this, but we have to be realistic here and ask you to brace yourself for news . . . that may not be what you were hoping for. But if you ever wanted to talk to someone, then please just know that I'm always here for you. I'll give you my private mobile number and my home number too. Call anytime. But until there's a concrete breakthrough, please try not to worry. Which I know is a bit like asking you not to breathe, but you'll try, won't you? You promise?'

'Well . . . thank you,' I manage to stammer. 'That's very kind of you.'

'I mean that, Angie. I'm here for you. No matter what the outcome of this.'

He leaves shortly after and, still a bit shell-shocked, I call Simon to fill him in.

A long pause while he digests it all.

'Jesus,' he eventually says in a weak voice, 'Crown knows something, or at least he's got wind that something we won't necessarily like is about to be confirmed. He has to have done. Why else would he have gone to all the bother of calling to the house to warn you?'

Exactly what I was thinking myself. Something is most definitely coming. Not sure what, but one thing is for certain. Whatever it is, it won't be a rose garden.

Outside Kitty's, 6.35 p.m.

The worst day yet, by far. Can't even eat, I'm such a ball of nervous tension and anxiety. Which for me is unheard of. Ordinarily Armageddon could well be nigh and I'm someone that would still be found gnashing into rasher sandwich with a side of fries.

It feels like such an interminably long wait for Simon to get home that eventually I crack, think, shag this, and head out for a quick, brisk walk to try to clear my head. Need to get out of here, need air, need to do anything other than sit looking at the four walls, working myself up into a crescendo of worry.

I'm barely gone a half-hour, but when I get back, there's

a police car parked right outside the house, with Simon's car right beside it.

Must be news, must be v. bad news, possibly the worst. And suddenly I can't breathe. My chest constricts and my heart starts palpitating as I let myself in and race into the kitchen.

Jack Crown is inside in full uniform now, standing awkwardly beside Simon and looking gravely over at me while Simon's on the couch, head in his hands. The minute I burst in, Simon reaches out to me and I instinctively go to him, sit beside him as he slips a protective arm around my shoulder, holding me tight.

'What's wrong?' I nearly yell at them both. 'For Christ's sake, tell me what's happened!'

'Jesus, Angie,' Simon says weakly, 'I thought you'd never get here. You have to prepare yourself.'

He grips my hand and I steel myself for what's coming.

'Will somebody please tell me what's going on?'

Crown sits down opposite us and looks at me with huge sympathy.

'Since I saw you earlier today,' he says, sounding like he hates having to say every single word, 'it seems there's been a development. I don't want you to get a shock, but I felt it was only right to come round here and tell you both in person.'

'To tell us what?'

'Can I get you some hot, sweet tea first?'

'No, please! I'd far rather you just told me whatever the hell was going on!'

'Angie, I'm really am so sorry to have to do this to you,' Crown says gently, 'but I'm afraid I have to ask.'

'Ask what?'

'Exactly how well did you know Kitty Hope?'

Nineteen and in love. He'd even asked her to move in with him. Which to her, back then, seemed like the height of real, proper romance. Movie love. And at the start, it had all been such a whirlwind. She'd never been in a proper relationship before, not like this, not with someone like him, so much older, so worldly and sophisticated. Fell for him hot and heavy right from the start, which, given how lost and vulnerable she'd been, took so very little on his part. A few dinners out, one or two trips away to places she'd dreamed of, but never seen. All he had to do was turn the full glare of his attention on her, show her a whole side of life she'd never seen before and she was his, all his.

It really was that easy.

It started out in the smallest of ways. Let's not go out tonight, he'd say back in their early days, let's just stay in, you and me. We don't need anyone else, do we? Besides, I want you here, all to myself. And something inside her would just melt. It's because he's such a die-hard romantic who loves you so much, she thought. You, who'd always felt yourself so unworthy of being loved. And now here's this man, who only wants to be with you and no one else. Whoever would have thought?

But as it turned out, she couldn't have been more wrong. Because slowly over time, so imperceptibly she barely even noticed at first, he gradually weaned her away from even her closest friends. And she was a girl who had loads of mates; attracted them naturally. So when things got bad and when she really needed help, needed someone to pluck her out of this, there was no one left to listen. Without even realising it, he'd isolated her from every single person that she'd ever known or cared about.

With one exception. A guy her own age she knew from

work, sweet guy called Sean, who'd frequently phone the flat and leave messages for her. All so pathetically innocent; they were just pals, nothing more. You free for a coffee or do you fancy a movie, he used to ask her, that kind of thing. Kids' stuff.

It led to trouble, though. It got so she could practically sense his eyes glowering at her every time Sean would call the flat and he'd hand over the phone. 'It's that git for you again.'

And over time, he gradually became more and more jealous and possessive, accusing her of flirting with Sean, of leading him on. If she ever stayed out late, the questions would be sure to start, thick and heavy. Were you with him? Did you kiss him, do you fancy him, is that it? So is there something you want to tell me? What's going on here that you won't admit? I don't do anything to upset you, so why are you putting me through this? Are you cheating on me behind my back? Why is it that I can't trust you?

Which was so ridiculous, it was risible. She'd laughed in his face and told him she was starting to feel like she was coming home to an angry parent, not a boyfriend. You don't own me, she'd spiritedly told him once, then for months afterwards marvelled at her own raw courage in doing it.

Wouldn't dare do it now. She'd have more sense.

First time it happened, she'd come home about an hour later than she'd said she would. Sixty bloody minutes, no more. But that was all it took. The very minute she walked in the door, she could tell by his silent sulking that there'd be trouble. Turned out he'd been gauging the length of time she'd been gone for so accurately, he might as well have had a stopwatch in his paw, like some kind of an Olympic training coach. And sure enough, the usual barrage of questions started. Who were you out with, was it him? I know it was, so you might as well just come clean. You can't lie to me, it's written all over your face.

She'd pushed him away, told him to stop acting like this, that she was seriously starting to get sick of it. Besides, she'd only been out with a girlfriend, that was it. Which, as it happened, was the truth. She and her mate Becky had met up for a quick drink after work and the two of them had lost track of time, end of story. She remembered looking him in the eye and telling him to lighten up, that she was starting to get seriously fed up with having to face the Spanish Inquisition every time she came home a bloody hour later than she said she'd be.

'Just back off, will you?'

She could still remember telling him that, before striding upstairs to let him cool down. Then defiantly throwing back over her shoulder, 'You do realise you're starting to sound like some kind of over-possessive nut job?'

But that was all it took. He came right after her, grabbing her leg as she was almost on the top stair and dragging her all the way back down again. Smashed her head off each banister rail as he pulled her towards him, then shouted in her face to own up to seeing someone else behind his back. And the more she screamed back at him, the more it continued, on and on. One slap after another, till she was aware of her face feeling soaking wet and a warm, sticky, metallic taste in her mouth. Took her a while to realise it was her own blood. Then came the blinding pain, so white hot and intense that it only stopped when she eventually blacked out.

He was actually apologetic after that first time. Utterly mortified, he told her, and she believed him. He did everything possible: bought her flowers, spoiled her, held her tight. Even rubbed antiseptic into the cuts on her face and tenderly put an ice pack on her swollen head. Jesus, I must be some kind of animal, he'd told her over and over. Your beautiful face, just look what I've done to your beautiful face. It was all the pressure he was under in work and he'd just cracked, he said. He'd never done anything like this before. Told her it was just because he loved her so much and was so frightened of losing her to anyone else.

It won't happen again, though, he swore blind. I give you my solemn word, this was the one and only time.

Never again.

A full hemisphere away, she woke up sweating and panicking, having to stop herself from screaming out loud in case anyone overheard.

She could control where she was. Could change her name, her whole identity, even, to protect herself. But try as she might, she could never stop the nightmares.

PART TWO

FORGET ME NOT . . .

Chapter Nine

Two years later

Cape Town was so beautiful at this time of year, Jean thought, stretched out on a sunlounger, her usual morning mug of extra strong coffee beside her. No humidity, not too hot, not too cool, just perfect, clear as crystal. On days like this, you could easily see all the way over to Table Mountain from the wraparound balcony of her third-floor apartment, where she lay surrounded by all the pots of forget-me-nots she'd planted. An appropriate flower, she always thought. For her.

It was just so peaceful here, blissful. Safe, even. She had to pinch herself every time she as much as allowed herself to use that word. Whoever would have thought?

She sipped at her coffee, nibbled at a half-eaten slice of yesterday's leftover pizza she'd taken out to the balcony with her, then glanced down at her watch. Only an hour's time difference between here and home, which sometimes made life a helluva lot easier. In little ways, like whenever she was on her way to work, she'd tell herself that Simon was probably doing exactly the same thing at roughly the same time. Imagined him in that silvery company Audi he was so proud of, the one she used to laugh at and tell him he looked like some kind of a gobshite pimp in.

Then she'd wonder what he was wearing, was he still going round in those sexy blue silk shirts she used to love so much on him? The colour brought out his green eyes, she always thought, remembering how she'd lazily run her hand up and down the back of his shirt while he was trying to get dressed early in the morning, loving the sensual feel of the silky fabric against her skin. 'Look at you, trying to molest me on my way out the door to work,' he'd grin suggestively at her. 'Insatiable woman.'

'Course, more often than not, the minute she caught that hungry glint in his eyes, she'd drag him back into the cosy warm bed beside her and make him late for work. Small wonder the poor guy managed to hold on to his job at all, with her around.

On her better days – days when she was feeling that bit stronger, a bit more like her old self – she could even bring herself to wonder what Simon's life was like these days. It had been two long years; was his life completely different now? Would he go out that evening? How had he spent last night? What would he do this weekend coming? And if she really wanted to torture herself, she'd allow herself to wonder who he'd actually go out with. It intrigued her, wondering who he was hanging round with these days. Did he still see any of her old pals, Sarah or Jeff maybe? Or had he gone back to palling around with that intellectually snobby, career-obsessed gang from his company that she used to call a crowd of stodgy old farts? To his face, the cheek of her.

But you don't understand, this shower drive me round the bollocking bend! She was always moaning at him on the nights they'd have to go to yet another one of Simon's excruciating work dinner parties. And if you think I'm putting on tights or a fecking dress to meet them, then you've another thing coming, mate. Listen, love, I know they're not the easiest, he'd patiently tell her, hauling himself out of the shower and towelling down that gorgeous body she loved so much, still glistening from the water and smelling divine. But then, Simon always smelled divine.

'Course he'd invariably try to stick up for all his work crowd, agreeing that they could sometimes be a bit of a challenge, but gently reminding her that at the end of the day, they were his colleagues and, like it or not, he was obliged to do the occasional bit of socialising with them.

But then that was Simon for you; her handsome, kind-hearted, loyal Simon who was physically incapable of hearing a bad word said about anyone. Just one of the things she loved so much about him. One of many. Just remember, though, he used to say to her, it means everything to me that you'll be there tonight. That you'll be there as my partner.

Note, use of the word partner, not just date. God Almighty, she should have been down on her hands and knees kissing the feet of a man who loved her so much, after everything she'd been through! But instead of being grateful to have such a loving boyfriend, what had she gone and done instead? Continued on and on with her bloody whinge-fest, that's what. How had the poor guy ever put up with her at all? There must have been times – and plenty of them – when she'd been a living nightmare to be around!

But in the middle of digging all this back up again, Jean would suddenly catch herself and glow a bit as one warmer memory did surface. The way Simon would look lovingly over at her when they were in the car en route to whatever night of torture happened to lie ahead. She remembered the gentle way he'd take her hand, lightly kiss the tips of her fingers and tell her how delighted he was that she'd come with him at all. Yeah, OK, so this lot can be a bit boring, he'd smile down at her, but you're not, are you? You'll liven tonight up, wait and see. Sure, you're the only woman I've ever met who could liven up a funeral parlour!

And so she'd tease him right back. When the car was stopped at lights, she'd lean into him, gently bite on his bottom lip in a way she knew drove him mental, and tell him that he'd just better make it worth her while when she dragged him back home afterwards. Because you owe me after this, big time, she'd tell him flirtatiously.

Because in spite of all her grousing, truth was it gave her a warm glow inside to think of just how much he genuinely must have wanted her to be there. The pride written all over his face when he'd introduced her to his colleagues, the way he barely left her side all evening. Never one to shy away from Public Displays of Affection, he'd always have a supportive arm around her whenever he could, playing absent-mindedly with a strand of her long, curly black hair. Showing her off, letting everyone see just how happy he was to be with her, even though she so obviously didn't fit in with any of them. This is the woman I love, he may as well have been signposting to the whole shagging lot of them.

Deal with it.

And then there was Angie, who she thought of incessantly, day and night. Her own warm-hearted, funny, big, bosomy, gorgeously insecure Angie. Sometimes, when she was grabbing a quick bite of lunch, she'd think about how Angie always loved her food and say to herself, look at me,

Ange! Here we both are, both still doing exactly the same thing at the same time! Ergo, not as far apart as you'd think! Might have seemed a bit daft as a coping mechanism, but on the bad days, it helped.

Last Christmas Eve, for instance, on Angie's birthday, she couldn't stop the tears from spouting every time she thought about what that girl must have gone through on exactly that same day, the previous year. What must Angie think of her now? Could she ever forgive her? Probably not, and in all honesty, you could hardly blame the girl. She was the closest thing to a best friend Jean had ever known and what she'd done to her and to all of them was monstrous, by any standards. She must have put everyone she loved and cared about through a living nightmare. She'd had to, for her own survival, she had absolutely no choice, but who'd ever understand that?

And who'd ever even want to speak to her again, even if by some miracle she ever could?

Jean checked her watch once more. Just seven in the morning here. Meant it was six at home. Perfect. Early morning edition of the papers should be already online. Hauling herself up, she slid open the patio doors, stuck her head inside to the living room and had a good listen. Total silence. Which was even better. Meant her flatmate, Paige, had already left for work, miraculously on time for once. Which meant she had a tiny window of privacy.

'Paige, you there?' She strained for the sounds of her in the shower, but no, still nothing. Paige Van der Kadavwe, to call her flatmate by her impressively unpronounceable full name, was also her supervisor at the Cape Grace Hotel while Jean herself worked as a chambermaid. Almost ten years younger than her, only twenty-four years old, and yet *already* working as a supervisor. And the way she was going, give her another year and she'd be a duty manager. Easily. Paige was one of those women who came with a naturally bossy streak and could probably do the job in her sleep.

'You know, I just don't get you,' Paige was always saying, crinkling up her forehead in puzzlement, the way she always did whenever she thought Jean was disappearing deep into herself again. 'You've been working at the hotel for well over eighteen months now, why won't you go for the supervisor's grade yourself? Everyone likes you in there, you know. You're really popular. You'd walk it!'

A tough one to wriggle her way out, so instead Jean would just laugh about her night job at The Monkey Bar on the waterfront, claiming the dosh there was far, far better, when you factored in tips. If you didn't mind working late night shifts that was, or dealing with nineteen-year-old students drunk out of their minds on Red Bull and alcopops. All of whom, by the way, had a fondness for discussing women's breast sizes and seemed to have a pathological deafness to the words, 'Drink up now, lads, it's closing time.'

And if Paige ever guessed that she was being lied to, she never let on.

But the truth was, someone like Jean was lucky to get casual work at all, and the lower a grade she worked at, the better. A supervisor's job was better paid, true, but it would have meant all sorts of interviews, background checks, a whole new set of visa requirements, not to mention a barrage of questions about all the glaring gaps on her CV. No, better to stay nice and low under the radar like she was right now. Safer by far. It was a mantra that ran round her head all the time these days, *safetysafetysafetysafetysafety.*

At all costs, no one must ever start asking questions.

And if that meant not advancing up career ladders or earning as much as she might otherwise have done, then wasn't it a price worth paying?

Besides, another lovely thing about this place: Cape Town was bloody cheap to live in. Took next to nothing to live like a lord, even on a humble waitress/chambermaid's salary. This jaw-droppingly luxurious flat, for starters. Rent about a quarter of what you'd expect to pay for somewhere with two bedrooms, both with ensuites, a living room you could comfortably play soccer in and a wrap-around balcony big enough to throw a party on, and still have plenty of room to avoid anyone who drove you mental. You're one lucky, lucky woman, Jean had to tell herself daily. A very lucky and a very safe woman. Helped her no end to get through bad days and, God knows, she certainly had enough of them to contend with.

Barefoot and silent, Jean slid open the patio doors, padded off to her bedroom and even though she'd the whole place to herself, she still took the precaution of closing over her door. What she was about to do took privacy.

The old, familiar surge of adrenalin as she grabbed her laptop from her bedside table, hopped up onto the bed, stretched her long, suntanned legs out in front of her and logged on.

Entered the password. Then clicked on the *Irish Times* webpage, like she faithfully did first thing every morning. Getting to be like her drug hit at this stage. Funny to think that back home she hardly ever glanced at a paper, and on the rare occasion when she did, it was either to read her horoscope or check out the TV listings. And now you couldn't stop her. What was it about news from home, however inconsequential, that still gripped her? Made her feel like she was still in touch in some way, she guessed, with . . . well, with everyone.

That she would or ever could go back home again was impossible, that much was certain, but even just keeping abreast of what was going on made her feel slightly less of an outcast. Somehow it put her in good form, made her feel that bit less isolated from everyone and everything, just by keeping up to speed with the news. Even when it was all boring as arse stuff about treaty referendums and the Euro and septic tank charges. It still helped.

The *Times*, she found was terrific for all hard news from home, but lamentably low on gossip or trivia. Greedily her eye scanned down the page, absorbing every tiny detail like she was on some kind of a read-and-destroy mission. Another glance down to the clock at the very bottom of the screen. Still only seven fifteen and her shift didn't start till nine; she'd plenty of time. So she logged onto the *Chronicle* website next, always reliably good for celeb shite-ology; who was seen out where and with who, that kind of thing. And from time to time she'd indirectly catch references of people she used to know. 'So and so, photographed with his new lady friend at the opening night of such and such at the Abbey Theatre.' And she'd smile and think, that smarmy git came into Byrne & Sacetti's once and hit on me, then never tipped.

A while ago, in the business section, she'd even seen a tiny mention of her old pal Sarah O'Reilly. Something about her sandwich bar chain now expanding into chocolate bars and getting some jammy big franchise out at the airport. Gave her a warm glow of pride, but then everyone knew Sarah of all people was going to do well. Sarah was the type who was born to run the world. It was practically bred into her, and the girl probably would have caused murder if she hadn't been making at least a six-figure salary by the time she turned thirty.

Once, only once, she'd caught a mention of Simon's company in the home news section of the paper. Not even a mention of him, just his company. There it was, in black and white, Crosbie Holdings. Something about one of their subsidiaries going into receivership. Took her two full days to get over it. Paige had to give her sick days off work and she'd been obliged to explain it all away with some lame excuse about suffering from panic attacks.

Incredible to think that just seeing the name of where he worked could have such an effect on her, even after all this time.

But then if it was one thing she'd learned, distance was nothing, silence was nothing, even two long years were nothing. Not to a heart still in smithereens.

She put on a pretty good act, though, most of the time. She could be tough, resilient even, outwardly at least. Could school herself to the way her life had turned out and keep reminding herself of the unthinkable alternative. But then some random landmark date would come along and set her back days, weeks, even, and yet again, Paige would have to give her time off work. His birthday, 17 August, for one. And 4 June, the date they first met. Christmas was always guaranteed to be a killer, Christmas Eve, especially, when she thought of Angie, her own warm-hearted, adorable, gorgeous Angie, and wondered if the poor girl could ever bring herself to forgive her.

Then one sobering thought would hit her square in the face. By now, both Angie and Simon would know everything there was to know about her. Absolutely everything. And she was certain of one thing: even if they did ever get to hear her side of the story, never in a million years would they understand how much it nearly destroyed her to have to leave them both. Because who could possibly begin to comprehend that? Who'd ever realise that much as it killed her, she had to do what she did?

Back to the papers and she clicked onto the *Post* next, a pretty evenly balanced paper when it came to news versus gossip. Big piece on last night's episode of *Britain's Got Talent*; apparently some lunatic had an act that involved him putting a saucepan on his head and doing an impression of a Dalek. Yawn. Kate Middleton visited a factory and wore yet another high street outfit. Oh, and had got thinner still. Double yawn. Justin Bieber, now on a tour of Germany, and girls are still screeching at him. Feck's sake, she wondered, had anything new happened at all since she left?

And just then, like a sign from up above, her eye chanced to fall on it.

A tiny notice in the far left-hand corner of the computer screen. Buried deep on page eighteen of the *Post,* on the classified page. So easy to miss, it was a bloody miracle she even spotted it in the first place. She blinked in disbelief; read it again, made sure she wasn't seeing things.

But no, there it was in black and white. She read it, re-read it, checked it again. Printed it off her computer, as though reading it on a sheet of A4 paper instead of on the screen might somehow make it not true.

Half a beat later, shock seemed to set in and she surprised herself by not being able to feel anything. Not yet, at least.

Still numb, almost creepily calm, she logged off, packed

her laptop away and started to get into her work uniform. Neat white shirt, crisp blue shift dress over it, white runners. Got dressed as though she were on autopilot, surprising herself that just by the simple act of focusing on the tiny mechanics, like pulling on a pair of socks and trainers, she could somehow function. You were supposed to wear tights the exact colour of Elastoplast into work as well, which she never did. Her own personal little rebellion.

She caught a quick glimpse of herself in the mirror when she was dressed. Her hair, the same hair that Simon used to love so much, was short now, cropped to the nape of her neck so the curls kind of grew outwards, which gave her more than a passing resemblance to Sideshow Bob in *The Simpsons.* She hated it and always winced whenever she passed a mirror, but it made her look completely different, which could only be a good thing.

No wincing this morning, though; she was too shocked, too catatonic to care.

She got her work bag together as usual, checked she'd her bus pass and swipe card for work, like she always did.

She took her usual bus to the Cape Grace Hotel, got a seat to herself and took out the A4 printout, reading it over and over again in the hope that somehow there was a mistake, that she was seeing things. But no, there it was in just a handful of terse sentences. Not even a particularly long piece, just a couple of lines at most.

No one could possibly know the effect those words would have on her. That one, single thing she'd been dreading for all these years.

But it was true. The worst, the very worst had actually come to pass.

And in the space of just a few minutes, the carefully ordered, secure existence she'd worked so hard to build up around her, started to crumble.

The following evening, Jean was at Cape Town International airport, strapping herself into her seat as the plane slowly began to taxi down the runway. Scarcely able to believe that she was really doing this. That she was actually, physically going home. *Home.* When she'd told herself so many times it was impossible.

God knows, just getting through check-in and security had been ordeal enough. She'd booked herself on a standard British Airways flight from Cape Town right through to London Heathrow, but she'd already overheard the odd Irish accent at check-in; the sound had filtered back down the queue to where she was standing.

Oh Christ, she thought, her resolve suddenly weakening, suppose she was recognised? Ireland was such a bloody village, everyone knew not only everyone else, but their first cousin and their neighbour's cat as well. Supposing there was someone here who she'd met before, or who'd recognise her from her old job at the restaurant back home? Or even worse, from all of that publicity there'd been after . . . well, after. Her heart seized, but then she bitterly reminded herself she better get used to it; there'd be a helluva lot more of that to come, on her connecting flight from Heathrow back to Ireland.

It had made her panicky, though, and for a long time she looked longingly back at the departures hall, wondering if she wasn't just about to make a horrible mistake. She was always doing mad, impetuous stuff on the spur of the moment. Had this just been some kind of insane blood rush to her head caused by delayed shock? Should she just bolt for it, now while she still had the chance?

But she didn't. Instead, she steeled herself to get as far as the check-in desk, telling herself that she could do it and that there was nothing to be afraid of, every time the queue inched forward. Just another few steps, she'd told herself, that's all. Take it nice and handy, one thing at a time. And eventually, step by step, she somehow made it all the way up to the top of the line. She handed over her passport, collected her boarding pass, then slipped off into the ladies loo, so she could splash a bit of cool water on her face and regroup.

It's been two long years, she told herself. Now just cop yourself on. As if anyone would even remember you after all that length of time! You think you're so unforgettable? Get over yourself. Besides, she thought, having a good stare at herself in the mirror of the ladies, just look at you now. Practically unrecognisable. It was only a lightning-quick, whirlwind trip, nothing more. She'd arrive back in Ireland, do what she needed to do, then hop back on the first flight out of there and back to safety.

And when she clung to that thought for long enough, somehow it calmed her.

The cropped, Rebekah Brooks curls nearly growing sideways out of her head did indeed make her look completely different. Plus ever since she stumbled on the news yesterday, she looked like she'd about thirty per cent less blood than normal. Over the past two years, she'd lost a lot of weight too, which made her face seem sort of sunken and hollow-eyed. God knows all the old sparkle had long since gone out of her eyes and her once pale body was now a deep shade of mahogany. 'Course there was still that bloody kink in her crooked nose, but there was no disguising that, was there? Under a giant pair of sunglasses, though, the face-covering kind where the lenses were the approximate size of two dinner plates, somehow it wasn't quite so noticeable.

She'd thought everything through and before she left the flat that morning, had even worried that her clothes could potentially be a giveaway; she who'd always been such a haphazard, careless dresser. But Paige had very kindly given her a loan of a neat, black suit, which she was wearing now, along with black pumps and a white blouse. She felt deeply uncomfortable and actually looked a bit scary, like she worked for a bank and had come round to repossess your house, but it certainly served its purpose. A few more deep breaths, a few mental reminders of why she was here in the first place and she was steady on her feet again.

Well, steady-ish.

The flight was full, but they still boarded everyone on time and, head bowed, Jean took her seat right at the very back, thankfully beside an elderly couple from Zimbabwe travelling on to London to see family. No more Irish accents in this part of the cabin, hallelujah be praised. She was careful just to smile and say next to nothing when the couple shook hands and introduced themselves, too terrified to even get drawn into casual conversation.

Almost like a talisman, she was still carrying that dog-eared A4 scrap of a printout with her and just as they started to taxi down the runway, she took it out again to re-read it for about the thousandth time. Like she'd been doing for the last twenty-four hours non-stop, still trying to let it all sink in.

'Ladies and gentlemen,' the British Airways stewardess

announced briskly over the Tannoy, 'in preparation for take-off, we ask you to ensure that all your hand luggage is safely stowed in the overhead compartment.'

Jean still gripped the printout in her hand, and just as they started taxiing down the runway, took one final look at it, nearly knowing it by heart at this stage. And there it was: in black and white. The only single thing that could possibly ever make her get onto this plane and go back home in the first place.

KENNEDY, Kathleen, (née McColgan.) At St Patrick's Marymount Hospice, Co. Cork. Formerly of Foxborough House care home, Co. Limerick. 25 September. (Peacefully, in her sleep.) Dearly beloved wife of the late James Kennedy, sister of the late Paddy McColgan and foster mother to Jean Simpson. She will be sadly missed by all her loving friends and staff at Marymount.

Memorial service Monday 29 September at midday. Rocky Island Crematorium, Ringaskiddy, Co. Cork. No flowers, please.

Mrs K., her beloved foster mum; the one person during her teenage years who'd shown her any care or kindness. The mother she'd never had and who it had broken her heart to leave behind.

And now she was gone.

Chapter Ten

If the first time it had happened had come as a shock to her; if it had been totally out of the blue, then the second time was calculated, almost preplanned.

It was almost as though he'd come in the door looking for trouble.

She'd finished work early and had been in the kitchen cooking dinner for them both: steak, onions and spuds, his favourite. But as soon as she heard him come home, she could almost sense there was something in the air; it was getting so she could nearly smell it. She knew by the slightly aggressive way he flung his briefcase down on the hall table and totally ignored her when she called out a cheerful, 'Hi! I'm in here!'

Right, she thought. He's just in one of his moods. He'll come round with a bit of TLC. He's just had a bad day, that's all, so I'll be nice to him, spoil him for the night. Besides, he was always telling her she was far too tough, too independent for her own good, so for this evening she'd be the perfect girlfriend. The kind of woman he was always trying to get her to be.

She remembered him turning on the telly when he got in; some big match was on Sky Sports that he'd particularly wanted to see. So she served him dinner on a tray in front of the TV, then plonked herself down beside him and asked how his day had been. No response back from him, though; he just kept looking blankly at the screen ahead of him, completely tuning her out. In time, she'd come to learn not even to dream of invading the same airspace as him when he got into one of those black moods, but back then, she was a complete moron who knew no better.

So instead of just backing off and leaving well enough alone, what did she do? Like some kind of kamikaze nut job, she'd asked him what was up and if she could help him in any way. Did he want to talk about it? All perfectly innocuous.

Or so you'd think.

But that was all it took. Next thing she knew she'd been flung back on the sofa, the force of his blow was that strong. Then she saw the tray of food – the dinner she'd gone to such bloody trouble over – being flung against the far wall, smashing the plate and sending peas, lumps of mashed potato and gravy flying everywhere.

'Are you completely blind?' he screamed right in her face. 'Can you not see I'm trying to watch this match, you stupid bitch!' Then he started pounding into her ribs, pinning her down so she couldn't move or even breathe. And the pain was utterly blinding this time; far, far worse than before.

But still she astonished herself by trying to fight back.

'Get off me!' she remembered yelling. 'Or else I'm calling the police!'

And then it was like something snapped in him. 'You do that and I'll fucking kill you,' he roared, going for her face this time. She tried to shove him off her, but he was so much bigger and stronger than she was. She remembered looking at the coffee table, wondering why it was at such a funny angle to her. It was only then she realised he'd just thrown her to the floor and she was looking at it from sideways on. And still the punching kept up right until she was about to black out with the pain. Every time he'd pause, she'd think that's it, it's over and then he'd start again, only with even more force. Her face felt so hot, clammy, numb . . . blood was spouting from her nose and pouring everywhere, and now he was punching her for all he was worth, roaring at her for destroying his carpet . . .

Suddenly she heard an urgent ring at the doorbell. His fist froze in midair for a second, then he barked at her to get up. She couldn't move, though, so he just abandoned her where she was and told her that if she as much as opened her mouth, she was a dead woman.

Even though her ears were ringing, she could still hear him go down the hallway to their front door and open it. It was Trish, a neighbour from the flat downstairs, wondering what all the hysterical screaming was about. Trish had three kids all under the age of eight, so for someone like her to start complaining about noise meant it really must have been something else.

'I got an awful fright and so did the kids . . .' she could clearly hear Trish saying from the bottom of the hallway. 'All that shouting and roaring . . . I was really worried . . . Is everything OK?'

'Absolutely fine,' she heard him tell her, cool as you like.

And he sounded so calm. Polite even.

'It's just I could have sworn I heard a woman's voice screeching out for help . . . It sounded an awful lot like Jean . . . So I just thought I should come up and check . . .'

'No, no, you must be mistaken . . .' God, he sounded so convincing, it was almost chilling.

'You're absolutely certain?'

Good on you, Trish. She wasn't letting it go. She must suspect something, she had to. Otherwise she'd have gone straight back downstairs to her own kids, wouldn't she?

The pain was near-blinding, but somehow Jean managed to haul herself up onto her elbow and did her level best to drag herself to the door, inch by inch, to beg for help, spattering a trail of blood behind her. Trish was a great neighbour, she'd get her out of here, she'd understand. Besides, the blood was pumping out of her nose now and she knew she needed an ambulance, fast.

But then just as she'd managed to drag herself as far as the edge of the sofa, his voice filtered back to her, stopping her dead in his tracks.

Because now he was laughing. Actually laughing.

'Listen, Trish, I'm absolutely mortified about this!' she could hear him saying. 'Thing is I've just been watching a movie on Sky and yeah, sure, there's a fair bit of shouting and a lot of violence in it all right. Sorry, was the TV on too loud?'

She couldn't hear Trish's reply.

'No worries at all,' he went on, smooth as you like. 'I'll turn it down right away and so sorry again if it gave you a fright. Serves me right for watching too many slasher movies!'

Jesus, now he was even making light jokes. How could he do that, the tiny part of her brain that couldn't register pain wondered. Act like the last ten minutes never happened? Was he some kind of Jekyll and Hyde monster? How could he sound so relaxed and calm now, when seconds ago he'd been screeching into her face and pummelling her to a pulp?

In the TV room, she'd still only managed to drag herself a pathetic three or four feet, nowhere even close to the door.

'Trish, help!' she tried to shout out, though she knew it was utterly futile. Her voice barely sounded like a tiny croak; no

one could possibly hear her. She could feel the blood from her nose oozing down the back of her throat and it was starting to choke her.

'In here!' she tried to yell out once more. 'For God's sake . . . Trish, can you hear me?' But it came out little more than a strangulated squawk that she could barely hear herself.

She'd had to be hospitalised that time.

'What in the name of God did you do to yourself?' a senior triage nurse in the A&E department had asked her worriedly, before referring her to a doctor for immediate attention, X-rays, stitches, the whole works.

'Course, he was there by her side, the picture of concern. Holding onto her hand, kissing it, telling her over and over again that she was going to be OK. All an act, her sane mind told her and a bloody convincing one at that. Time and again he kept saying how sorry he was, how he'd just snapped for some reason and how he swore it would never happen again.

'You can't leave me, Jean,' he'd whispered to her, as she lay drifting in and out of consciousness on a hospital trolley, out of her mind, almost floating on soothing waves of morphine.

'I'd die without you and you'd die without me too. We love each other too much to let this come between us. I'll get help, I swear I will. I'll do whatever it takes for you to forgive me.'

Her heart wanted to believe him so badly, it frightened her.

So when she felt strong enough, she looked the junior doctor in the eye and lied to her. The same lie she'd rehearsed over and over in her head.

'I've just taken up amateur boxing,' she'd croaked weakly.

'And had a rough fight tonight. That was all. It was no one's fault but my own.'

The doctor looked long and hard at her.

That the truth? She seemed to be asking silently. Because if you need help, all you have to do is say so.

It's the truth, she hoped her eyes said back. And if the doctor could tell it was a howler of a lie, she didn't question it any further.

'How badly hurt is she?' she heard him asking.

'Apart from the blood loss and bruising, she's got three cracked ribs. But a far bigger worry is her nose. It's been broken in three places. I'm afraid without expensive plastic surgery, it'll never be back to the way it was.'

As soon as visiting hours were over and he'd had to leave, she'd made a silent vow to herself. When I'm well enough, when I eventually get out of hospital, then that's it, I'm leaving. She'd heard that old phrase countless times: hit me once, shame on you, hit me twice, shame on me. Just never in her wildest dreams thought it would apply to someone like her, that's all. Someone who'd always fought her own battles in life, someone who'd always been so tough and feisty and independent. How could this possibly happen to her?

After all, she was such a strong person, everyone kept telling her. Wasn't she the girl famous for not taking shit from anyone? The one who always stood up for anyone who was being bullied or downtrodden?

And now just look at her. Look at what he was slowly turning her into.

She was probably the last person you'd ever think something like this could happen to, and yet here she was, lying semi-comatose on a morphine drip in an A&E department, with a smashed nose so sore she could barely breathe through it.

I'll go home during the daytime, she faithfully promised herself, when he's safely out at work. Then I'll pack up my things and just take off. Somewhere he'll never find me. I could even change my name, just so I'm really on the safe side.

In the end, she didn't leave him, though. Not that time.

Or the time after that, or the one after that again.

And just look how that turned out.

'It's all right, honey,' she heard a gentle voice say beside her, 'it's OK, wake up. You were just having a bad dream, that's all.'

Jean came to, opened her eyes, petrified.

But somehow it was OK.

She was still on the flight to London, except it was pitch-dark outside now, cabin lights had been dimmed and half the passengers around her were conked out asleep. She looked over to where that lovely elderly lady from Zimbabwe sat beside her, worriedly patting her hand.

'I'm so sorry,' Jean said, still groggy and realising that her borrowed blouse was stuck to her with cold, clammy perspiration. 'Hope I didn't wake you.'

'No, you're fine, honey. I was watching the in-flight movie anyway. You were talking in your sleep, though.'

Shit, no, no, no, she thought.

'You mentioned someone called Joe? You kept saying his name over and over.'

Jesus, no . . .

'I'm really sorry for disturbing you,' was all she could manage to stammer out.

'Anytime, lovie. I'm not a great flyer and I don't sleep that much anyway.'

'Well . . . thanks for waking me.'

'No problem at all. You sure must have a lot on your mind.'

'Yeah. Yeah, you could say that.'

They arrived into London Heathrow just before seven in the morning; a miracle, the lovely lady beside her kept saying, considering how dire the weather was outside. 'So you can say goodbye to sunny South African skies for a little while then,' she'd smiled, nudging Jean and pointing out the cabin window towards the gales and torrential rain that seemed to be raging all around them. 'Instead, I guess we get to enjoy some traditional British weather for a change!'

Jean smiled back at her as politely as she could, thinking, if a heavy storm is all you have to worry you, lady, then you're one lucky woman.

She still had a good few hours to while away before her connecting flight on to Cork airport. Which was more than worrying, to say the least. Because once she'd claimed the small bag she was travelling with and changed terminal, there was another problem ahead. The weather outside seemed if anything to be getting worse. The rain was battering up against the windows of the departure lounge now, worse than rainy season in Calcutta. She swore she could even see a flash of lightning. Brilliant.

Just then, she happened to look up at an overhead monitor and her heart sank even further.

There it was on the screen right in front of her: 'FLIGHT EI 723 LHR – CORK. DELAYED. PASSENGERS ARE ADVISED TO WAIT IN THE LOUNGE FOR FURTHER UPDATES.'

And, on cue, a fuzzy announcement came over the Tannoy.

'Ladies and gentlemen, this is to announce a delay on all departing flights from Terminal One, due to adverse weather conditions. Please continue to wait in the lounge and check overhead monitors for further updates. We sincerely apologise for any inconvenience caused.'

Not the best for Jean's already raggedy nerves, needless to say. Now a short connection had turned into a wait of God only knew how much longer. And now suddenly she was in the land of pale, freckly skin and Irish accents. Where anything could happen, where anyone might recognise her.

Anxiety started to make her paranoid, and by the time she'd arrived at the lounge beside her connecting flight's boarding gate, she was starting to feel a full-blown panic attack coming on: heart palpitating, eyes blurring, chest walloping cartoon-like, the whole works. Forcing herself to stay calm, she made her way to a tiny coffee shop close by, took a quiet seat in a tucked-away corner where she was certain she wouldn't be seen and did her best to regroup.

You're being ridiculous, she kept telling herself. As though the more often she said it, the likelier it was to sink in. It's been nearly two long years, for God's sake! You honestly think people will still remember after all this time? You really believe someone will see your face and put two and two together? You've more chance of winning the EuroMillions lottery, she thought, than of some random stranger seeing you here and wondering why it is that you look a bit familiar. So just stop beating yourself up, cop the feck on and pull it together.

Besides, you've come this far. You've been a lot of things in your life before, but you've never been a coward and you're not chickening out of this now. Plus, you'll need every reserve of strength you have to get through the funeral. So just get over yourself.

Then to really calm herself down, she fished out the by-now battered and raggedy A4 printout from the depths of her jacket pocket and spread it on the table in front of her.

You see this? This is the reason why you're here, she sternly reminded herself. The one and only reason.

This was the only woman she'd ever thought of as Mum, and there was no power on earth that would stop her from paying her last respects. Absolutely nothing, no matter how high the risk.

God knows, she felt badly enough that she couldn't get in touch with Foxborough these past two years, but then, that was out of the question. A phone call from a South African number enquiring after Mrs K. would immediately arouse suspicion and could so easily be tracked. Even an anonymous email enquiry to the home was fully traceable, she knew. Every computer had a unique IP address that could be tracked down and it was a risk she just couldn't afford to take. She'd written to Mrs K. every chance she got though, and then would cajole anyone at the hotel who was travelling onto Europe, Australia or the States to mail letters for her whenever they were passing through. Knowing that Mrs K. wouldn't be able to read or even focus on them, but hoping that someone at Foxborough would be kind enough to read them out to her. She was always careful never to say where she was, and she knew the postmark wouldn't give her away; she just wrote that she was OK, that all was well but that she missed her dreadfully.

To her shame, she'd done next to nothing else for Mrs

K. over the last two years, bar alternate between thinking about her and worrying over her. Knowing that at least in her condition, the poor woman wouldn't be able to grasp the enormity of what had happened. Wouldn't even be aware that she'd stopped visiting her, that she really was gone. Poor consolation, but still. It got Jean through more than a few dark nights of the soul. So being there for her today felt like the least she could do, no matter how big a gamble she was about to take.

She went over it all in her head again, for about the hundredth time: the plan she'd worked out so carefully. She was still OK for time, because even if her flight was delayed till much later on that night, the funeral still wasn't until midday the following day.

First, she'd hire a car at Cork airport and drive all the way to Rocky Island in Ringaskiddy, Co. Cork, where the memorial service and cremation was to take place. She'd done all her research, had even printed off an AA route map, and figured, all going well, that she could manage the drive in well under two hours.

She was pretty certain there wouldn't be anyone who'd know her at the church. How could there be? She worked out that poor Mrs K. had been moved from Foxborough to the hospice in Youghal some time ago, probably so she could be closer to Cork University Hospital. 'Course, there was always the slim risk that someone from Foxborough might travel down to pay their last respects, but it seemed doubtful anyone would. They were always so understaffed and overworked in there, taking a day off to travel all that distance was highly unlikely.

The main thing was that he wouldn't be there. How could he be? He knew of Mrs K.'s existence alright, but rarely even asked about her and had never once come with her on a visit. For God's sake, he didn't even know Mrs K.'s full name, how could he possibly just turn up? Even if by some weird chance, he'd happened to see the tiny notice in the paper, the woman's full name would have meant absolutely nothing to him. He'd never remotely interested himself in anything to do with Jean's past. It was her present and, worst of all, her future, which was all that concerned him.

A good, strengthening thought. Just cling to that, she told herself, and you'll live to tell the tale. Half a bottle of icy cold water later, she felt stronger, more like herself.

Yet again, she went over it. It was simple, really. She'd arrive as late as she dared to the church, when everyone else had gone inside for the service. Stay well at the back where she wouldn't be seen, then slip away before everyone else got up to leave. No lingering around and, above all, no entering into conversation with anyone she didn't know. Get in, get out, fast. Do it for Mrs K.

And she could, she knew she could. Once she stuck to the plan, she'd be OK. The more she said it over and over to herself, the more she started to believe it. Everything would be all right. Her exit strategy was all worked out. With any luck, she'd be back on the road to the airport, safely out of there and back to her life of obscurity in no time.

She'd come this far. She could do it.

After all, she had no choice.

ANGIE.

Chapter Eleven

27 September, 8.15 a.m.

BIG, red-letter day in the life of Angie Blennerhasset. Huge. If I ever came to write my own autobiography, today would probably take up an entire chapter. Our new business, The Chocolate Bar, is, as of today . . . drumroll for dramatic effect . . . officially up, running and open, available for all your needs beverage- and chocolate-related! I'm so beside myself, I'm actually running around like an over-excited nine-year-old, having a sugar high on Christmas morning.

Mind you, Sarah's taking it all far more professionally than me, and in a heroic attempt to calm me down, reminds me we've still got our big interview with the Business section of the *Daily Post* to navigate our way through first. Which, by the way, is a proper photo shoot with an actual, professional photographer . . . I know, I can scarcely believe it either! Me, the Queen of the Flake-Heads, actually being featured in a business section, read by busy, important, briefcase-wielding types? It's an amazing victory lap for Sarah and me and – with apologies for the pettiness of what I'm about to say – a serious smack in gob for everyone who laughed and belittled us over the past two years, as we crawled our way up.

Because just take a look at me now . . . swanning up Grafton Street to meet a journalist and photographer who want to run a full feature on the business, like I've been doing it all my life! Yes, me, big loser Angie, who once aspired to scrubbing floors on film sets, in the vain hopes I'd eventually work my way up to becoming the female equivalent of James Cameron (except maybe without banging on about the bleeding *Titanic* quite so much).

'Course, I still love and miss the world of film production so much it hurts, but eventually I had to grow up and face hard, cold facts. God knows, I'd more than my fair share of looking at things square on over the past two years, and this, in a funny way, was almost the least of it. Eventually, though, I made the v. painful decision that when it came to my first career choice, the utmost I'd ever most likely aspire to was a glorified tea-lady and general all-round go-for.

In fairness, it's not entirely my fault. There just are no work opportunities in the film industry, unless you uproot and go out to LA. And even then you *still* end up as a glorified tea-maker, except all the accents are American and chances are the tea is green and caffeine-free, full of antioxidants.

Wasn't easy, mind you, giving up on long-cherished hopes and dreams, but sooner or later the time comes to all of us when we have to cop on to ourselves. And I had to decide either to make something out of my life, or else stay on the dole moaning, till I was old enough to collect the state pension.

So I chose to move on.

And as Sarah never tires of reminding me, the *Daily Post*

feature is a seriously huge deal for the two of us. Not only as PR for our new business, but as a sort of badge of pride/endorsement for us both too. As she quite rightly says herself, we've been through so much over the past two years and we've worked so bloody hard; so if we're not going to pat ourselves on the back, then who is?

In fact I often think back to the sheer amount of grief the pair of us each had to put up with, back in those early, start-up days. Sarah from the banks and me from . . . well, I'll come back to that in a minute. Have to say in Sarah's defence, though, God help any banker that gets in her way now; she's got to be so bloody well able for them. I've sat in with her on more than a few v. scary, high-powered meetings with branch managers in the past, and the girl would nearly astonish you. Goes in with the attitude of, 'You're all basically a shower of morons if you don't even consider investing in a small, but up-and-coming growing business opportunity! It'd be akin to turning down a licence to print money, and mark my words, you'd all end up laughing stocks! Far, far worse than when Simon Cowell turned down Take That, on grounds the lead singer was too fat!'

Less swaggering personalities like me sit cowering in the corner, cap-twisting, as my mother says, embarrassed and beyond apologetic at having the bare-faced cheek to look for an actual cash loan. Wondering when the part comes where they tell us the loan application has to be signed in blood under full moon with the sound of bloodhounds baying in background. But not our Sarah. Don't think I've ever in all my born days seen any living creature like her. Seriously, Angela Merkel could do Sarah's correspondence course in assertiveness and still manage to pick up a trick or two.

The *Daily Post* glossy business feature, however, would be more in the nature of a personal validation for me. Mainly because of the serious amounts of shite I was forced to take back in our start-up days from my delightful sibling, the perennially supportive Madeline Blennerhasset. I really thought the girl would burst ulcers from laughing when she first heard about what we were up to, all of two years ago. Can still hear her grating, nasally voice sneering at me.

'A coffee shop called The Chocolate Bar? Is it possible that you're being serious? The way you're headed, Angie, you won't be happy till you're working as a cleaning lady! Mark my words, it's a slippery slope.'

Really, really hate to gloat and I know it's v. small-minded of me. But mark my words, after a few drinks at tonight's launch party, chances are I'll end up dancing rings around the old witch, chanting, 'HA! In your face!'

And yes, am aware there's such a thing as being gracious in victory, but on a day like today, sod that for a lark.

Westbury Hotel foyer, midday

The journalist who's arranged to interview us is already here ahead of me, with Sarah sitting pretty on the sofa beside her. Journalist turns out to be absolutely lovely, by the way; she's an older lady dressed head to toe in floaty white linen, who introduces herself as Clara, shakes hands warmly and says she's really looking forward to the big launch party tonight. She thanks us profusely for the invite and says her little girl, who adores our chocolate, wishes us the best of luck too, and is very much looking forward to treating herself to a few of our special dark chocolate caramel surprises when she can.

'That's lovely to hear, thank you,' Sarah smiles graciously. Then, ever with an eye to getting a good plug in, she goes on, 'and maybe you'd tell your little girl that our suppliers are about to set up monthly children's workshops, where kids can spend a full day seeing how the chocolates are actually made, then eat all they like at the very end. It'll be a magical day out, perfect for children's birthday parties.'

'Well, I'll be sure to pass that on,' Clara says a bit uncertainly, 'but when I say she's my little girl, she's actually thirty-four.'

Then, all apologies, she steps away from us, to take an urgent call from her editor on her mobile phone.

The minute she's out of earshot, I give Sarah a warm bear hug, even though I only saw her a few hours earlier at work.

'Look at you, Ange, you look a million dollars!' she beams at me.

'Ah, would you ever give over!' I nudge her back playfully. 'You're just getting far too used to seeing me behind a counter with my hairnet on, that's all!'

We've both changed out of our work gear and are all dressed up like two dogs' dinners for this, Sarah in an elegant black shift dress from Karen Millen, with her hair neatly tied back; v. Kate Middleton-going-to-inspect-the-troops sort of look, if you're with me. But then, Sarah's just born to wear Karen Millen; she's got a handspan waist and is absolutely doll-sized, just like you have to be to even fit through the door of that shop.

As for me, given my new career and in spite of all my best efforts to shift a few pounds for today, my waistline slowly seems to be engaged in coup de corps, trying to take over my whole body. (And as an aside, I defy anyone to spend all day working round the yummiest chocolate yet discovered by man and *not* gain weight, but there you go. It's somewhat in the way of being an occupational hazard.)

Anyway, it's not easy finding clothes that cover a multitude and yet look good on me, but as a very special splash-out present to mark the day, I decided to really push the boat out and treat myself. So I'm now all togged out in a long, floaty maxi-dress from Reiss, with a dotey little matching cardigan to shield the public from having to gawp at my fleshy, dinner-lady arms. Feels great on, and again, at Sarah's insistence, I even had a blow-dry this morning, something I *never* do. Well, in my line of work, it tends to be a big waste of time, given the restraints of hairnets. Not certain what I look like, but I can tell you one thing with absolute confidence. At this moment in time, I feel like I'm officially on top of the world.

'Isn't this just a dream come true?' Sarah squeals excitedly.

'Oh, babes . . .' I start to say, but end up just lamely trailing off instead.

Almost impossible to even put into words, but it's been such a long, long time since I felt this positive about myself. Amazing, wonderful sensation, like I've finally come full circle and I'm bloody determined to squeeze every last drop out of it. Sarah and I have each had so much to deal with on every level over past two years and today is nothing short of a major celebration.

I've this overwhelming urge to yell at everyone I meet: 'Look! We've done it! And in spite of everything, by some miracle, I've come out the other side!' I do a lightning-quick spotcheck of my feelings and realise something. That I'm actually happy. Really, genuinely happy. Now whoever would have thought?

Never thought I'd be happy again, not after what happened and certainly not after everything that was thrown my way, not two short years ago. And it turns out I couldn't have been more wrong. But then, I suppose that's the thing about life. Just when you think it's all headed down the toilet, that's when it'll surprise you most.

I'm way too overcome by it all to even articulate all this to Sarah; instead, I settle for just squeezing her arm and smiling warmly back at her. Besides, pretty much everything we've been through, we've been through together, shoulder to shoulder, side by side.

She already knows what I'm feeling without my even having to say it aloud.

12.15 p.m.

Clara eventually wraps up her phone call with many, many red-faced, flustered apologies, then switches on her tape recorder and kicks off with her first question.

'Well, now, ladies,' she smiles, 'firstly, can I just say what an inspiration your story has been to women everywhere. A good news story like yours coming out of the economic gloom could hardly fail to put a smile on anyone's face, now could it?'

'Course I beam, while Sarah just nods and takes all this in her stride. But then out of the pair of us, Sarah is v. much the visionary and won't be happy until we've achieved world domination. It's pretty much the main reason why she and I work so well as a team.

'So,' Clara goes on, 'let me start by asking you, what was it that first gave you the idea to set up The Chocolate Bar?'

I let Sarah field that one. It's like an unspoken agreement

we have. Although the business is an equal fifty-fifty split, she always talks about the nuts and bolts of it, but when it comes to the actual product, that's when it's over to *moi*. In other words, she's the money gal, I'm the one you chat to about all things grub-related. But sure, who in their right mind wouldn't be happy to chat about chocolate all day? Sure that's not work, it's more like my hobby at this stage. And believe me, I've the cellulite to prove it.

'Easy,' Sarah says, sitting bolt upright like she's about to read the nine o'clock news. 'As you know, my family have a franchise of sandwich bars . . .'

'Yes, I remember reading about that . . .' Clara smiles, all encouragement.

'So you could say I effectively was born into the catering industry,' Sarah goes on smoothly and confidently, almost like she's rehearsed this. Which knowing her, she probably has, in front of a mirror and everything. Sarah's always thoroughness itself. Secret of success, she says. Fail to prepare, prepare to fail, etc. is her motto.

'But then,' she continues, 'over time, I slowly started to notice something. A few years back when the credit crunch turned into a full-blown recession, and then when the economic meltdown first began to hit hard, customers unsurprisingly began to cut back on their take-out lattes and low-fat mochas. Instead they'd make their own coffee at home and take flasks into work with them, or else do without. Which is absolutely as you'd expect. It's completely understandable and, unfortunately for us, how people behave whenever money is tight.'

'Of course,' Clara smiles and nods along.

'But here's what I began to pick up on. Customers were still coming into us, but instead of ordering their low-fat

Americanos to go, they'd make straight for the sweet counter. It was as though everyone was suddenly cutting back on luxuries, but still allowing themselves the odd, inexpensive little treat, like one or two handmade chocolates that still only cost less than fifty cents each.'

'So, Angie, when did you first come on board?'

Right then, over to me.

'Well, Sarah first came to me about two years ago. She'd had this idea and asked if I'd be interested in getting involved. At the time, I was already working in one of her family's sandwich bars and really surprising myself at just how much I loved dealing with the public.'

'She's a born natural at it!' Sarah chips in loyally. 'It's like Angie is everyone's friend. We've got customers who seem to come in just for a natter with her! You should see her. They tell her everything, even the most personal things. You wouldn't believe it. There she is, day after day, doling out chocolate and relationship advice . . .'

'A perfect combination, if I may say so,' Clara smiles warmly.

I grin like a prize eejit and get back to the question.

'So anyway, Sarah had spotted a tiny kiosk up for rent out at Terminal One in the airport . . .'

'. . . And a knockdown rent, at that, because the location was so out of the way, no one else wanted it,' Sarah interrupts, but then whenever she and I get talking about how we started up, we both get over-excited and tend to overlap each other.

'Everyone said we were nuts to even consider investing in such a rubbishy location . . .'

'. . . Only Sarah here managed to negotiate even more of a rock-bottom rent for us . . .'

'. . . But at that stage the banks were refusing to lend to us, so I had to borrow start-up capital from my family . . .'

'Same here,' I say, 'which we used to invest in securing a contract with Burke's handmade chocolates . . .'

'. . . That they'd supply exclusively to us and us alone . . .'

Meanwhile, poor old Clara's been looking from one of us to the other, Wimbledon-style, frantically trying to keep up.

'So initially, you opened up at the airport,' she says. 'Must have been incredibly hard work at first.'

Sarah takes over that one and I nod along with her, remembering all too well what a slog it was back in those early days. No messing, we'd both be on the road at four a.m. to get out to the airport and open up, ready for all the early morning commuters. And we'd stay there, sometimes till well past ten at night, astonished at just how much trade we were still doing. V. tired, hungry airline passengers all wanting a coffee to perk them up and a slice of The Chocolate Bar's double mocha choccie biscuit cake to go along with it, were nearly beating a path to our door. The perfect carb hit.

We both reminisce fondly as Clara checks the tape recorder in front of her. Amazing times. It was v. strange at first, experiencing success when I'd become so accustomed to nothing but failure. But then, this was something different, something special and we both knew it. We seemed to somehow catch a wave, we'd trapped lightning in a bottle, however modestly we first started out. Within six months, we'd our start-up loans paid off, and after our first year we'd even cleared enough profit to start looking at expansion.

So, propelled along by Sarah's can-do attitude and my genuine love and belief in our product, we expanded into a bigger location out at the airport. A proper unit this time, in a far better location, in the flashy new duty free hall at Terminal Two. Word of mouth took over and suddenly we were getting glowing little mentions in the papers, including a review from v. well known and highly regarded food critic. Neither Sarah nor I could believe it when he wrote a lovely piece saying that by far the best part of travelling out of Terminal Two now was the chance to have a latte and one of our handmade double Mocha whip chocolates, all for only two Euro. (Divine choccie, by the way, one of my faves, definitely makes it into my product all-time top ten.)

We framed the review and somehow just knew we were on our way. But even though business was booming and we were starting to do very nicely thank you, Sarah still had an eye on us growing bigger still. So when a lease came up for renewal in the city centre, we just went for it. Which is what tonight's all about. The official grand opening of The Chocolate Bar's second branch on Dame Street, right in the heart of the city. Amazing location, couldn't ask for better. Means we not only cash in on all the tourists but also it's a great catchment area for the busy city lunch trade, as there's so many offices around there.

But if there's one thing I've learned it's this. No matter how old you are, no matter how little dosh you have on you, no matter where you're from or what you do, chocolate really is the world's great unifier. We get kids in, we get their grannies, we get back-packers from the furthest corners of the planet, we get businessmen in suits, we even get homeless people, but then we've a policy that we'll give them any out-of-date stock that we're only chucking out anyway. Which was my idea. (There but for the grace of God, etc.)

And then there's a natural break in the chat. Sarah sits back into the comfy sofa and glances over at me as if to say, well that's it, that's pretty much brought her up to speed, hasn't it? What's left to talk about now?

Seems Clara still has a few more questions for us, though. She adjusts her tape recorder, then looks keenly at both of us.

'OK then, that seems to be the business end of things covered,' she says, 'so now I'd like touch on something a little bit more personal, if I may. Just so our readers can get a clearer picture of who you both are. As people.'

Who we are 'as people'? As opposed to what? I suddenly think. Who we are as gorillas? For a moment, Sarah and I look across at each other, a bit mystified. Then she shrugs at me as if to say, well the publicity's not doing us any harm, so let's just play along.

'You both seem to work such incredibly long hours,' Clara says and we nod vigorously. Certainly no denying that one. 'So I suppose I was just wondering, does that leave any time in either of your lives for a relationship? Can I begin by asking you, Sarah?'

Am relieved beyond belief that she started with Sarah. And I'm now sitting here with a clenched arse, only praying she won't ask me the same thing.

The normally unflappable Sarah falters just a tiny bit, but if you didn't know Sarah, you'd never cop it, she's incredibly cool. It's only me that picks up on a tiny bit of discomfort, something in the way she shifts slightly on the sofa. But then, Sarah's single, has been for the longest time and says that now she's turned thirty, she's officially starting to get just a tiny bit panicky. She has one bullet-proof strategy, though: never, on pain of death, to let it be known that she's officially single and looking.

'Well, as you say,' she says eventually, eyeballing Clara, 'I find that with the hours we work, it's just so difficult to even see friends, never mind sustain a relationship.'

Good gal, I think. Great answer.

'In fact, our pals are all saying the only way they'll ever get to see us is if they call into The Chocolate Bar every day!' I chip in, in a futile attempt to back her up.

'Plus you have to bear in mind,' Sarah goes on, 'I'm in my car at the crack of dawn and it would be really unusual for me to get home before ten in the evening. 'Course, by then I'm just so whacked that even if George Clooney knocked on my door, I'd probably end up just yawning into his face . . . ha, ha!'

She laughs just that bit too much, then looks to me as if to say, 'Get this one to change the fecking subject, FAST.'

Sure enough, Clara's over to me now.

'And, if I can turn to you, Angie, would you agree?' she asks. 'Is it impossible to have a relationship, given the schedule you both work? Are you married? Or with a partner? Or maybe seeing anyone right now?'

Silence.

And for the first time since the interview started, I'm at a total loss for words.

Because I've never talked publicly about this before and am not even a hundred per cent certain that I want to. Our close friends and family all know, of course, but it's a totally different thing announcing it to the media. Besides, is all just so new, it's barely even been six months . . .

'Angie?' Clara interrupts my chain of thought, patiently waiting on an answer.

'Well, em . . .' I half mumble.

'Yes, as a matter of fact,' Sarah answers firmly for me. 'Yes, she is in a relationship. With someone lovely, who treats her like the princess she is.'

I shrug back at Clara as if to say, that answer your question? 'Cos that's all you're gonna get, lady.

'So then you didn't seem to find it difficult to meet someone with the crazy hours that you put in?' she asks me directly.

'Well, you see, we'd already known each other for a long time before The Chocolate Bar ever came into being,' is all I say.

'They were and are great friends,' Sarah says. 'Which is by far the best foundation for any relationship, really. I mean . . . just look at Prince William and Kate.'

'Right then,' Clara says thoughtfully, and I think, phew. We're off that highly mortifying subject, thank you, God.

'Well, in that case, ladies, there's just one more thing I'd like to ask you both, just before our photographer gets here,' Clara goes on, and for a split second I relax, thinking it's back to talking about the business. Has to be. Major sigh of relief all round.

But no, turns out I'm spectacularly wrong.

'Sticking with your personal lives for a moment, if I may . . .'

Shit, what now?

'I'd like to ask you both about that waitress who went missing around two years ago. Kitty Hope, wasn't that her name?'

And suddenly, it's like no air moves.

We weren't expecting this. And it's not bloody fair to spring it on us out of the blue! I thought we were just here to plug The Chocolate Bar? My shoulders instantly seize and I swear I know without being told exactly what's coming next.

'Am I right in thinking that you were both friends with her? And that you both were initially involved in the search to find her?'

Sarah looks over to me and I can see the worry in her eyes, wondering how I'll take it.

'Yes, we were,' is all I say quietly.

'Thought so,' Clara nods, shoving the tape recorder that bit closer to me now. 'There was a huge amount of coverage about it at the time and when I Googled you both, I could see that both of your names had been linked with the case. It must have been an awful time for you. All happened over Christmas and New Year, if I remember.'

This time Sarah and I just look at her stonily without saying a word. Subtext, can we just drop it, please?

But no, Clara's still not done with us.

'How is the case—' she begins, but I don't let her finish.

'That case has been closed for a long time,' I interrupt her in a tone I hope conveys, 'and that's as much as you're getting out of me, missy.'

'All that coverage,' Clara muses thoughtfully, 'and then suddenly, the whole thing was just dropped. I can still vividly remember all those posters and flyers all over town. She was such a gorgeous-looking girl too. It did strike me as very strange at the time, though. The way the whole thing just seemed to be abandoned. '

'No,' I tell her. 'Actually, when you know the facts, it wasn't a bit strange at all.'

'Any further comments to make?'

Sarah picks up on my silence and smoothly as ever, takes over.

'Can I just get in a plug for our new line of champagne truffles?' she tactfully lobs in, anxious to get the interview back on track. 'Special gift boxes are available for only nine ninety-five. Ideal for any birthday gift.'

Thank you, God, Clara allows her to fill air with truffle chocolates and Baileys liqueur mini bites while I sit still, just waiting for my pulse rate to come back down into double figures. It's just there've been so few mentions of the whole thing in so long, that when that particular ghost is invoked, it never fails to completely knock me for six. Even now, even after two long years, even after everything that's happened since.

And there's so much I could tell Clara, if I chose to. I could tell her that Kitty Hope's disappearance was sudden, yes, but for her, as we now know, not something entirely unexpected. I could open up to her about the agony of those first few days and weeks when we were all left completely in the dark, not knowing what had happened to her or where she'd gone and, of course, presuming the very worst. How it was exactly like a dazzling bright light had just gone out of my life.

I could talk about the deep shock, shock on an almost cellular level when that Detective Sergeant, Jack Crown finally unearthed the truth and broke it to us. The relief I felt that Kitty was OK, and yet the anger that she could even think of putting us all through that. That she'd been living a lie all that time and never once had told anyone, not even me.

Then with time, came a slow dawning of understanding and even a little pity. That the girl honestly felt she only had one way out and so when the need arose, of course that was the course of action she chose. I could tell Clara that just because we don't talk about her any more doesn't mean I don't think of her, often. Yes, what she did was cruel and unbearably painful, but at times, I can see where she was coming from; can even understand that she honestly felt she had no other choice.

Besides, she may have hurt all of us desperately, but my own conduct since hardly stands up to criticism either, now does it?

I've broken an unwritten rule of friendship and my only defence is, well, Kitty broke it first.

I could tell Clara the facts, all of them. That we found out the whole truth and nothing but the truth just weeks into the search. I could tell her what was waiting for me when I got home that horrible night, the full import of what Jack Crown had to tell us. The shock of it, the anger I felt at first.

I could say that not long afterwards, I even got a postcard from her.

I'm fine. I'm sorry.
Please take care of him for me.
And maybe one day I'll get to explain.

And that was it. After seven years of friendship, that was all I got. Three lousy lines. She'd been careful to cover her tracks, too; the postcard had been mailed from London and yet we were certain that wherever she'd pitched up, she'd never materialised there. So we figured she must have got someone to post it for her, to keep her whereabouts a secret.

Yet another secret, I should say, in whole catalogue of them she'd been carrying around.

Most of all I could tell Clara that she's actually got her facts completely arseways.

And that her name wasn't even Kitty to begin with.

It was Jean.

As long as she lived, Jean would never forget sitting alone in the bathroom that night, perched on the side of her bath, eyes glued to a minuscule screen on a Clearblue pregnancy test.

She couldn't be, she thought, half out of her mind with frantic worry. Not someone like her, surely it wasn't possible? For God's sake, she was only twenty-two years old! With her whole life ahead of her, etc. etc. Last thing she needed right now was this. She still felt like such a big kid herself, how could she possibly start facing into parenthood?

Come on, come on, come on, she willed the thin, plastic stick she was holding with one hand, while mopping cold, clammy, panicky sweat off her forehead with the other.

Be negative. Just be negative. Please, for the love of God, be negative.

Besides, her reasonable mind told her, it really can't be possible. He'd told her a long time ago that he couldn't have kids, something to do with chicken pox he'd had as a kid. Which was the only reason she hadn't bothered with birth control as diligently as she should have been. So barring this was some kind of Immaculate Conception, how in the name of arse could it have happened?

Because men lie, the same nagging voice in her head told her. And gobshites like you are always there to believe them.

She glanced back down to the skinny white stick she was clinging to.

And as soon as the one single word she'd been dreading slowly began to appear, it was as though her whole life suddenly shrivelled in front of her.

Maybe it wouldn't be half as bad as she'd feared, she desperately tried to reason with herself at first. After all, he hadn't had an episode, or one of his 'outbursts', as he referred to them, in a long, long time now. Quite the opposite, in fact; for months, he'd been nothing but contrite, mortified, apologetic even. Had seriously upped the romance in their relationship too, and lately had consistently been surprising her. Being so utterly attentive and caring, it was actually unbelievable. Bringing her home big bunches of ridiculously expensive roses after work, buying bottles of wine to have with dinner, whisking her off for romantic weekends away, just the two of them. Constantly telling her over and over again just how much he loved her, how he'd die without her.

And she really did love him, course she did. Besides, ever since . . . well, ever since his last 'outburst', everything was now completely back to the way it used to be. For the past few, magical months it had all been so romantic and wonderful, like when they'd first got together, years before. So she slowly started to relax, allowing herself to get swept up in it all, falling in love with him all over again.

What happened was just a blip, she'd half-managed to convince herself. Has to have been. Because just look at us now! Love's young dream all over again. Well, in his case, love's middle-aged dream, but still.

Mind you, every time she looked in the mirror, there were reminders staring right back at her. The stitches on her forehead had healed and healed well, as had all the bruising, but then there was still her nose . . . Well, the least said about that, the better. She just had to accept that she was left with it this way and that's all there was to it.

She'd been dreading telling him her news. Mainly because this was exactly the kind of thing that could send him over the edge; that could so easily trigger one of those dangerous, terrifyingly black moods.

So as soon as he got in from work, she decided to get it

over with quickly and cleanly. Made damn sure to do her best to sweeten him up a bit first, though; no harm in a bit of insurance. She handed him a glass of the expensive whiskey he loved and cooked up steak and onions for him, his all-time, desert-island favourite meal.

Then, heart pounding in her chest, she took his hand and forced herself to say the words, the speech she'd been rehearsing so carefully in her head all afternoon. There was a short, stunned silence as her whole future balanced precariously on a knife edge, and she knew as soon as she finished that the next few minutes could change the entire course of her life.

In a heartbeat, he could so easily flare up, might even claim it wasn't his, even though there was absolutely no question about who the child's father was. Worst of all, though, was the very distinct possibility that she could end up back inside an A&E. With another pathetic, transparent story to tell the medics. 'I accidentally fell down the stairs,' or similar. Yet again.

Instead though, a miracle happened and his reaction utterly astonished her. He was absolutely overjoyed, jubilant, got up to swing her round and said in that moment, she'd just made him the happiest man on the planet. Said he always knew the doctors who'd diagnosed his infertility must have got it all wrong. Sure what do doctors know anyway, he'd laughed. He stayed up half the night with her discussing baby names, schools, you name it.

He'd even asked her to marry him.

All she wanted was to run away somewhere and do it quickly and quietly abroad. But nothing would do him only to make as big an occasion as possible out of it. After all, we're only getting married once, he'd told her, so let's go all out. Waste of time, she'd told him spiritedly. Live bands and bridesmaids and stag nights? Sure who'd even bother to come? Mates from the restaurant she was working in? That was a laugh!

He didn't like her working night shifts now. Instead he wanted her home in the evenings when he was there, so he could take care of her properly. This is the only time you and I ever get to be together, he used to say to her, and while on the surface it may have sounded romantic, she knew deep down it was complete rubbish; the two of them were together night in, night out. Weekends, bank holidays, you name it. The only other person either of them really saw was the other one; they were joined at the hip. Like having a social circle of just one other person.

And while she loved him and adored being with him, especially when things were as good as they had been lately, there were still times when she wished she could do normal things with pals her own age. He was thirty-five, but she was only twenty-two, for God's sake. These were the years when she should be out there having fun, she told herself, like any other normal girl her age. But she knew if she did what it would inevitably lead to, so more and more often she just stayed put.

Far easier all round.

These days, she mostly worked early mornings instead of late shifts, and whenever there was a night out or a party happening with her co-workers, she knew far better than to ask him along. And eventually, to even bother going herself. From bitter past experience she knew it just wasn't worth the hassle, the constant questions, the mood swings. Best not to rock the boat, she reasoned. Besides, things were so good between them ninety-nine per cent of the time, weren't they? 'Course they were.

And as for family, who did she have she could possibly invite to her wedding? She had only one person who counted as family, now in a nursing home, miles away. And yes, his parents were alive and well, but relations were strained to put it mildly and he hardly ever saw them. Rarely even spoke about them. Besides, he seldom let her out of his sight these days, which left precious little time over for his family. They spent every spare minute together, until eventually she looked around herself one day and, to her surprise, realised just how isolated she'd become. How scarily dependent she now was on him. And now, in time, how dependent her child would be.

But she'd told Becky her big news about her engagement and about the baby, of course. She'd known Becky for years. They'd shared a foster home when they were just kids. Over the years, they'd lost touch, but found each other again when they ended up staying in the same hostel, trying to get work, trying to scrounge enough cash together to get out of there.

Two heads, they figured, were always going to be better than one, so between them they got work in a fast-food burger bar and worked their way up from there. By putting in for every extra shift that they possibly could, they'd even managed to afford the deposit of a month's rent on their very own flat. Where the pair of them had an absolute ball, working hard, but crucially, playing even harder.

But ever since she'd moved in with him, that had all changed. Becky just didn't like him and never had.

'It kills me to have to tell you this, Jean,' she'd say time and again. 'But I wouldn't be a true pal if I just sat here and kept my trap shut. And I'm sorry, hon, but Joe is just far too controlling for his own good. What's really weird, though, is that you don't even seem able to see it! Does the guy ever give you a single minute to yourself? God, that fella would follow you into the bloody ladies if he could!'

Jean would sit quietly opposite her with her whole face burning, but saying nothing. Knowing deep down that kind-hearted old Becky thought she was only doing the right thing. Even if she didn't really have the first clue about the depths of their relationship. How these days they were now like trees whose roots had slowly become entwined. Utterly inseparable.

'Sorry to bang on about it,' Becky went on, really driving her point home, 'but I just don't like Joe. Never really did. And, yeah, I know you always say you're madly in love and that he treats you like a queen. And of course, after what you and I've been through, it helps that he's not short of a few quid and has a decent place to live. But you're not yourself around him, not your real self, and I just don't think it's right.'

Jean had wanted to get up and stride out the door at that, but forced herself to stay put and listen. Becky means well, she told herself. So just hear the girl out. You've been through so much together, you owe her at least that.

'For God's sake,' Becky went on, 'you're normally so confident and full of fun and messing! You used to be so different, Jeanie. You were easily the wildest person I'd ever known, someone who could stand up for herself and who didn't take any crap from anyone! But around him you turn into this timid little voiceless mouse, this person that I barely even recognise half the time. I'm sorry to have to be the one to say it and I know how serious things are between you, but that's just the way I feel. If I was going out with a complete dickhead, I know you'd have the guts to say it to me.'

And so, inevitably after that conversation, she and Becky had drifted apart, just like she had with all of her other friends. They'd completely given up arranging nights out where Joe would just glare moodily across the table at them and pretty soon, even Becky understandably got fed up with his rudeness down the phone if she chanced to call the flat and he answered.

It was utterly pointless, Jean knew, to ask Becky or any of her work gang to celebrate her engagement to a guy they'd absolutely no time for.

Sad, she thought, to be only twenty-two years old, up the duff and effectively friendless. Made her all the more dependent on him and she was someone who'd been independent her whole life.

Was it a bad sign, she sometimes wondered, that there were times when she'd to remind herself she was in love?

Chapter Twelve

The Chocolate Bar, 6.15 p.m.

Mother of Divine, I can barely get my head around it, but the place is completely thronged! There must easily be a hundred and fifty people, maybe more, all crammed in here like sardines. I cannot *believe* the turnout. This is by far the biggest premises we have and you want to see it right at this moment, there isn't room for a kitten. Even the street tables under a canopy outside are jammers . . . it's AMAZING!

The PR girl we hired for the night is running round the place carrying a clipboard and generally acting like some kind of blow-dried missile in a pair of slingbacks, corralling the social diarists and food bloggers who've come to – we hope – give us a little name-drop and say kind things about us. Social diarists and bloggers, she's been lecturing us all week, wield considerable amounts of clout in this town and therefore must be treated like minor royalty and not be allowed to leave without having incredibly generous goodie bags thrown their way.

Swear though, every time I catch her eye, the PR girl looks nearly ready to ditch the clipboard and burst into a jig of pure joy. Because, after all, it's just an ordinary midweek night, and never in our wildest dreams did we imagine we'd get this kind of a turnout.

This is just unbelievable! It's actually like a bleeding furnace in here now; even the insides of the windows are sweating and I'm sure my carefully applied make-up (well, v. special occasion and all that) is now well and truly dribbled down to somewhere round my collarbone. The launch party officially kicked off at six o'clock and already I can tell that I'll have to re-order stock first thing tomorrow. The goodie bags were snapped up within minutes, one or two cheekier punters even asking if we'd any going spare, and all the complimentary trays of chocolate pyramids we'd dotted around the place as tiny little samplers, were all scoffed approximately fifteen seconds after we opened our doors. Now guests have started buying individual chocolates and the till hasn't stopped ringing all evening.

Lovely, lovely sound; the pinging noise the till makes when it's opening. Don't think I'll ever tire of it.

I catch Sarah's eye, where she's standing over in the corner, chatting up one of our suppliers – a v. good-looking guy of about forty, by the way, who's been the subject of much debate amongst us recently as to whether he's gay, married or straight and single. No wedding ring, but as Sarah says, that means shag all in this day and age.

She sees me looking in her direction and grins broadly back. This branch is gonna work, her eyes seem to be saying. Our biggest risk to date is about to pay off, in spades. Think you might just be right, I try to mouth back at her, but then I'm dragged off in yet another direction to chat to yet another 'highly influential food blogger'. (All the PR speak is starting to rub off on me a bit, too.)

'I think this is going to be a great success for you,' the poor girl has to almost shout at me to be heard over the din.

Wow, think to myself. Because it's a major momentary reality check. Did I ever think the day would come when the word 'success' was uttered in the same breath as my name?

7.00 p.m. on the dot

Speeches. Been dreading this all day and know I won't be able to really relax and get a decent glass of vino into me till the torture is ovah. Tried my level best to get out of it, but our slightly bossy PR girl said not a chance, it's expected that each of us say a few words.

Sarah's up first. Hush descends and all you can hear in the background are passing waiters politely asking guests if they'd like their wine glasses topped up. And as you'd expect, Sarah's completely terrific, cool and competent with efficient cue cards in front of her, a bit like a politician. Name-checks everyone she should, thanks her family for their support, emotional and financial, then moves on to thank each of our investors individually for their faith in us, not to mention their generosity.

As she's chatting, I do a quick scan of the crowd and spot Mum and Dad centre stage, Mum looking as Ann Widdecombe-like as ever in a sensible tweed suit and even more sensible shoes to go along with her sensible hair. But then my mother, bless her, went blithely into the frump-osphere aged around fifty and pretty much decided to stay there. She catches my eye and I wave over to her, then she nudges a woman beside her and stage-whispers, 'Yes! That's her standing right over there, that's my daughter, you know. The co-owner!'

Yet another massive reality check. Mum actually, actually, actually being proud enough to lay claim to me in public!

Dad's beside her, taking photos on the camera I bought him for his last birthday and looking fit to burst with excitement. He gives me a big, confident thumbs up and I wave back at him. It's a lovely, lovely moment that I want to savour, just so I can relive it later on.

Sarah's still chatting confidently away into the microphone in front of her, so I scan the crowd yet again.

But no sign of The Man yet. Which is odd.

Because he's always on time, he's the punctual one out of the two of us; if left to me, we'd never have a snowball's chance of making a dinner reservation in time. On a v. rare date night (and believe me, in this weather, it's once in a blue moon that the two of us actually get to go out at all) I'm usually so tired, I'm incapable of even organising myself to leave my flat and arrive at the restaurant in time. Drives him nuts, he says, though he always says it lightly, jokingly.

I get a momentary surge of disappointment that he's not here for our big launch, which quickly turns into worry. Which escalates at the speed of light into full-blown panic.

Maybe something happened to him in work? Something major that delayed him? But then if that's the case, why didn't he just call me to say so? And then supposing something even worse happened to him, like he was involved in some kind of horrific accident on his way here? And is now lying unconscious on a stretcher in an A&E somewhere, unable to even get a message to me?

But then that's something my own personal history has left me scarred by. These days, whenever someone is even a tiny bit late to meet me or doesn't phone when they say they will, I automatically assume the very worst.

There you go, two years on and the legacy left behind by Kitty Hope still has the power to reach out and clutch me by the throat.

Sorry, I meant to say Jean. Keep forgetting.

Weird, though. That's the second time today that her ghost has resurrected itself. Strange.

Of course he's not lying in an A&E, I tell myself. But then, I'm invariably my own worst enemy when it comes to The Man, and immediately start doing my own personal Olympic sport: jumping to extreme conclusions. And then of course, all the self-doubting kicks in . . .

If he's a no-show tonight, then he's definitely not interested . . . I just misread all the signs, that's all . . . Whole thing is just a big non-starter . . . And, by the way, I was a roaring eejit to ever have thought someone like him would ever be interested in me anyhow! Didn't I, deep down? 'Course I did. Always felt I was seriously punching above my weight with him and now here's the proof . . . staring me slap, bang in the face . . .

Suddenly, I'm aware there's expectant silence all round and now all eyes seem to be focused on me.

'Ladies and gentlemen,' Sarah is saying, game-show-host style, 'let me proudly introduce the single best reason why The Chocolate Bar is the success story it's been . . . my amazingly wonderful friend, the one and only Miss Angie Blennerhasset!'

Oh shit, anyway. Time for my shagging speech.

Thunderous applause as I stumble my way in slightly too-high heels to makeshift podium where a v. scary-looking microphone waits for me. Everyone's now focused up this way. A terrifying moment. I'm suddenly aware of cameras flashing in my face, and everyone staring expectantly up at me. So I begin hesitatingly, not unlike Colin Firth in *The King's Speech*, eyes darting towards the door in case The Man turns up late. Which would be marginally better than him not turning up at all, but still.

'Ladies and gentlemen,' I say into a microphone that whistles bit gratingly every time I breathe into it. It made Sarah sound like an authoritative politician; makes me sound like a toothless hag of about seventy. 'Thanks so much for coming along and . . . em . . .'

I break off a bit here, suddenly hit by a bout of nerves.

Make a joke, my subconscious mind screeches at me. Just make them laugh, say something, say any shagging thing, but for God's sake do something to fill the dead air . . .

'Well . . . em . . . I hope you all enjoyed the free chocolate?'

Mumbles and murmurs of grateful appreciation all round and I have to wait a while before there's hush again.

'Look . . . the thing is . . . well, let me put it to you this way.'

I take a deep breath here and somehow try to find my way. Something The Man once said suddenly comes back to me. If you've got something to say in public, he told me, then it's always best just to speak straight from the heart.

Right then, from the heart. Here goes.

'Can I just say that two years ago,' I begin falteringly, 'I was on the dole, living at home with my poor, long-suffering parents, with not a bean to my name and about as much chance of getting a proper, paying job as I had of winning the Lotto jackpot. And then . . .'

I'm about to say '. . . and then Sarah O'Reilly bounced up to me, waved her magic wand and somehow managed to change my whole life around,' but just at that moment, I spot him.

Yes, I think jubilantly, he *is* here after all! The Man's actually here! Not only that, but he's been here all along, by the looks of him! I must have just been so busy running around like a blue-arsed fly that somehow I hadn't spotted him through the throng.

He's standing over by our cabinet display, looking, no other word for it, just *beautiful.* Tall, dark and classically handsome, lightly tanned from the fabulous Indian summer we've been having, and still in his work suit. Carrying a massive, oversized bunch of pink stargazer lilies, my all-time favourite flower, bless him.

As ever, just seeing him, actually here for me, to support me, almost takes my breath away. I could v. happily stand here staring at him all day. The guy really is that extraordinary-looking. Like a Greek God with a Roman Emperor profile, and yet by a country mile the kindest, most caring, unassuming soul I know. I almost go a bit weak-kneed, like some pathetic, teenage One Direction groupie whenever I see him. Can't help it. He's that much out of my league, it's unbelievable.

But it's only been six months, I tell myself. Stop mentally planning the wedding, Angie! Early, early days!

And yet here he is and he's here for me. Even though I've been so busy, I never even noticed him arriving. With *flowers.* For me. When's the last time a man actually went and bought flowers for me? Can't even begin to answer that one.

Just the sight of him somehow gives me the confidence

to propel me through the rest of the speech. Suddenly words start to foam at my mouth and, with renewed vitality, I tell the room that once Sarah and I teamed up as a partnership, I never saw the inside of a dole office again. I even touch wood as I'm saying it, which gets a big laugh.

I tell everyone that even in this crappy economy, where every single day seems to bring yet another bad news story, miracles can and do still happen. Because isn't our story the proof? I say that if someone like me can get off the dole and actually make a success of a small start-up with absolutely no experience whatsoever, then anyone can. I tell them all that when we first started out, I knew next to nothing about the world of business, unless watching *Dragon's Den* and *The Apprentice* counted. I tell them that two short years ago, I used to use the business section of the papers at home to line the cat's litter tray. More laughter at that. Then I tell the room that all you need to succeed in a business like ours are two essential ingredients. A partner exactly like Sarah – calm, level-headed ying to my panicky, insecure yang – and a lifelong love of all things chocolate-related. Once you've those locked in place, I say to the whole room, then the sky really is the limit.

I wrap it up by thanking everyone, Academy Award style, from investors and suppliers to family, friends and well-wishers. Then, in a wobbly voice, I turn to find Sarah, who's in the front row, looking like she's trying v. hard not to tear up.

'Thank you for being you,' I tell her sincerely. 'Thank you for your extraordinary drive and ambition and for encouraging me everyday to go that bit further. Sarah O'Reilly, I'd run a mile in my highest heels for you, I'd give you my last handmade chocolate . . . and if you were a fella, I'd probably marry you!'

There's a big laugh at that and a v. generous round of applause, so I decide to quit while I'm ahead. And as the clapping shows no signs of slowing down, I look over at The Man, who's looking intently back up at me.

Thank you, I mouth silently at him and he winks back at me. Couldn't even bring myself to name-check him in my speech; I knew I just wouldn't have the self-control not to end up looking like an overflowing water feature. So I just content myself with gazing at him, in all his gorgeousness instead.

Thank you for being the reason I can get out of bed these mornings, I say silently across the room to him. Thank you for being my best friend.

I swear it's as if he understands me. He grins back up at me, proudly. And I don't need to be able to lip read to know what exactly what he's mouthing back at me.

Thank you for bringing me back to life.

7.44 p.m.

Finally, finally, finally the crowd clears enough for me to make my way over to The Man. He's been chatting to a group of people that I don't know, but breaks away when he sees me coming and smiles warmly.

'Congratulations,' he twinkles down at me, 'these are for you.'

I blush a bit as I take the massive bouquet of lilies from him.

'Thank you, they're absolutely stunning,' is all I can manage to say back.

'Your speech was great, by the way. Well done.'

'I . . . well . . . I wanted to thank you as well, that is, I tried my best to, but I ended up just stumbling . . .'

'Hey, now, none of that! I thought you did brilliantly. I know how petrified you were about it but to see you up there, you'd never have thought so. Not a nerve in your body. Like you've been doing this your whole life. And as for Sarah, it genuinely wouldn't surprise me if that girl ended up in politics someday. She was born to run a small country, she really was.'

So touched he said that. I look gratefully up at him, wishing he'd kiss me or that I'd the guts to kiss him in front of all these people, but I know it won't happen. Funny, he can be so affectionate whenever we're alone together, but never in public. Shame really. I mean, I wasn't exactly looking for him to swing me up in his arms in front of everyone, sweep the counter display to the ground and roughly throw me across it for a passionate clinch, but a little, minor bit of hand holding would just be so lovely, tonight of all nights.

That's all. I'm only saying.

'So how does it feel,' he smiles down at me, 'to be a successful business owner? Two Chocolate Bars under your belt already and both set to go from strength to strength?'

'It's . . . well, it's hard to get my head around,' I tell him. 'All down to Sarah, though. You know what a tornado of efficiency she is—'

'Credit where it's due,' he interrupts me gently. 'Remember, you're a team. None of this would work without equal input from both of you.'

I beam proudly back at him. Then think, oh sod this anyway, I don't care if he's not demonstrative in public, shag it anyway, I am, and if I want to kiss him, then why can't I? We seem to get feck all alone time together these days with all the mental hours I've been working, so can't we act like a proper couple, just this once? I run my hand playfully up and down the lapel of his jacket and he doesn't pull away. Then I'm just about to lean in closer to him, when a voice from behind stops me.

'Very crowded, isn't it? And this is only Prosecco they're serving, not actual champagne. Just so you know.'

O-kaaaay. Only one person I know speaks in that affected, pseudo-West Brit accent that used to grate on my nerves so much, but now makes me want to laugh. Funny, the confidence a small bit of success gives you. I turn round to see my sister, Madeline, with her mouth pursed into a v. irritated-looking cat's bum shape, playing with her iPhone and looking like it's anathema to her to even have to make appearance. The only person here who I actually noticed refusing a free chocolate goodie bag earlier, lest she gain a couple of ounces in weight. And I know right well she's only here in the first place under strict instructions from the parents; otherwise it would physically choke her to stand by and watch the one-time loser kid sister she loved nothing better than lording it over, now actually making something of herself

'Yes, it's certainly crowded all right,' I smile sweetly back at her. 'But then, it is a *launch* party, Madeline. The general idea is to get as many people in as possible.'

'Aren't you going to introduce me?' she says, indicating The Man, who's looking at her with that dangerous, dark glint he gets in his eyes, which I know means that he's on the verge of smirking. Right then, only one thing for it: get it over with and out of the way as quickly as possible.

I mutter my way through introductions and am just about to drag The Man away from any further Blennerhasset torture, when Madeline stops me in my tracks.

'I'm sorry,' she's saying to The Man. 'It's so noisy in here, I didn't quite catch your name. What was it again?'

The Man smiles easily, confidently.

'Oh, didn't you?' he says. 'It's Simon, actually. Simon Ashby.'

Chapter Thirteen

1.30 a.m.

So here we are, Simon and me, in his car after the launch party, the dinner after the launch party and the drinks that followed on after that again. It's stupid o'clock and I'm a bit drunk after one too many glasses of pretty much whatever floated on a tray past me. Had to, tension reliever. In fact, I was so nervy before the do, I think I'd happily have drunk car battery acid if I'd thought it might calm me down.

Now normally, whenever it's just me and Simon alone, there's always an easy, comfortable silence between us. The kind of air-time that you never feel the need to fill, not when you're with your best mate. But for some reason, instead of having to be scraped off the ceiling from the high of how well the whole night went, I'm just the teeniest bit on edge, now that it's just the two of us and the night is finally over. Just wondering how the whole romance boyfriend/girlfriend bit will all play out at this, the final furlong of the evening.

I've been so busy getting ready for the launch, and in putting finishing touches to our Dame Street shop, that he and I have hardly had any alone time together at all recently, let alone a date night. And even if we ever do manage to meet up, even for a quick drink, then chances are he'll drop me straight home then head on back to his own house.

Or should I say, Kitty's house, because . . . yes, two years on and he's still living there. But whatever we do, as Sarah says, we won't mention the war. For God's sake, none of us are even at the stage when we can start referring to her as Jean yet, let alone tackle him on that one.

Fact is, though, Simon refused point-blank to leave Kitty's house and when the lease was up, just automatically renewed it with the landlord. I told him v. forcefully at the time that I didn't feel it was healthy for him, that as long as he continued on there, he was still living in the past, but he was having absolutely none of it. Just shrugged his shoulders at me and said that he 'still wasn't ready to leave'. 'Course I've tried on countless occasions since to change his mind, as have Sarah, Jeff and all of his own mates too, but you know how stubborn fellas can be with their heels dug in.

'Place just suits me,' he'll shrug, then wax on about how close it is to his office, how handy for town, blah-di-blah.

So I just have to continually bite my tongue, while never actually saying anything.

The whole thing just seems so wrong to me, though. Feels completely arseways, in fact. A bit like the guy has chosen to perpetually live with a ghost.

It goes without saying that I can't stay over in that house at all, ever since he and I got together. Can't even bring myself to call over there to see him, like I used to, back in the day. V. hard to describe, but somehow it's as if Kitty's still there, in every single room, in the pores of the walls, even. I swear I can feel her presence surrounding me and looking down on me all the time.

I never felt like this going there before, but in the past few months it's like every time I open a cupboard and see her favourite jacket hanging there, or else the flowery wellies she used to wear in the rain, I get an instant pang of guilt that feels exactly like chronic indigestion. As if she's watching me and Simon too, watching us together, seeing everything unfold under her nose. Just like in *Rebecca,* except she's very much alive and living a whole new life somewhere on this planet.

Indescribably weird.

Mind you, the place is a helluva lot tidier now than it ever was when Kitty lived here, but, that aside, her things are still exactly where she left them the day she vanished. Or more correctly, the day she walked out. Simon not only won't touch a thing, but refuses to let anyone else either. Kind-hearted Mrs Butterly from next door even offered to shift some of her old clothes to the Oxfam shop on Camden Street, but he wouldn't hear of it.

So now all of Kitty's clothes still hang in the wardrobe, exactly where they've always been. Her cosmetics and face creams and hangover tablets are all still in the bathroom cabinet. Even a stack of her books and CDs are all still in the spare room, waiting for her. Like she's about to turn the key in the door and stroll in any minute, saying, 'Oh, hi, everyone. Jeez, was I really gone that long?'

You never know, he keeps telling me, one day she could be back for it. Like he's still clinging to that frail little wisp of hope, even though he knows it's useless to. Even though I've pointed out to him on countless occasions the complete and utter insanity of what he's saying. Because whatever corner of the globe Kitty's in right now – and the last trace we had on her was in Morocco, of all places – one thing is certain. Given what we now know about her, that girl ain't waltzing back into our lives, not ever.

Sorry, I meant to say Jean. It's v. difficult to keep remembering, though; to me she always was and will be Kitty Hope.

Anyway, I just can't hack being in that house with her ghost hovering around any more. God knows, it was hard enough when we first found out the truth about her, but it's next to impossible now. Every time I even walk down the street where she lived, past her neighbours, who all did so much to try to help find her, I almost start palpitating. Got to the stage where I was even getting antsy just phoning Simon there. I swear I could almost see Kitty's hazel eyes flashing at me and hear her voice reverberating round my head.

'This is your idea of looking after him for me? You couldn't get a man of your own, so you went and nabbed mine, when I was out of the way? What kind of a best friend are you anyway?'

And yes, I'm fully aware of the irony of her saying that to me, after what she put us all through. Completely ridiculous, I know. It's like I'm somehow cheating behind a former friend's back, even though that friend was a person who never really existed.

Beyond weird.

So when I first started renting my own flat a few months back, I confidently thought I'd safely lay that problem to rest. In all my gobshite-ery, I genuinely figured that now Simon and I would have somewhere neutral to hang out in, somewhere free from painful memories at every turn.

It's a gorgeous little flat, too, in the newly kitted-out Granary Building on Cow's Lane, right in the heart of Temple Bar and only a stone's throw from our Dame Street Branch. (LOVE using that word! I'm now using it every chance I get! Branch, branch, branch, we're a business with actually proper *branches* . . .) Plus it means I can stroll to work and open up first thing every morning. Dirt-cheap rent, too, and I was blessed to land it at all, given the huge demand for city-centre rentals.

I really had high hopes that Simon would love it as much as I did, because it's absolutely everything that Kitty's house isn't. Hers is a typical Corpo house, old and showing its age more and more every year, with all the problems you get with old houses that aren't meticulously maintained.

Whereas my new little flat in the Granary is the total exact opposite: light, modern, spacious, airy, with central heating that actually works and a north-facing bedroom that was deliciously cool in the summer heatwave we just had. As if that wasn't enough of a carrot to dangle in front of Simon, the flat also has fairly sizeable balcony on the third floor, that looks out right over Temple Bar, down onto all the buzz that's happening underneath.

And believe me, in Temple Bar there's *always* a buzz. Twenty-four seven, a bit like a mini city-within-a-city-that-never-sleeps. On my street alone, there are two theatres, countless bars and God knows how many pop-up restaurants that seem to sprout like mushrooms. Always busy, always bustling and packed out round here, even on week nights. Amazing to see; really lifts the spirits. As if by some weird osmosis, it's somehow possible to pick up on all the youth and energy and messing and craic that's going on, just a few floors down beneath you.

Sure, admittedly, it can get a bit noisy late at night when the heavy boozers start falling out of the pubs underneath and screeching words like 'waaaaankeeeeeeeer!' at each other. Plus, I've frequently walked home late at night after work to find a naked man chained and handcuffed to the lamppost beside my apartment block, who'll politely claim that he's absolutely grand, thanks, just on a bender of a stag night, but that he's confident his mates will be back to free him up v. soon.

Apart from that, though, it's a fab place to live. Boy heaven, I thought when I first viewed it and snapped it up instantly. It even has giant flatscreen, for feck's sake! But of course, back then, I naïvely thought Simon would love it here as much as I did. That I could gradually wean him away from Kitty's house and introduce him to delights of living in a lovely, modern ghost-free home. Bit by bit, I thought. It's a slow, step-by-step process.

But no, nothing doing, at least not yet. Oh, sure, he'll come back here with me, have dinner, watch TV, have a perfectly pleasant, quiet evening in. But then Cinderella-like, come the wee small hours, he'll scarper off and retreat back to his lair.

It's hugely frustrating and after six full months of it, I'm starting to get a teeny bit worried. But then, as Sarah wisely points out, we've only been together a few months, it's early days and we're still v. much finding our way round each other, as a couple who crossed over the best friends line.

Awkward, icky days.

Fact is, though, ever since I moved in here, he's stayed over a grand total of *three* times (not that I'm counting or anything). And, by the way, I use the term 'stayed over' v. loosely; we went to bed all right, but he has yet to actually stay the night and still be here when I wake up next morning.

'Should really get home,' he'll invariably say, 'work tomorrow, need to get a clean shirt, etc.' Even at weekends, always the same shagging story.

'But it's Saturday!' I told him once, trying to hide my bitter disappointment.

'Yeah, I know,' he told me, fumbling in the dark to get dressed, 'but I just wouldn't mind waking up in my own bed, you know how it is.'

And I nod and smile through my teeth and tell him it's fine, but in truth, I'm lying. It's not one bit fine at all. Feck's sake, we're meant to be in first flush of lurve here! These are supposed to be the idyllic months when it's all sex and talking and laughing and dates and romance, aren't they? Before reality sets in and we get to the stage of rowing over whose turn it is to put the bins out and unclog hairs from shower tray.

And I know I'm v., v. lucky to have such a loving, caring, ridiculously kind, generous man in my life. Not to mention a guy who's so out-of-my-league good-looking. I'm constantly hearing all my customers' horror stories about life at the dating coalface and I'm all too well aware of how rare it is to have a man who I'm so completely compatible with on every level.

But still. Somehow, I can't help feeling slight bit cheated. Whatever way you look at it, it's a tad demoralising to think that your brand-new boyfriend would rather be with a ghost than with a real, live, three-dimensional person. We're just like best friends who just happen to sleep together every so often. Friends with benefits, if you will.

And even that's a major source of deep concern for me,

as I'm constantly wondering if he's looking at my wobbly bits and comparing them with Kitty's lithe, toned, perfect body. Best you can say about me in the nip is that I'm plus-sized and healthy-looking. Botticelli-esque, as my gym-obsessed buddy Jeff v. kindly describes me. Not that I'm suffering from body-image issues, but the fact remains I'm a good, sturdy 34FF, which just to put in context, is same size Jordan was *before* her breast reduction. And believe me, it's no fun, constantly comparing myself to Kitty, who was beautiful and built like a sparrow, and wondering if Simon's unconsciously doing exactly the same thing every time he has to look at my lardy bits.

Not easy, competing with anyone's ex, but when the ex in question might as well be a bloody poltergeist – and a skinny one at that – it's no joke, take it from me.

Early days, Angie. Tread softly . . .

And now here the two of us are, parked not far from my apartment block and on our way up there 'just for a little nightcap'. I'm linking onto him, hobbling along in my ridiculously high heels on the cobblestones, still clinging to the stunning bouquet he gave me earlier. But after all the chat and the sheer mentalness of tonight, we've both gone quiet now. We arrive at the door of the Granary Building, then get the lift up to the third floor, where my flat is. I unlock the front door, we head inside and he collapses exhaustedly down in the sofa, loosening his tie and kicking his shoes off.

I find myself staring at him, just wanting to admire him in all his sexiness. Even at this hour of the night, even though he's as wrecked as I am, even though he's still in his work suit, he still manages to look so shaggable and handsome and – sorry, but there really are no other words to describe him – just gob-smackingly beautiful.

Oh feck this, I can't resist for one more minute. I shoehorn myself out of unforgiving heels that have been at me ever since I put them on earlier this evening, bounce down beside him on the sofa, snuggle into him and lightly kiss the tip of his nose.

'Thank you,' I whisper, a bit drunkenly.

'What for?' he smiles.

'For being there tonight. For braving the Blennerhassets out in force. For the beautiful flowers. For everything.'

'Hey, it was your night; 'course I was going to be there to support you.'

He slips his arm round my shoulder now, so I move onto kissing his cheek, pressing myself up against him, loving the feel of how hard and taut his body feels beside me. Wishing he'd just kiss me back. Kiss me properly.

'Tell you what,' I murmur in what I hope is a seductive-sounding voice, 'I've a lovely bottle of Merlot in the kitchen, how about we take a glass each into the bedroom with us?'

'Erm . . . look, Ange, would it be a hassle for you if I just had a coffee?' he asks, pulling away from me just slightly, so slightly anyone else would hardly even notice. But I do. 'It's just I've a meeting early in the morning and . . . well, you know yourself.'

Take it easy, Angie, don't overreact and remember, early days . . .

'No problem,' I tell him, a bit disappointedly, sitting up straight now. I even manage to stretch a smile tautly across my face as I say it. But then as I'm fast learning, 'you know yourself' = Simon's polite code words for 'which is why I won't be staying the night here tonight'.

No, he'd rather sleep the night back in Kitty's house with a ghost.

And I hate the thoughts of bringing it up, particularly not tonight, which is meant to be a celebration, but I'm also aware I still haven't told him about what happened at the interview earlier today.

Didn't want to have to invoke that particular ghost, tonight of all nights, but I know deep down that I have to. I'm physically incapable of keeping secrets from Simon. Apart from anything else, it only gives me heartburn. Only reason I haven't said anything up till now, is that with everything else that's been going on this evening, I just never got the chance to mention it.

But Simon and I have one hard-and-fast rule in this. Absolutely no keeping anything from each other. We've both had enough secrets unwittingly kept from us in the past to ever want to go there again. So we just don't. Simple as.

I get up to organise coffee and late-night snacks as he picks up yesterday's paper that's still lying on my sofa, and idly starts to flick through it.

'By the way,' I tell him over my shoulder on my way into the kitchen, faux-casually. 'I forgot to tell you how the interview with the *Post* went earlier.'

'Oh, yeah, that was this morning, wasn't it?' he calls back in to me as I click on the fancy espresso maker Sarah gave me last Christmas and let it bubble to life.

'Yup, in the Westbury.'

'So how did it go?'

Momentarily, I stop fishing round the back of my tiny kitchen cupboard for clean mugs and come back into the living room, where he's still glancing through the paper.

On second thoughts, I think I'd rather be face-to-face with him for this.

'You want to hear the good part or the bad part?'

He looks up from the paper at me now as I perch on the edge of the sofa beside him.

'Good part first.'

'Good part is that we should get a fair bit of publicity out of it.'

'Come on, Ange, that's better than good,' he grins. 'That alone is worth its weight in gold these days. So what was the bad part?'

'Bad part was that I left there with a really sick feeling in the pit of my stomach.'

He's looking right at me now, the dark green eyes focused in that intense way that he has.

'What happened? Journalist give you a hard time?'

'No, no, nothing like that. The journalist was really lovely . . .'

'What then?'

'Well . . . she started asking all sorts of questions that I just wasn't prepared for.'

'It sounds to me like you've absolutely nothing to worry about,' he says, stretching his long legs out in front of him and stifling a yawn. 'It can't have been as bad as you think. That's what journalists do, after all. Main thing is that it's a big plug for The Chocolate Bar. Isn't that the only reason you agreed to do it in the first place?'

'No, I mean she started asking *personal* questions. Really personal stuff.'

'But that's just journos for you. They want to really get a decent angle on you. All perfectly normal. The woman was only doing her job. I wouldn't let it get to you. '

'Simon, you don't get it. This one had done all her Googling and . . . well, she wanted to know about Kitty.'

And now there's silence while he digests this.

I study him closely, but it's v. hard to get a read on his face.

'So what did you tell her?' he eventually asks.

'I didn't. I just faffed around a bit, then Sarah thankfully took over and changed the subject.'

Now he's up and on his feet, coming round to where I'm standing by the sofa's edge.

'Come here to me,' he says softly, and I do, folding myself in his arms, as ever, loving the deep, musky smell of him. He presses my head against his chest and we stay like that just for a moment.

'Tell me the truth. Did you get upset when she brought up Kitty's name?' he asks, tilting my chin up to him and looking down at me.

'No,' I tell him, 'it was just . . . a bit of a shock, that's all. I mean, can you imagine how it felt when this complete stranger, who seemed to know all about what had happened, just started asking out of nowhere why the case was closed now? It just . . . it suddenly brought it all back to me, I suppose, that's all.'

'I know, I know it did,' he murmurs, pulling me tightly into him again.

I run my hands up his chest and snuggle into him, thinking: don't move, please don't move. Not sure about you, but I could stay like this for ever.

'You wouldn't be human if something like that didn't get to you,' he says softly. 'But you have to try to let it go. OK?'

'OK,' I mumble into his shirt.

Just then the bubbling sound from the espresso maker starts getting louder and he pulls away from me.

'Come on, Ange,' he says, 'you've had a long day. Here,

let me get the coffee, then I want you to relax and try to put the whole thing out of your head. You're just overwrought with all the pressure you've been dealing with, and that journalist caught you off guard. That's all. OK? Trust me.'

I nod and smile, suddenly aware of just how much I've had to drink and just how bone-tired I really am, now that all the adrenaline of the day has finally worn off. Honestly, I think I could sleep for two weeks straight. So I haul myself back to the sofa and sink comfortably down into it.

'Do you fancy a cheese toastie?' Simon calls out to me from the kitchen.

'Ha! Is that some kind of trick question?' I shout back at him, perked up a tiny bit at the thoughts of food to come. 'When have you ever known me to refuse a cheese toastie? With a big mound of brown sauce on it, please!'

(My own personal theory is that there is no savoury dish on earth that can't be improved by the addition of Chef HP BBQ Sauce.)

'Sit back and relax, it's coming up!'

He's dead right, I tell myself, smiling and stretching out on the cream linen sofa, trying my best to blank out the interview earlier and the very mention of Kitty's name, which can sometimes feel exactly like a cold, icy hand landing on my shoulder. I'm just exhausted, that's all, and that journalist knocked me off kilter, nothing more.

Then suddenly I realise . . . it's been so, so long since Kitty's name cropped up, but that's already the second time today I've ended up talking about her; once at the interview and just now with Simon.

And it's not that I'm superstitious or anything, but they do say these things go in threes.

Oh, would you just listen to yourself, I think, doing my best to snap out of it. This is why they say forget the past, and just concentrate on the here and now. Besides, that guy in the kitchen currently rustling up supper for the two of us is the single best thing to come out of all the drama and heartache Kitty put us through two long years ago. I'm the luckiest woman alive to have such a gorgeous, caring man in my life who'll make me a mug of coffee and a cheese toastie when I'm feeling a bit wobbly after a long day. And yes, I do realise just how blessed I am to have him. What a catch he is. And then I have barefaced cheek to moan just because he won't stay over with me at night?

'Where's the barbecue sauce?' Simon calls out to me, and I know I should get up off my lazy arse and get it myself, though I'm far too wiped out to move a muscle. I spend all day in work running round after everyone else and now I'm enjoying the rare experience of being waited on hand and foot.

'Try the bottom shelf in the fridge,' I yell back at him.

'Have it!'

I can hear him clattering away in the kitchen so I make to clear a space on the coffee table in front of me for the grub. Then I pick up the paper he left lying on the sofa beside me. Yesterday's; never even got a chance to open it. I have a quick flick through while he's still clattering around in the background. The news appears to be . . . Well, that there's no news really.

Kim Kardashian attends a concert wearing a dental floss dress shocker. Yet more bad news about the Euro crisis, which by now feels like it's been going on for approximately a decade at this stage.

Just to pass time, I flick idly down through it to the TV listings page, in case there's a late-night movie we can snuggle up to on the sofa together, (hope momentarily triumphing over experience).

But just then, almost completely by accident, my eye falls on the very back page. The last place I'd ever normally turn to: the death notices.

It's just about the tiniest column you'd ever see; a complete fluke my eye even fell on it at all.

I blink, in case I misread. Read it again. And again.

No, no mistake then. There it is, right in front of me.

KENNEDY, Kathleen, (née McColgan.) At St Patrick's Marymount Hospice, Co. Cork. Formerly of Foxborough House care home, Co. Limerick. 25 September. (Peacefully, in her sleep.) Dearly beloved wife of the late James Kennedy, sister of the late Paddy McColgan and foster mother to Jean Simpson. She will be sadly missed by all her loving friends and staff at Marymount.

Memorial service Monday 29 September at midday. Rocky Island Crematorium, Ringaskiddy, Co. Cork. No flowers, please.

I try to call out to Simon, but my voice won't make a sound.

You see? Always knew these things came in threes.

Chapter Fourteen

29 September, 6.30 a.m.

Simon and I are in total agreement. We're going. Together. To the funeral. All the way down in the bowels of deepest Cork. It's absolutely the right thing to do, no question. God knows, I did little enough for poor Mrs K. over the past two years (I was so busy with work, I barely had time to see own family, never mind Kitty's), but Simon's a far better all-round human being than I am any day.

Not that I'm saying he went down to visit her every other weekend, nothing like that, but once every so often he'd just disappear off the radar on me, not answering calls for a full day, that sort of thing. 'Course I'd instantly spiral off into a tailspin of worry, but then given my history of loved ones taking off on me, it's all perfectly understandable. Then when he'd materialise again, he'd just shrug at me and say that on impulse, he'd hopped into his car and driven all the way down to Foxborough to check in on her.

It got to the stage where I'd know without his even having to say anything. I'd just *know.*

There's only one thing I don't get, I told him repeatedly

till it must have sounded like I was nagging the guy for doing nothing more than being a kind-hearted person. Why all the secrecy? Why not just tell me what you're up to in the first place? It would save me all the bother of worrying, when you just take off without saying anything to me. I don't get it; we tell each other everything else, anyway. So why keep this to yourself?

And then, the blindingly obvious eventually hit me. It's just another way for him to somehow keep Kitty's memory alive. Bit like the eternal flame you see flickering away at JFK's grave. Mrs K. is the last link with Kitty and I suppose that by keeping in contact with her nursing home and checking in on her every so often, he was, in small way, clinging to another porous little wisp of hope. That if Kitty were ever to come back, Foxborough would doubtless be her first port of call.

But a bit like him still living in her house, it gradually became something we just stopped talking about after a while. Pointless to. As Sarah wisely points out, you know what fellas are once they've got both heels firmly dug in.

Anyway, this carry-on kept up for a good year and a bit, but then a few months ago, at around the same time Simon and I first got together, all changed. Mrs K.'s condition suddenly worsened and she was moved to a hospice down in Youghal, Co. Cork. An excruciatingly long drive from Dublin, it would take you half the day just to get there. So, not as easy for Simon just to bounce into his car and take off on a whim. But every so often though, he'd make a point of phoning the hospice, just checking in on Mrs K., asking after her, that kind of thing.

Which was as it should be; absolutely the right and proper thing to do.

Like I say, though, the only niggling thing that ever got to me was all the bloody secrecy attached. For instance, I'd walk into a room and he'd abruptly hang up phone, then look shiftily at me, and again, I'd just know without being told. Got so I could smell it.

'How's Mrs K. doing then?' I'd ask gently. Rarely getting more than a monosyllabic answer.

'Same,' he'd shrug, before leaving the room.

It's his very last link with Kitty, I'd remind myself. And he ain't about to sever it anytime soon. Best I can do is accept it and learn to live with fact that Kitty is never too far from his thoughts.

Which, come to think about it, makes me bit like second Mrs de Winter in *Rebecca*, minus all the psychological bullying from Mrs Danvers.

The character that's so boring, no one even bothers with her Christian name.

Simon's car, on the v., v., v. long road to Rocky Island. Not having had the time to eat any brekkie. 8.15 a.m.

Simon's worryingly silent for most of the journey. Not a brooding, intense silence, more like the guy's just lost in thought and completely miles away. Every now and then, I reach out to squeeze his hand like the supportive girlfriend I'm trying v. hard to be.

He doesn't exactly pull away, but doesn't take my hand either.

God knows where. (All I can see is motorway, a Statoil garage with Spar attached and a load of plastic bags fluttering past in the breeze.) 9.25 a.m.

Quick petrol pit stop. Haven't first clue where we are, or how far we've got to go. And my bum's actually like a bag of spanners from sitting so long. As Simon's filling the tank, I run into the garage to buy us two take-out coffees and a bagful of rubbery Danish pastries. 'Course the coffee is vile, watery and tasteless. This shower have some bloody cheek, I think furiously. They should be done under the Trade Descriptions Act for having the barefaced neck to try and pass this tepid dishwater off as latte! It's not even in same *league* as the coffee we serve at The Chocolate Bar, but I digress.

(Sorry. Working in on the go snack trade has given me a v. competitive edge. Note to self, STOP.)

Back inside the car, I hand Simon over what passes for coffee.

'For you.'

'Lovely, thanks,' he says, gratefully taking it from me.

'You fancy a Danish?'

'How are they?'

'Plasticky. Total crap.'

'Might pass in that case. But thanks anyway.'

Having finally opened up a conversation of sorts, I decide to go for it.

'So . . . em . . . how are you holding up?' I ask tentatively.

'Oh . . . you know.'

Jesus. It's like pulling teeth. No, in fact, it's more like trying to pull a train uphill with my teeth.

Also, hard as it is to believe, these are the first few words we've exchanged since leaving Dublin. If you could even classify the above as him actually speaking to me.

10.44 a.m.

OK, I've officially had enough! This is it; break point. I can't take one more second of all this brooding, intense silence. It's *seriously* starting to get in on me now. On the grounds that I've a fairly good idea what's going through his mind, I decide that a quick, pre-emptive strike is the only course of action open to me.

'Simon?' I tentatively say after another excruciatingly long-drawn-out silence, worthy of a Pinter play.

'Mmm?' he says, absently. Totally focused on the road ahead.

'You do know what you're thinking about is pointless, don't you?'

'Why? What am I thinking?'

'About trying to kick start the whole search for Kitty again,' I suddenly blurt out, in spite of myself. 'To tell her about Mrs K., I mean. I know it's on your mind, so let's just bring it out into the open.'

Jeez, it's actually a relief to finally talk about the elephant sitting in the back of car with us.

'I'm right, aren't I?' I ask him gently.

'Yeah, yeah, you're right,' he sighs. Eventually.

'It's just . . . well, I don't think I could handle seeing you go through all of that again. And I can tell you, I certainly wouldn't be up to it. Simon, you and I did absolutely everything, for God's sake; we even hired a private detective, just to see if we could somehow find out what corner of the world she was holed up in . . .'

'I know,' he nods tersely, eyes trained on the road ahead. 'I already know all of this.'

'. . . And still, we got absolutely nowhere.'

'Please, Angie. You don't need to remind me.'

'Look, all I'm saying is, don't do this to yourself. We've agreed that what's done is done, it's all in the past and it's time to move on. So can't we just get to the funeral, mourn the woman and look on today as the final bit of closure that we both need? That's all I'm asking.'

He doesn't answer me, though. Just stares straight ahead like an angry taxi driver whose last fare never tipped. Then kicks the car up a gear and starts driving even faster.

Almost as if he can't wait to get there.

Rocky Island Crematorium, Ringaskiddy, Co. Cork, 11.50 a.m.

We arrive a bit early. Rocky Island Crematorium turns out to be impressively new and a pretty good size too. It's absolutely nothing like I'd expected. Problem is, though, there's just a v., v. tiny turnout. I can tell it'll be small, because ours is one of only six cars in the car park. A warm, friendly priest at the steps of church politely asks if we're family of the deceased? Friends, Simon tells him. So few people are here, though, we're all invited to sit up the very front.

I cast a quick look around: ten people here, tops. A few nurses, looking like they've come over from the hospice to pay their last respects. Right behind me, there's an elderly, distinguished-looking guy who nods and smiles at them and who the nurses all sit up straight for. A senior consultant at the hospice, I guess again.

12.07 p.m.

Funeral's in full swing. And suddenly I'm hit with a huge pang of sadness. Kitty always spoke of Mrs K. as being such a warm-hearted, generous human being. It's heart-wrenching to think that, at the woman's funeral, there's next to no one here. Just a handful of hospice staff who, chances are, barely even knew the poor woman, myself and Simon. A pathetic send-off for someone who was once so loved. I've a big, salty lump in my throat just thinking about it.

I cast a quick glance up at Simon, but he's firmly focused ahead. Utterly unreachable.

12.10 p.m.

There's a gentle thudding at the very back of the crematorium. So soft, you'd barely even notice it. Wind probably. It's only September, but it's still v. blustery today in Cork. I glance round, half wondering if it could be another mourner come to pay their respects who's just a latecomer. Another medic from the hospice, maybe?

It's not, though. Turn around to see a woman standing in very back row, but the crematorium is so big and she's so far away from me, I can't make out her face.

I can tell she's tall, though, whoever this one is. Has her head down. Dressed head to toe in an elegant black suit. Strange, weird haircut, almost like it's growing sideways out of her head.

Huge Jackie O sunglasses that cover her whole face.

Next thing, my whole body tenses up as, out of nowhere, a wild thought hits me square in the face.

Jesus, it couldn't be! Could it?

Kitty? Come to pay her last respects, after all this time? And just the idea alone instantly makes my throat constrict and the sweat start pumping out of me. Another quick, sneaky look behind, though, and on second thoughts, I'm convinced I got it arseways.

Not her. Definitely not. Sure, how could it be?

Breathing a bit easier now, I cop myself on and force myself to look ahead and focus on the service, instead of imagining ridiculously far-fetched scenarios.

Utterly mental, ludicrous thought anyway. As if.

12.17 p.m.

Can't stop myself taking surreptitious glances back though.

Because it's intriguing. I'm certain Mrs K. didn't know anyone in Cork, how could she? By the time she was sent here, she was way too ill to make any new friends. Maybe the woman in black is some kind of off-duty medic, just not in uniform? I turn round again. But now, as well as the dinner-plate sized sunglasses, the woman in black now has a Mass missalette stuck right in front of her face. So it's impossible to get a good, clean look at her, whoever she is.

Bit like movie star that doesn't want to be recognised.

12.18 p.m.

That doesn't want to be recognised . . .

And those words keep playing like a loop in my head. Because . . . why would anyone come to a funeral and not want to be recognised? Bar they'd just had plastic surgery and were anxious to cover up the bruising?

12.19 p.m.

No. It couldn't possibly be. Could it? No. One hundred per cent definitely not.

12.20 p.m.

That is, I'm pretty certain it's not.

12.23 p.m.

Still can't stop myself from sneakily glancing back every chance I can. The woman in black could be anyone, but there's just something about her posture that's vaguely familiar . . . She can cover her face all she wants, but she can't disguise that long, lean figure.

And only one girl I ever knew was that tall and that much of a skinnymalink . . . All of a sudden, I find myself getting a bit weak and have to slump back against the pew while forcing myself to breathe.

In and out and out and in. . . .

12.30 p.m.

OK, so after much fanning of my face with the missalette, I'm feeling a bit more like myself again. Besides, I'm wrong, course I'm wrong, how could it be otherwise? Trouble is, though, by now I'm pretty certain the woman in black, whoever she is, has clocked me glancing back at her the whole time. I just know by the way she won't look ahead towards the altar, like everyone else.

In fact, she keeps looking back to the door and now I'm half wondering if she's about to make a run for it.

12.33 p.m.

I nudge Simon, who glances over at me. It's a noisy bit in the service, the priest has his back to us and is v. busy sprinkling the coffin with holy water while Panis Angelicus plays in the background. Everyone else has their heads bowed around us.

I hiss urgently across to Simon, 'Check out the very back row. The woman in black.'

He does as I ask. Then looks back at me blankly.

'Well?' I ask him, nearly wanting to shake him by the shoulders at this stage.

'Well, what?'

'Did you get a look at her?'

'A look at who?'

Head almost spinning, I turn back one last time. Except now there's no one there.

Nothing to see except church door swinging slightly in breeze, as though someone's just left.

And left in a hurry.

Chapter Fifteen

Rocky Island Crematorium, Ringaskiddy, Co. Cork

With her heart practically walloping off her ribcage and her breath coming in short, jagged, painful bursts, Jean tried her best to breathe in some of the fresh, blustery air outside the crematorium. Anything to try to calm down a bit.

Angie had seen her. She was certain of it. To say she nearly had an anxiety stroke when she walked into that vast, cavernous church and saw Angie and Simon sitting together, companionably side by side up in the very front row, was an understatement.

From what she could see, given that she was wearing ridiculous shades that must have made her look like some kind of mafia crime boss on witness protection, Angie, her beloved Angie, hadn't changed a single day. Still the same open, trusting face, still as pretty and plump and bosomy as she always was. Her heart physically twisted in her ribcage when she saw the girl looking back in her direction every two minutes.

What must she think of her now? After everything she'd been put through?

And then there was Simon. Tall, handsome, completely unchanged. Jesus, even standing at the top of a church and with his back to her, the very sight of him almost reduced her to a jelly-legged wreck. How could she possibly begin to explain to him, of all people? She knew what she'd done was unforgivable and knew him too well to hope that even given time, he'd stop sticking pins into a voodoo dummy of her and maybe even forgive her.

And yet somehow, she'd have to try to find the words. Because this time, there was no getting out of it.

Enough with the running. Enough with all the lies and deceit.

Here was her one and only chance to try to make amends. She'd run out on them once, she couldn't do it a second time.

It was time to lay the past to rest once and for all.

Sure enough, approximately two minutes later, Angie and Simon were first out of the crematorium and back in the fresh, blustery breeze gushing in from the Atlantic. No doubt attracting more than a few raised eyebrows from the rest of the tiny congregation for their hasty exit.

They'd barely even come through the heavy, swinging church door when Simon suddenly stopped dead in his tracks.

But this time, she hadn't bolted at all.

Instead, here she was, leaning against a car, looking right at them. The woman he'd once wanted to marry, all that time ago.

Just waiting for them, for both of them.

And finally ready.

PART THREE

They'd decided – or rather, he'd decided – to get married just a few weeks after she'd discovered she was pregnant, in Las Vegas, of all places. So both wedding and honeymoon could be an all-in-one deal, so to speak. A quickie in-and-out job in The Little White Wedding Chapel. Just think how romantic it'll be, he kept telling her. We'll be able to tell our grandchildren that we were married by an Elvis lookalike. It'll be hilarious, it'll be fun. And you're the one who's always saying we never do anything fun, aren't you?

Now that he'd reacted so amazingly well to the pregnancy and now that she'd had time to process it all herself, she was actually thrilled. Happy. Looking forward to being a mother, even if it was unplanned and she was a bit on the young side. But aside from being an excited mum-to-be, the early stages of pregnancy were taking their toll and the truth was she'd never felt more physically drained in her life. He was so looking forward to the wedding trip whereas she was actively dreading having to travel so far. She was far too tired these days, too nauseous even to think about flying anywhere, let alone on such a long journey. And to Vegas? Sin City, of all places? Whereas all she wanted was to sleep, nibble on dry toast, occasionally stick her head down the loo and cry.

Her doctor told her she was about seven weeks gone at that stage and she felt . . . and looked . . . like total and utter shite. Everything was making her sick. Food? Forget about it. Even the sight of a dry cream cracker was just about the only thing that wasn't physically turning her stomach. Then there was the tiredness, so acute these days that she was almost getting to be like a narcoleptic. Back in the day, she'd been a girl who could go out partying all night, then put in a full day's work the next day, scarcely batting an eyelid. Whereas now she was falling asleep practically anywhere and everywhere she could. On buses, in the car, even walking down a busy, packed street; sometimes she'd suddenly start yawning and know she'd have to be lying flat on her back in bed within the next five minutes.

She begged him to change his mind, to postpone the whole wedding/honeymoon thing till well after the baby.

'After all, what's the big rush?' she kept asking him over and over, but he was having absolutely none of it.

'Come on, this is Vegas, baby!' he kept telling her. 'It's going to be the trip of a lifetime! We're getting married in style and that's all there is to it.'

Utterly useless, she knew of old, even trying to argue with him when he'd dug his feet in like this.

There was something else too. Over time, she slowly started to wonder – and worry – whether the whole pregnancy thing was all starting to get in on him a bit. Already he was beginning to gripe on about how inattentive she was being when he got home in the evenings.

'You're not seriously going to bed at half-eight at night?' he'd say.

'Hardly much I can do about it, now is there?' she'd snap back at him, hopping hormones making her even more feisty than she was normally.

'Sorry, Jean,' he'd say, instantly backing down and hugging her. 'Just . . . I feel I never really get to see you these days. I miss my best girl, that's all.'

But we'll have a ball in Vegas, he told her.

And sure enough, practically from the minute they arrived, he was in seventh heaven. Wanted to grab some food immediately, then hit the casino, in that order. To humour him, she managed to make it as far as the restaurant, but when he ordered clam chowder and prawns with his whiskey, and when the smell wafted its way up to her, she could take no more. Hand clamped over her mouth, she bolted to the nearest bathroom and threw up all round her. Then, of course, was barely able to crawl back up to their hotel room to lie low for the rest of the night.

She first sensed a mood change when he eventually followed her back up. It was hours later, well after two in the morning, and she figured he'd been at the casino the whole time, but she was wrong. Instead he'd fallen in with a gang of lads over from Luton on a stag night and when they'd found out he was about to get married too, the heavy boozing really got under way.

He conked out on the bed beside her, the smell of stale whiskey on his breath turning her stomach. She pretended to be asleep, but then felt him urgently tugging at her nightie underneath the covers.

Christ, no, she'd thought, don't let this be happening. He couldn't possibly want a drunken quickie now, not when she was so ill and half asleep anyway? But he did. Forced himself on top of her, breathing heavily, crushing her under the sheer leaden weight of him.

'Stop it, Joe!' she'd pleaded. 'I can't . . . I'm not well enough . . . I think I'm going to be sick . . . Get off me!'

He'd pulled back and looked at her in surprise.

'For God's sake,' he'd growled darkly, 'lighten up a bit, will you?'

'I mean it, get off me right now!'

'You expect us not to sleep together on holidays? When we're meant to be getting hitched in a few days' time? We're in Vegas and we're supposed to be enjoying ourselves!'

Seeing all the warning signs, she knew well enough to back down and not escalate things. Managed to sooth him down a bit, even.

And when she turned her head away and blocked out the overwhelming nausea every time he thrust against her, it was all over in a flash anyway.

The following night was different, though. She'd stayed in their room, too tired and ill even to think about hitting the casino with him. But then of course, having slept most of the day and with her body clock out of synch and all over the place, she was sitting up and wide awake when he eventually got back to the room, at well past four in the morning this time.

'How'd you get on?' she'd asked, but it was a superfluous question. That familiar black-eyed look on his face told her everything she needed to know. He'd had a thunderous night at the roulette table, as it turned out. Good, she'd thought defiantly. Maybe that'll get all this casino crapology out of his system once and for all.

'Trust me, you don't want to know about my night,' he'd grunted, heading for the mini-bar and helping himself to a large Scotch. 'So just take my advice and back off.'

'You know something? Maybe it's no harm,' she'd bravely suggested from where she lay stretched out on their gigantic, honeymoon-sized bed.

'What did you just say?'

She should have recognised that key change in his voice, but unusually for her, she didn't.

'Joe, come on,' she'd said reasonably, mistakenly thinking she was somehow making things better. 'We've a new baby coming and I only make a pittance in the restaurant. We both work too bloody hard for you to just fling it all away at some bloody roulette table!'

It all happened so fast, the next few minutes were all a blur. She was aware of a woman's voice screaming out, then shocked to realise the sound was coming from her. She remembered being dragged to the ground and systematically kicked all over, ribs, legs, stomach . . . Oh dear God, not her stomach . . .

'Did I just hear you right, you stupid bitch?' he was screaming, incandescent with white-hot rage now. 'You have the cheek to tell me how to spend my money? When you contribute absolutely nothing bar your pathetic salary?'

'Stop it, the baby . . .'

'You were nothing when I met you, just a tuppenny halfpenny waitress working in a dive bar for tips and I gave you everything! You only live in a decent flat because of me; you're only in this five-star hotel because of me. And now you've got the nerve to tell me what I can and can't do with my own money? You jumped up, presumptuous little . . .'

Last thing she remembered was the warm, sticky feeling of blood trickling from between her legs onto the expensive deep white carpet, before blacking out.

When she eventually regained consciousness, she was in hospital, but unlike the last time, not an A&W ward. No, this time she was in a maternity hospital. Spring Valley on

Rainbow Boulevard, Nevada. Weird, she remembered, looking out the window with nothing to see but desert all round.

'We're all real sorry 'bout what happened to you, honey,' a nurse with a Southern drawl breezed in and told her. 'You were only about ten or eleven weeks gone, is that right? But you know, don't despair, sweetie. Plenty of women who miscarry first time round go on to have perfectly healthy, normal pregnancies. I see it happen all the time in here. Besides, you're so young, you can always try again!'

She'd fallen getting out of the bath, was what he'd told the hospital staff. A complete freak accident. While he'd been down in the casino. He'd just come back up the room to check on his fiancée and found her lying there. He was utterly devastated, he told them. Really laid it on with a trowel. He'd even thrown in the fact that he'd had to call off their wedding, garnering yet more sympathy for himself.

Nor were there any flowers from him this time. No hand-holding, no mortified apologies, no faithful promises that he'd get help and that this would never happen again.

And so lying there, weak as a cat and unable even to sit up in bed without broken ribs stabbing painfully into her sides, she began to think. To formulate a plan. A way of escape. Because she had to. She'd thought of escaping many times before, but this time was different. This time it was for real.

But whatever she decided to do, it would have to be soon.

When she was finally deemed well enough to travel and flew safely back home, she went straight down to visit her beloved Mrs K., who at this stage, was barely able to even distinguish Jean from the rest of the staff, God love the woman. Her poor, worn-out brain really was disintegrating that fast.

The two of them sat alone in Mrs K.'s peaceful, quiet room and Jean had calmly told her everything. About the whole, nightmarish trip, about her aborted wedding, about losing the baby, about the reason why she'd miscarried, everything.

'I have to get out,' she'd whispered, knowing that the chances were she was effectively talking to herself. Mrs K. was so completely tuned out these days, she barely even knew who she was herself half the time, let alone who Jean was.

'Because I'm scared. And I was never the type to give into fear . . . But this is different . . . I've never been this afraid before in my whole life. And I've never felt this trapped. I have to go, to take off. Before it happens again.'

And the more she thought about it, the more do-able it all seemed. After all, you saw this kind of thing happen all the time in movies, didn't you? So what was to stop her from completely reinventing herself? Then moving to a new city, somewhere miles away, where he'd never find her? He'd always vaguely threatened her that if she ever left, he'd come after her, that he'd spend the rest of his life tracking her down. He almost made it sound like it would become his life's mission and, God knows, the guy was certainly obsessive enough to do anything.

But supposing . . . the Jean he knew were to just vanish? Suppose she just ceased to exist any more? It would make her practically impossible to track down, wouldn't it? And, after all, the only other link he'd have to trace her would be via Mrs K., but he rarely if ever bothered asking after her and had never once even gone to visit her.

Which had always suited Jean; she liked keeping this part of her life private.

Besides, he never even knew Mrs K.'s real name, hadn't once asked. She remembered him making a disparaging comment once about how she was 'only ever your foster mother and, at that, only for a short time, so why do you bother traipsing all that bloody way to see her?' At the time, she'd snapped back at him and they'd ended up rowing about it, but now she was glad of it. Glad he knew so little about Mrs K. Because if she were to disappear, she knew that she was bound to be the first person he'd want to see or interrogate. The first link to her.

Amazingly, this was where her luck held. As it happened, Mrs K. was due to be moved to a new care home, in Limerick this time. A super-posh one by the name of Foxborough House, apparently, where Alzheimer's care was the best around. And crucially, where no one would ever have heard of one Jean Simpson. It couldn't have been more perfect. Meant she could still go to visit, just under a brand-new name and no one would be any the wiser.

The more she talked out loud about it to Mrs K., that warm, peaceful sunny day, the more she knew this was her one and only chance. She knew him of old, knew he'd leave no stone unturned to track her down, so therefore her strategy had to be foolproof. She had to disappear into thin air.

The old Jean had to go. No other way to do it. She'd take a brand-new name, put together a whole new identity. She'd move away too, back to Dublin, maybe. Mainly because a) it was big enough that she could just disappear and be anonymous, and b) he hated the place and never went near it, if it could possibly be avoided. Galway was his city; it was where his business was based, where he'd lived his whole life. It was where Jean and he had met and eventually moved in together. It was bound to be the focus of his search.

There was something else, too, that worked in her favour. She knew right well he'd be too cowardly ever to go to the police and mount a big search operation for her. Because the first thing they'd surely do would be to start sniffing around, asking all sorts of questions. And how long would it take them to realise she'd been in and out of A&E units for the past two years? That she'd presented with a whole string of injuries and a litany of the most pathetic excuses the staff must ever have heard? They'd surely put two and two together and he'd only end up implicating himself. As it was, these days after one of his 'outbursts', he'd spend more time cajoling her into not going to the police than he ever would apologising to her.

No, she was safe from that, she was certain of it.

And there was yet another thing going in her favour. There was a customer at the diner where she worked, Harry McGlade, who came in for a big fry-up brekkie all the time. Had a nickname everyone called him by, 'McGlade, the Blade'. A real character, a man with friends in low places, if ever there was one. Used to use the diner as a sort of dining room-cum-office.

She'd been serving him coffee one day and overheard him having a conversation with a 'business associate' about how easy it was to obtain fake passports. Ones that were so realistic, not even the most thorough immigration official could ever possibly see through them. So she made up her mind. She'd ask him for help, knowing full well she could rely on his discretion.

One thing was for certain, though. She had to move fast.

She'd even decided on her new name. Kitty, after Kathleen, Mrs K.'s Christian name. And Hope for a surname. For what she was about to do, she'd certainly need hope in bucketfuls.

'So . . . what do you think?' she asked Mrs K., who'd been lying propped up against the pillows, looking frail, pale under her parchment-thin skin, bone tired and half asleep. Jean

didn't expect an answer, couldn't even be certain if she'd taken anything in properly.

'I mean, of course I'd be able to come and visit you in Foxborough House, except I'd go by a different name, that's all. But it would still be the same old me.'

But then Mrs K. astonished her by opening up her cornflower-blue eyes wide, taking Jean by the hand and squeezing it tightly.

'Do it, love,' she whispered weakly. 'And just remember, you'll be a long time dead!'

Chapter Sixteen

Outside Rocky Island Crematorium

An aching silence as all Jean could bring herself to do was gape at the ground while Simon and Angie stood stock-still, shell-shocked. Neither of them able to really take in what it was they were actually seeing.

Someone just say something . . . Jean silently willed, aware of them both drinking her in, from head to foot, jaws hanging somewhere around their collarbones. From out of nowhere, she suddenly thought about just how changed she must look to them now, with the drastically chopped hair, dressed in clothes a million miles removed from the kit she used to traipse around in. Her first instinct was to turn and run, but somehow she forced herself to stand there, while silence crackled between them like so much static electricity.

In the background, she was dimly aware of other mourners slowly trickling out from the crematorium and into the cool, blustery day. She could hear voices wafting back; surreally talking about perfectly normal stuff like going somewhere for lunch now and arranging lifts back to the hospital in Youghal, and wasn't it shame there'd been such a tiny turn-out?

In the end, it was Simon who took the lead. Stepped forward and locked eyes with her. Such a deep, penetrating look, full of confusion and pain and something else Jean couldn't quite read.

She tried to force out a sentence, but to her frustration absolutely no sound would come. And now all she could do was mutely look from him to Angie, back and forth, desperately trying to read them and not able to, at least not clearly.

In the end, though, Angie saved her all the bother, by bursting into big, gulping, noisy tears. Simon immediately went to her side, slipped his arms around her shoulders, then turned back to look at Jean.

'I think we should go somewhere we can talk. I think after two years, the very least you owe us both is that.'

They drove in convoy to the nearby picture-postcard seaside town of Cobh, Jean leading the way, though she hadn't really the first clue where she was going, Simon and Angie following closely in their car behind. As if she needed to be watched carefully, almost as if they were afraid she might just put her foot to the floor and try to escape on them all over again.

Which stung, but then if that was how they felt, could she really blame them?

Shaking, she drove into Cobh and pulled over at the first hotel she spotted. The WatersEdge; appropriately named, she thought, as quite literally you could have dived over any one of the balconies dotted around it and landed directly into the swirling sea below. And if things went badly for her here, she thought wryly, she might end up doing exactly that.

In tense, awkward silence, Simon led the way through reception and on into the bar, which given that it was lunchtime, was fairly busy, then outside onto a terrace that directly overlooked the harbour. Completely empty, apart from the three of them. A perfect setting for a final act of contrition, Jean thought numbly.

They took a table and settled themselves, Simon and Angie sitting opposite Jean, almost as if they'd come to interview her. She hadn't anticipated how much of a united front they'd be and, again, figured she deserved it all. The waves of hostility practically rolling towards her were bad enough, but if anything, she figured it was lucky they weren't physically hurling furniture across the terrace at her.

A passing waitress offered lunch menus, which they swatted aside.

'Coffee OK for everyone?' Simon asked, as Angie just nodded mutely, twisting a hanky Simon had given her round in her hands, over and over. Jean managed a tiny nod back at the waitress too, though she knew right well the very smell of coffee would turn her stomach. A half-pitying smile back from the waitress, who'd doubtless clocked that this lot definitely weren't locals, but more likely passing visitors, dressed as only people who'd just been attending a funeral on Rocky Island could be.

And given the friction that was practically pinging between the three of them, Jean figured that the waitress would quickly put them down as distant relatives, who were now about to have the mother of all barneys over a deceased relative's will. You could nearly see a worried thought balloon over the poor, hassled girl's face that read, 'Better have security on stand-by, just in case this lot start sticking forks into each other's eyes.'

Strange, Jean thought from out of nowhere, to be sitting here faux-polite, with the two people she'd once been closest to out of anyone in the world. The first man who'd shown her what true love really was and the best friend, who she'd treated so—

She stopped herself. There'd be time enough later on for all of that.

Once again, Simon took the initiative.

'Look . . . em . . . Jean,' he began, stumbling over her name, like he had to keep reminding himself she wasn't Kitty any more. 'Thing is, we know pretty much everything there is to know by now.'

Jean nodded, and suddenly it was as though the world had shrivelled down to just this tiny table. Somehow she forced herself to make unbroken eye contact; a far better punishment for her that way. Though poor old Angie, she couldn't help noticing, now looked like she was going to be physically sick. All Jean wanted to do was reach across the table to her, slip her arm round the girl's shoulders and tell her everything would be OK. Like she'd done a thousand times in the past, whenever soft-hearted Angie was getting a bit weepy and upset over some bastard who'd mistreated her.

But then that was another thing she'd forfeited, wasn't it? The right to ever call herself a best friend, or any kind of friend, ever again.

Simon coughed, cleared his throat and continued.

'The police filled us in . . .' he started, then hesitated.

'I can imagine,' Jean said softly.

'. . . Well, they pretty much fleshed out a lot of your back story.'

He looked straight at her now, unflinching. Nothing, she thought, not a recognisable scrap of that old look he'd get in his eyes when he used to look at her. Like a total stranger treating her with a polite but cold disdain. She'd fully expected it to be bad, but not quite as bad as this.

Well, what did you expect anyway? a voice inside her head asked. Welcome home banners, a parade and a happy reunion, great-to-see-you, don't-leave-us-again, knees-up all held in her honour?

Yeah, right.

'As you can imagine,' Simon was saying, businesslike, clipped, 'it didn't take the police too long to find out all about Jean Simpson. And very quickly afterwards, we came to realise exactly what you'd done. That you'd just changed your name, your whole identity.'

Jean nodded, taking it on the chin, willing herself to stay strong. There'd be time enough later on to collapse.

'We even know the reason why,' he went on, and she may have been mistaken, but could have sworn that this time, there was the slightest break in his voice as he said the words. A tiny chink . . . Maybe of understanding?

'That you were trying to protect yourself, to escape from . . .'

Yes, she'd been right! Because now it was Simon's turn not to finish a sentence. So Jean obligingly did it for him.

'. . . from an abusive relationship,' she said calmly.

Then Angie spoke up. 'For God's sake, Kitty, why couldn't you have just told one of us?' she suddenly blurted out, twisting Simon's hanky round and round her finger, face snow white from shock. 'You and I were best friends! We told each other everything! Couldn't you have trusted me?'

Seeing Angie was agitated, Simon reached out to her and gently took her hand, which seemed to calm her down momentarily.

'Sorry,' she tacked on weakly at the end. 'I keep meaning

to say Jean, not Kitty. Pretty hard not to; to me you'll always be Kitty.'

'I understand,' Jean said softly, wanting nothing more than to sit beside her and tell her it would all be OK, but knowing she'd doubtless be brushed aside. 'And you have to believe me when I tell you that it broke my heart to have to do what I did. Hardest thing I've ever done. Hardest thing I've ever had to do.'

'Two years!' Angie glared over at her, really starting to get angry now, as all that pent-up frustration finally reached an outlet. 'You wait *two long years* to come back to us and explain? Have you even got the first clue what you put us through? We did absolutely everything humanly possible to try to find you, we organised search parties with all the neighbours, we might as well have moved into the Garda station, we spent so much time there, we even littered the whole city with flyers looking for you! Have you any idea of the worry, the stress we all went through that miserable Christmas? Which, by the way, lasted for weeks, right up until the police unearthed the truth about you . . .'

'Shh, shh, it's OK,' Simon gently told her and at that, she seemed to stall a bit.

'I can only imagine,' Jean whispered. Knowing it was next to useless to try to say much more.

'And in all this time, what do we get from you anyway? A lousy postcard? That's it? After everything we went through together! Did we really mean so little to you? That you were just able to stroll out of our lives without a backward glance and probably even without giving us a second thought?'

'Angie, you have to believe me, that's not true . . . You've got it all so wrong . . . You have no idea . . .' Jean leaned across the table towards her, willing her to listen.

'Well, if I have it all wrong,' Angie swallowed hard, eyeballing her and sounding stronger now, 'then I guess you'd better fill me in. Please, go ahead,' she threw in, a bit sarcastically, which was so uncharacteristic of her. 'After all, we've waited this long, haven't we?'

Then Simon spoke, sounding at least calm, if nothing else. 'Thing is . . . Jean,' he said, and if he accidentally stumbled over her name again, it was hardly surprising. 'We know where you were coming from, we can even guess at your reasons for keeping so much from us for so long, and ultimately, for doing what you did. But what we don't understand is why. Why then? Why that Christmas night, of all nights? The day before Angie's birthday? And only a few days before you and I were due to go away on holiday together? I think the very least we're owed after all this time is a full explanation. Don't you?'

Jean nodded, though said nothing. Because how in the name of God could she ever even hope to begin? She looked from Simon to Angie and from Angie back to Simon again; Angie all teary and emotional, Simon rock-still, ashen-faced.

No way out of this. No more running. They were right: they deserved the truth, the full truth and nothing but. She was about to say, 'You'll hate me for it,' but shut herself up in time. A superfluous statement if ever there was one. They already despised her; sure, how could they not?

'If that's what you want,' she eventually said. 'But I warn you, you won't like it.'

'Christmas Eve, two years ago,' Simon said, insistently. 'How about you just start from there?'

They both looked at her intently while Jean sat back, eyes half shut, trying her best to bring to the surface a memory she'd tried for so long to suppress.

Christmas Eve. And sure enough, little things slowly started to come back to her. The way Christmas was without doubt the most exhausting time to work at Byrne & Sacetti, but somehow that particular night was very different. Ordinarily, after a late-night shift, Jean remembered how she'd practically crawl out of the place, dead on her feet with bone tiredness. But not that night.

'This'll sound completely mental to you both,' she began falteringly.

'Just try us,' Simon told her coolly. Christ, he certainly wasn't making this any easier for her. A horrible, tense pause as Jean tried to read his face. But it was useless; all she could see was cold, flinty anger practically coming off the guy in waves now.

'Well, it's weird, but I can still remember how happy I felt. Just this overwhelmingly feeling of deep contentment and optimism about the next few days and how magical it was all going to be. I'd just finished up in work and not only was I officially on a week's leave, but I was so looking forward to treating you on your birthday the next day. Remember?' she said, looking directly at Angie.

A tiny sniffly nod from Angie was all she got in reply.

'It was my full intention to give you just a brilliant, no-holds-barred pamper day at the Sanctuary Spa, Angie, you have to believe me. Then I was so excited about heading off on holliers with you,' she said, this time looking directly back at Simon, willing herself to meet his eyes.

But then I always looked forward to anytime you and I were together, she wanted to tack on, but couldn't. Jesus, this was so much harder than she ever could have thought! She so badly wanted to say that she'd honestly never felt as happy in her whole life, as she'd done during their time together; her gorgeous, handsome, loving Simon; at least that's how she'd always remember him, regardless of his feelings for her now. So frankly she wouldn't have cared where they were headed for Christmas or what they were doing over the holidays, just as long as they were together. If he'd told her they were booked to spend two weeks sleeping rough under a bridge in Tubbercurry while busking for food scraps during the day, she'd have burst out laughing and gone along with it. As far as she was concerned, bring it on.

God, there were times back then when she had to pinch herself every time she even thought about Simon. How in the name of God had someone like her ever got so lucky? Someone so damaged, who vowed she'd never trust another man again, as long as she lived? Then out of the blue, to somehow find a man like that, a real, rare diamond, a complete gentleman, who treated her so amazingly well. Who'd even grown to know every single one of her faults and who, astonishingly, still seemed to love her in spite of everything.

And there was something else she needed to say too. Something else that was putting that added spring into her step as she practically bounced along dark, deserted Camden Street, that icy cold night, humming 'Santa Claus Is Coming to Town' under her breath. Earlier that day, she'd been rummaging round the spare room at home when a suitcase belonging to Simon that had been perched precariously on top of a wardrobe, came clattering down on top of her. And out fell a package, a small, square, beautifully wrapped little box. She knew right well she should have left well enough alone, but curiosity got the better of her and, in spite of herself, she opened it up to peek inside. A ruby engagement ring, tiny and so, so perfect. Suddenly an instant wave of something near akin to euphoria came over her . . . Jesus, she didn't even need to think of what her answer would be, when he asked her!

Hardly appropriate to mention it now, though. To put it mildly.

'Em . . . are you OK?' Angie asked her in a tiny, worried voice. 'Are you sure you want to continue?'

'Yeah. Sure.' At least, she'd certainly try. 'Well, I can't remember how far I'd got down the street after I left work,' she went on as clearly as she could, 'but I do remember, just on impulse, going to whip my mobile out of my bag to text you.' A quick glance up at Simon, but apart from the slightest flush, he stayed statue still.

'Way too late to call you, of course; besides, I knew you were in Galway with your family at the time and I didn't want to wake you. I just figured it would be a nice little surprise for you in the morning if you woke to find a late night message. Just saying something light and breezy, that's all.'

Like, I love you, she had actually been going to text him: she remembered clear as crystal, but didn't say. Couldn't.

'Anyway, I do remember stopping in my tracks on the pavement and whipping round this backpack I had, to fish my phone out. But when I started to rummage round for it, for the life of me, I couldn't find the shagging thing. Then I remembered. 'Course I wasn't able to, it was still in my locker in the staff room where I'd dumped it earlier, wasn't it? So I knew I'd have to go back for it. No choice.

I wasn't working the next day and wouldn't get the chance again. It was late, but I had a set of keys to get in. Besides, I figured Joyce would still be there. Well, either Joyce or Sacetti himself; one of them was bound to still be around, doing up the tills before finally clocking off for the night. One of them was always around. Sometimes,' she half smiled, 'I used to secretly think they might even sleep in the place overnight.'

'So you went back?' said Angie.

'Yeah. I remember just turning back the way I'd come, amazed at how quickly the streets had cleared of drunk Christmas revellers and just how deathly quiet it was by then. There was just the odd car zipping past me, but that was about it. I remember checking the time on a clock above a pub close to the restaurant. It was just coming up to two a.m., which of course meant the main door to Sacetti's would be locked, barred and bolted; I'd have to use the staff entrance. '

Angie just nodded and took it up for her. 'Which was down a tiny alleyway that ran alongside the whole building. But were you not terrified? Going down a dark alleyway on your own at that hour of night?'

'If I'd known what was waiting there for me, I certainly would have been,' Jean said wryly. 'But at the time, no, I wasn't.'

But then, she thought, that was one small advantage of surviving what she'd come through: you knew you'd never know fear like that again, so therefore you didn't sweat little stuff like being on your own down a dark alleyway late at night. Piece of cake.

'Go on,' said Simon curtly, jaw clamped tight, almost like it was wired shut.

The build-up was straightforward enough; but this would surely be the hard bit. Taking a deep breath, she steeled herself.

'I can remember . . .' but she broke off here. Because suddenly this was tough, far tougher than she ever would have thought.

'Want me to get you some water?' Simon asked, and she nodded gratefully .

'Take a breather,' Angie said, eyes brimming over with concern now. 'We know this must be horrendous for you.'

'No, it's OK, I'll keep going,' she told them, willing herself just to toughen up a bit and get it over with. Easier said than done, though; after all, these were memories she'd long since filed away in a corner of her brain, sealed off and labelled 'Do not enter'. Still, though, it was better they knew, far better just to get it all over with. They were right. She owed them at least the full story.

'And then . . .' she tried her level best to pick up where she'd left off.

'Yes?' Simon asked tersely.

'. . . Well, I remember seeing this black Jeep parked right opposite the staff entrance, but the windows were tinted and it was so dark, I wasn't able to make out the driver. Initially I wasn't worried; I figured it was just a minicab Sacetti had waiting to take him and Joyce home, nothing more. In fact, I remember half wondering if I'd be cheeky enough to try and scrounge a lift myself. Anyway, I fished the staff room keys out of the bottom of my bag and went up to the entrance. I was nearly there, almost home and dry; I can still distinctly remember having the keys in my hand to get inside, I was this close to safety . . .'

She had to stop herself here. The rest was just too painful.

If she'd just been a bit faster, if she'd got inside the building quicker, she might have made it. God knows, she'd certainly spent long enough over the past two years beating herself up about it. And still, even after all this time, the nightmare would resurface.

That voice suddenly coming from directly behind, stopping her dead in her tracks.

A man's voice, one she hadn't heard in years, instantly turning the blood in the veins to rock-solid ice.

'Hello, Jean.'

No one called her Jean. No one had, not in years. She wasn't Jean any more, she was Kitty.

There was only one person she could think of who'd ever call her by that name. Slowly, trying very hard not to show any kind of fear, she turned round and there he was. Smiling, actually smiling, like he was delighted to eventually have found her.

'So this is where you've been hiding out on me all this time.'

There was total silence round the table now, all eyes focused on her. Then Simon ordered water for her and when it appeared, she gratefully took a sip.

'Your ex was there, wasn't he?' he asked, and was she imagining it or did he sound a bit less cold now? 'Joe McGuinness.'

'Yes.'

'Oh, Jean!' Angie burst out. 'Why couldn't you have made a run for it, or at least tried to? Surely there might have been someone on the street who'd have stopped to help you?'

She shook her head. 'Because it was useless to even try. Shocked and all as I was, I knew that much. For God's sake, he had a car; he'd have been after me in a matter of seconds. Besides, there was a tiny part of my mind that told me it was probably in my best interests to play him along. For a while, at least.'

'But why?' Angie insisted. 'I don't get it, after everything that guy put you through?'

'Because I needed to know exactly how much he'd discovered about my new life. I had to find out just how long he'd been on to me. After all, he'd already tracked me down to where I worked, so did that mean he now knew where I lived too?'

She didn't tell them what else she had to find out. Did he know who her new circle of friends were? Did he know about Simon?

'So you see, I had to know, to find out everything. I had to be able to gauge exactly how threatened my whole new way of life was before I could do anything at all. Believe me when I tell you it was against my better judgement, but I went quietly. I knew of old that it was always easier if you didn't put up any kind of a fight with this guy.'

And so two minutes later, she stepped up into the Jeep beside him and allowed him to drive off into the night.

'This is the part that none of us knows,' Angie says, almost on the edge of her seat by now. 'So where did he take you?'

'To this apartment that he'd taken on a short lease in a complex right behind Christ Church Cathedral,' Jean told her. 'I remember thinking it was very Celtic-Tigerish altogether; it had its own private lift in the basement car park, that swished you all the way up to the top floor to the place he was renting. Which was bad news for me, meant we met no one on our way in, saw no one. Which meant no one knew I was there.'

'Go on,' Simon said tersely.

Taking deep breaths and by some kind of superhuman effort, managing to keep outwardly calm, Jean willed herself to keep going.

'Well, the next hour answered pretty much every question I needed to know. It turned out that he'd been searching for me for years and eventually he'd shelled out a fortune on a private detective to track me down, which of course terrified the living bejaysus out of me. Because if that was the case, and if I really had been so untraceable all that time, then what had finally given me away? I was beside myself to know. He was drinking whiskey, I remember, and so I just sat there letting him talk on, though I made bloody sure to keep his glass well topped up.'

She looked over at them both and saw that Angie was vigorously nodding her approval.

'You see, I figured the drunker he was for this, the easier it would be for me. Besides, by then, I was burning up to know exactly how he'd found me and in the end it turned out to be something so mundane . . . '

'What was that?' Simon asked, looking at her keenly.

'Well, it seemed that out of nowhere, and when he least expected it, the private detective had chanced on this lucky break. A colleague of his just happened to be in Byrne & Sacetti one night and mentioned there was a waitress there who answered the description of a woman he'd been looking for. Fitted the picture to a T. Same height, build, eye colour, same crappy, bushy hair, same kink in the nose; absolutely everything seemed to match. Except the name.'

'And?' Angie asked, ashen-faced by now.

Jean paused and took another sip of water before going on. 'Well of course, I just felt nauseous at that; I mean that it was something as haphazard and open to chance that finally led him to me. I can remember how every instinct in my body told me to turn and bolt for the hills, but I knew I just had to stay and learn more. So he kept on drinking and talking and I let him. And I was glad I did, because it turned out there was at least one thing in the whole sorry mess that I had to be grateful for. The more he rabbited on, the more I realised that it had only been a matter of days since he'd traced me to the restaurant. So I was hoping against hope that there hadn't been time to do much more scouting round since then.'

'Why was that so important to you?' Simon asked.

'Because I wanted to keep you all safely out of this. I had to.'

'But that's what I don't understand,' he insisted. 'Why couldn't you just have told us the truth?' Then with just the tiniest break in his voice he added, 'Don't you know I'd have moved heaven and earth to protect you from him?'

She shook her head firmly. 'You couldn't have,' she answered him simply. 'No one could. You've no idea what he's like. He'd ruined my life once before and wouldn't stop until he'd done it all over again. This is a man who had been sabotaging my friendships for years. He'd do it all again. Jesus, he'd have seen it as his life's mission. He wouldn't have let up until he'd driven us apart. All of us,' she said, taking in Angie this time.

'Well, I can't accept that,' Simon said, shaking his head. 'No one has the right to upend anyone else's life. We'd have made sure that never happened. Got the police involved if necessary. We'd have done anything. You had other options open to you, besides just running away. Plenty of them.'

'Did I?'

Impossible to tell them how she'd really felt that horrific night. She shuddered involuntarily a bit just at the memory. How everything around her, even familiar things, suddenly seemed to be so frightening, pointy and terrifying. How threatened she suddenly felt, even in a city she'd come to feel so happy in. And now it was all over. Had to be. She knew that for certain. The wonderful, happy new life she'd carved out for herself was finally over. Like a magical dream that she always knew would have to end one day, when hard, cold realities suddenly had to be faced. He'd seen to that the minute he discovered where she worked and what her new name was. Kitty Hope's days were numbered the minute she saw that black Jeep parked at the side entrance to Byrne & Sacetti.

Simon was wrong, she didn't have any choice.

'Kit— sorry, I mean, Jean,' Angie said, looking plaintively across the table at her, 'if you can, please keep going with the story. Remember, we've tried to second-guess what actually happened that night so many times, I have to find out the truth.'

Jean sighed and picked up where she'd left off.

'So there I was, trapped in this ridiculously plush apartment with . . . with—'

Another sip of water just at having to invoke that name, before she could even go on.

'Take your time,' Simon said.

'And he just kept talking on and on, really began his charm assault in a big way, just like I knew he would. God,' she added bitterly, 'he even recycled some of the same tired old clichés I'd been listening to him pedal out years before. Begged me for another chance. Said over and over how sorry he was for everything that had happened between us in the past. Told me how much he hated himself for ever hurting me. Swore on anything that moved it would never happen again. Said that it didn't matter where I went or where I took off to, he'd always find me. 'Course, I almost wanted to throw up at that and had to fight hard against the urge to smash the glass he was cradling and slam it into his face. But then I kept reminding myself, getting out of there safely was the number-one priority, wasn't it? It was in my best interests to let him talk on and so that's what I did.'

'But how did you manage it?' Angie blurted out, 'I mean, how did you eventually get away from him?'

'Fed him enough drink to fell an army,' Jean said dryly. 'He was never really able to handle it anyway, so every time his glass was even half full, I'd take good care to top it up to the brim with whiskey. And sure enough, the amount he'd had to drink eventually made him doze off. So that's when I did it. I just tiptoed out the door, miraculously made it out of the building and safely down in the lift to the street outside.'

'And absolutely no one saw you,' Simon said, shaking his head.

'Not a soul. It was well past five a.m. by then and still pitch-dark, but my luck was in. A taxi with its light on was just driving down the street, so I flagged it over and hopped in. Better yet, the driver was a foreign national who didn't seem to speak much English and who certainly had feck all interest in finding out my entire life's history, like most Dublin taxi drivers. Last thing I'd have wanted.'

She didn't say it aloud, but it was there all the same,

unspoken. If she was about to go through with her emergency plan, she needed to be utterly untraceable.

'So where did you go?'

'I got the taxi to take me home and asked the driver to wait.'

'You mean you went back to the house?' Angie asked, stupefied.

'Had to. No choice. So I bolted inside, raced upstairs and went to . . . to this hiding place I had . . .'

Shit. That had been even harder to say than she'd reckoned on. A pause while she tried to filter away the panic that her body could still recall with near digital clarity, even if her mind had edited it out after all this time.

'By that I mean . . . a safe place . . . one I'd buried my whole past life in, just in case an emergency ever happened.'

'Which was where exactly?' said Simon, flushing furiously.

'In the bedroom.'

'Where?'

'You'll love this,' she told him sardonically. 'Under a wonky floorboard, covered with this tatty red rug on the floor that I'd bought with you at a flea market years before.'

'Jesus,' Simon muttered under his breath. 'You mean all that time you had stuff concealed down there?'

'Had to,' she said slowly. 'My real passport, for starters, real birth cert, official documents and this tiny running away fund that I'd stashed there: cash I'd squirrelled away over the years just in case the unthinkable ever happened. And then of course, it did.'

Simon's hands, she noticed, were balled into fists by now and she was just wondering if she should leave it at that when a very red-eyed Angie piped up.

'For God's sake, I've waited two bloody years to hear the end of this! Don't stop now, what next?'

So Jean kept going. Editing out the bit where the only tiny, sentimental indulgence she allowed herself was to say a silent prayer for Simon and Angie before banging the hall door behind her and leaving for good.

'Well, my luck held,' she said. 'It was so early in the morning, the street was deserted and the lights were all out along every house beside mine. Thank God there was no one to see, no neighbours up and about, absolutely no witnesses. So I told the taxi driver to take me to the airport and twenty minutes later, we were there.'

She remembered vividly how sheer numbness and shock seemed to get her through. Somehow got her out of the taxi, into the terminal building and over to the first ticket desk she saw that was open. Like a person who'd mentally rehearsed a fire drill time and again, and who knew exactly what steps to take when the need arose.

'When we got there,' she went on, 'I just went up to a ticket desk and they told me that the first available flight they had out that morning was at six a.m., travelling to Amsterdam.'

'Amsterdam!' Angie nearly gasped. 'I don't believe it! The police traced a lead we had that placed you there! We even went through CCTV footage of you at the airport! At least, it was someone who looked a lot like you . . . but it was a bit blurry, you know . . . and we convinced ourselves it wasn't you.'

'Why Amsterdam?' Simon asked her coolly.

'I don't know,' she said, shaking her head, 'it just appealed. I figured everyone had really good English in Holland, so I'd be fine, I'd get by for a bit. And in the event of a search,

I thought it was unlikely that word of my disappearance would spread as far as the Netherlands. I just thought it was somewhere I could lie low and think about what to do next. You have to understand I wasn't thinking straight. I needed time, I needed space, I needed to somehow get my head together.'

'And so you just hopped on the plane without a backward glance,' he said, jaw tense.

She couldn't answer. Couldn't even finish what she'd been about to say.

Because it was only when she was actually on the flight and watching Dublin airport from a safe distance as the aircraft slowly began to taxi away, that the panic attack she'd been holding at bay finally overcame her.

She remembered thinking about Angie, her own lovely Angie. It was her birthday that day and now look what she'd gone and done to the poor, blameless girl. A true pal, who'd shown her nothing but love, loyalty and friendship.

Then she thought of Mags, Jeff and Sarah, all the gang. All the amazing friendships she'd forged over the years. What would they think of her? When they realised she'd just buggered off on them, without a single word of explanation?

She still wasn't able to think about Simon, though. Not while she was still in shock and trying to process so much. She remembered surprising herself at not even being able to feel pain yet. Instead, there was just the dull expectation of pain to come.

She remembered vividly the aircraft thundering down the runway, building up speed for take-off. And how she allowed herself one final look out the window behind her, before she burst into tears and allowed the enormity of what she'd just done to sink in.

Because Kitty Hope was no more. She'd arrived at the airport as Kitty and would land in Amsterdam as Jean.

And, somehow, bring herself to start a whole new chapter in her life.

Chapter Seventeen

30 September, The Chocolate Bar, 9.45 a.m.

'So, Angie, come on, tell me everything! Dish the dirt! Quick, while we've got time before the elevenses brigade all start to descend on us!'

I'm in our Dame Street Branch, being grilled by Sarah, during a mercifully quiet mid-morning lull.

And she is categorically not – repeat NOT – letting me off any hooks till she's wrung every last, tiny detail out of me.

'For starters, how did Kitty look?'

'You mean Jean, don't you?'

'Yeah, yeah, I keep meaning to say Jean. Sorry, force of habit.'

'I know. I still can't get my head round it either,' I tell her numbly.

'You still haven't answered me! So, does she look exactly as she always did? Or has she put on any weight? Maybe . . . gained a few pounds across the midriff?' Sarah asks hopefully.

'No, she's still the very same,' I answer, laying out whole new layer of double chocolate with dark organic mint filling at very front of our counter display, along with a sign saying 'Sample stock, feel free to try!' Knowing they won't last longer than approx. three minutes in here.

'The very same? How exactly? For God's sake, Angie, I need details here!'

'You know, tall, super-skinny . . . Oh, but she's had the hair all chopped off. Looks kind of . . .'

'. . . kind of what? Weird? Makes her look . . . a bit older, maybe?'

Now I know Sarah means well, but I honestly don't think she'll be happy till I tell her that Kitty – sorry, I keep meaning to say Jean – now has thighs the size of the Port Tunnel from stuffing herself with nothing but McDonald's and subsequently spending the past two years living in a haze of guilt-induced oblivion. Sarah's school of thought is that it's the v. least she could have done, for what she put the rest of us through.

'The thing you have to understand is,' I try to explain, 'I was just completely knocked for six . . . And still am really. Just to look back and see her standing there at the back of the crematorium . . . I'm not joking, it was like coming face to face with a ghost. To be honest, I'm amazed I was even able to be coherent around the girl. Never mind taking in how she looked, and whether or not she was carrying a couple of extra pounds.'

Must still be in utter shock, I think to myself. It's the only reason I'm even half functioning today, but then, as I know of old, habit tends to be a terrific deadener for getting you through.

Sarah suddenly flings down a tea towel she's ostensibly been drying espresso cups with, and furiously turns to face me.

'Well, I don't know about you,' she says, 'but half of me wants to hug the girl and the other half wants to wring her neck for what she made us all suffer through. I'm furious and curious at the same time, if that makes the slightest bit of sense.'

'I know,' I tell her patiently, 'and if it's any consolation, so am I. But, believe me, I don't think any of us could possibly make her feel anything even approaching the hell she's gone through herself. I mean, we can't begin to appreciate the anguish she's been suffering ever since she left. Can you just imagine what it's been like for her, all this time? Not being able to check in on Mrs K., not being able to explain things to any of us, just walking out on her whole life like she did. You should see her now, Sarah, it's . . . Well, it's actually weird.'

'Weird how?' says Sarah, brightening.

'It's not just the way she looks, it's her whole persona. She's changed. You have to prepare yourself for quite a shock when you see her.'

'Details, please.'

'Well . . . remember how whacky and wild she used to be? That mad, restless energy she always had about her? How funny she was and how she never seemed to give a shite about getting into trouble or anything?'

'How could I forget?' Sarah says dryly, folding her arms and momentarily abandoning the espresso mugs. 'You're forgetting, I'm the girl who went with you on that famous night to meet her in a pub for "just the one". And woke up the following morning in Holyhead, with possibly the worst hangover ever known to man, thanks very much.'

'Well, it's . . . it's like that incredible, insane spark there was about her has just been put out. Totally extinguished.

All that devilment and craic and messing and the way she used to behave . . . it's like that was a whole other person that we used to know in a whole other life. And now there's a woman in her place who looks vaguely like the Kitty we knew and who even sounds like her, but this time she's called Jean and is . . . somehow . . .'

'Somehow *what?*'

I rack my brains trying to come up with right word.

'Sadder. Like a fragile girl who's had all the life and spirit sucked out of them.'

Which seems to satisfy Sarah, for the time being, at least. But then I don't actually think she'll be happy till Jean has crawled in here on her hands and knees, wearing sackcloth and ashes with a shaved head, pleading to make amends for everything.

'It was just hearing her whole side of the story was so heart-rending,' I go on. ''Course, we knew fragments of it from what the cops were able to tell us two years ago, and were already able to piece a lot of it together. We knew that a woman called Jean Simpson had been through the A&E unit in Galway so many times that staff were starting to get suspicious, and that they'd guessed about the nightmarish relationship she must have been trapped in . . .'

I break off here a bit. Just remembering back to that horrific night two years ago when I went back to Kit—*Jean's* house to find that copper Crown sitting there with an ashen-faced Simon. And then having to sit and listen to what he told us. Exactly what it was that the police had discovered as soon as they'd run background checks on one Jean Simpson.

And it's amazing, but I'm still shuddering at the memory.

Even from a safe distance of years, it still has the power to send an ice-cold shiver down my spine.

I glance over to Sarah who's looking expectantly back at me, impatiently waiting for further elaboration.

'Look,' I say lamely, 'We've all spent so much time speculating and counter-speculating. It was just finally getting to hear the whole thing from Jean's point of view that . . . that made me see it all a bit differently, that's all.'

'And what exactly is there to see differently here anyway, I'd like to know? Oh, Angie, you're not going to turn into a big mushy marshmallow on me, are you? Need I remind you that Jean, or whatever we've all got to start calling her now, just flitted off and left the rest of us here worried sick about her! God, we did everything possible to try to find her, you name it! And all the time, she's holed up in Amsterdam? And not a phone call to any of us in all that time, not a letter of explanation, absolutely nothing! So don't you even think about going all soft on me now, missy, because I'll tell you something,' she goes on, now packing dirty coffee mugs into the dishwasher with such ferocity that I'm afraid she'll start flinging them up against the wall in a minute. 'I know exactly what I'll say to that one if she ever has the nerve to face me. I'll look her right in the eye and . . . and . . .'

'And say what exactly, hon?' I interrupt her gently. 'Because, believe me, I honestly don't think you could possibly make the girl feel any worse than she already does. If you could only have heard her yesterday! Your heart would have broken for her, it really would. Just to sit there and to finally hear her telling her side of the whole thing . . .'

I trail off lamely here, unsure how to articulate what else is on my mind. Because I'd guessed, of course, but never really realised to what extent Jean was afraid. The terror she must have felt that Christmassy night when she vanished; one minute feeling so safe and secure with everything in life to look forward to, and the next, stuck down a dark alleyway with her very worst nightmare suddenly standing face to face with her.

'To be honest,' I tell Sarah, 'I think the girl has spent the past two years having some kind of nervous breakdown. I don't think she even knew what she was doing the night she took off. She was in complete meltdown; she wasn't thinking straight. I think she'd worked out her emergency plan years before and just followed through numbly, without even stopping to think about the consequences. And then spent the next two years of her life regretting it, though Jean's not the type to wallow. She just accepted this was the price she paid for her safety, and got on with it.'

'Easy enough for her to just "get on with it". But what about you? You were the best friend she had. Did she honestly expect you just "to get on with it" too?'

Still haven't quite worked out the answer to that one myself, so I turn away and get back to plonking out chocolate samples on the display case.

'And another thing,' Sarah mutters unconvinced, but I can tell by the fact she's stopped bashing crockery round that she must be a bit calmer now. 'Jean really should have trusted us back then. She could have told us the truth. She didn't have to live a lie all those years, not around any of us. We would have been on her side, for God's sake. We would have helped her.'

'Yeah, but in a funny way, she was only doing it to protect us, if that makes any sense.'

'How do you mean?'

'Well, that guy she'd been living in such terror of, Joe, well . . . he'd spent years and years just sabotaging her friendships and slowly isolating her from everyone who ever cared about her. So of course, when the worst started to happen and then kept on happening all those years ago, Jean looked around and found herself utterly alone and friendless. I think she was petrified of the same thing ever happening again. Of the same old pattern repeating itself with us.'

Sarah is looking over at me with 'still remain unconvinced' practically stamped across her forehead, so I keep on trying to drive my half-arsed point home.

'Look, Jean's really been through the mill,' tell her firmly, 'all I'm asking is that you just give the girl a chance to explain it to you. Doesn't she at the very least deserve that? She's changed her flight, but she's still planning on going back to Cape Town in a few days anyway, and she came here specifically to try and put the past to rest. Which you have to admit, was brave of her, if nothing else. You've got to give her that. So all I'm saying is, would it kill you just to meet her halfway? For old times' sake, if nothing else.'

'In other words, you've decided just to forgive her and let her waltz back into your life? Is that what you're saying?'

'I honestly don't know.' Only the truth.

'But of course, there's still one last and final thing,' Sarah goes on, dishwasher abandoned as she looks even more keenly at me this time. 'Something that's not quite so easy to explain away. If I'm allowed to refer to the elephant in the corner, which both of us have successfully managed to avoid so far.'

Swear I know what's coming next without being told.

'Sorry, babe, but I have to know. What about Simon in all this? How does he feel about her sudden resurrection?'

And now I clam up a bit. Then look hopefully towards door, praying a customer will come in and put end to the awkward turn this conversation's suddenly taken. But no such luck; the brekkie rush is over and we tend not to fill up again till after 10.00 a.m., when customers usually need their sugar/caffeine hits to see them through the rest of the morning. I glance around anxiously for some untended-to job that needs doing to extricate myself from having to answer, but Sarah's straight onto me.

'Angie? Come on, love, don't just clam up. I only wanted to make sure that he was OK, that's all. And that you were too, of course. I mean, that's the woman that he'd wanted to mar—'

OK, at that I interrupt her bit waspishly before she even gets a chance to finish her sentence.

'Look . . . I honestly don't know how Simon feels about it, OK? So can we just leave it at that?'

Bleeding hell! I love Sarah dearly, but honestly, there's times when she's like a dog with a bone, till she prises an answer out of you.

'And I'm assuming that Jean knows nothing whatsoever about the two of you? As of yet, at least?'

'Well . . . we were both still coming to terms with seeing a ghost for the first time in two years, so no, Sarah, our respective love lives didn't really enter in the equation, thanks for asking all the same.'

Didn't mean to sound quite that snappy, not when she only meant well, but truth is . . . the real truth is, I'm worried bloody sick about whole situation with Simon.

Before we left yesterday, Jean had told us she was staying

on in Cork for a while, so she could tie up any loose ends at the hospice where Mrs K. passed away. But then, in yet another surreal moment, she said now that she'd spoken to us, that maybe she should come up to Dublin, just for a couple days before she went back to Cape Town. 'To try and make my peace with a few more people,' was how she put it, so simply and humbly that it nearly broke my heart. 'So maybe after I'm gone, we can all finally put the past behind us.'

'I'm still staying in the house on Berkeley Street, by the way,' Simon had told her, icily for him, I distinctly remember thinking.

And then it was Jean's turn to look shocked, though she said nothing.

'So if you needed to collect a few of your things, you can,' he tacked on, by way of explanation. 'I'll leave a key with a neighbour, and if you call when I'm in work, that would probably be best.'

Implication v. clear: so I don't have to be alone with you at any time.

I don't think I'd ever heard Simon speak so coldly to another human being before. V., v. weird. Like he was just one tenant politely asking the previous one to clear out the last of their crap, whenever.

'Thanks, I appreciate that,' was all Jean said quietly in reply, leaving me in a puddle of worry and anxiety about what lay ahead. For her, for Simon. And, by implication, for me. And if I'd thought Simon was silent and lost in thought on the drive down, that was a bloody party compared to his thin-lipped silence the whole way back to Dublin.

So how the hell did this happen anyway, was all I could think angrily, staring out the car window on the interminably long drive home.

How did I suddenly end up in the middle of a love triangle? And not only that, but, I've a horrible feeling, on wrong end of it?

10.05 a.m.

Suddenly the bell rings out above The Chocolate Bar front door and I look up, grateful for any kind of interruption. At this point, I'd v. happily have had the red carpet out to welcome a visit from Health and Safety this morning, I need distraction so badly.

It's one of our regulars, lovely, a friendly girl called Madge who works in a shoe shop across the street and usually comes in every day at this time for caffeine and a chocolate-hit. V. chatty and I just know by the watery, red-eyed look of her that she needs to talk about her boyfriend.

'Angie, thank Christ it's quiet in here this morning. I need your advice so, so badly!'

I instantly switch into work mode, efficiently frothing up her cappuccino just the way Madge likes it and whipping a slice of our chewy double chocolate biscuit liqueur cake from the display case, her usual mid-morning treat. Sarah senses her one-on-one grilling with me is finally over and efficiently click-clacks her way into store room at the back, to get organised for a supplier's meeting she's got out at our airport branch this morning.

'So tell me, love, what's the spineless bastard gone and done on you now?' I ask poor old Madge sympathetically. Such a big relief to focus on someone else's disastrous love life; certainly takes my mind off my own.

I should explain. Madge is in an on-again, off-again relationship with a guy who, if you ask me, continually treats her like shit and openly sees other people, thereby propelling poor old Madge into me, bawling and needing a sympathetic ear, a cappuccino and a slice of our double chocolate biscuit liqueur cake in that order, as she says herself, 'to get her through'.

You do realise all you're getting from that fella is booty calls, I've told her till I'm blue in the face, though I strongly suspect it's a big waste of time. In Madge's stronger moments, she'll nod and agree and vow to delete his number from her phone and never talk to him again. Till next time it happens, of course.

'Oh, Angie,' she says, bleary-eyed, 'what would I do without you! You're so amazing, you always seem to know whenever I caved and ended up going round to his flat . . . at half-eleven last night!'

Not due to any psychic gift on my part, might add, it's just that she swears off this git, then weakens and ends up taking a booty call from him at approximate week-long intervals. Could nearly set your watch by it.

Madge plops herself up on a seat at the counter bar beside me as I slide her an extra frothy cappuccino and a slice of said cake in all of its chocolatey gooeyness.

'Thanks, Angie,' she says gratefully, sticking a fork down into it, 'this is exactly what I need after a night with that useless, uninterested, noncommittal . . . Jeez, I'm pathetic, aren't I? When will I ever learn? When will I finally start reading the signs?'

'Just eat up, hon,' I tell her calmly. 'And remember that a slice of double chocolate biscuit liqueur cake is a known cure for everything. Homesickness, loneliness, heartache, you name it, that cake will soothe it all away. Proven fact.'

On she chats and, to be perfectly honest, I'm v. grateful

for the diversion. I spend the next fifteen minutes doling out wise, sage advice whenever I can get a word in, such as, 'Trust me, the more you ignore him, the more he'll come running after you. Remember, you're a fabulous prize for any guy and it's his job to try and win you! Just stay strong, honey, that's all you've got to do. And no harm while you're at it, to start seriously looking for someone who actually *wants* to be with you.'

She talks on and I let her, though truth is, my thoughts are wandering now. Funny, I think. How easy it is to dish out pearls of sound relationship wisdom to someone else, and yet how hard it is to get my head round what's going on in my own love life.

When Madge reluctantly gets up to leave, I slip into the store room at the back and check my phone, yet again. Haven't spoken to Simon since he dropped me home, after the long drive back up from Cork, at all hours last night. And of course I knew it was big waste of time asking him into my flat, so I didn't even bother. Instead just said to call me anytime if he got a bit wobbly.

'You've had a huge shock,' I gently told him, before I hopped out of the car. 'And so have I. But just remember we got through a worse shock two years ago by sticking together and that's the only way the two of us can possibly get through it this time.'

He didn't answer, though. Just kissed me lightly on the forehead and didn't even wait to see that I'd got into the building safely.

Soon as my feet barely touched the pavement, he was gone, speeding off into the night, without so much as a goodbye.

Chapter Eighteen

Still in The Chocolate Bar, 8.55 p.m. (And yes, we do stay open till then, as a matter of fact. Late-night shoppers for one thing, always a v. lucrative passing trade for us.)

Been on my feet here in work all day and I'm so, so relieved that it's almost closing time. Normally the days here go by in a blur, I'm that busy, but somehow, not this one. Legs are aching. Head's pounding. I need a) a hot bath, b) a takeaway Thai green curry and, most of all, c) to talk to Simon.

Just to talk to him, that's all. I've steadily been working myself up into a crescendo of anxiety all day and have to know where he's at in his head and what he's doing. Hardly too much to ask, now is it?

I mean, I am still his official girlfriend, aren't I?

9.01 p.m.

I've just let Jamie head home for the night. (A lovely work experience guy we took on, who's proving to be an excellent barista, and as Sarah's v. quick to point out, incredibly handsome into the bargain – never any harm.) I pull on my jacket, grab my bag and am just about to start switching off lights and turning on the alarm when, suddenly, the door opens.

Groaning inwardly, I look up, expecting to see some late-night customer chancing their arm and desperately needing some v. long and complicated order involving low fat/skinny/soya-blend latte, or a complex combination thereof. Or else – hope against hope – maybe it's him? It's Simon, who's maybe popped in to take me home and to see how I'm holding up? Maybe?

But it turns out to be neither.

I couldn't be more shocked to see Detective Sergeant Crown standing in front of me, freckly and sandy-haired, all strapping six feet two of him.

9.03 p.m.

'Angie,' he says, apologetically, while I just stare up at him like some kind of a mute gobshite. 'Do you remember me? Don't tell me it's been all that long!'

'Yes, Sergeant, I remember you.' Like I could ever forget?

'Look, I'm so sorry for barging in on you this late at night . . .'

'That's OK, but as you can see, I'm just about to lock up. We're closed, I'm afraid. But we're open again from seven tomorrow morning . . .'

'Don't worry,' he smiles, 'I haven't come in looking for coffee and cakes. Delicious and all as they look . . .'

Then what in hell are you doing here? I ask myself, totally at a loss.

'And congratulations, by the way,' he says, looking around, nodding slowly and taking the whole place in. 'On the success of your business, I mean. It's a real credit to you.'

'Thanks,' I manage to say. Immediately thinking to myself, Jeez, is this about that parking ticket I still haven't got round to paying, the last time I borrowed my mother's car? Or maybe he's here to check I'm not bootlegging hard liquor under the table after hours, like Chicago in Prohibition era, circa 1922? So is this what the coppers are doing now, making door-to-door calls on foot to suspected miscreants like me?

All instantly superseded by an even bigger worry. It could hardly be anything to do with Jean, could it? She only arrived back in the country yesterday morning for the funeral service . . . No, it couldn't be.

'Actually, I was out at your airport branch only recently,' Crown chats on easily, 'on my way to see Ireland playing Poland in the World Cup qualifier.'

'Oh, right,' I manage to say, still at a complete loss. 'So . . . em . . . what did you think?'

'Oh, it was a disaster. Just painful. What can I say? Grown men sobbed like babies.'

'*Excuse* me?'

'Sorry,' he grins, 'I meant the match. No, The Chocolate Bar was a welcome beacon for a gang of five lads all nursing minging hangovers on our way home, I can tell you. But the game itself was a complete whitewash.'

'Oh, right,' I just nod back at him. Why is this guy here? And what exactly does he want from me?

'Well . . . em . . . sorry about the match not going our way, but it's certainly a big relief to hear that The Chocolate Bar didn't let you down.'

'The thing is, Angie,' he says, taking a step closer to where

I'm stood over by the counter, handbag clutched to my stomach like I'm an old lady petrified of getting mugged. 'I needed to speak to you. Have you got a minute, by any chance? Maybe we could chat in here, if that was OK with the lady proprietress?'

'Eh . . . yeah, sure, have a seat.'

I've already piled chairs on top of tables, all set to be mopped down first thing in the morning, but he deftly takes two down and invites me to sit down opposite him.

Silently I do as I'm told, intrigued. Start to take him in as he eases into the chair opposite me, really have good gawp at him. He's changed a bit, I decide. Has gained weight but luckily for him, he's got the height to take it. I remember when I first met him, I had him pegged as some kind of a remote automaton type, emotionless and cold; the type of guy who worked eighteen-hour days, had no friends and spent his weekends running marathons. Then it comes back to me how great he was as we came closer to solving the mystery of The Lady Vanishes. How he called to the house and offered me support and help and a friendly ear. How strong and how comforting he'd been and how shite I felt for being such a narky bitch to him, way back when we'd first met.

He's out of uniform now and dressed casually in jeans and a light sweater and looks exactly like the sort of fella who'd come in here, grab a table and happily while away an afternoon reading the sports pages and stuffing his face with pies. Sort of fella I can relate to, in other words.

Hard to forget the last night I clocked eyes on the guy. Still imprinted on my brain, in fact, almost like it's tattooed behind my eyeballs. I can still recall it with frightening clarity, I can even feel the rising nausea at back of my throat when I walked into Kit— *Jean's* sitting room and found Simon sitting there looking like death, with Crown standing opposite him. I remember Crown asking me to sit down too, even offered me sweet tea. Being kindly, human and so concerned. Then he stunned me by asking exactly how well I'd known Kitty? I remember being gobsmacked at even being asked, but that turned out to be absolutely nothing compared to what was to follow. And to finding out that Kitty Hope never really existed.

To this day, I can still recall the shock. This, I can clearly remember thinking, must be what it feels like to live your whole adult life as one person, then to suddenly, out of a clear blue sky, be told that you're actually adopted. Exact same feeling of being deceived, duped and lied to, for an entire lifetime.

And it was all down to simple, plodding police work in the end. Not even a particularly big mystery at all. When police ran routine background checks on one Kitty Hope, nothing came up. Which was unusual. So they dug a little deeper and grilled Simon and I that bit more, particularly about Kitty's elusive younger years. Time and again I told them it just wasn't something she went into, ever, but then out of nowhere, something completely random struck me. The name of a complete dive bar where she'd worked for a while, when she was far younger. Worst job in history, I suddenly remember her drunkenly laughing on a night out we were having. But still the name of the place of it wouldn't come to me.

Smiley, I told Jack Crown, though thinking absolutely nothing of it at the time. Smiley something, Smiley bar maybe? And I clean put it right out of my head again. Because after all, it was just a throwaway, casual remark of Kitty's from years ago, how could this possibly be of any significance? But as Jack later told me, in cases like these, there's no such thing as a flippant remark. So of course, the coppers quickly located Smiley's, discovered it was in Galway and shifted the focus of their search to there. But absolutely no trace of anyone called Kitty Hope. Which really alerted suspicions. Then one of the barmen vaguely remembered a girl who looked an awful lot like the girl in the photo police showed him, but who had a completely different name. Jean, he thought. Old staff records quickly were searched and suddenly we had, as coppers kept telling us, the breakthrough we'd been waiting for.

Then police got a tip about someone else who'd known Jean back in Galway at the time, another waitress called Becky. Turned out she and Jean had worked together back in Galway years before, but Becky had since moved to Glasgow and was completely unaware of all the coverage of a missing girl called Kitty Hope. But she was eventually traced and when questioned said that she had indeed known Jean Simpson, not long before she'd pulled another disappearing stunt not dissimilar to this one. And there was more. She had strong suspicions that Jean Simpson was in an abusive relationship with one Joe McGuinness, though she stressed that Jean was always at pains to deny it.

When coppers started to run deep background searches on Jean Simpson, they didn't take long to discover that she was a regular patient at Galway University where she'd presented over the years with just about every injury you could think of, from a smashed nose, to broken ribs to a fractured pelvis. Joe McGuinness was quickly traced and brought in for questioning, but insisted these were all as a result of sports injuries, although suspicions were raised. Still more questions were asked, though as Crown pointed out to us at the time, without Jean herself physically present to press charges against the guy, there was damn all they were left with, only conjecture and guesswork.

The police then traced her passport under Jean's real name and got as far as Holland, then, not long afterwards, to Morocco, of all places. But searches for her went completely cold after a while and as far as the coppers were concerned, that was that. Case closed. They could accurately guess at why Jean had taken off and why she'd reinvented herself, they only question we'd no answer to was where had she gone?

And I've barely had any contact with Crown at all since. He kept in touch for a while afterwards, and would phone every so often with updates on Jean Simpson, but as leads on her grew thinner and thinner, the case just seemed to be shelved. And for my part, I never really felt I should keep in touch with him either. Well, didn't seem to be any need, did there? We'd finally got to the bottom of the mystery, discovered the extent to which we'd all been had, there was nothing else to do but try to get on with the rest of our lives without Kitty, as best we could. We knew that wherever this new woman called Jean was, at the very least, she was safe.

I look back to Crown, who's sitting awkwardly opposite me now and fidgeting a bit, like he's not quite sure how to begin this conversation.

'Angie, the last thing I'd ever want to do would be to startle you,' he eventually begins, looking at me with worried blue eyes. 'And I'm sorry to say at this hour of the evening that it's a work call.' Then he adds with a small grin, 'Much as I'd love nothing more than to sample some of those divine-looking chocolates you've got on display.'

'Call in any time, Sergeant,' I say automatically. 'Be happy to give you one, on the house.'

No harm in keeping him sweet. Just in case I'm wrong, and he actually is here about the unpaid parking fine.

'Call me Jack, by the way. Please.'

'Jack.'

'The thing is, there's been a development in your friend's missing person's case. Look, Angie, I really hope this isn't going to be a shock to you, but we've just had notification from Border Patrol and Immigration at Cork airport that a woman travelling under the name of Jean Simpson was reported passing through the airport about thirty-six hours ago. I'm sorry about the delay in getting this information to you, but of course, I had to resurrect her file and check everything out thoroughly before I came to you with this.'

'It's OK,' I interrupt. 'We already know. Simon and I, that is.'

I give him a brief, potted version of the events of yesterday, tell him about seeing Jean at the funeral and what she told us afterwards, as we all sat together in that tiny waterfront bar. Without doubt, the single weirdest moment of my whole life to date. Three former best mates, all sitting and looking from one to the other, like complete strangers. Then seeing Simon's fists clenched inside his pockets, as Jean told us the full, unexpurgated version of exactly what that bloody monster Joe McGuinness had put her through.

While I'm at it, I make sure to lay it on pretty thick about that sub-human git and Jean's exact reason for her even contemplating doing what she had to in the first place. I tell him that the girl quite honestly felt she'd no choice. It was either survive or smother. So she chose survival.

'I see,' Crown nods slowly when am finally finished yabbering on, looking a bit relieved, to my surprise. 'Well, I'm certainly glad that none of this is coming as a shock to you. Or, I hope to your friend Simon.'

Friend. V. ironic description of him at this point in time, I think to myself, but keep my mouth shut. Somehow sensing there's still something more to come.

'But I'm afraid that's not all.'

Ha! Knew it. I find myself sitting up now, thinking, so . . . what next? What can possibly be left to tell that she hasn't filled us in on already? Jean's really the illegitimate love child of the Grand Duchess Anastasia, last of the Romanovs, and Lord Lucan?

'As soon as the news landed on my desk,' Jack goes on, 'of course I went to alert both you and Simon. He wasn't answering the contact number I have for him, but I did leave a message for him. You've changed your mobile number since it seems . . .'

'. . . But you were able to trace me through The Chocolate Bar?'

'Yup. I'd seen a fantastic review in one of the papers when you first opened up here and remembered you so well. You must be very proud. You've achieved so much since the last time I saw you.'

'Thanks, but . . . you did say there was something else?'

'Yeah, and I'm so sorry to have to land this on you. But unfortunately I will need to see Jean Simpson at her earliest possible convenience. So I came here to ask that if you heard from her, that you'd let me know immediately. I hate troubling you, only I can't stress how important it is.'

'It's no trouble, but . . .'

Suddenly, I start getting bit defensive on Jean's behalf.

'Now just hang on a minute, Jack. You're not thinking of arresting her or anything? Because you just couldn't! I mean, she hasn't actually done anything wrong! OK, so she changed her name, but she did it for her own protection! That's hardly a crime, is it? You can't just haul her in and . . . And clamp her in handcuffs and lock her up for what she did! She's only just buried her foster mother and she's unbelievably fragile . . . Plus, the girl's already in bits over all the worry she caused us back then, she genuinely is. You wouldn't make this any worse for her, you couldn't! It would be . . . cruel! And . . . a miscarriage of justice!'

And now, suddenly, Jack's grinning, actually grinning at me, like he thinks this is hilarious and I'm a prize moron. A big, broad, freckly, warm grin.

'Angie, would I be right in thinking that you watch a lot of those crime dramas on telly? Of course Jean isn't in any trouble. Come on now, do you honestly think we'd put the woman through any worse than she's already been through? We're police all right, but we're not entirely inhuman and void of all emotion, you know.'

'But . . . you said . . .'

'Jeez, I thought you were about to start banging on tables and demanding to ring your lawyer there for a sec.'

'So why is it that you need to see her then?'

'Because as soon as I heard news of her being back in the country, I naturally ran a trace on Joe McGuinness, as a matter of urgency.'

No, no, no, no, no, no, no.

'You did *what*?' I snap across table at him. 'Because if he ever got wind of the fact she was back in the country, you can be sure she'd join a convent of nuns and move out to Namibia on witness protection!'

'Wait, Angie,' he says, making 'calm down' hand gestures at me. 'Just calm down and hear me out. You have to understand that I needed to know where the guy was. In case she ever wanted to press charges against him, I'd have to have tabs on him. Our first priority at all times is to keep any woman who we suspect has been in an abusive relationship as safe as we possibly can. Plus, there's the distinct possibility that he could track her down for himself, and God knows what could happen then. As you yourself said, he'd done it once before.'

'And what happened? What did you find out when you ran the trace?'

My head's starting to thump now and I'm beginning to feel cold, clammy beads of worry-sweat slowly trickle from under my arms right the way down to my ribcage.

'Well, you see, this is why I'm anxious to speak to Jean as soon as possible. To tell her she has absolutely nothing to fear from that guy any more.'

'*What?*'

'It seems that roughly six months ago, McGuinness's company went to the wall, owing well over a million. He has a list of creditors he owes money to the length of your arm. But instead of dealing with the problem upfront or possibly even declaring bankruptcy, he upped sticks and emigrated to New Zealand.'

I slump back into my chair, gobsmacked.

'In other words . . .'

'I'd be astonished if Jean Simpson ever so much as hears from McGuinness again in this lifetime. If he ever shows his face in the country, there's a long list of creditors he owes a fortune to, not to mention a probable fraud case pending against him. In other words, she's as good as safe now, Angie. I need to see that woman to tell her that after everything she's been through and put her friends through, she's finally free.'

I try to speak, but for some reason, no words will come out.

Dame Street, right outside The Chocolate Bar, 10.15 p.m.

Jack's still here, even stays with me as I finally lock up and switch on the alarm, etc.

'It's getting late and I know you must have an early start in the morning,' he says, helping me to pull down the security shutters outside the place. I'm actually v. grateful for his help, the shutters weigh a bleeding tonne.

'Generally, I'd be up at about six-ish,' I tell him, as we start to walk down the street together, passing gangs of revellers smoking outside a pub that's belting out 'Moves like Jagger'. 'Funny thing is, though, after a while you just get used to the total sleep deprivation. Bit like having a baby, I imagine.'

He smiles down at me. And again, it's a nice, warm smile.

'Well, you've certainly been through the emotional wringer over the past few days, Angie. You must be absolutely exhausted. Least I can do is offer you a lift home, if you'd like? My car's just here. Yet another advantage of being a cop. You can park wherever it suits you.'

The feet are nearly blistered off me and think if I have to walk one more step, I'll possibly end up taking off my shoes altogether and going home barefoot and I won't even care. Taking a lift from Jack is a total no-brainer.

Outside my building on Essex Street, 10.31 p.m.

Temple Bar is always mayhem, but it's really, seriously heaving tonight. There's an exceptional number of stag nights on the prowl, plus gangs of college students on piss-ups, are screeching at each other at top of their lungs and calling each other wankers. V., v. glad to be inside a snug, warm car. And I keep having to resist the urge to stick my head out the window at the whole shower of messers and yell, 'Look at me, I'm with a copper! A very senior detective, as it happens! He could arrest any one of you at minute's notice and on a whim! Now shut the feck up and let me get some actual SLEEP tonight!!'

'Fantastic place to live,' Jack nods towards my building, as we pull up beside it in his neat little Peugeot. 'So central and handy for everything. Must be amazing to have the whole city centre right on your doorstep. You could eat out any time you wanted or, better yet, just take a short stroll and see a different movie every night of the week. That would be my idea of heaven, but then I'm a complete movie buff.'

'Are you? Me too. Went to film school and everything.'

'Film school? Wow, very impressive,' he smiles, glancing over at me. 'And living here, you must get to the cinema all the time, I'd say. I envy you.'

I have to resist urge not throw my head back and guffaw at that.

'Are you kidding? Nothing I'd love more, but right now I'm doing well if I get to see a decent flicker every couple of months, what with work being so mental. And even if I do get a night off, I'm so bush-whacked, I usually just end up crashed out in front of the telly watching *I'm a Celebrity* or similar, and eating crappy take-out grub.'

'Tell me about it,' he smiles, and again, it surprises me by being a big, open, warm smile. 'I think I could recite the take-out menu from my local Dominos Pizza in my sleep.'

OK, time for me to go.

'Well, thanks so much again for the lift,' I tell him, unfastening seat belt and hopping out of the car.

'Sleep well,' he says, leaning forward and starting to fumble around the glove compartment. 'Don't forget to let me know when you hear from Jean next, OK? Here's my card, with my direct number and my mobile on it, just in case you need it.'

'Ta very much,' I say, sticking my hand back inside the window and taking the offered card from him.

'You're welcome,' he grins, then waits till I'm safely inside the building. A nice touch, I think. Polite.

Two minutes later, I'm back upstairs in my cosy, warm little flat, greeted by an ever-growing mound of ironing still waiting to be attacked.

Strange, strange evening, I think, kicking off my shoes and going into my tiny galley kitchen to make tea. Crown 'call-me-Jack' turning out to be so different from the way I first had him pegged, all of two long years ago. Plus, never thought I'd say this, but actually being so easy to chat to outside of a cop shop.

You know, normal, ordinary, down-to-earth.

I stick the kettle on, then flush a bit remembering back to all the times I was so downright rude to his face while roundly abusing him behind his back for, as I saw it then, not doing enough in search for Jean. I can even remember Simon calling me on it and urging me to be a bit more civil to him.

Now? I feel a tad guilty over that. Especially seeing as

how the whole police search turned out to be a classic waste of time and police resources, you name it.

Because Jack Crown was . . . no other way to put it . . . warm and friendly tonight. Easy-going and laid back. Relaxed and even funny. Not the same person I first had him pegged down as at all. I shrug; decide that sometimes I'm v. happy to be wrong about people, then head to the hall table, to fish my phone out from the bowels of my handbag.

I dial Simon's number, to fill him in. Dying to finally talk to him. I've so much news, I feel like the latest edition of something.

It rings. And rings. Rings again. So I leave a voicemail message, asking him to call me the minute he gets this. Then every ten minutes after that, I keep jumping, thinking I heard it beep beep with a message and that it's him and that he'll just get in his car and come over and we'll talk the night away and that everything will be just fine.

But my phone stays resolutely silent.

Chapter Nineteen

Most bizarre experience yet, Jean thought, walking down Berkeley Street, where she'd once lived and been so happy for such a long time. Beyond strange being back, when she could still remember the terror she'd felt on that very last night she left here. How afraid she was that Joe would somehow trace her, may even have followed her, even though she knew it was highly unlikely then and even less so now. Jesus, but it still sent a flare of panic through her, even saying his name. And it caught at her throat to think that coming back home to Ireland had actually taken her this far, when she'd vowed to get on and off the island as fast as she possibly could.

What made it all doubly weird was that there was precious little she didn't remember about Berkeley Street; she'd certainly played it back in her head enough times, so often in fact, she could practically recognise each and every crack in the paving stones. Back in Cape Town, even being able to remember tiny little things could be a real comfort; it helped no end to get her through the worst days.

She'd remember the neighbours, one by one, right down to lovely, warm-hearted Mrs Butterly from next door and all seventeen of her grandkids, or whatever it was at last count. And the warm, loving way she almost saw herself as a surrogate mammy for Jean. How she'd hammer on Jean's door every Sunday at lunchtime and say, 'Come on in and have a bit of roast beef with us, love. Put a few pounds on you! Sure, I've seen more weight on a butcher's pencil.'

Then there was the way her grandsons would team up with gangloads of other local kids and turn the whole street into one giant soccer pitch, more often than not smashing the odd neighbour's window while they were at it, then making a run for it, screeching, 'Wasn't me, honest, it was him!' for all they were worth.

Jean smiled a bit at that one. Funny, the tiny things you missed.

It was just gone half-nine at night, late-ish to be calling, she knew, but she couldn't risk Simon's not being there. Because she had to talk to him, just this one last time. Somehow she had to try to explain to him, even if she'd never be able to make him fully understand. Nothing on earth, she knew, could possibly be worse than the hard, cold, flinty way he'd practically glared at her yesterday.

She couldn't – just couldn't – bring herself to fly back to Cape Town and know that he was living his life in another hemisphere and thinking ill of her. So now here she was, in good faith, prepared to make peace at any price, or certainly to try. And if he didn't accept her heartfelt apology or maybe if he even refused to hear her out, then at the very least, she'd have made a bloody effort, wouldn't she?

Taking a deep breath, she stood outside her old house, girding her loins and only praying that he'd answer. She pressed the doorbell and took a good step back, waiting. Marvelling at how little the place had changed in two years, from the outside, at least. Except, if anything, it looked more cared for than it ever had when she'd lived there, which admittedly wouldn't have been all that hard. Windows were gleaming, the brasses on the door had been polished; there was even a neat row of geraniums planted in a box outside. All Simon's doing, no doubt, she smiled quietly to herself.

But then, he was always the neat, organised, efficient one, not her. He was the one who always put out bins, remembered to pay bills on time and made sure there was fresh milk in the fridge. Whereas, left to her, the electricity would regularly get cut off while they sat shivering in winter, with no gas to heat the place and nothing to live off except a box of stale corn flakes.

Still no answer, so she took a deep breath and knocked this time, knowing right well he was home; his car was parked outside. Same car he'd had from two years ago, she thought, as this time another very different memory surfaced. But then it was hard to forget all the times he'd driven her back home from yet another one of his boring work dos and the way she'd suggestively lean over and start kissing him while he was behind the wheel, just for the laugh. Purposely trying to distract him, teasing him. There were even a few nights when things got so hot and heavy between them, that they'd ended up having a quickie shag on the back seat, parked on the side of a deserted country road.

She blushed a bit at the thought, wondered if it was something he still remembered too, then looked up sharply, as the door was opened.

Simon. Arms folded, not even registering surprise, almost as if her visit hadn't been entirely unexpected. And for a split second, it was like time stood still. A throbbing moment while she looked at him and he looked right back at her and no one spoke.

Shit, she silently cursed herself. What had happened to her carefully worked-out speech? She knew she had literally dozens of these mortifying, sackcloth and ashes, 'prodigal daughter returns and begs forgiveness' scenes ahead of her, and what's more, with dozens of other people. So why now, face to face with the one person she'd probably hurt the most, did she have to go completely blank?

Simon, ever the gentleman, though, made it that bit easier for her.

'Jean,' he nodded flatly. 'You should have let me know you were coming round.'

Subtext: so I could have made sure I was in a different county.

'Sorry about that, but I wanted to make sure you were home,' was all she managed to get out in reply. Subtext read and clearly understood. If you'd known I was on my way, chances are you'd be half way up a faraway mountain by now. Anything rather than face a one-on-one conversation with me. So this was my one and only option.

'You're here for your things, no doubt,' he said coolly, stepping aside to let her in.

'No, actually. I came here to talk to you.'

She went into her old hallway, struck by the twin illusion of familiarity and estrangement, like she was remembering it all from a *déja vu.*

'Oh my God!' she couldn't help exclaiming as she followed him on through to her old sitting room. 'Everything's almost exactly as it used to be . . . Simon, you even hung on to my old books!' she added, as her eye fell on a pile of English course texts she'd needed for her night classes.

It was completely uncanny. Apart from the place looking a helluva lot tidier than it ever had when she was around, it was largely unchanged. Her pictures were still on the wall, her plants were still in full bloom on the windowsill, looking well watered and cared for. All the furniture was exactly the way she'd always arranged it, which basically meant that everything pointed towards the telly. She could even see a stack of her old DVDs piled in a corner, as if she'd just dumped them there, then wandered off to do something else.

You'd swear she still lived here. You'd almost think that the past two years hadn't happened and that she'd just hauled herself home from Byrne & Sacetti, stuck a pizza in the microwave and was about to plonk herself down in front of the telly, tin of beer clamped in one hand. God, all the scene needed to finish it off was that little stray cat she used to feed, Magic, to amble in on the scrounge for grub, like she used to all that time ago.

'I think you'll find everything's here for you, all present and correct,' Simon said, coldly this time, pointedly not asking her to sit down or, God forbid, even offering her a mug of tea. Again, very disconcerting, in a house so familiar to her. And which still felt so much like home.

'If it would make it any easier for you, I'll clear out of your way and head out for a bit,' he added. 'Give you what, say an hour to get your things out of here? That enough time for you?'

'The last thing I'm here for,' she said hesitantly, 'is to pick up stuff belonging to me.'

'You sure? Because no doubt you'll be needing at least some of it, for your new life in Cape Town,' he almost snapped the words out. Which again, caught her offguard.

Just standing here, listening to Simon who was ordinarily so mannerly and polite being this cutting towards her, was far, far worse than she ever could have imagined.

'All of your old clothes are all upstairs in the spare room, you'll find,' he said, standing well away from her, right over by the door, as if he couldn't even bear to share the same airspace as her.

'But if you're looking for your car, I'm afraid we took a decision to sell it about a year ago. No choice; it kept getting clamped and eventually was towed. It was costing a fortune in parking bills and as we figured the chances of you ever coming back for it were slim to none, selling seemed like the best option. We kept the cash safely for you, though, in case you ever needed it.'

'Simon,' she interrupted, 'if you think I'm here about my old car or looking for cash or, God forbid, a few mangy bags of old clothes, you're much mistaken. All that crap is just so transient. It means absolutely nothing to me.'

'Then why are you here, *Jean*?'

She wasn't mistaken. He'd almost spat out her name.

'If I possibly can . . . to try to talk to you.'

She'd walked over to him and was right beside him now. Standing tall, determined that she wouldn't start falling apart, not when there was so much still to say. Plenty of time for that later on.

'Well, let's not expect the impossible, probably best not to,' he said, tersely. 'Besides, we already spoke yesterday. You explained exactly why you took off that night. Nothing more to say, I'd think. Wouldn't you?'

'I mean I wanted to talk to you, alone, and I'm not leaving here till you at least hear me out,' she told him, and in a weird way, now that she was home, she could slowly feel like some of her old spirit was somehow seeping back to her. Now that she'd come face to face with him, she felt a bit stronger. More in control. Feck it, she'd come this far, hadn't she? She wasn't leaving now without saying her piece.

'Simon, walking out on you and Angie was the single hardest thing I've ever had to do in my whole life. You have to believe me! Not one single day has passed since when I've not thought about you, wondered how you were getting on, all the time knowing you must despise the sight of me for what I'd put you through. And I know it's way too late in the day for apologies, and the last thing I'd ever expect would be your forgiveness, but if I could at least try to make you understand—'

'Understand what, exactly?' And this time he was actually raising his voice, something she'd never heard Simon do before, in all the time she'd known him.

She looked blankly at him, momentarily stunned into silence.

'I asked you a question,' he fired angrily at her. 'What is it exactly that you miraculously expect me to understand? I couldn't bring myself to say this to you yesterday, not in front of Angie. It wouldn't have been fair to drag up the relationship you and I once had with her there. But have you the slightest idea what it was like for me back then? You disappear off the face of the earth, we rip our whole lives apart trying to track you down, worried sick about you, then the police land in on us and we discover that, all this time, you'd been living a complete lie! You and I had been together for eighteen months and you never even thought to tell me that Kitty wasn't even your real name! How exactly do you propose trying to get me to understand that, Jean? Please, I'm all ears! Very curious to hear you explain that one away!'

'I was frightened!' she almost yelled back at him, feeling a surge of elation now that she'd finally found her voice. 'I was absolutely bloody petrified! You ask if I knew how things were for you, but have you the slightest idea of what *that* was like for me? I'd had my whole life ripped apart before and I wasn't prepared to let that happen to me again! So forgive me for taking what I thought was the only option that I had open to me, so I could keep myself safe. And to keep you and Angie safe, too. Yes, I came to Dublin with a new name and I know I deceived you and that it was wrong of me. But I thought at least that way I'd manage to protect myself. Then I met Angie, so of course she only ever knew me by my new name. Same when I met you.'

'So you thought it was acceptable to let us believe a complete lie? Or when you've lied as often as you have, does it become like second nature?'

'Simon, just hear me out! I know it was a despicable thing to do, but in a funny way . . . it almost stopped mattering after a while. I figured, OK, so I happened to be calling myself something different, but at the end of the day, I was still the same person, wasn't I? After all, my whole personality hadn't changed; all I'd done was tweak a couple of official documents, that was it. At least, that's how I saw it.'

'You couldn't have trusted me?' he asked, really looking at her intently now, first time he'd done that since she'd arrived. 'Couldn't have told even me the truth? Didn't you know that I'd have done everything I could to protect you? No one would have threatened you while I was around, no one. Surely you knew that I'd have taken care of you?'

His voice cracked a bit here and he broke off, as if emotion was finally getting the better of him.

'It wasn't a risk I could take,' she answered simply, glad that at least they weren't yelling at each other any more. 'Besides, it wouldn't have been fair to lumber the whole burden of my past onto you. You didn't deserve that.'

And anyway, she could have added, you couldn't have protected me, no one could. Because Joe – Christ, how she hated even having to invoke his name! Well, he'd still managed to find her, hadn't he? He'd still traced her all the way to Byrne & Sacetti. So no one could have kept her safe from then on. And the rest was history.

'Oh, no, I may not have deserved *that*,' Simon was saying dryly, sarcastically. Again, so unlike the old Simon. 'Whereas my girlfriend just disappearing into thin air, leaving police to tell us the truth about her, was something that I *did* deserve? Or that Angie deserved? Is that what you're saying?'

'But it wasn't like that! Believe me, I know what I put you both through is indefensible and if I had my time over, I'd do things so differently. I just didn't want you thinking that it barely cost me a thought to do what I did, because you couldn't be more wrong!'

'But you've been gone for almost two years, Jean! And in all that time you couldn't have picked up the phone to explain all this to me?'

She shook her head, willing herself to lock her voice into its lowest register and, above all, to stay calm.

'But where would I even have begun?' she asked him softly. 'And yes, when we were together, there were times . . . plenty of times . . . when I'd contemplated telling you. I hoped and prayed that you'd understand, but the thing was . . . well, the longer we were together and the more serious things got between us, the harder it became. It was wrong of me, I know that, but I honestly didn't know how on God's earth I could tell you that I'd been living a lie all that time. Besides, we were so happy together, so rightly or wrongly, I figured, why not just live in the now and enjoy ourselves? Then of course, after I'd gone, I knew that it was only a matter of time before the police would have discovered everything there was to know about me and I knew how deceived you'd feel. Best thing all round, I thought, was for me to just disappear, to dissolve like a Disprin. Believe me, I thought I was doing you a favour. I thought you were far, far better off without me.'

'You know what the worst part of all was for me?' he asked, all of a sudden looking so very tired and worn to a shred by all of this counter-accusation and bitterness.

She knew exactly how he felt.

'Tell me.'

Now he was walking over to the sofa by the TV, then slumped exhaustedly down onto it, rubbing raw, red eyes with the palms of his hands. Almost like he'd had enough of this row and just wanted peace, wanted out.

'Do you remember you and I were due to go away on holiday together, about three days after you disappeared?' he said, sounding that bit softer now. Bit more like the old Simon.

''Course I do,' she said gently, instinctively moving over towards him. 'Skiing. To Austria.'

Those first few days after she'd gone, there was little else she thought about.

'Well, I had – oh God, where do I even begin? Let's just say, I had a surprise planned for you. A very special one. At least it was special to me. At the time, that is.'

She stood silently and let him talk on, glad that at least he seemed a bit calmer now.

'I was planning to take you off on the Orient-Express,' he went on, pointedly not looking at her. 'Then on to Paris. Had it all worked out to the nth degree, worse eejit me. I'd booked us into the Crillion Hotel, I'd arranged a candlelit dinner at Maxim's and then, the plan was— '

She found herself holding her breath.

'Simon, please, you don't have to . . .'

And suddenly he was looking right at her. Green eyes boring into her.

'I was going to ask you to be my wife,' he said simply. 'And what's more, I think you may even have had some idea that it was coming.'

She stood beside him and flushed, correctly guessing what he'd say next.

'The ring, Jean,' he said, looking coolly at her. 'The engagement ring. You found it, didn't you? Just before you disappeared?'

'Yes,' she nodded simply. 'I came across it. Not on purpose, though. It was a complete accident; I wasn't rummaging or anything like that at all. It was just that a pile of your clothes fell down on me from on top of a wardrobe and when I went to put everything back, there it was. I'm sorry . . . I know I shouldn't have, but as soon as I saw it, just had to know what was in that beautiful ring box. And it was breathtaking, Simon, it really was.'

'Glad to hear you thought so,' he said curtly. 'Certainly didn't look that way to me at the time.'

She looked keenly back at him, desperately wanting to sit down beside him and grip his hands in hers, so he couldn't keep on avoiding her gaze. Not knowing what to say next.

The speech she'd so carefully rehearsed was completely choked out of her. She'd no words left; she'd nothing.

Say something, she silently willed Simon. At least throw me a lifeline here. For old times' sake, if nothing else.

'Jean,' he eventually said, after sighing so deeply, it was almost like it was coming from the soles of his feet. 'It seems your sole purpose in coming here was to try to make yourself feel better for what you'd put us all through.'

Unfair and so wide of the mark, she thought to herself, but let it pass. Chances were she deserved it. Deserved a lot worse.

'But you need to know,' he went on, 'that your actions had consequences. Did you ever once stop to think about how it must have looked from my point of view back then? One minute, you're here and it's Christmas and you're all excited to be going on holidays with me, next thing you've vanished into thin air, leaving Angie and me like two headless chickens running around trying to find you, all the time imagining the very worst. Then out of the blue, I discover that you'd stumbled across the engagement ring. So three guesses what conclusion I jumped to?'

'Please, you don't have to—'

'No, I heard you out and now it's my turn. Up until you and I got together, you apparently were famous for running to the hills each and every time you as much as sensed that a guy was getting serious on you. I'd heard you and Angie telling so many stories together, giggling about the time one particular boyfriend wanted you to move in with him and what did you do? Bolted in the opposite direction, as fast as you could, apparently.'

'That's not fair! I had bloody good reasons for backing away when I did!'

'So what was I left to deduce, Sherlock?' he said bitterly. 'That you'd found the ring and your old pattern had just repeated itself. As it had done so many times in the past. So just try and imagine how that made me feel, if you even can. I was about to put my whole heart on the line for you and what do you do? The minute you get an inkling of what's coming, you just take off.'

'But that wasn't the case at all, Simon! Surely you know that by now! That's what I've been trying to tell you!'

'Shame it's coming two years too late,' was all he said, eyeballing her coldly.

Waste of time, she suddenly thought to herself. What was she even doing here any more? She'd tried her best to talk to him and got exactly nowhere. He wouldn't listen, wouldn't even try to. She'd expected a lot of things, but was never quite prepared for the level of anger he still held against her. There was nothing more to say, except goodbye.

'I should go,' she said simply, hoping for some kind of reaction, but getting absolutely none.

'I'll see you out.'

He rose to his feet and led her on down through the tiny, dark hallway to the front door.

'Where will you stay?' he asked, politely enough. Like he was talking to a complete stranger whose welfare he wasn't particularly bothered with.

'I booked into a hotel in town. Cheap and cheerful, but then I'm not here for very much longer.'

'How much longer?'

'It's an open-ended ticket, though I hadn't even planned on staying this long. But I imagine I'll be out of your hair by the end of the week.'

Cape Town awaited. Serving fries and cheap beer to tourists and picking up manky towels from a hotel room floor awaited. Living the life of a student in a shared flat at the grand old age of thirty-three, while kids far younger than her effortlessly by-passed her in work, awaited. She had to go back, had no choice, she knew that. She'd made her bed and now had no choice but to lie in it.

She just hadn't banked on realising just how much she missed the pull of home and how hard it would be to leave, that was all.

'Anything you want to take with you from here before you go?' Simon asked coldly.

'No, thanks.'

'And what are your plans for the rest of your stay?' he asked, holding open the hall door for her as she stepped outside into the street.

Again, if you were eavesdropping, you'd swear she was some random tourist who'd stopped and hammered on the door, to ask for directions to the nearest pub.

'There's a lot of people I need to talk to,' she told him. 'With Angie top of the list. If she'll hear me out, that is.'

Did she just imagine a tiny change in his expression when she mentioned Angie's name? Or was she imagining it?

'I'm sure she will,' he eventually said. 'Angie is one of the sweetest, warmest human beings on this planet . . .'

'I know that.'

'. . . And she never stopped caring about you or sticking up for you, you know. Not in all this time.'

'Nor I about her.' Or you either, she wanted to tack on, but couldn't.

'Probably something you should know before you meet her, though,' he went on, and she thought she may have imagined it, but swore she sensed a slight gear shift in his voice.

'Is it about her new business, with Sarah? The Chocolate Bar? Amazing news, but then I always had faith that she'd do well. I used to think the only person who didn't have faith in Angie, was Angie herself.'

Angie had told her all about it yesterday, before they'd left for Dublin, and Jean had genuinely felt so thrilled for the girl, inordinately proud of her.

'Now all you need is a good man in your life to complete the picture and you're away!' were the last words she'd said to her, not sure why Angie flushed a bit before driving off. Maybe there was someone on the scene for her? Jean hoped so. No one deserved it more. And it would be a lucky man who landed a gem like Angie, that was for certain.

'No,' Simon said, 'it doesn't concern work. As a matter of fact, it's about her private life.'

'I knew it!' Jean smiled, actually sounding animated for the first time since she'd got here. 'I knew there was a man on the scene for her!'

And now she definitely wasn't imagining it. Simon was looking at her differently. Almost a bit guiltily, she thought.

Two minutes later, walking shell-shocked back down the street, she finally knew the reason why.

Simon and Angie.

The man she loved and her one-time best friend.

And there was absolutely nothing she could do about it, bar go back to Cape Town and somehow try to battle on as best she could.

Chapter Twenty

My flat, crack of bleeding dawn

Frenetic phone calls have all started, now that word's gone round on the tom-toms. First call is from my buddy Jeff, at bloody six in the morning. (Jeff's a v. early riser. Has to be, all the work he does applying slap on early morning brekkie TV shows, where he's gigging as a freelance make-up 'artiste'.) Plus I'm about the only person he'd dare ring at this hour, but then he knows right well I'll probably be already up, washed, dressed, out the door and on my way to open up The Chocolate Bar by now.

The very second the mobile on my bedside table rings, I'm instantly awake, thinking, *please be Simon, please be Simon . . .*

'Angie? It's me! Did I wake you?'

It's not Simon. I try v. hard to keep the deflation out of voice. Not easy, though, given that I'm half awake and am only capable of sounding remotely human after two cups of super mocha grande latte, with muffins and jam on side, etc.

'Oh, hi, Jeff,' I manage to yawn down phone. 'No, don't worry, I've got to get up for work shortly anyway.'

'That's what I thought,' he says, sounding ready to burst if he doesn't get the inside scoop v. soon. 'Anyway, I'm in the make-up room out at *Good Morning Ireland* and can barely concentrate on my Mac primers and Chubby Sticks till I find out exactly what's going on! So come on, babes, tell me everything! How have you been holding up?'

'Oh, I'm all right. I suppose. You know,' I tell him groggily.

'Dunno about you, but I'm finding all this so stressful.'

'*You're* finding it stressful?'

'Well, yeah, of course! One half of me is delighted that Kitty is back safe and sound, while the other half of me is in flitters till I know how all this is going to play out in the final reel.'

'Jeff! It's too early to talk about final reels . . . Please! I need caffeine for this conversation!'

He's not listening, though.

'Because I just can't get my head around all this drama! The returned ex-girlfriend, the man who used to love her and the new woman in his life who also happened to be her erstwhile best friend . . . God, it sure as hell beats any plotline *Coronation Street* could come up with! But then, you know me! I'm always saying that real life trumps fiction every single time.'

He warbles on as I haul myself up onto one elbow and try to act like I'm alert and awake.

'So what are you going to do?' Jeff's demanding in one ear. 'No pressure or anything, Ange, but I've already told the whole make-up room and we're all beside ourselves to know.'

What indeed?

'Just like in *Rebecca*,' he adds dreamily. 'The absent influence that casts a shadow over a fledgling relationship . . .'

'Excuse me, it's absolutely nothing like *Rebecca* at all!' I tell him stoutly, bloody well wide awake now.

'Though mind you, at least in *Rebecca* the ex had the good grace to be buried underwater. Not alive and well and suddenly back to cause the second Mrs de Winter yet more trouble.'

Running down Dame Street to work, v late by now. Scarily late

I bump into Sarah outside Chocolate Bar, who's pulling up the shutters and unlocking the place. And yet somehow – typical Sarah –managing to look like she just stepped out of a beauty salon, with immaculate hair, tank-proof make-up, high heels, the whole works. In one quick up-and-down look, she takes in the manky, dishevelled state of me. (Haven't slept and I was so v. late getting up this morning, I had to choose between washing my hair and/or brekkie. Unsurprisingly, brekkie won out.)

'There you are, honey! Are you OK?' she says, giving me a big, warm hug.

I already filled her in on all developments over the phone last night, including Jack Crown coming here just before I locked up. So she knows that Jean is finally safe and that McGuinness piece of pond scum can never harm her again.

'And what was Simon's reaction? When you told him that Jean is safe, I mean?' she asks, as together we whip up the clattery shutters and let ourselves inside to set up for the day. Which usually involves switching the alarm off, getting the espresso machines up and running, then nattering at length about last night's telly.

'I haven't. That is, I tried to . . . I mean, I called him and everything, but he never got back to me.'

'*What?* You mean you never heard a peep from him last night? Nothing at all?'

'No, and now I think I'm being dumped Irishman style.'

'What's Irishman style?'

'You know. When a guy just starts acting weird on you, not returning any of your panicky calls and generally making you feel like you're turning into a stalker, just for trying to make contact. When he's theoretically supposed to be your boyfriend. Then eventually, you're supposed to cop on that you've actually been, or are about to be dumped. It's what all Irishmen do when they can't bear to have the face-to-face chat with you. Act weird for a bit and hope you'll be good enough to do the dumping for them. Classic coward's way out.'

'Can't quite believe that of Simon,' Sarah says, shaking her head worriedly. 'Mr Perfect? Who's always so attentive to you?'

'Well, you'd better believe it, hon,' I mutter exhaustedly, heading into the store room to pull on my Chocolate Bar apron and a v. unflattering hairnet. Don't mean to sound this cranky, it's just that the whole thing has the head scalded off me.

'Just like in *Rebecca*,' Sarah sighs, her face the picture of concern now.

'No! It's nothing like in *Rebecca!* Nothing at all!'

And as an aside, I wish everyone would bloody stop trying to cast me as the second Mrs de Winter! I'm seriously bloody fed up with it. Enough!

8.50 a.m.

Phone rings. Finally, finally, finally, it's Simon. I've had my mobile stuffed in my apron pocket just in case, and nearly drop it into a jug of frothy soya milk, I'm so anxious to answer. He apologises profusely for not calling last night and fills me in on the reason why.

'So . . . Jean called over to see you?' I ask him in a v. small voice, slipping into the store room for maximum privacy and leaving Sarah on her own to deal with customers.

Subtext: do you still love her? And does she still love you? And why am I once again getting the sick feeling that I'm on the arse end of a love triangle here?

'She was trying to make her peace,' he says flatly.

'And?'

Silence.

No, I think furiously, no more with the long-drawn out silences! I'm sick to the bloody gills of them!

But now Simon's doing what he always does when faced with emotionally awkward questions. Just goes frustratingly quiet on me, so of course, I end up warbling like a complete moron, just to fill dead air.

'Because you know, I'm first and foremost your friend here!' I tell him. 'I care about you and of course I know just how difficult this must be for you. But it's not exactly a barrel of laughs being in my shoes either, trust me.'

'I know that, Angie,' he eventually says, after a pause worthy of Chekhov.

I take a leaf out of Sarah's book. And decide on direct confrontation.

'Well then, I suppose the big question is now, what are we going to do?'

I so badly want him to say: I'll tell you exactly what we're going to do, love: you and I are going to skip town, take the first flight out of here and spend the next two weeks on some remote desert island with absolutely no internet or mobile signal. Just till all this shite dies down. Then we'll just go right back to where we used to be. Happy and untroubled.

He doesn't, though.

'Look,' he eventually says, 'I'm in the office and just about to head into a meeting, I can't really talk properly now. But I'll call you later, OK?'

'OK,' I say, though I'm actually thinking, you fecking well better, mate. I'm seriously starting to get sick of all this lack of communication and 'just bury your head in the sand and wait till it all blows over' carry-on.

Who in right mind would put up with that? I mean, who'd even want to?

'Oh, just one more thing,' he says.

'What's that?'

Be ready at the airport with your bags packed and meet me there in an hour, with your passport tucked under your oxter? Yes, I think, clutching wildly at the hope, I'm so there . . .

'I have a feeling Jean may want to see you too. She's here to make peace, so don't be surprised if she pitches up at The Chocolate Bar anytime soon.'

'Well, bring it on. Quite apart from everything else I have to tell her that Jack Crown called here last night and said if she got in touch, I was to contact him.'

I fill him in v. quickly on the reason why.

Another agonising silence while I fret about what conclusion he's coming to.

'So she's finally safe then?' is all he says. Flatly, in a monotone. Like I've just given him the latest shipping forecast.

'Yeah, it seems so.'

'And just before I go . . . the thing is, there's something else you should know, Angie. I told her about you and me too.'

Jesus. Now the legs suddenly feel like they'll buckle under me.

'I thought it was only fair and right,' he adds. 'Just because she kept secrets from us for so long doesn't mean we have to.'

'OK. Well, yeah, absolutely.'

'Shit, look, I'm so sorry about this, but my meeting's about to start, I really have to go. Let's talk later, yeah?'

'OK. Later.'

But in the meantime, what am I supposed to do? Wait around and see if Jean will just stroll in here and clobber me over the head with a large skillet for seeing Simon now?

Jean . . . I think as a fresh wave of worry hits me. Why did she come all the way up to Dublin anyway? Suppose she's really come this far just to try and get back with him?

The worst pang of all comes when I think about Simon, though. Which leaves me exactly nowhere. Except waiting to see what he's going to decide. And if it comes down to it, whether he'll choose her or choose me.

And I've an incredibly prescient gut feeling that I already know what the outcome of that will be.

Chapter Twenty-One

The Chocolate Bar, 10.30 a.m.

The phone rings in store room. Jamie, our new barista, answers it while I'm wiping down tables after a particularly mental brekkie rush. Sarah's gone out to the airport to crack the whip and keep a beady eye on things. (She's convinced staff nicking chocs is becoming an issue out there, though personally I can't really blame them. I'd do the v. same myself. The goodies here are just too addictive.)

'It's for you, Angie,' Jamie says, coming back to man the espresso machines.

Bowels instantly turn to water.

'Who is it?'

'Didn't say. Some woman looking for you.'

But I know, just know, deep in my womanhood exactly who it is and why she's calling. And for once, I'm right on the money. I pick up phone and suddenly it's like putting the clock back two years.

Except I'm talking to someone called Jean, not Kitty at all.

12.50 p.m.

'So what exactly did Jean say to you?' Sarah shrieks at me, when she gets back from her fact-finding mission out at the airport and I fill her in.

'Just that she wants to meet for lunch today, so we can talk. And that was it really.'

'That can't have been it! You mean she didn't say anything at all about you and Simon?'

'Well, what exactly could she say? I mean, yeah, I know I've broken this unwritten commandment of friendship, but in my defence, she bloody well broke it first, didn't she?'

What I don't tell her is that I'm actually having such serious doubts about Simon and the way he's been carrying on, that I'm half tempted to pull a disappearing stunt myself, till all this crap is long behind me. I was just about to text him to let him know I'd be meeting her, then I thought to myself, why even bother? So he can just not reply to yet another one of my messages? I knew deep down it was a complete waste of time. And if he wants to bury his head in sand till this all blows over, then shagging well let him.

'And did you tell Jean that Jack Crown needs to see her urgently?'

'Didn't get the chance. Just then a clatter of customers all came in together and it got so noisy in here, I could barely hear myself, let alone anyone else. Besides, that's a conversation to be had face to face, don't you think?'

'So where are you meeting her?'

'The Exchequer Bar,' I tell her, unsure really of why I even suggested it, only that it's a) public, in the event of furniture flinging, b) close by The Chocolate Bar, in case

I've the sudden urge to make a quick getaway, and c) somehow I can't imagine ever meeting Jean for lunch in anywhere other than a pub. Back in old days, Kit— sorry, keep meaning to say Jean, would only ever eat lunch in bars.

'Hmm. Good call,' Sarah says. 'Nice and close by in the event of your needing backup or reinforcements.'

'Can you spare me in here for an hour or so?'

'Of course! Don't even think about rushing back till you and she are sorted, one way or another. Take all afternoon, if you'd like. I'm here and I'm going absolutely nowhere, in case you need backup or support.'

'You're an angel, hon.' I smile gratefully at her.

'Or I could come with you, if you'd like me to?'

'Thanks, but I think I really need to see her alone. Just this once. If you don't mind, that is.'

'No, don't worry, I understand. Just can't bloody well *believe* I was out when she rang,' she goes on, whipping off her jacket, pulling on her work pinny and starting to get a bit worked up now. 'Because I'm telling you, if it had been me who answered that phone . . .'

'Don't worry, you'll get your chance to talk to her very soon,' I tell her nice and soothingly. Always best way to deal with Sarah whenever she's getting a bit wound up.

'I mean, when you think about it,' she says, efficiently going to the till to count the morning's taking so far, 'here we are, and we've all learned to somehow live without her, and now what? Do we just unlearn the past two years and start over? Are we suddenly just expected to reintegrate her back into our lives and just pick up where we left off? Easier said than done, you know.'

'Hon, I know . . .'

'And another thing; if she as much as thinks that she's got any right to come between you and Simon, she'll have me to answer to. That's no idle threat, by the way.'

'But in the meantime, just stay here with your phone to hand and if I text you with an SOS, don't think twice. Just come running.'

Exchequer Street, 1.00 p.m. on the dot

Thank God, the pub is only round the corner from The Chocolate Bar, so I've only a v. short distance to race, to get there on time. Completely on impulse, I whip the card Jack Crown handed me last night out of my handbag and call him. He answers after about two rings. I fill him in and tell him I'm just about to meet Jean.

'Great,' he says warmly. 'That's terrific news. Good of you to let me know.'

'It's no problem.'

'So can you get her to call me as soon as possible? You can tell her why and that it really is urgent. Tell her I'm in Harcourt Street all day, if she'd like to drop in instead; or if she'd prefer me to meet her somewhere else, that's fine too. Main thing is that I get to talk to her. She needs to know the full facts and the sooner the better. The girl deserves to have her mind put at rest.'

'Don't worry, I will,' I pant breathlessly down the phone. 'And thanks for the lift home last night, by the way.'

'Anytime. Always a pleasure to meet a fellow movie buff.'

I think it's the first time today I've actually managed to crack a smile.

'And by the way, Angie?'

'Yeah?'

'If you wanted to come into the office with Jean later on today, you'd be more than welcome.'

'Oh. OK then.'

''Course, I can't promise the coffee here would be up to The Chocolate Bar's exalted standards, but I'll do my best.'

Exchequer Bar, 1.05 p.m.

Jean's already here ahead of me. Waiting for me in a quiet table for two, tucked right away at the very back. A good, suitable spot, I think distractedly. Nice and private. I wave over at her as I weave my way through the lunchtime throng. Still not able to get head round how in one way she looks so different and yet in another, she's exactly the same.

She's wearing jeans today and a v. sober-looking plain black sweater. Inconspicuous-type clothes. The kind of gear Kitty would have laughed at and probably claimed she looked like she was trying to sell life insurance. But then back in the day, Kitty would have gone round wearing the lagging jacket off the boiler if she was let. Her short, tight, cropped hair is so difficult to get used to as well. It's utterly bizarre; a bit like looking at a close relative of someone you once knew intimately.

Jean gets up when I come over and there's a tense pause as two of us just stand looking at each other. Like two actors in a bad play who've forgotten their lines. And suddenly, I just choke up. Just at the thought that this was the one single person who I was closest to in the whole world for such a long time, and now we're like two distant acquaintances tiptoeing politely round each other.

'Sorry I'm late,' I eventually manage to croak out.

'Hey, I'm just happy that you agreed to meet me at all,'

she says quietly, sincerely. 'I wanted to talk to you on my own. There's just . . . well, there's things I need to say to you that I just couldn't, at least not in front of Simon. You understand, I hope?'

I nod as we sit down, then of course nerves get the better of me, so I immediately start gabbling. Tell her all about Jack Crown, that she needs to contact him and, more importantly, the reason why.

There's a v. long silence as Jean just slumps back against her chair and exhales deeply, somehow trying to take it all in.

'So, you understand, you're finally safe,' I tell her insistently, half wondering why she doesn't look a bit more relieved. Not that I expected her to get up and start dancing jigs and reels on tables or anything, but come on, this surely is good news, isn't it?

'Joe McGuinness has emigrated to New Zealand,' I find myself repeating, really pressing the point home. 'And according to Jack, it's highly unlikely he'll ever show his face in this country again. For one thing, he owes far too much money. It seems the guy's gone bankrupt, he's in debt up to his oxters and there's even talk of a pending fraud charge against him. And secondly . . .'

But I break off here a bit.

'Secondly what?' she asks weakly, suddenly white-faced underneath her suntan.

'Well . . . I know Jack is hoping that you'll make a statement. A full statement, about everything that happened to you.'

She visibly winces at this, but I've started so I'll finish.

'It's all for your own protection,' I tell her gently. 'Just in the unlikely event that McGuinness ever did track you down again, so that he can be prosecuted and brought to trial for what he's done. Because Kit— Sorry! It's bloody hard trying to call you Jean the whole time. You'll always be Kitty to me.'

A faint smile from her.

'You think that's weird? Try being me,' she says wryly.

'Jean,' I say, a bit more confidently now, 'the thing is, you can't keep doing this to yourself any more. Never mind to others around you. You can't just plant down roots somewhere, make friends and then walk away from it, all over again. You certainly have no reason to any more. You're safe, you're really safe! Finally. And what's more, you always will be. The running is over. All those lies and deceptions are in the past. It's time to move on for good. And come on, aren't you the girl who used to preach to me that we'll all be a long time dead?'

I actually think she might start getting teary now, which I'm not sure I could handle. Because she never used to; was famous for it.

'Did I ever really used to say that?' she says, shaking her head. 'Pity I couldn't have practised what I preached.'

'Jean,' I ask her, beside myself to blurt out the one question that I've been burning to ask her, more than anything, 'why did you stay with him all that time? With McGuinness, I mean. You could have left him before, when he first . . . well, when things first turned nasty for you. You could have got help. You had only to ask, hon.'

She focuses on the middle distance and it takes her an age to answer.

'I spent countless nights asking myself that very same question, believe me. But you've no idea what it was like. The pull he had over me back then, how entwined our lives were. I was someone who'd basically been alone and fighting her own battles since about the age of sixteen and suddenly this older man walks into my life and says he'll take care of me. And he did; when things were good between us, they were unbelievable. It was, I suppose, a first love thing for me, but God, it actually got to a point where I really thought my whole life wasn't worth living without him. And I know that makes me sound so frail and pathetic and weak, like one of those women you'd see on daytime TV trying to defend an abusive relationship by coming out with crap like, "But I love him!" But there you go, it's the God's honest truth. And if it could happen to someone like me, who was always such a battler, it could happen to anyone.'

I lean over and instinctively give her hand a tight squeeze.

'I completely understand,' I tell her softly, 'though for what it's worth, you could have trusted me back then. When we first met and got so friendly, I mean, you could have told me, you know. I'd have done everything I could to protect you. Sure, you were my best pal. I'd have done anything for you.'

'You were the best friend I ever had,' she says wistfully.

'I know it won't be easy for you,' I tell her, feeling like I'm slowly winning her over. 'Talking about it, I mean. After so long. But if you'd like, I'll even come with you to the cop shop. And I promise, it won't be half as bad as you think. Jack Crown is a nice guy, trust me. He's on your side and he's one of us.'

Still in the Exchequer Bar, 1.25 p.m.

Feck lunch anyway, we've moved onto the G and Ts. Dunno about Jean, but I sure as hell need one to get me through this. I knew it was only a matter of time before the giant elephant in the room reared its ugly head and sure enough, after a big, nerve-calming gulp from the glass in front of her, Jean turns to me. Not v. hard to guess what's coming next.

'So,' she says, meeting my gaze head on in that fearless way she always had. 'You and Simon.'

I clench my bum and look anywhere except at her. But what she says next absolutely astonishes me.

'Look, Angie, I'm going to be out of your hair in no time. And that's a promise. But before I go, I want you to know that I'm genuinely happy for you. Both of you. I mean that so sincerely. Jesus, would you ever look at me when I'm trying to say this?'

I bring myself to meet her eyes and see she's smiling back at me. Actually *smiling*. A big broad smile too, a genuine smile, not a fake Miss World runner-up one. No, I think wildly, this isn't supposed to happen . . . She's surely supposed to be overturning tables and accusing me of being a big boyfriend stealer! I wasn't expecting niceness and encouragement!

For some reason, I'm completely incapable of saying anything back to her, though; it's like my jaw is suddenly wired shut. She's not supposed to be this sweet about it, no matter what she did on us two years ago.

'Angie, you're one of the loveliest and most loyal women I've ever had the privilege of knowing,' she says, taking my hand now and pressing it affectionately. 'No one deserves happiness more, absolutely no one. And Simon . . . well, he's the best there is. So I suppose what I'm trying to say is that, in spite of everything I put you through, I just couldn't leave without wishing you well. Both of you.'

'That's . . . well . . . what I mean is, thanks, I manage to stammer. For being so understanding about this whole mess.'

'Well, what did you think I was going to do? Accuse you of being a boyfriend stealer and start smashing gin glasses into your face?'

Exactly what I'd thought, as matter of fact.

And now she's laughing, her big belly laugh too, giving me a lightning-quick, momentary flashback to the old Kitty and the way she could always find the humour in anything.

'Sure, what right have I to start laying down the law with you or with anyone else, for that matter?' she says. 'Christ, I count myself lucky you still agreed to meet me today. And as for Simon, I thought he was going to physically throw me out of the house when I went round there last night. He's so bitter, so angry. Still.'

'Just give him time,' I tell her. Although I find myself not automatically able to tack on, 'because am certain he'll get over it and get over you and all will be rosy again.'

'Anyway, I hope you'll both be very happy,' she's v. generously saying. 'You're two lovely people who deserve no less. So, I just wanted you to know that there's someone all the way down in Cape Town wishing you well. ' And now she's raising her glass and actually toasting us as a couple.

I just shift uncomfortably round in the seat.

Because suddenly this is all starting to feel v., v. wrong. Jean's making it sound like Simon and I will be engaged in a matter of months and will go on to live happily ever after, in a suburban starter home with an interest-only mortgage and a shedload of crap from IKEA.

So why am I not feeling that too? And moreover, why don't I feel as upset about it as I was so certain I would?

But that's when it hits me square in the face. As soon as

I've somehow finally managed to catch onto one of the worries that have been swirling round my head, suddenly I can make order out of chaos and can see with perfect clarity. See everything.

Because the truth is that Simon and I were a bit like two bereaved people who grew closer and closer, to somehow help each other get by. When Kitty first disappeared, I suppose we were both in a kind of state of mourning, and now that there's no need to grieve her loss any more, I find myself looking at him with brand-new eyes. We're fundamentally two friends who crossed a line that I now seriously doubt we should ever have gone near in the first place.

Jean's looking back at me now, a bit puzzled and confused. Probably wondering why I'm gone so quiet all of a sudden. Why I'm not acting like one half of a loving, devoted couple.

'If it makes the slightest difference,' I eventually find words enough to tell her, 'all we mostly did was talk about you.'

Still in the Exchequer Bar, 2.55 p.m.

Two gin and tonics later and suddenly it's like the past two years have just rolled away. We're chatting away just like we used to, somehow managing to keep approx. five conversational balls up in the air all at once. Jean (and it's only now I've finally got used to calling her that) is filling me in all about her life in Cape Town, which sounds on the surface so exotic and glam but which she swears is anything but.

She chats away about the Cape Grace Hotel where she works as a chambermaid by day and which she says is a fabulous place to work; you were valued and respected, even in the humblest job like hers. But there was a major downside; they'd nearly be sending you off for counselling if you didn't bounce in seven days a week singing 'Oh, What a Beautiful Morning' at the top of your lungs.

Then she makes me smile when she talks about a stunningly gorgeous flatmate she shares with called Paige, and how panicky she's getting about blokes in spite of her effortless beauty, given that she's living in a city where everyone's so bloody good-looking it's a level playing field. If you happen to be six foot tall, look like Georgia Jagger and weigh approx a hundred and three pounds, that is.

'So what about you, then?' I nudge her. Bit cheeky, I know, but then the gin and tonics are finally starting to make me v. confident now. Also, everything's out in the open anyway; what's left for the girl to hide?

'Come on, Jean, I've told you everything, so fair's fair! Fess up time; is there a lovely man on the scene that you want to tell your Auntie Angie about?'

She nearly guffaws into her drink. A tiny gesture, but one so exactly like the way she used to, that I suddenly feel an overwhelming urge to give her a big bear hug.

'Have I a boyfriend? Are you taking the piss?' she grins.

'Come off it, I don't believe you! You always had fellas salivating over you everywhere you went! And the more you ran away from them, the more they'd chase you. It was unbelievable. To this day, I've never seen anything quite like it!'

She doesn't answer me, though. Just shakes her head then starts crunching lump of ice from bottom of her drink.

'Well, no offence, but I'm certainly glad I don't live in Cape Town,' I shrug back at her in the silence. 'If you're single, then what possible chance would someone like me have, surrounded by all those glamour hammer-y ones? It's bad enough here in Dublin!'

'But you've got a partner now. A lovely one who treats you like the goddess you are.'

'Oh. Yes, of course. Yeah, I do.'

I find myself going a bit quiet at that. And then I wonder . . . is it a bad sign that she had to remind me?

Now on our third gin and tonic, 3.40 p.m.

Yeah, yeah, I know, I'm a shameless lush for getting sozzled in the day, but somehow I don't care that I have to go back to work; we're just having way too much craic here. Every now and then, I keep half-heartedly getting up to leave, pleading that it's not fair to leave Sarah in The Chocolate Bar high and dry and just bunk off for the afternoon, etc, etc. But then Jean will just yank me back down beside her and tell me to stop acting like such a bloody head girl; that one boozy lunch won't kill me.

Just like old times.

Besides, Sarah v. kindly texts to see how I'm getting on and to check that no back-up, SWAT teams, etc. are necessary. She also stresses that I'm to take rest of the day off, that between herself and Jamie, everything's under control, bless her.

The chat's seriously loosening up now. Not even certain how it happened, but we're now yakking about the old days, swapping stories, telling tales out of school. Girl talk.

Turns out to be the best afternoon I've had in I don't know how long.

5.10 p.m.

Phone rings, and it's Jack Crown. I apologise to Jean but explain that I have to take it, it's important.

'Angie?' he asks, and I have to strain a bit to hear him, it's that noisy in here by now. 'Are you OK? I just wanted to check up on you. Everything all right?'

'Waaaaay better than all right, everything's bloody fantastic!' I slur a bit down the phone. 'I'm here with Jean and it's brilliant, we're having such a laugh . . . catching up with each other, telling stories about the old days . . .'

'You sure you're OK? You sound a bit . . . ahem. Well, you know . . .'

'Never been better!'

'Look, I just wondered if you got a chance yet to ask Jean to come into the station to make a statement. But if you can't talk, I understand. Don't worry, I'll call you back later.'

'Em . . . look . . . Oh . . . just hang on a minute, would you?'

I fill Jean in. It's that copper I was telling you about, I mouth silently at her. Wants you to go in to him, as soon as you can. Whaddya think?

What, now? Jean mimes back at me.

Yeah, now.

She thinks for a minute, then knocks back the dregs of her G and T and grabs her coat, all set to leave.

Come with me, she mouths, scooping her backpack up off the floor.

As if I'd let you go in there alone, I mime back.

'Let's get it over with now, then,' she says out loud, looking defiant. Strong. Much more like the girl I used to know. And love.

'Atta girl.'

'Besides, the drunker I am for this, the better.'

'That sounded like a yes?' Jack says hopefully into the phone, pulling me back to the call.

'We're on our way,' I tell him.

'Just tell me where you both are, and I'll send one of our lads to pick you up.'

'You did say this Jack Crown would go easy on me, now didn't you?' Jean says, suddenly a bit anxious. 'I mean, he's a nice guy, isn't he? Because if he starts giving me any shit about what I did, I'm so out of there.'

'Trust me, he's not going to. And yes, Jack's very nice. Actually, lovely.'

Chapter Twenty-Two

5.25 p.m.

Drunketty-drunk, drunk, drunk. Jean and I are sat in the back of an actual squad car, being whizzed at speed through traffic all the way up to Harcourt Street Garda HQ. V. exciting, I have to say, like being a paid extra in a cop opera. Also, hysterically funny. Jean keeps rolling down the window every time we're stopped at traffic lights, sticking her head out and screeching, 'Help! It's a terrible miscarriage of justice! I'm being held against my will! Call my TD, call a parish priest, get Sky News here, do anything, just help meeeee pleeeease!!!'

Am convulsed with giggles till the stony-faced copper driving us tells us to stop messing or else the pair of us can get out and walk.

Harcourt Street Station, 5.35 p.m.

Jack's just inside the main entrance, waiting on us. He helps Jean out of the car, shakes hands and introduces himself. And is gentle and sensitive with her, I notice, which of course is absolutely the right way to handle her. Weird, but for all

Jean's messing and larking about earlier, now that we're actually here, it's like the enormity of what lies ahead has really started to hit home. And somehow Jack seems to sense this, so he thanks her for coming in, promises her that it'll all be over before she knows it and reassures her that she's absolutely done the right thing. For her part, Jean just nods and manages a smile, head held high, looking like she's ready to face anyone. A firing squad, anything.

'Well, I've come this far,' she tells him stoutly, so much like her old self. 'So let's just do it.'

Then Jack comes over to me, grins and in a second seems to guess that the pair of us have been merrily boozing away for the whole afternoon.

'Enjoy your lunch then?' he asks, mouth twitching downwards.

'Eh . . . lovely, thanks,' I say, trying my level best to sound sober.

'Come on inside then, ladies,' he smiles. 'And I think we might just get you both some strong coffee before we start.'

'If it's OK,' Jean says, 'I'd really like Angie to sit in on this too?'

'Of course. If that makes you feel more comfortable.'

'I kept secrets from my friends for long enough,' she says, as we're ushered down a long, snaking corridor. 'And all that ends today.'

Police interview room, 5.55 p.m.

Just myself, Jean, Jack and an older Bangarda who introduces herself as Stella and instantly puts us at ease by explaining she's a liaison officer, specially trained in dealing with domestic abuse cases. Lovely woman, and I can practically see Jean instantly warming to her. She has that firm-but-fair wise-mammy thing going on; you could v. easily see this one putting manners on any man who ever dared inflict even a quarter of what poor Jean had to suffer through.

It's completely weird. Turns out to be exactly the same interview room where Simon and I sat time and again, all that time ago. Being here with Jean beside me now somehow brings it all full circle.

And by the way, I must have waltzed in here like Liz Taylor after a skinful of gin, because the next thing, a tray of coffee is brought in and Jack makes sure that the two of us drink it down to the very last drop.

6.40 p.m.

I'm seriously sobering up now that Jean's finally making her statement. And in spite of the fact I've already heard her tell it before, is somehow even more harrowing second time round. Jean's amazing, too; sounds fearless, brave, not a bit like a victim at all. She talks about the abuse, the pain she went through, and how trapped she felt; how she really had been boxed into a corner and that there was absolutely no one for her to turn to for help. And how that was almost worse than anything else: the complete and utter isolation. My heart goes out to her when she talks about discovering she was pregnant so young, then losing the baby so violently. And how eventually that decided her enough was enough. She made up her mind to grab her chance and to get away the second she could, and if it meant changing her whole identity, then that was a small price to pay.

Stella nods along, like she's not only heard it all before,

but possibly even heard far worse. And Jack is terrific, so sympathetic and understanding. Keeps telling her to stop and take a breather if she's feeling a bit wobbly.

But Jean just shakes her head defiantly.

'I've been waiting a very long time to have my say, Sergeant,' she says, 'please don't stop me now.'

'Could I ask one thing?' Jack gently asks her, shoving the pile of official-looking files he had in front of him aside for the moment.

'Fire ahead.'

'You came to Dublin and started calling yourself Kitty Hope,' he says, blue eyes unflinching. 'We have all that. But what's really puzzling me is, why not travel even further afield? After all, you were still less than a three-hour drive from Galway where McGuinness lived, why not go abroad then and put even more distance between you?'

And for the first time since we got here, Jean surprises me by actually smiling.

'The reason,' she says, 'is sitting right here in this room.'

Everyone turns to look at me and I find myself flushing a bit.

'Because I met you,' Jean tells me, simply. 'Do you remember? In that kiphole of a call centre where we slaved away in those little rabbit hutch cubicles? And we started hanging out together and in no time, it was like the pair of us were just inseparable. Angie introduced me to the loveliest bunch of people and, well . . . we were just having such a ball, I couldn't bring myself to leave. I had never meant to stay in Dublin for so long, I'd only ever intended it as a temporary place to crash out in while I got a few quid together and moved on . . . but after I met Angie . . . well, I just couldn't leave. Or walk out on this amazing life that suddenly opened itself up to me. I felt happy for the first time in years and yes, of course I know it was a shitty thing to lead everyone on like I did and to lead everyone to believe that I had this whole other name, but believe me, I thought I had no other choice.'

I'm actually starting to well up a bit now.

'Besides,' Jean goes on astonishingly calmly, 'Joe McGuinness loathed and despised Dublin, always did. He owed a lot of people money here, so he used to avoid the place like the Black Death. And with a whole new name for myself and a new social circle, day by day, I just got used to being safe. And of course, the longer I stayed, the more difficult it became to ever leave.'

'Well, we really appreciate your honesty,' Jack nods approvingly at her. 'And I know how incredibly difficult it must have been for you to talk about what happened to you all those years ago. But Jean, rest assured, our primary job is in keeping you safe. So in the unlikely event of McGuinness ever targeting you again, he'll find himself in front of me in no time. And with a list of charges against him the length of my arm. Don't you worry, I'll personally see to it.'

'God,' she says, throwing her head back, 'I can't tell you how long I've waited, just to hear that.'

'One last thing, though,' he says, going back to the mound of case files he was working off earlier. 'In the early days of the search, we were able to track Jean Simpson from Amsterdam to Morocco, but the trail just seemed to thin out after then. So, tell me this. How on earth did you get from there all the way to Cape Town without us knowing about it?'

'You're sure I won't be arrested for this?' she asks him a bit cheekily, sounding so like her old self, it's heartening.

'It's not exactly what you might call . . . eh . . . legal.'

'Ah . . . just off the record,' Jack smiles easily, sitting back, stretching his legs out and folding one chunky arm over another. 'I've been curious for a while now. And I promise, it'll go no further than this room.'

'Well, I took a night train to Algeria,' Jean says, 'and let's just say there are many ways of avoiding passport checks on African trains, even now. Border control tends to be a helluva lot more lax than it would be in Europe or the States. Happens all the time. You see people like me pretending to be asleep when they come round to check your documentation for one thing, or else hiding out in the loo . . . it's really not all that hard, trust me.'

'Well, you certainly had me fooled,' Jack grins across at her, then leans over the desk and stage whispers, 'and strictly off the record, of course, fair play to you.'

Jean keeps talking, one of those stories that could only happen to her. How she fell in with a right pair of likely lads from Germany who were travelling by car overland all the way to Zimbabwe, so she hitched along with them and her luck seemed to hold. No one asked any questions, but reading between the lines, it seemed that this pair were every bit as anxious as she was to avoid any kind of official border control checks. And had discovered that just by using interminably long back roads, it wasn't entirely impossible. Took months to get to Zimbabwe, but from there onto Cape Town had been the easy part.

And as Jean's telling her story, embellishing it the way only she can, I notice something else about her.

Funny, I think to myself. In the past few days, so much of the girl I once knew is starting to return, now she's back on home soil. That spark, that magic wildness slowly seems to be somehow re-igniting in her. It's actually beginning to make me think she rightfully belongs here, not a whole hemisphere away from us. Here, where she once had a life and where she could so easily again if she wanted to. Not stuck at the very bottom of Africa, picking up dirty towels from hotel bathroom floors by day, or else serving chips and chicken wings to a load of drunk tourists by night and hating every minute of it. Terrified that she might have to bolt again at a second's notice.

In fact, by now I'm seriously starting to wish that she'd reconsider going back to Cape Town. Just doesn't sit right with me somehow.

Jean eventually finishes up and surprises me by not looking a bit upset or shaken, more relieved now that she's finally had the chance to tell her story.

'Well, we really can't thank you enough.' Jack says, wrapping it up. 'But if it wasn't too much for you, would you mind if I just read the statement back to you? Just to make absolutely certain that there's nothing you want to change or add in, that's all.'

'Hey, I've come this far,' Jean says, sitting back and letting out a long, exhausted sigh, now that it's finally over.

'Well done,' he says. 'Five more minutes, that's all I need, and then I'd safely say you girls are in need of a good strong gin and tonic. You certainly deserve it.'

'I like him,' Jean says, turning to me, not caring that Jack can hear. 'Always thought coppers were meant to be boring beyond belief, but this guy's one of us. Oh, and just in case you were wondering, that's actually meant as a compliment,' she throws cheekily back at him.

'Praise from Caesar!' Jack says wryly, mouth twitching down like he's trying v. hard not to smile.

And as he patiently reads her statement back to her, I drift off a bit. That is, drift off a bit and start wondering if he has a girlfriend.

Just wondering, that's all.

7.10 p.m.

Statement is finished, everyone's v. happy with it and now Stella asks if she could possibly have a little bit of time alone with Jean. She tells us that there's a lot to talk about and even mentions the possibility that Jean could opt for counselling if she wanted to. Jean readily agrees and I take that as my cue to leave. We hug each other tight before I go.

'Thanks, Angie,' she says simply. 'Couldn't have managed this without you.'

'I'll wait outside for you.'

'No, hon, honestly, I'll be fine. Beside, this could take a good while, so go on home and rest; you've had a killer of a day. And I'll call you later on, OK? I promise.'

Jack v. kindly sees me out, then just as I'm about to leave, stops me in my tracks.

'You certainly seem a little more like yourself now,' he smiles.

'Eh . . . how do you mean?'

'Oh, nothing. Just when you and Jean first came in here, I thought maybe you'd em . . . well, let's just say that a liquid lunch might have been involved. Would I be right?'

I laugh back at him. And after all the tensions of the past few days, it's actually genuine, relieved laughter now that somehow everything seems to be just fine.

'Jack, I honestly don't think either of us would have managed to get here in the first place without just a teeny drop of liquid fortification. And come on now, would you really blame us?'

'You feeling OK now?'

I do a quick audit. Then realise that I'm bloody starving. Liquid lunch, my arse; Jean and I ate nothing, just drank whole afternoon away. Come to think of it, I've been so uptight, I haven't eaten since the crack of dawn, unless you count a few sneaky choccies I wolfed down behind Sarah's back at work.

'You know, Angie,' Jack says, correctly interpreting my silence, 'I'm finishing my shift now and I was about to grab a quick bite to eat on the way home anyway. Don't suppose you fancy joining me, do you?'

Harcourt Street, strolling towards Jack's car, 7.15 p.m.

A warm, sunny evening. And for the first time in days, I've a lovely, peaceful feeling of being completely relaxed and at ease with the world (although mind you, that could well be the after effects of all the gin wearing off).

Simon flitters through my mind, as he so often does. I half wonder if I should call him, fill him in on what's been happening, maybe even invite him along for something to eat?

But some inner voice tells me not to. Besides, I've already called him so many times today and am still waiting on a pile of phone calls, not to mention countless texts, to be returned. Don't think I could handle hearing his voicemail message yet again. Enough. I need serious face stuffing first. And I'll think more clearly after that. Always do.

'You know, I'm really delighted you agreed to come for grub,' Jack smiles down at me, shoving a clumpful of the thick, fair hair out of his eyes. Cute little gesture, I find myself thinking distractedly.

'You're doing me a favour!' I smile back. 'Believe me, I'm bloody starving!'

'No, it's not that. What I meant is . . .' He looks ahead of him now.

'Yeah?'

'Well, now, I could have the wrong end of the stick here, of course . . .'

'What do you mean?'

'OK, put it this way. When you and I first met two years back . . . now, I could be wrong, but . . .'

'But what?'

'But I somehow got the impression you weren't exactly a big fan of mine. Would I be right?'

Slight awkward pause. Two options here: tell the truth, or else be polite and lie my way out of it. Seems to be a day for confessions, so decide on plan A.

'Well,' tell him as he turns to look at me, waiting on an answer, 'the thing is, Jack, I'm really sorry if I came across as being a bit brusque with you back in the early days, but you have to understand I was just . . .'

'Say no more,' he smiles. 'You were stressed and worried out of your mind. It was a rotten time for you. I get it.'

'Exactly. So if I ever came across as being, well, a bit rude or anything . . .'

Bless him, he saves me the bother of having to finish that excruciating sentence.

'Don't worry a bit, Angie. Happens all the time. No one ever likes having to be the harbinger of bad news, and in my line of work unfortunately it's an occupational hazard. God, I'll never forget that awful night I had to break the news about Jean to you and your friend Simon. There are days when I hate my job and, believe me, that was one of them.'

I fall silent and keep pace with him, remembering that night with a shudder too.

'Anyway,' he says just as we reach his car. 'I just wanted to make sure you didn't have me down as the big bad wolf any more, that's all I was asking.'

'No, not at all,' I smile back up at him.

And drift off again. Wondering, just casually, if a catch like this could possibly be single.

Elephant and Castle Restaurant, Temple Bar, 9.10 p.m.

God, I've always loved this place! I was *seriously* chuffed when Jack suggested it; major brownie points for him. It's kind of my local, actually, just a stone's throw from where I live, and it really does serve *the* best chicken wings in town. And another bonus too: Jack turns out to be a proper eater, not just a food picker like . . . well, like Simon for one, who spends more time toying with food rather than actually getting it into him, with the result that I just end up finishing his grub for him. Whereas this fella, on the other hand, eats like a trucker on death row, who hasn't seen food in weeks and who's now about to have his last meal. Might sound odd, but it's actually a major plus point in my eyes.

Anyway. After a v. serious amount of face-stuffing, the two of us fall into an easy, companionable banter.

'So come on then, Angie, gimme your top ten movies of all time,' Jack grins, sitting forward and looking attentively at me. 'And no pressure or anything, but you did go to film school, so I'm expecting this to be seriously impressive. But feel free to throw in at least one or two mainstream releases just so I don't feel like a complete dimwit, will you? And not just the less obscure movies of Akira Kurosawa, if you don't mind. No offence, but Japanese art house wouldn't exactly be my strong suit.'

I laugh back at him.

'Ah, now! A top ten list is a helluva lot more complicated than you think,' I say, dipping the v. last of my too-delicious chicken wings into what remains of a blue cheese sauce. Bloody mouth-watering.

'Explain, please?'

'Well, for starters, that's way too broad a field. Many, many sub-divisions exist here, you know. Like, for instance, do you mean top ten thrillers, top ten war movies, Westerns, romantic comedies, musicals, historical movies? Kindly deal in specifics, please!'

He laughs back at me and between us we somehow narrow a long, long list down to approx fifteen. Even find ourselves agreeing on loads. Which is actually surprising, because normally I can never get anyone to agree with my own personal all-time favourites.

'So Hitchcock's *Vertigo* is in then,' Jack says, waving over to the waitress for dessert menus.

'But *The Hurt Locke*r is out?'

'Definitely. *Hurt Locker*'s very worthy, but ultimately boring. Rule one, Thou Shalt not Bore.'

'Seriously over-rated. Totally agree.'

'And out of curiosity, where do you stand on movie actors?'

'Of all time, throughout movie history or present day?'

'Start with present day.'

'You go first.'

'Well, it's not a popular theory and no doubt someone clued in like you, who's actually studied at film school, will roar laughing at me, but I've always thought Tom Cruise was just an all-round terrific actor . . .'

'Snap! Totally agree with you! I mean, did you see him in *Magnolia*? He was stunning.'

'And hysterically funny in *Tropic Thunder*.'

'It's just that no one actually likes him. Not even his wives.'

'Are you an RPatz fan?'

Shake my head. 'Sorry, Jack. Again, not a popular theory, but the guy can't do it. A pretty boy flash in the pan, but sadly no more.'

'Completely agree. He's no DiCaprio, that's for sure. In ten years' time he'll probably be . . .'

'. . . Doing infomercials for shaving mousse or similar.'

'Couldn't have put it better myself. Mind you, if my teenage niece overheard this conversation, she'd have the pair of us stoned to death.'

I throw my head back and guffaw laughing.

Essex Street, just outside my apartment, 10.35 p.m.

Jack drops me home. Absolutely insists, even though I only live a stone's throw from the restaurant.

'Angie,' he says, just as I'm about to hop out of the car. 'Can I ask you something?'

'Sure, go ahead.'

'Well, em . . .'

But he peters out. And there's silence now. Slightly awkward silence, like he's a bit nervous. Which is strange. First time all evening he's been a bit tongue-tied with me.

'Thing is,' he goes on hesitatingly, 'and I'm sure you're probably busy . . . I mean, I know you're up to your tonsils with The Chocolate Bar and everything, but you see . . . Now only if you really fancied it that is . . . and please just feel free to say no if you want to . . .'

I wasn't imagining it! The guy is *definitely* acting bit weird and uncomfortable! And now I find myself looking at him fondly. It's actually endearing.

He takes a deep breath and really goes for it this time.

'Thing is, Angie, there's a new Sam Mendes movie opening tomorrow and I just wondered if you fancied coming along with me to see it? Only if you'd like to, and of course I totally understand if you're busy.'

I smile gratefully back at him. And now it's my turn to be a bit hesitant.

'Jack,' I say falteringly, 'thing is . . . well . . . I've had such a laugh with you tonight and, believe me, there's nothing I'd love more than a lovely movie night this weekend. But you see, it's a bit more complicated than that . . .'

'Don't tell me! You're married? Living with someone? Engaged? Go on,' he grins, 'tell me, I can take it.'

'No, none of the above! But I am seeing someone. I mean, I sort of am. I mean, I was . . . But now it's all a bit . . . Oh, look, it's just that I kind of think I'm seeing someone and it just wouldn't be fair on him, really. I hope you understand.'

There's just a half-beat of a pause as I try to gauge his reaction. Hard to tell if I'm imagining it or not, but . . . somehow he looks a bit . . . a bit what? Resigned? Disappointed, even? Or am I reading this arseways?

'Sure I do,' he says easily. 'And like I said, no worries at all. But can I just say one thing before you go?'

'Sure.'

'Of course, it's absolutely none of my business, but if you only *think* that you're seeing someone, chances are you're not.'

Chapter Twenty-Three

10.40 p.m.

I let myself into the Granary Building, hop into the lift and hit the button for the third floor. Still thinking about Jack Crown, if I'm being honest, and about the fun I had this evening and how entirely unexpected the last five minutes in his car had been. Then it occurs to me, I think I've had my phone on silent ever since I was back in the police interview room with Jean, so I switch it back on again and realise it must have been ringing all night.

Mother of Divine, eighteen missed calls. *Eighteen.* Millions of messages and texts all from either Sarah, Mags and Jeff, all in varying degrees of panic and wanting to know three things. Am I OK, is Jean OK, and what happened this afternoon? Each of them stresses that I'm to call the very second I get their message, which means I'll probably be on phone till approx sometime after 4.00 a.m. tomorrow morning.

I let myself into the flat, all resolved to have a lightning quick shower first, then to hit the phone and give everyone the latest bulletin. But when I come in, I discover the lights are already on in my hallway.

Which is odd. I most definitely didn't leave them on when I went to work at sparrow fart this morning.

I open the living room door and there's Simon, just waiting for me. Looking sheepish. Like he's got something to say.

'Angie,' he says, standing up as soon I come in. 'I'm so sorry about this, but I had to come and see you. I had to talk to you.'

And I think it's the one and only time he's ever even used the key I had cut specially for him.

10.50 p.m.

He follows me into my tiny galley kitchen as I automatically go to make coffees for us. I fill him in about today and he instantly looks relieved; the guy's shoulders visibly unstiffen when I tell him that Jean has finally made a police statement and that her safety is now as good as assured.

'That's certainly good to hear,' he says, gratefully taking the mug I offer him and following me into the sitting room. We both plonk down, him on the sofa, but for some reason, I'm careful to take the armchair opposite, not our normal seats at all. Usually we'd be side by side cuddled up, but not now.

Steel myself, gird my loins.

Who'll go first, though, that's what I want to know.

And in the end, it's him.

'Thing is, Angie,' he eventually begins, a bit hesitatingly, 'I came to say that I'm sorry.'

'You're sorry? What for?' I ask, suddenly wrong-footed. This wasn't the conversation I expected, not by a long shot!

'For acting like such an arse these past few days. Ever

since . . . well, you know the answer to that one. The whole thing's just knocked me for six, Jean being back, I mean, and . . .'

'Simon,' I gently interrupt, 'you don't need to say another word. I completely understand. For God's sake, you wouldn't be human if the whole thing didn't take its toll on you. And for that reason . . .'

I find myself breaking off here, even though I'm absolutely rock-solid certain of what I'm about to come out with next. Just never, in a million years, thought I'd be the one to say it, that's all.

'The thing is,' I tell him, willing myself on. 'I think it's best if you and I take a bit of a break.'

OK, so it may have sounded a bit blurted out, but at least I've said it. At least it's out there.

'A break?' he repeats, looking at me intently and blinking. A lot.

'No, in fact, that's not what I mean. What I'm trying to say is that . . . Simon, you're terrific. You're one of the most amazing people I've ever met and you and I were doing brilliantly as pals. But we crossed a line we shouldn't have ever gone near. Don't you see?'

I try to get a read on his face, but somehow I can't. Then suddenly, I find myself thinking back to all the stuff about him that I made excuse after excuse for, but which actually drove me completely mental. Because there was so much here that deep down I knew I was only ever tolerating. How he'd never stay over here like a normal boyfriend, the infuriating way he'd just drift off into space on me, how he point-blank refused to leave Jean's house, so that I instinctively knew he was happiest living with her memory.

A sudden sense not only of lightness, but of v. deep relief

floods over me, now that it's all out in the open. Because I'm doing the right thing. I'm certain. After all, all I was effectively ever doing with him was wallpapering over cracks and, sure, what's the point in that?

I smile warmly over at him.

'You understand, Simon, don't you? It's just I value you too much as a friend to let this drag on any longer. So can we start again please? And just go back to the way we used to be? Friends?'

He says nothing, just looks over at me fondly for what seems an age. Then in one quick movement, he gets up, pulls me to my feet and hugs me tightly.

'More than just friends, Angie,' he says into my hair. 'Best friends. You're my best friend and I'll never let go of my best friend.'

Then I pull back a bit, so I can face him properly.

'But there's something I need you to do first.'

'Anything. Name it.'

'I need you to make peace with Jean.'

He can't meet my eye now, but I press on anyway.

'That's why she's still here,' I tell him firmly, 'and that's all she asks. Simon, you have to listen to me. Because if you don't, you'll regret it for years to come.'

'You think?' he asks softly.

'I know. Look, I know where she's staying and I've got her new phone number. Just go and see her, that's all I'm asking. It's the right thing, you know it is.'

Chapter Twenty-Four

Saturday, The Chocolate Bar, 5.45 p.m.

Place is absolutely thronged. Lovely, lovely sight. Doubt I'll ever tire of it. Sarah and I have barely come up for air all day and still there's absolutely no sign of customers even beginning to thin out.

I'm dead on my feet at this stage and I know even the indefatigable Sarah must be feeling it too. Not helped by fact that we all had a sort of, ahem, reunion with Jean last night, at her hotel. The whole gang of us; myself, Sarah, Mags and Jeff.

Which actually turned out to be an amazing, magical night. Just like old times. I'd thought it might be a tad awkward, I think I was afraid that accusations and counter-accusation might follow, but there was absolutely nothing. Just a gang of old pals, reconnecting. Thrilled to somehow find each other again, after all this time and in spite of everything that had happened. Even the perennially diehard Sarah, who'd been saying all along that half of her wanted to hug Jean while the other half wanted to throttle her, only had to take one look at the girl, remind herself of what she'd suffered through, and it was like the past completely melted away.

One drink at Jean's hotel somehow turned into three drinks, then some eejit (and I'm sheepishly ashamed to admit it may have been me) suggested going on to the Odessa Club, a v. late night haunt, 'just for a nightcap'. Subsequently, I distinctly remember being poured into a cab at stupid o'clock by Mags, with me groaning that I'd to be up for work, first thing in the morning. 'Course, Mags just roared laughing at me as she slammed the taxi door shut and said, 'HA! Serves you right, Ange! So now you know exactly how it feels to be a stay-at-home mom who functions on four hours' sleep a week, if she's lucky! Welcome to my world, baby!'

Now I love Mags dearly, but she can have a v. cruel streak sometimes.

Brilliant, brilliant night, though. At least the bits I remember of it. Jean, as usual, was the ringleader, the nucleus that the rest of us somehow always seem to revolve around. And it was just so wonderful to see her almost back to her old self. Would really gladden your heart. At various stages throughout the night, we were all at her to change her mind about going back to Cape Town, and once or twice I even thought we might just have persuaded her, but then she'd just deflect the subject and get back to talking about one of us instead.

Knew without her saying anything, though, that it's all down to Simon. You certainly don't have to be Sherlock Holmes to figure that one out. And on the subject of Simon, by the way, it seemed that by the end of the evening, the whole bar were aware that he and I had parted amicably. Total strangers kept coming up to me in the loo and saying things like, 'Hey, I heard you and your ex had the first recorded case of an actual civilised break-up, congratulations!'

You'd have to laugh. And the very fact that I want to laugh, I figure, has to be a v. good sign.

Only fly in the ointment was that Simon himself never showed. We each called him numerous times during the night to try and drag him out, but no, absolutely nothing doing.

'Jesus, that fella will die of stubbornness!' Mags groaned after about our fourth phone call to him.

'Just give him time,' Jeff wisely counselled. 'Guy's still in shock.'

'But there isn't time, that's the problem!' I hissed. 'Jean's saying she's heading back to Cape Town on Sunday. That's only two days away and he still hasn't made peace with her yet! And I'm worried. Really worried. This just doesn't feel right to me.'

'Why? Jean seems to be doing really well now, isn't she? And after all, Simon's a big boy. He'll do what he wants, when he wants.'

'Because . . . well, I suppose I just like a Hollywood ending, that's all. And this is most definitely not a Hollywood ending!'

Silence, then Sarah who'd been thoughtfully focused on the stem of a wine glass all this time, suddenly piped up.

'So what about a Hollywood ending for you then?' she came straight out with, nearly nudging me off my bar stool. 'With that lovely guy Jack Crown, I mean? Have you finally copped on to yourself yet? Are you going to call him and say you changed your mind about going on a movie date with him after all?'

This, by the way, had been a major subtext of all gossipy chat tonight, both to my face and behind my back. Jeez, it was actually hilarious; to think that someone like me, who had absolutely no love life to speak of for so long, now suddenly had all of this going on? One guy barely out the door, and this lot already trying to shove me into arms of someone new? I mean, when did I suddenly turn into some kind of a temptress?

'Because for God's sake, Angie!' Sarah went on, way too loudly for my liking, and not giving a shite that we were practically entertaining the whole bar by then. 'Jack Crown is an absolute dote! And you've millions in common with him and . . . Oh, look, if you don't pick up the phone to him and tell him you've changed your mind about going out with him, then I've a good mind to do it for you. Because clearly you need me to make all romantic decisions on your behalf!'

'Remember what a complete bitch you were to him when you first met?' Jeff laughed.

'Eh . . . yeah, thanks for reminding me.'

'You distinctly said he had all the personality of a vacuum cleaner.'

'Don't suppose we could change the subject?'

'Just goes to show you. Phrases about judging books by their covers spring to mind. You had Jack down as this emotionless automaton and how wrong were you? Sounds like he couldn't have been sweeter to you, or to Jean these past few days.'

'You said he's mad into movies . . .' Mags chipped in.

'. . . And you love movies . . .'

'. . . Plus he's obviously single . . .'

'. . . And as of about twenty-four hours ago, so are you . . .'

'Have to say, I'd love it if you went out with an actual proper detective sergeant,' Sarah said. 'Always very handy to know a copper. Just think, none of us would ever have to worry about penalty points or parking tickets again.'

'You lot are unbelievable!' I hissed at the lot of them, beetroot red in the face by then, I was sure. 'Jeez, me and Simon only just called it quits; will you let me catch my breath here for a bit? I'm . . . you know, in a transitional period. I'm grieving the end of a relationship here!'

'No you're not, you're out on the piss.'

'You haven't stopped giggling and messing ever since you and Simon called it a day.'

'It's like a big load's been lifted from you.'

Surprisingly it was Jean, who'd been quiet up until then, who stuck up for me.

'Hey, you lot, just back off a bit and stop pressurising her,' she told the others firmly. 'Give the girl a break, would you?'

'Thanks, love,' I remember slurring a bit drunkenly over at her.

'S'all right,' she shrugged. 'But you just trust me, hon. If Jack's the right one, he'll wait for you. You're worth it. If two people are really meant to be together, there's nothing on earth that can keep them apart.'

Silence at the table, then suddenly was aware of everyone focusing on Jean now. I was pretty certain I knew what they were all thinking too. But who'd be the one to come out with it? Did a quick audit and decided that I was just about drunk enough to.

'The ins and outs of my romantic dilemmas are all very well and good, my dear,' I said to her, turning to face her full on, so she couldn't avoid my gaze or change the subject. 'But . . . what about the right one for you? Are you seriously telling me you're going back to Cape Town and leaving someone behind, someone who I think you still really care about? Where's your happy ending, that's what I want to know.'

And the mood completely shifted at the table. Suddenly it was deadly quiet, all eyes on Jean. But she calmly knocked back the dregs of the G and T in front of her and evenly eyeballed everyone right back.

'Well, not everyone gets what they want, do they? Besides, after what I've done, I don't really deserve a Hollywood ending. After all, plenty of people live their whole lives and never get one, so why would someone like me? Beside, just being here, with all of you lot is just so . . . Well, let's just say I may not exactly get a happy ending, but I certainly have been given a Hollywood beginning!'

Saturday evening,The Chocolate Bar, 6.40 p.m

. . . and I'm in the middle of serving four customers at once, all v. complex orders involving many, many chocca-mocca whips (house speciality, incredibly popular), low-fat lattes and what seems like a mountain of individually wrapped handmade chocolates to go. Meanwhile Madge from the shoe shop across the road has come in after work, wanting hot chocolate with whipped cream and a good bitch about her on again/off again non-boyfriend. And is seriously demanding my attention, even though I'm run off my feet and just can't give her all the time she wants. At least not yet.

'You're not listening to me, Angie!' she whinges from where she's perched up at the counter.

'Yeah . . . just a bit busy here, hon, be right with you!'

'I really need your undivided attention!'

'And you'll get it just as soon as I serve everyone else, I promise!'

Next thing, Sarah comes back from carrying an order over to a table and sidles up beside me.

'I think you've got a visitor.'

I look sharply up and around me, but for the life of me, can't see anyone I know. Way too packed in here for starters.

'Just come in, back of the queue, eleven o'clock . . . Over there!' she hisses.

I glance down the snaking queue, past a line of women with buggies, and giggling teenagers laden down with shopping bags . . . and that's when I spot him.

It's Jack. Off duty, in v. casual pair of chinos and a light blue sweater. Which actually looks lovely on him, I suddenly think out of left field. A great colour on anyone blue-eyed and fair-haired.

The queue's so long and snaking, though, that it'll take him ages to get to me. Which is good, which is great. Gives me time to figure out exactly how I feel about this.

'So?' says Sarah, who's standing right up beside me now, hands on her hips, like she means business.

'So what?' I ask, then bury my face over at the cappuccino machine in the hopes she'll go away.

'Well, Jack's obviously come to see you! Because why else would he be here?'

'I dunno, but here's a wild guess. Maybe because he happens to want a coffee?'

'Don't pretend to be stupid!'

'Look, when he gets to the top of the queue, you serve him, will you?' I ask her. Not even sure why. Just suddenly I don't know what to think.

'Over my dead body!' she says crisply. 'In fact, not only will you serve him, you'll flash him your brightest smile and remember at all times that straight, single men in this town are a bloody rarity.'

'Straight single man, did you say?' Madge pipes up from her barstool. 'Where, where?'

'You see?' says Sarah, triumphantly. 'In her own sweet way, even Madge agrees with me.'

'Can you please stop broadcasting this to half the shop?' I mutter at her, burying my head in the cappuccino machine and busying myself with about three different orders at once.

'I'll do far worst than that if you don't cop onto yourself! Now you just listen to me, missy. You're going to tell him you're delighted he dropped in because your circumstances have changed since you last saw him and that now you'd be delighted to do a movie night.'

'A movie night with who?' Madge wants to know. 'What are you pair whispering about?'

'With this lovely guy, who, by the way, has a terrific job and who's right at the back of the queue,' Sarah hisses back to her.

Shit, now Madge is swivelling round to have a good gawp at him.

'The blondie-haired guy at the back? But he's absolutely lovely!' she says. 'Good, solid chunky build; me like! If you don't want him can you introduce him to me?'

'Jesus! Back off the pair of you! And will you please keep your voices down!'

'You're being deliberately obtuse now,' Sarah says, in her best schoolmarm manner. 'Perfectly good guys like that don't grow on trees, you know.'

'So he's interested in Angie then?' Madge says, yet again a tad too loudly for my liking.

'Yeah, definitely. No question. Took her for a bite to eat the other night, then asked her to a movie and everything.'

'Shhhh!' I hiss menacingly at the pair of them.

'And Angie turned him *down*? Why?'

'On account of this other guy who she was seeing, but she's not any more. So you see, now there's no problem.'

'Oh. That's romantic!' Madge sighs. 'Why can't something like that ever happen to me? One fella out the door and another one already on standby!'

OK, this is getting far too loud for my liking and now other customers in the queue are starting to earwig in. The only plus is that it's so noisy and clattery in here, Jack can't have heard. At least, not yet. If the pair of them shut up now, I might . . . MIGHT . . . just come through this and live to tell the tale.

'So, when he gets to the top of the queue . . .' Sarah's saying bossily.

'Excuse me, when who gets to the top of the queue?' says a middle-aged woman sitting beside Madge, with a pile of shopping bags at her feet, who's sipping elegantly on a peppermint tea. 'I'm sorry, but this is all just so intriguing and I have to know. Who exactly are you all talking about?'

'The guy at the very end. Over by the door,' Madge helpfully tells her. 'Looks a bit like Simon Pegg.' Jesus, she even points him out for maximum mortification.

'Shut up, the lot of you, or he'll hear!' I hiss at the lot of them, but it's a big waste of time. Now they all just start yakking over me, like I'm not even here.

'He's a detective sergeant,' Sarah tells them both proudly.

'Oooh, lovely. Always handy to know a Guard,' middle-aged woman says.

'Guards? Where?' says a youngish guy with a buzz-crop haircut and a pile of tattoos, who's now at the top of the queue.

'It's OK, apparently he's only here 'cos he fancies Angie,' says Madge. 'He's not here in an official capacity, in case you were worried.'

'In that case, can I get my Americano to go?' says buzz-crop guy, a bit worriedly.

'Certainly, sir. Now can I serve anyone else?' I ask, my voice about three registers higher than normal, in a desperate attempt to change the subject, but it's no use.

'He's lovely and tall, isn't he?' middle-aged lady says, pointing, actually pointing, Jack out now, in case there was any doubt about who the lot of them were gossiping about. 'Always much preferred taller men myself.'

'So what are you going to say when he gets to you?' Madge wants to know.

'I don't know what. Because the chances are I'll have run out of here in the next four seconds if you lot don't keep quiet!'

'Just tell him that you're now available for movie dates any time at all in the near future,' Sarah says bossily. 'Just say the words in that order, or if you don't I'll bloody well do it for you!'

'Good idea!' says middle-aged lady. 'A night at the pictures just sounds so romantic, and maybe dinner afterwards?'

'Can I please point out that I'm wearing a hairnet and my uniform?' I hiss at this fecking Greek chorus the lot of them have turned into. 'Hardly much of a turn-on, now is it?'

'If he really likes you, he'll be well able to see past the hairnet,' says a young mum at the counter, with one kid in a stroller and another with his nose pressed up against the counter top demanding chocolate.

'And you know, he did already ask you out, so he's hardly going to turn you down, now that it's your turn!'

OK, there's just no way Jack can't have heard that. I throw a surreptitious glance down to the back of queue, but . . . Shit! Suddenly catch his eye and he waves. Then he mouths up at me, 'Like the hairnet, by the way!'

Feckfeckfeckfeckfeck! He did hear!

'You should definitely tell him you'll go to the movies with him,' young mum is saying now, as the whole shagging queue behind her start to tune in for a right good listen. 'Good men don't just grow on trees, you know.'

'And she won't be young for ever!' middle-aged lady chimes in agreement.

Look back down to Jack, who's grinning, actually grinning, like he's getting a great kick out of all my discomfort.

'Is that him?' says a teenage guy behind young mum, pointing back to Jack. 'Because he can swap places with me if he wants. Get to you that bit quicker. Anyone mind?' he politely asks the queue behind him, who say nothing, just nod and smile. No doubt enjoying the fecking side-show.

And now for the first time since this whole bowel-witheringly mortifying episode started, I'm dimly aware that the place has suddenly gone v. quiet.

Next thing, Jack is striding confidently up to the top of the queue and smiling a warm thank you at the teenager, who immediately switches places with him.

'Hi,' he grins cheekily across the counter at me.

'Hi.'

'Don't think I've ever been so royally entertained while standing in a queue before.'

'Eh, yeah, sorry about that,' I mutter, am sure by now flushing like a forest fire.

'So . . .' says young mum, who's right beside both of us, looking eagerly from Jack to me, 'don't you have something to say to this gorgeous guy?'

'Yeah, go on!' says a voice from a table at the back of the shop. 'We're all waiting here! Put us out of our misery!'

Mortified, awful, stilted silence, then Madge pipes up from her barstool, 'Jesus, Angie, if you don't, I'll bloody do it for you!'

Loud burst of laughter from the queue while I make a mental note to strangle her later.

And now it's like every eye in the whole place focused on me and me alone.

No getting out of this.

Deep breath. Go for it.

'Jack,' say in a wobbly voice I barely recognise as my own, while beads of perspiration roll down my ribcage, 'I'm really sorry I couldn't make it to the movies with you the other night . . .'

'But?' he says, and when I look into his eyes, I realise he's teasing me. He's standing tall now, arms folded, twinkling down at me, loving every second of this. Challenging me to go on. 'You were saying, Angie?' he asks innocently. 'Do please go on. I'm all ears here. As are all of these good people.'

'But . . . if there was any chance you were free to go another night . . . then . . .'

'Then what?'

'Then that would be lovely!'

Then he leans over the counter and in an exaggerated gesture like something straight out of a romantic comedy, he takes my hand and kisses it tenderly.

'Ladies and gentlemen,' he says to the room, utterly confident, not a nerve in his body, 'I'm absolutely delighted to announce that this gorgeous young lady and I will finally be going on a date sometime soon. Stay tuned for further developments!'

Wild applause suddenly breaks out when he leans across the counter again and this time kisses me smack full on the lips.

And that was it.

That's how I got my Hollywood ending.

Chapter Twenty-Five

Sunday

And in a few hours' time, Jean would be on her way back to Cape Town. No getting out of it and certainly no putting it off any longer. She'd specifically asked/pleaded for a low-key exit from the others; no tearful airport goodbye scenes, no hand-wringing in the departures hall . . . Nothing at all. She just wanted to slip quietly away under the radar and be done with it. Mind you, poor old Angie kept ringing her mobile every half-hour, tearfully wondering if she'd changed her mind and if there was anything at all that could be done to persuade her to stay, but Jean wasn't for turning.

Friday night had been so wonderful, though, she thought, shoving the last of the clothes she'd borrowed from her flatmate, Paige, into the depths of her suitcase and neatly zipping it shut. It had been beyond price to hang out with Angie, Mags, Jeff and Sarah again, just like old times. Like nothing had ever happened to drive them apart. No recriminations, no guilt-trips, just a gang of old mates reconnecting. Amazing. Just like she'd imagined it would be, all those long lovely days and nights back in Cape Town.

Better, in fact. Far better.

She glanced at the digital clock by the beside table in her hotel room. Just gone two in the afternoon. Good. She still had piles of time to get to the airport – hours, in fact; her connecting flight to London wasn't till much later on that night. But she might as well get there good and early and just while the time away till she left. She'd purposely kept herself busy all morning; the busier she was, she figured, the less time she had to think. Even made a point of going back to Byrne & Sacetti earlier on, just to stick her head in and, if at all possible, to see Joyce, the co-owner, and Sacetti himself. To explain.

And was so glad she had. Not only did she get to see the lovely, unchanged Joyce, but was astonished to find how many of the old staff she'd worked with were still there. She'd even been given a warm round of applause when she came into the staff locker room, and could happily have stayed there for hours, just catching up with old friends, old faces, remembering old times. Marvelling that someone like her could possibly have been so missed. Would have been unthinkable to her just a few short days ago.

'I wish to God you'd change your mind about going back to Cape Town!' Joyce had hugged her warmly as they were saying one final goodbye. 'I could really do with having you back here again. You were like my right hand in here. Place was never the same after you left, you know. Far less fun, for starters!'

Jean laughed and thanked her, but reassured her that her mind was made up.

'That your final answer?' Joyce had asked. 'Or do I see you wavering even just a tiny bit? Go on, I'll even throw in a pay rise!'

'Final answer,' Jean had grinned, grateful and touched beyond words at the kindness of the offer.

She'd dearly loved to have gone back to her old street off the South Circular Road, just to say hello to Mrs Butterly and some of the old neighbours who'd always been so brilliant to her. But knew it was out of the question; for starters, it was the weekend and the chances of Simon being around were high. Last thing she wanted was for him to see her or hear about her visit and feel like he was being staked out.

She'd tried her best with him and got precisely nowhere, and it was ten to twelve now: time to check out and leave. And even though it felt so wrong, even though every nerve-ending in her body was screaming at her that she should rightfully stay, she knew it was out of the question. She just couldn't bring herself to live in the same town as him, knowing that he cursed the very sight of her. How could she possibly hang around with mutual pals, knowing that she might so easily bump into him at any minute? Knowing that everything she either said or did would surely get back to him and vice versa? Complete non-starter. She'd made her bed, nothing for her now but to lie in it. She'd done it before and somehow she'd have to find the strength to do it again.

One last and final check of her hotel room to make sure she'd left nothing behind, then she slammed the door shut behind her and went down to reception to check out. Don't allow yourself to sink under, she told herself sternly, just get to the airport quickly as you can and, remember, mission accomplished. You came here to make peace with everyone and you almost succeeded.

Even more amazingly, instead of accusations and guilt being lobbed at her, she'd met with nothing but warmth, kindness and a genuine feeling that she was forgiven. That she was still loved. Missed, even.

Well, by everyone except one person. And, she reminded herself, with her leaving the country tonight, there was very little more she could do about that now, was there?

She checked out and was just wheeling her little carry-on bag through reception for the last time when out of the corner of her eye, she saw a familiar face that suddenly made her stop in her tracks.

The world kept spinning on its axis, guests kept brushing past her in a rush either to check in or else get the hell out of there, but all she could do was stand stock-still, rooted to the spot.

No mistake. Definitely him. He stood up the minute he saw her coming and for a long, long time, they both just looked across the busy foyer at each other, as the normal Sunday afternoon business of a city-centre hotel went on all round them. She swallowed, willing her legs not to buckle from under her, and next thing he was over beside her. Looking intently down at her, in that same way that never failed to make her melt.

'It's you.'

'It's me.'

'But, I don't understand . . . what are you doing here?'

Simon took her by the elbow and gently steered her to a quiet corner where he sat her down, then slid into the chair opposite.

'I . . . well . . . the truth is that I don't really know the answer to that one,' was his uncertain opener, green eyes boring into the back of hers. 'At least, not yet I don't. All I knew was that . . . well, I knew you were leaving today and . . . thought, maybe you'd like a lift to the airport?'

'Be lovely, thanks.'

Ten minutes later, she'd checked out and was sitting in the passenger seat of Simon's car, just like she had so many times before. Silence for a long time while he just looked directly ahead, totally focused on the road.

'You know, Simon . . .' she eventually said.

'Yeah?'

'I've hours to kill before my flight. How do you fancy a walk, maybe? If you had time, that is. Maybe we could go to . . . you know, where we used to? With the thing by the place . . .?'

He turned to look at her.

'All right then,' he nodded. 'Sure. Why not? Let's go to where we used to. With the thing by the place.'

Ten minutes later, they were at Pigeon House Pier by Sandymount Strand, a gorgeous, perpetually deserted beach where they'd walked together so often in the past.

'You know, I'm glad we're doing this before I go,' she told him simply, as they strolled down the beach and towards the water's edge. 'And I'm glad you called to the hotel. I'm just . . . I'm glad, that's all.'

'Me too.'

Then he looked over at her for ages, like what he was about to say was tough for him beyond belief.

'Because the thing is, Jean . . .'

'Yeah . . .?' She found her stomach clenching, just sensing that something big was coming.

'Well, in spite of everything that was said the other night, and in spite of what's happened, I really felt that I should come. I couldn't just let you leave without seeing you. Even if it may be for the last time.'

Her heart leaped at that. And even if it didn't exactly

sound like she'd been forgiven, at least he was starting to thaw. A bit. Maybe. Which was better than nothing. Back in Cape Town, she could possibly even school herself to live with that.

They strolled on side by side for a good while in silence, like there was so much to say between them that it was impossible to even know where to begin. Jean remembering back to all the times they'd done this walk before, arms wrapped around each other, laughing, skitting, messing, loving each other's company. Loving each other, full stop.

'You know,' she eventually said, more to break the awkwardness between them than anything else, 'back in Cape Town, I'm often reminded of the beach here.'

'You are?'

'Yeah, sure. I often go walking along the Waterfront, near the hotel where I work. It's by far my favourite part of the place and even on the bad days, somehow the sea air and just the sight of the Waterfront itself never fails to lift me out of myself. If that makes any sense.'

He nodded like he understood.

'So what's Cape Town like, then?'

'Oh, you'd love it. You'd have great fun trying out all the restaurants and tapas bars and just strolling around enjoying the buzz of the place. It's one of those cities that's big and beautiful and bustling . . .' She trailed off here, though. Thinking, I'll be back there this time tomorrow. And all of this will be just a dim and distant memory.

'Look, can I ask you something that's been on my mind?' he said, interrupting her thoughts.

'Sure, go ahead.'

'Well . . . why Cape Town? I mean, of all places? It just seems so very far away, that's all.'

'Well, to be perfectly honest, I think that was the main attraction when I first got there. You know I can still remember not long after I first arrived, taking this boat trip out to Robben Island.'

'Where they held Mandela?'

'Yeah,' she nodded, then added dryly, 'well, in Cape Town, you kind of have to see Robben Island, it's a bit clichéd, but it's almost expected of new visitors. Like the South African equivalent of drinking Guinness, or kissing the Blarney Stone. Or else getting sloshed out of your mind and throwing up in Temple Bar.'

He smiled a tiny bit at that. Encouraging.

'Thing is, though,' she went on, 'I remember just about everyone else in our tour group going on and on about how appalled they were at the conditions there. Marvelling at everything that poor old Mandela had to put up with for twenty-seven long years, in a cell barely big enough to fit a child's mattress. And it was weird, but all I could think was . . . not me. You could lock me up in here, I figured, and all I'd feel was safe. If anything, you'd have been doing me a favour. Then I overheard this American tourist saying how lonely Mandela must have been, cooped up here for all those years. And of course everyone in our tour party nodded in agreement, but I just wanted to screech at them that they'd got it all wrong. Because that's the deceptive thing about loneliness. You'd think it would be a bitter feeling, but it's not. As a matter of fact, it's kind of addictive once you get used to it.'

They'd stopped walking now and Simon was standing opposite her, drinking in her every word.

'And . . .' Jean went on, voice breaking a bit as she stared out at the tide, stared anywhere except back at him, '. . .

before we took the ferry back from Robben Island, I remember looking back out across the sea towards the V & A Waterfront in the distance and all I could feel was just this incredible deep sense of security, if that makes the slightest bit of sense. I thought, just look at me now. I'm at the southernmost tip of the world. No one could or ever would find me here. I figured it was a bit like Tiffany's in New York and that nothing bad could ever happen to me, as long as I stayed there. Safe, out of harm's way. And after a while, it became almost like a daily little affirmation I'd say to myself. No one could or ever would find me here.'

Besides, she thought, but kept it to herself, at the end of the day, there were really only three people from her old life that she missed. And now, one of them—

She tried mentally to finish that sentence, but the words just wouldn't come.

'So I guess . . . what I'm trying to say is,' was all she could manage to get out now, 'is that when I first arrived there, I think I was having a meltdown. A breakdown of sorts, if that's what you want to call it. I needed to feel safe and to answer your question in a very roundabout way, I think that's why I chose Cape Town.'

Simon looked at her for a long time before they turned and walked on a bit further. And the silence between them throbbed. It was getting chilly now; the wind was whipping up a bit, so she pulled the jacket she was wearing closer round her. Remembering back to all the times they'd stroll along here and the very minute she started getting cold, he'd immediately wrap a big, warm comforting arm round her, to warm her up.

All an age ago now.

'You know, there's something I wouldn't mind getting off my chest too,' Simon eventually said, looking over at her now.

'What's that?'

'I suppose . . . well, I just want you to know that I felt awful about the way I behaved towards you when you called over to the house the other night. I acted like such a complete shit and, after all, all you were trying to do was explain . . .'

'Oh, come on, it's completely understandable,' she said simply. 'You were angry and you'd every right to be. Besides, I should never have just barged in on you like I did. I just wanted to try to make you see my side of what had happened, that was all.'

'I know, and it was only when you'd left, and then over the past few days, that I've finally got round to accepting that. But you have to understand, it's been . . . I just . . . I mean . . .'

'You don't have to say it . . .'

'. . . Jean, you know there was a time when I'd have thanked God on bended knees to have you back here again.'

She didn't answer. Couldn't.

'But it's just been so . . .'

'I know.'

'. . . And you understand the way I felt . . . And the plans I had for both of us, back then . . .'

'Sure I do.'

'. . . I mean . . . the engagement ring and everything . . .'

'. . . Which was so beautiful . . .'

'. . . Then finding out the truth the way we did . . .'

'I know.'

'. . . All that deception . . .'

'. . . It must have been . . .'

'. . . Just like a betrayal.'

'. . . Sure.'

'. . . And then to have it all suddenly resurrected, out of the blue like that . . .'

'. . . I can only imagine . . .'

'. . . And just when I thought I might be able to move on, to finally let go . . .'

'. . . Which you'd every right to do . . .'

'. . . But you have to understand that ever since that funeral, I've been in pieces.'

'. . . Which is completely understandable.'

'. . . So if I behaved badly towards you . . .'

'. . . You don't even need to go there. It's OK.'

Bloody hell. She even surprised herself by smiling. Because this reminded her of old times and the way they could read each other's minds, finish each other's sentences, the way their thoughts somehow always kept pace with each other, the way each would know exactly what the other was thinking without a single word ever being said.

Simon was walking close by her now, just inches away. So close she could almost smell him.

'You've no idea just how much it's thrown me,' he was telling her now, gently. Sounding far more like his old self. 'Just knowing you were in town the past few days. I haven't been able to eat or sleep, I'm worse than useless in work, and now . . .'

'Hey, come on! This is me you're talking to. And I understand, I promise. I mean that so sincerely.'

A pause as they both just looked at each other. Don't stop, just please, please keep talking, she willed him as he held her gaze. But nothing. He looked distracted, like he was trying to pluck up the courage to say something else, but somehow couldn't.

Right then, over to her.

'Well, it was lovely of you to take me here. And even better to see you before I leave,' she said, making to leave. 'But if I don't get to the airport very soon, I'll be going nowhere.'

And now he was standing right in front of her, blocking her path.

'Then go nowhere,' he said simply, eyes burning. 'Stay.'

'What?'

'Jean, the thing is, I don't know what the future holds. I wish I could process everything that's going on in my head and I know it's going to take time. But one thing's for certain. None of us wants you to leave, and what's more I don't think you yourself do either.'

'But what about . . .?'

'You and me? Why don't . . . well . . .'

'. . . Unless . . .'

'. . . I mean, it's just a thought, that's all . . .'

'. . . But maybe if there was some way . . .'

'. . . We could just take things . . .'

'. . . One day at a time?' she finished the sentence for him hopefully.

'Yeah. One day at a time. And maybe . . . In time, we might be able to work our way up to . . . Maybe having a drink sometime? Down the line, I mean.'

'I'd like that.'

'I'd like it too.'

Then she smiled, as a big lump in her throat nearly threatened to choke her. He took her hand, pressed it tightly and just looked at her for a long, long time.

‘In that case, there’s one more thing, Jean.’

Her heart leapt.

‘What’s that?’

‘Take your airline ticket, rip it up and throw it away. And stay. Definitely stay.’

Two months later, Women's Aid Advice Centre, Wilton Place, Dublin

'. . . And now can I invite you all to join me in a warm round of applause for the incredibly brave Jean Simpson, who so kindly came here tonight to share her story with us!'

The whole room round her broke out in spontaneous clapping and floor stomping, and Jean beamed. She'd been volunteering for Women's Aid for a few weeks now and yet every time she told her story, she never failed to be astonished by the response. What was even more amazing was that these were women just like her, women who in many cases had far more harrowing tales to share than she had.

God, nights like this, she had to almost pinch herself! To think that she'd actually made it this far, when just two short years ago she'd felt so powerless? Like such a victim. It was the one thing she'd hammer home relentlessly, time and again, every time she got up to speak here. You may feel utterly alone and friendless, but, trust me, you never are. Pick up the phone to me, she'd tell the room, anytime. And I'll come running. And I'll understand, and what's more I'll help.

'So just before we wrap it up for the evening,' Emily, tonight's organiser and a tireless director of Women's Aid announced, 'does anyone here have any questions they'd like to put to Jean?'

A hand shot up and Jean saw that it was a pale-faced, underweight-looking young girl, sitting right up the very front.

'Jean . . . em . . .' but she broke off here, like she'd come this far, but couldn't bring herself to go that bit further.

'Just relax and take your time,' Jean told her soothingly, remembering back to the very first night she'd got up to speak here and just how petrified she'd been. 'And remember,' she added encouragingly, 'we're all in the same boat here. Sure, otherwise we'd be down the pub.'

Pale Girl smiled a bit at that and taking a deep breath, willed herself to talk.

'Well . . . the thing is . . . would it be all right if I asked you about your life at the moment?' she said softly, nervously. 'It's just that you sound like you really went through the mill and I wondered if you were in a good place now, that's all? Do you ever feel afraid? Or does that fear live with you for ever? Because . . .' She broke off a bit again here.

'It's all right, love, take your time,' Jean said, instinctively going over to where this slip of a thing sat and squeezing her hand.

'Well, you see . . .,' Pale Girl went on, and it was only when Jean was up this close to her, that she realised the girl was actually trembling. 'It's just . . . living in fear for me is the worst part. Even though I'm out of the . . . well, the situation I was in, I just feel like I'm constantly looking over my shoulder. It's scarred me and I wondered if these scars will ever heal.'

She looked up at Jean with big, watery blue eyes and Jean gave her a bear hug.

'What's your name?' Jean asked gently.

'Ingrid.'

'Well, Ingrid,' she answered gently, 'the main thing is that you're here. And trust me, that's the first step towards healing. As for me . . . well, I'd be the first to say that I've been incredibly lucky. My abuser went bust and was forced to leave the country. I've made a full police statement against him now, so even if he did return, which is unlikely, he'd have a whole barrage of questions to face. But I completely recognise that a lot of women in similar situations aren't as fortunate as I was.

'So to answer your question, I suppose I'm just grateful every day now. Whole weeks go by when I don't feel frightened, then I remember I've nothing to be frightened of. I feel safe, secure, even happy, and I promise you that you will too. In time. That's all it takes, trust me. Because I used to live my whole life in fear and dread, just like you. But it took what I went through to make me realise that I was actually living at all. Sure, I was safe in Cape Town, but it was only ever half a life. My abuser took so much from me, he took my whole past, but over my dead body was I letting him get away with robbing my future!'

Ingrid smiled tearily and nodded as another round of applause broke out. Next thing, a hand shot up, this time from the very back of the room.

'I've a question for you,' called out an older woman who Jean couldn't help noticing had a suitcase at her feet. Like she'd come to Women's Aid to find safety and wasn't leaving without it. Her heart immediately melted. There, but for the grace of God, etc.

'You changed your whole identity to escape your abuser,' said this lady. 'But why did you stay away for so long? You must have missed your family and friends here so much, especially when they found out the truth about you. Were you in some way punishing yourself?'

'It's a hard one to answer,' said Jean, 'and even harder to explain to those I left behind, believe me. But all I can really say is this. I had a meltdown, a complete and utter meltdown, that's the only way I can describe it. And for what it's worth, I learned that sometimes you can only really find heaven by backing away from hell.'

The woman nodded in understanding and thanked Jean for her honesty.

Half an hour later and that week's meeting had broken up. Emily, the organiser, thanked Jean warmly and invited her to come along next week too.

'If you're not too busy working at Byrne & Sacetti, that is, of course,' she added.

'Be delighted to,' Jean smiled. In fact, try and stop her. It was never easy, coming here and speaking about what she'd been through, but when she saw how much support she was able to give to other women just like her, she'd started to develop a powerful sense of motivation about their meetings. And OK, so maybe she couldn't put the clock back, but she certainly could do her level best to help anyone who found themselves in the same situation she had, all those years ago. In a weird way, it was almost healing, cathartic even.

'It's just wonderful to have a young, confident, fresh voice here, someone who's lived through what these women are going through now and who came out the other side to tell the tale,' said Emily. 'We're all so pleased that you're one of our volunteers, love. I hope you know that.'

'It's the least I can do,' Jean told her sincerely. 'Besides, all I do is talk straight from the heart. And tell them that if it can happen to someone like me, someone who was always so gobby and strong and independent, then it can happen to anyone.'

'Well, we're certainly all delighted to have you on our

team,' Emily said, holding open the door for her as they both stepped out on the busy street outside. 'Can I offer you a lift home?'

'No, thanks, I just live close by.'

'Till next week then, and thanks so much again!'

Jean said her goodbyes and strode quickly through the city centre and down into Temple Bar, which was even more thronged than usual, given that it was a Friday evening and a rare sunny one at that. Pavement cafés were packed and customers were spilling out of bars onto the street, to soak up the last of the autumn rays.

With a spring in her step, Jean headed up towards Angie's flat, where she'd been sharing with her for the past few months. Working incredibly hard, both of them, but having the time of their lives every single chance they got. And now that Angie and Jack were officially seeing each other, it was like having a new pal to hang around with too. Jack was terrific, Jean decided; she really liked him. Bonkers mad about Angie and a very welcome addition to their little group.

She picked up her pace, turned a corner and suddenly arrived at the place she'd been looking for.

And there he was, with his movieplex good looks, handsome as ever. Sitting at a tiny pavement table, with two drinks in front of him and an empty seat beside him. Just like she knew he would be.

Waiting for her.

'Hello there,' Simon said, instantly lighting up when he saw her approach, just like he used to.

'Hi.'

'Lovely evening, isn't it?'

'Beautiful.'

'How did tonight go?'

'Went well, I think. And how are you?'

'At this exact moment, I'm surprisingly good,' he grinned back at her.

She laughed, folded her arms and tilted her head back to really have a good look at him, to drink him in.

'Thing is, Jean,' he eventually said, 'here I am, all alone at a table for two and . . . well . . .'

'Yes?' she teased.

'. . . And . . . I was just wondering if . . . maybe . . . you'd like to have that drink now?'

Claudia on . . . her inspiration for writing *Me and You*

Ask any author and they'll all tell you the same thing. One of the questions you get asked most often is, 'where do you get all your ideas from?' And the slightly clichéd but honest answer is, from anywhere and everywhere. For instance, one time I just happened to overhear half a conversation in a Starbucks queue. The woman was utterly convinced her boyfriend was seeing someone else behind her back. Her best friend was beside her and I'm not joking, was trying to convince her to get onto his mobile phone company, to try and blag a set of his most recent monthly statements.

'But they'd never give out that kind of information,' Worried Girlfriend stammered, 'no matter what I told them!' Then she desperately tacked on, 'wouldn't they?'

'Course they would,' her pal insisted, so authoritatively that you'd swear she did this every day of the week. 'It's dead easy! You just call the phone company and pretend you're his mother! Then you say something like you're really worried he's got in with a bad crowd and is going to end up either an alcoholic or else on drugs. You know, improvise a bit; use your imagination. Trust me, they never say no to a concerned Mammy!'

The girls collected their lattes and moved off to a table out of earshot, but it made me wonder what other pearls of wisdom the pal would pass on next. By the time she was finished, I'd visions of her convincing Worried Girlfriend to camp outside the boyfriend's house with a long lens trained at his bedroom window. And that they should start checking out ebay in case there was any surveillance equipment for sale on the cheap. Just in case.

God bless coffee shops. Trust me; they're an absolute minefield for novelists everywhere!

But with *Me and You*, it was actually a tiny article in the paper that initially set me off thinking. There was an interview with the head of the missing persons unit and one of the things he revealed absolutely intrigued me. He said that in well over ninety per cent of cases, people go missing voluntarily. Well, of course, that line alone totally grabbed me. I started to wonder what it was that would make someone just walk out on their whole, entire life. I mean, can you imagine? Just turning your back on family, friends, work, home, everything you'd built up over years . . . and checking out.

And the more I researched it, the more hooked I became. I got in contact with the Missing Persons Association and the head of the organisation, a lovely man called Aquinas Duffy, was incredibly helpful and generous with his time. And gradually, the deeper I dug, the more intriguing the stories became.

It seemed like every single week, the news brought a fresh story of a different person who'd gone missing. And of course, a percentage of these stories sadly had tragic consequences, making the headlines for the most gut-wrenching reasons. This is utterly devastating and heart-breaking for the families concerned, but that wasn't what I wanted to focus on with this book. Enough, I felt, had been written about such cases elsewhere. Instead, I wanted to write about a heroine, who for reasons beyond her control, unwittingly finds herself in a situation where she feels she has no choice but to up sticks and go.

And so, as a result of all my research, I eventually met up with a young woman who we'll just call Susan for now, and she very kindly – and bravely – told me that she was happy to share her story. Because about four years ago, she went missing voluntarily. She was twenty-four years old at the time and had been working far from home, but had found the going much tougher than she'd expected. Susan had thought moving to a new city on her own would be exciting, and that she'd quickly fall in with a new gang of mates to hang around with. Just like something out of *Sex and the City* she said, smiling at me. But it didn't work out quite like that; in her new job, people barely gave each other the time of day, they were all so stressed out of it, and it was incredibly hard to forge new bonds from scratch. Susan says she's a naturally shy person, so it was extremely difficult to get to know people who were at best cliquish and at worst, just too busy to take on a new friend in their lives.

After a while, Susan began to feel worthless and alone. And worst of all, that there was no one for her to talk to. Over the weeks and months that followed, she began to sink deeper and deeper into herself, until she reached a stage where she felt unable even to get out of bed in the mornings. She recognises now that she was suffering from the early stages of depression, but at the time all she felt was that the four walls around her were closing in on her and that if she didn't do something, she'd surely suffocate.

'So,' she told me, 'I walked. I needed to get away. It's impossible to explain, but I just wanted to put as much distance between me and this life that I hated as I possibly could. Something had to give and, mad though it may sound now, at the time this just seemed to me like the right way to go about it. I wasn't thinking about all the worry and unnecessary stress I was causing to my family; I wasn't thinking, full stop.'

Susan took a flight to London, checked into the cheapest hotel she could find and lay low. And of course, in no time, the alarm was raised. Her family back home became concerned at not having heard from her. She wasn't answering her phone and wasn't turning up for work either. Her parents contacted the police and through passport records at the airport, it didn't take the police long to trace her to London. After that, her mobile phone gave away her location pretty quickly. In the meantime, money had started to run out for Susan and she knew herself that sooner or later, she'd have to come forward. She knew it was just a matter of time before her old life caught up with her.

'But in a weird way, it turned out to be the best thing I could possibly have done,' she told me. This, she now feels, was a classic cry for help and so help is exactly what she got. And for the first time in years, she began to open up about the black dog of depression that had been smothering her for so long. She's in a far better place now, she tells me, and thankfully her whole life has moved on.

'When I disappeared,' she added, 'part of me knew that I was only causing huge unnecessary worry to my family. But that's the thing; you can't see the wood for the trees. You have to understand that you're in complete meltdown, and all you can think of is that you want to walk away from it all.'

But *Me and You* isn't just about a girl who goes missing. It's a love triangle too, and that was very much what I wanted to focus on when Kitty/Jean returns back to her old life to find that everyone else has moved on, except her. But here was the thing; do love triangles ever end happily?

I spoke to countless people – women mostly – and the general consensus seemed to be that, while it's no fun being on the wrong end of a triangle, sometimes realising that your partner is just never going to stop obsessing about his ex can be the very spur you need to move on. And to accept that, try as you might, the relationship is going absolutely nowhere. A tough lesson to have to take, isn't it?

One friend had a particular gem; she was madly in love with her too-perfect boyfriend, who she claimed was just the nicest man on earth. But that was the trouble; he was almost too nice, too easy-going, too unable to see what was going on around him. Because he had an ex you see (don't they all?), who was still very much a fixture in his life. To the extent that she was constantly on the phone to him, or else hanging around his flat. On one famous occasion, Mr Perfect Boyfriend was taking my pal out to a special occasion posh restaurant for Valentine's Day . . . and his ex decided to tag along too.

'She was feeling really low you see,' Mr Perfect patiently explained. 'So what could I do? Course I had to include her.' Anxious to be seen as unthreatened by this and complete fine with it, my pal just kept her cool, and nodded and smiled, albeit through gritted teeth. But this was far from being a one-off; in fact time and again, needy-ex-from-hell kept finding more and more ingenious ways to sabotage Mr Perfect's budding new relationship. If he and my pal were due to have a romantic dinner together, she'd be sure to pick that night of all nights to have a panic attack, so he'd just have to drop everything and run to her side. And by the way, as my friend pointed out, this was a girl who seemed to be able to time her panic attacks so they conveniently coincided with any night she and Mr Perfect planned to be together. Some coincidence, no?

If they were having a cosy night in front of the telly

with a bottle of vino and a pizza, just the two of them, you could almost guarantee his phone would ring. Guess who?

'So of course after a few months of this carry on, 'my friend said, 'My patience started to wear thin and I just reached breaking point. I really appreciated that my lovely boyfriend was so caring and concerned about his ex, but the fact was that she was manipulating him and he was completely blind to it. I wanted to shake him by the shoulders and ask him why he couldn't see this, but of course then I would have ended up looking like the one who was being a complete bitch. Which, I suppose, is what his ex wanted all along, I'd safely guess. In retrospect she played it all so well and ultimately got what she wanted, which was me out of the picture. We broke up amicably enough and I really wasn't surprised to hear that within no time, he'd got back with her. But then, she was determined not to let him out of her life and would have gone out of her way to sabotage any fledgling relationship he may have had.'

You see what I mean? Ask any author and they'll tell you. The stories and inspirations really do come from just about anywhere and everywhere . . .

Claudia on . . . editing and deleted scenes

Ok, time for an extra-special treat. Thing is you see, I always feel so sorry for my lovely editor. Mainly because I'm a shocking over-writer and have a horrible habit of delivering first draft manuscripts that are so ridiculously long, they could almost double up as door-stoppers. Which is where the amazing Claire Bord steps in, and works tirelessly on pruning back my initial meandering scribblings down to a more manageable length. You know, something that's less likely to give you shoulder strain when you're carting the book around.

Anyway, this always involves losing scenes which sadly, just have to head the way of the cutting room floor. But I just wondered if you'd like to have a sneaky peek at one of them? Which, ahem, got as far as the first draft, but then had to be jettisoned in the interests of publishing a book that would actually fit on a bookshelf.

So this particular deleted scene takes place in part one of the book, when Kitty has first gone missing and poor old Angie and Simon are left running around like headless chickens. While researching this, the police told me that one of the things that can often hamper any missing person investigation is a load of psychics and mystics all creeping out of the woodwork and claiming that they've got valuable information that's guaranteed to help with the case. As they have to take any information seriously, hours of police time is wasted in pursuing these and most end up as little more than wild goose chases.

But I wondered what would happen if, in total desperation, Angie went to visit one of these psychics and if the information she got turned out to be frighteningly accurate and on the money?

Read on and you'll see what I mean!

The Deleted Scene

12th January
7 p.m.
Madam Rita's

I'm not sure what exactly I expected, but it sure as hell wasn't this.

I'd half expected Madame Rita to work from some run-down bijou-type artisan cottage, with cats combing all over it and with a smell of incense hanging in the air so strong it would make you gag. A bit like in Grey Gardens.

So I can't quite believe it when Jeff pulls his car into a space outside an office block on the quays in town. One of those giant concrete monstrosities that got flung up in the building boom, and now sits virtually empty. Like a ghost town, where they probably pay *you* to rent office space instead of other way round, they're that desperate for tenants.

The second surprise is Madame Rita herself. Again, I'd been carrying a mental picture of a wafty, slightly dotty eccentric old lady; you know, a batty old dear who goes around in flowing Kaftans and a turban. Not unlike Margaret Rutherford playing Madame Arcati in *Blithe Spirit.*

(David Lean, 1945. Completely brilliant, still funny and fresh. May even suggest it to Simon for our next movie night. Absolutely no romance in it, just gags all the way. He'd enjoy.)

But it turns out I'm wrong again. When we work our way up to the fourth floor and knock on her office door, Madame Rita turns out to be a neat, efficient, middle-aged woman, well dressed with lovely soft blonde highlights and not a Kaftan or turban in sight. She's dressed a bit like a secondary school teacher wearing an elegant beige suit with sensible shoes. Which slightly disappoints me; I'd nearly have preferred an out-and-out oddball that we could all have a good snigger at later on.

Madame Rita has a gentle, understanding manner about her too; she smiles warmly, offers us some green tea and sympathises with us for what we've been through, her cloud blue eyes unflinching and very sincere. Now of late, I've noticed that when most people offer sympathy, they get awkward and tongue-tied and often come out with the wrong thing, but not her. So far, so good.

Then she ushers the pair of us from the reception area into her office and invites us to sit down. Her office turns out to be an actual proper office with a Mac computer, fax machine, printer, copier – the works – and not an incense stick or a stray cat in sight.

Very tasteful altogether, and all I can think as I look around is that there must be a fair few quid in being a professional psychic.

7.10 p.m.

Reading starts. Madame Rita sits down opposite us and rubs her temples. Jeff and I sit opposite, on tenterhooks. Jeff the very picture of concentration; me more awkward, not knowing where to look.

'I'm afraid I must ask for silence now please,' she says softly, 'while I tune into your spirit guides.'

Tuning into our spirit guides takes a lot longer than I'd thought though and every time I catch Jeff's eye, it nearly sends me onto the verge of giggling. But a scalding look back at me from Jeff has a sobering effect though. I keep forgetting he's inclined to take all this stuff very seriously.

'You come to me with deep concerns,' Madame Rita eventually says, eyes closed, like she's deep in meditation. 'About a very dear friend . . .'

OK, so far, so Googled.

'By any chance did you bring along something that once belonged to her?' Madame Rita suddenly asks, snapping her blue eyes wide open.

'Oh, emm . . . Yes, right here,' I tell her, fumbling around the bottom of my handbag for a cardigan that Kitty used to wear a lot. Vintage Kitty; it's oversized, in pillar box red and was so big it would nearly have fitted two of her into it. I distinctly remember she used to wear it with a denim mini and deep green tights, then go round laughing at herself and asking if she looked bit like a Christmas tree.

'This was Kitty's,' I say. I hand it over and Madame Rita fondles it like a James Bond villain stroking a cat, eyes closed.

Another larky glance from me to Jeff, trying to goad him into having a good snigger. But he's having none of it, just sits bolt upright and shoots me another one of his head boy glares for daring to act the messer.

'Yes,' Madame Rita mutters softly to herself, 'yes, yes, I see . . .'

'Emm . . . See what?' I interrupt. 'Anything we should know about?'

'Shh! Please dear, I really do have to ask you for quiet. You must understand I'm trying to concentrate!'

'Sorry,' I mouth back, nearly having to suck my cheeks in at this stage to stop me from convulsing.

'There's a piece of jewellery,' Madame Rita mutters softly, almost like she's off in a trace. 'A ring. I'm seeing a beautiful antique ring, it's a ruby I think . . . Yes, definitely a ruby . . .'

Jesus. Instantly I sit up like I've just been electrocuted. Suddenly she has my attention.

'. . . with two diamonds on either side . . .'

And now I'm in shock. Because that's it. That's exactly what Simon's engagement ring looks like.

'. . . It was intended as a gift . . . was meant to be a surprise, I feel . . . but somehow, Kitty came across it . . . she didn't mean to . . . it was an accident . . .'

'. . . And she panicked?' I interrupt her urgently. Jeff shoots a look at me as if to say what the hell are you on about? Because no one, absolutely no one, knew about this. Just Simon and me, that's all. He'd asked me to keep quiet about it and so I did.

A very long pause.

'No,' Madame Rita eventually says, so softly that I nearly have to strain to catch what she's saying. 'No, there was no panic . . . I'm not feeling anxiety, I think your friend was in a good place . . . I can feel her excited, happy to find it even . . . She carries a great love in her heart for the man who was about to give this ring to her . . .'

But . . . that makes absolutely no sense! If Kitty didn't bolt because she freaked out about getting engaged, then why did she go at all? And more importantly, where to?

'Do you know where she is now?' I blurt out, on the edge of my seat now.

'I feel . . . she's absolutely safe,' Madame Rita murmurs, 'Yes . . . she's secure now . . . I can tell you that for certain . . . She had to go, you see . . . very much for her own protection though . . . It had to be done . . . the poor girl had absolutely no choice . . .'

'Protected from what?' Jeff and I say in unison.

'. . . I'm feeling fear,' Madame Rita says, trance-like, 'Huge fear . . . she'd been carrying it with her for a very long time . . . something to do with her past . . . maybe someone from her past . . . I get a sense of her running from something or someone . . . someone who was determined to find her again . . . to track her down at all costs . . . and track her down they did. I can feel her panic . . . but she managed to get away . . . She was so worried that this day would come and was well prepared . . . and he can't possibly harm her where she is now . . . she really is quite safe . . .'

None of this is making the remotest bit of sense! And yet my heart is physically twisting in my ribcage with what I'm hearing.

'So where did she go to?' I blurt, nearly wanting to hammer on the table with frustration. 'Where are we not looking?'

'. . . I can feel sun on her face . . . I think she's somewhere warm . . . close to the sea . . . abroad . . . Yes, I can hear others around her speaking in English, but with very different accents . . . your friend has travelled a great distance. You won't find her though . . . she doesn't want to be found . . . but you must understand that she didn't want to leave her life here behind, I feel a huge reluctance on her part . . . This has been the hardest thing she's ever had to do in her life . . . It's all been a massive wrench for her . . . but she didn't have a choice . . . none of this was her fault, you see . . . she had to do this for her own safety . . . she's tried to do it before too, I'm almost certain . . .'

OK, so now my chest is pounding now and I'm about to break out in a clammy, cold sweat.

'And will she come back to us when she's ready?' I gulp.

Another aching pause, then Madame Rita starts to shake her head.

'. . . No, no I'm not feeling it . . . at least not for a long, long time . . . I feel that in this life, if you ever do see her again . . . she won't be Kitty Hope anymore . . . that girl is gone . . . she'll be someone different . . . I see two faces . . .'

Jesus, two faces? What is Kitty anyway, Clark Kent?

'She'll be a whole new person . . .' Madame Rita whispers, 'in fact, she IS a whole new person . . . and you must be prepared... Also you mustn't be afraid to let go . . . just let go . . . move on . . .'

I'm completely at sea here. Kitty, a whole new person?

'. . . But there's news coming . . . very soon too . . . You mustn't be shocked by what you hear though . . . just remember that your friend is quite safe and well . . . remember that, no matter what you may hear . . .'

A second later, Madame Rita opens her eyes and calmly hands Kitty's jumper back to me.

'Well?' she asks me, cloud blue eyes blinking like she's just woken up from a deep sleep.

'Was that any help to you both?'